Run, Cindy, Run!

HUNTED FOR SECRETS SHE DOESN'T HAVE

Lana McAra

VENDELA

Paperback Edition ISBN: 979-8-9993526-6-8
Hardcover Edition ISBN: 979-8-9993526-7-5
Ebook Edition ISBN: 979-8-9993526-8-2
Library of Congress Control Number: 2025916548

Cover design by r2cdesign

Endorsements for *Run, Cindy, Run!*

"Just what lovers of action-packed espionage thrillers laced with a gripping tale of betrayal, bitter-sweet love, war, blackmail, deceit, secrets, and money should be looking for. … I loved this magnificent work."

~ **Keith Mbuya**, Reader's Favorite 5-Star Review

"Tightly written and action-packed, *Run Cindy Run*! kept me wanting more right to the very end. Be prepared when you dive into this. You won't want to stop."

~ **David L. Hancock**, Producer of *House of the Dragon*

"On a par with Dan Brown, minus all the symbolism… #unputdownable."

~**Ann Crawford**, author of *Bazoomerangs*

"The ending was good! Now I'm wondering what everyone else would do with access to the codes!!"

~**Terry Jackson**, US Navy Veteran

This was an absolutely captivating thriller. McAra does a great job with describing things in such a way that you feel like you're right there watching everything unfold. I love Cindy, she's a great MC. A thrilling read that you won't want to miss!

~**Liliyana Shadowlyn**, The Faerie Review

"Tom Clancy meets Mary Higgins Clark. *Run Cindy Run!* is fast-paced with just enough romance to make you care."

~**Anastasia Alexander**, Best Selling Women's Fiction Author

"*Run Cindy Run!* gripped me from the start and never let go.

~**Peg Moran**, editor

Other Titles by Lana McAra

Reaping the Whirlwind by Rosey Dow (Christy Award winner)

The Englewood Medium Mystery Series by Lana McAra

   Shaken But Not Stirred

The Cowboy Romance Series: Old West History . . . With a Mystery by Lana McAra

   Tara's Dilemma

   Lisa's Defiance

   Layla's Luck

   Sally's Secret

   Ellie's Enemy

   Angie's Deception

   Katie's Fiction

   Penny's Folly

How To Write a Novel That Sells by Lana McAra

This book began long ago as a collaboration.

Though it has since taken on new form,

I honor the spark lit in those early pages—

and the creative spirit of Andrew Snaden,

whose contributions remain part of its foundation.

Table of Contents

Run, Cindy, Run!

Chapter One

Rochester, New York

Shortly after dawn, Cindy Lestrade lounged in bed, scrolling through social media on her phone, enjoying the lazy brain fog of an early Saturday morning. Her phone chimed. "Brad!" she said, a laugh in her voice. "You're up early."

His voice sounded strained. "What's up, baby?" he asked. "I just woke up with this horrible feeling…"

Banging noises came from downstairs. Her mother screamed, "Run, Cindy! Run!"

"What the…?" Scrambling out of her blankets, Cindy dashed to the window, pushing her dark curls away from her face to see clearly. Twenty feet below, six black SUVs filled the circular driveway. Two men in black stood guard by her front door, the letters FBI in yellow on their backs.

She said to Brad on the phone. "The FBI is here…"

Before she could say more, her bedroom door flew open, and two scowling giants holding guns burst in. "Give me the phone!" the dark-haired one barked.

Cindy hit speakerphone and dropped the phone to the floor. Hands up, she leaned back against the windowsill.

The agent picked up the phone. "Levitt," he said, holding it out to the guy with the big gut. "Look. Brad Hillcox," he said, ending the call. Her home screen came up with the photo of Cindy and Brad with their arms around each other. The agents shared a knowing look.

Did they know Brad? Cindy's heart pounded. She pressed her hands over her chest. Why were they here?

Two more men came in. They all wore blue gloves. The four men turned over her mattress, pulled clothes from the closet and dropped them to the floor. The contents of her dresser drawers added to the pile, then jewelry and makeup. Levitt turned to the corner hutch where her collection of porcelain dolls stood in careful rows. Almost worthless now, some of them had cost hundreds of dollars back in the day, except Mary Sue who was her birthday present when she was six years old. That was twenty-two years ago.

Mary Sue had started her collection. She had worn-out paint on her pink cheeks, black hair, and a painted-on smile. Her hard face had glowing green eyes and, beneath that, a soft huggable body. Mary Sue was her favorite.

"Perez," Levitt said. "Those dolls might be the ticket."

Her mind whirling, Cindy melted against the window, willing herself to be invisible, until Perez pulled out a knife and gutted Lady Ophelia. He pulled out her stuffing, tossed the doll to the floor and reached for Marie Antoinette.

"No!" Cindy shouted. She grabbed Mary Sue from the top shelf and sprinted to the door. She was gone before the guys in her room reacted. Levitt shouted, "Stop her!"

Cindy's bare feet pounded down the arched hallway. She lunged into her parents' room. Her face slammed into yellow FBI letters on a black jacket. The agent spun, then held himself in check half a second before he drove a rifle butt into her face.

"Leave her alone!" Alice Lestrade shouted. Her slim form came upright from a Monterey chair. She was still in her pink dressing gown. Cindy rushed into her mother's arms.

Red-faced, Levitt strode towards Cindy, his hand outstretched. Cindy clutched Mary Sue to her chest. She slipped behind her mother's stiff back.

"Give it to me!" Perez demanded, coming around the other side.

Cindy looked for a way to escape.

"What's going on?" the agent with the rifle asked.

"There may be something inside the doll," Levitt told him. "She let us rip open the others. She's protecting this one."

"I've had her since I was a kid," Cindy ground out through clenched teeth. "There's no way you're going to hurt her."

Perez and the guard grabbed Alice Lestrade and yanked her away from her daughter. When Levitt reached for the doll, Cindy whipped around to press her body against the plastered wall, pinning Mary Sue to it. The FBI agent spun Cindy around. Mrs. Lestrade screamed. Delivering a well-placed kick to his groin, Cindy sprinted toward the door.

Perez's heavy hand bit into her upper arm. Cindy stumbled, and he pinned her to the white carpet. Wild with fear and fury, Alice Lestrade broke free and sank her teeth into the back of his neck. The other two agents dove in to help, and the bedroom became a frenzy of screams, curses, and flailing limbs.

Grant Collier's deceptively boyish face had a grim cast as he followed the macadam driveway through an acre of manicured lawn. Under cover for almost two years, he had gained the trust of the Lestrade family while Homeland Security investigated Harrison and Alice Lestrade for treason. Grant wasn't even an operative. He was a CIA analyst. Because he spoke five languages, he was assigned as a CIA liaison to Homeland, translating raw data as it arrived and passing it along. He was also trained in negotiation, which usually happened over the phone, even in emergency settings. Up until the Lestrade case, he was primarily a desk jockey with small assignments in the field.

The local director had pressured him to go undercover this time because of his computer skills. Computer genius, Harrison Lestrade, had shared software technology with America's enemies. If Grant could access Lestrade's home computer, the feds might get enough evidence for an arrest. Up until now, that hadn't happened. He needed more time, and his time just ran out.

Rounding a curve, Grant stomped the brake to avoid smashing into six black sedans in front of the Spanish-style villa. Cursing silently, he thumped the steering wheel with his fist. His operation was completely blown. All he could do now was damage control.

Collier knew every detail of the white stucco house with arched doors and windows. Below the red clay-tile roof, he could see shadows of men moving about the bedrooms on the second floor. He knew which belonged to Cindy and which belonged to her parents. The estate was more than a computer scientist could afford. That had drawn attention that Harrison Lestrade would have been smarter to avoid.

Collier had the small build of his Asian DNA, but he could bench press 225 and ran seven miles a day. He crossed the tile patio in three bounds, flashing his ID. The guard let him pass. Hoarse screams came from upstairs. The living room plaster had a gaping hole beside the fireplace, and the cover of the baby grand piano was wide open, its lid hanging in mid-air.

He dashed up the curved staircase, using the iron rail to boost his momentum. In the master bedroom, Perez and an African-American agent had Alice Lestrade pinned against the bedroom wall. She was writhing and crying, desperate to get to her daughter.

Cindy's cheek smashed into the floor. Her curly hair looked like a tangled mop on the white carpet. Levitt had his knee on her back, digging under her. Cindy's face was blue, soaked with sweat and tears.

"Get off of her!" Collier bellowed.

His face also covered in sweat, Levitt looked up. "Not 'til she gives me the doll."

Collier's sharp kick knocked Levitt off her. He said to the agents holding Mrs. Lestrade, "Let her go."

Perez released the woman and moved toward Collier. "Now wait one minute. You've…"

Perez's head snapped back as Collier grabbed his windpipe. "I'm not negotiating with you morons. The girl has nothing to do with it. Now get out!" He turned Perez loose.

Perez gulped and rubbed his throat. The agents released Alice Lestrade. She rushed to her daughter. The women retreated to the safety of Mrs. Lestrade's bed, crying in each other's arms.

Sending killing glances at Collier, the FBI agents shuffled out of the room.

Grant Collier righted an antique chair and placed it near Cindy. Sitting, he reached for her hands, expecting that she might throw herself into his arms, but she shied away from him. Her eyes had doubt where love was the last time he saw her. Was it only yesterday?

"You okay?" he asked.

Without thinking, he gently brushed a tear from her cheek. What was he doing? The game was over. Gazing into those shimmering emerald eyes, he felt a deep, fierce dread.

"What's going on, Brad?"

How could he tell her that the candlelight dinners, the wild nights, and loving looks were part of a federal investigation of her parents? He let his eyes drift over her flushed face, down to her quivering lips. He felt like pond scum.

Cindy silently begged him to make it all right.

He took a breath and forced himself to speak the awful truth. "My name is not Brad Hillcox. I'm a member of a law enforcement agency that's investigating your father."

"Investigating Daddy? For what? He works for the Department of Defense. He's no criminal."

"I'm sorry, but I can't answer that."

"You aren't a teacher." She said it as a statement.

"No." Why did he feel so guilty for doing his sworn duty?

Cindy turned translucent white. Was she going into shock? He wanted to take her in his arms and hold her.

Still staring at him with a disturbing blank expression, Cindy reached for Mary Sue. "Everything was a lie." She swallowed convulsively. "All… all part of your job."

Collier leaned back. "No. No, Cindy." His throat tightened. "It wasn't all a lie."

"The dates? Did you use your money or the government's?"

His silence gave her the answer.

She raised her hand. A sharp crack echoed off the walls.

He jerked away. His cheek was on fire. He clamped his jaw. He still had a job to do. He couldn't afford to have feelings. He strode out of the bedroom before she could see the pain in his eyes.

In the hall, Cindy's bedroom door stood ajar. He caught a whiff of Elige perfume. He had to get out of here.

When he reached the bottom of the stairs, six FBI agents watched him.

"Face looks a little red there," taunted Levitt.

Collier ignored him.

"Got any more hearts lined up to break?" asked Perez, scoffing.

Collier shouldered between them, refusing to be baited.

"Hey, how was it being undercover with her?" Levitt called after him, laughing. The other men snickered.

Collier spun and landed the heel of his hand on Levitt's nose. Blood gushed down the front of his uniform.

Collier's cold stare went from man to man until each stupid grin vaporized. Finally, he turned again to Levitt. "Where is Harrison Lestrade?" Lestrade was the computer genius who had developed an independent missile that could fly across an ocean and hit a For Rent sign propped in a window. Its detonation would take out two city blocks.

Levitt's voice was muffled by his handkerchief over his nose. "He wasn't here."

Collier's top lip curled into a sneer. "Oh, that's obvious. You've torn the whole house apart, and the only suspect you came up with was a baby doll. Well, hot shot, if you'd bothered to touch base with me, I could have told you Harrison wouldn't be home. After this fiasco, he'll be out of the country within hours. That man has the power to bring this nation to its knees. Don't you think he has an escape plan?" He clenched his fist, begging one of them to make a move. "You've destroyed two years' work."

His shoes crunched across the debris until he reached the door. He paused. "Let me make this perfectly clear: If any one of you so much as lays a finger on that girl, I'm coming after you and not only with my fists."

The East China Sea

Eighteen months later, a hundred miles off the coast of Taiwan, ship's Captain Zheng Zhengqui barked an order to his second in command, and The People's five-hundred-fifty-foot guided missile cruiser yawed sideways. Zheng's lips compressed into a hard line, anticipating the glory in store for China. No more missed targets or fouled detonations. Thanks to their newly updated systems, their weapons now equaled those of Russia and NATO. Best of all, today The People would give Taiwanese President Tsai Ing-wen a long-promised wake up call.

Zheng had orders to put half a dozen cruise missiles directly over Taiwan and destroy an old freighter offshore—a demonstration to take the starch out of the Taiwanese navy. One day, Taiwan must reunite with Mother China. Zheng's chest puffed out. That day was just ahead.

With his ship parallel to shore, Zheng entered the tiny control room where four officers sat at the control hub of the ship. Closing the door behind him, Zheng called out, "Lock onto the target!" The weapons officer's fingers danced along the keyboard. He turned toward his captain and gave a stiff nod.

Two seconds later, the ship's communications officer spoke into his headset directly to Beijing. "All ready." The young man looked at the captain and nodded.

Zheng's lower teeth showed as he called out the equivalent of "Fire!"

Two cruise missiles vaulted from the ten-thousand-ton ship, the backlash making it rock. Zheng's gleaming gold buttons pulled taut against the blue serge. This was a great day for China.

Four minutes after the launch, a low grating sound erupted from every loudspeaker on the ship. Red lights flashed on the weapons station. With the captain behind him, the weapons officer had his face two inches from the monitor, his fingers a blur of motion over the keyboard.

Zheng leaned over him. "What happened?"

The officer kept typing.

"What happened, you fool!"

"Sir," his voice trembled, "the missiles veered off course."

Zheng's throat closed. His jaw was a vise. This was an outrage.

A moment later, the officer's voice rose to a shrill whine. "They've turned toward us!"

Zheng rushed to his failsafe button, a large red knob under a plexiglass dome. He entered a code and the top popped open. Feverishly entering code after code, he kept looking at the screen. Nothing changed. The missile was ten miles out. Five miles. Desperate, Zheng pushed the yellow self-destruct button.

With a roar, both missiles exploded. The glory of Mother China fizzled into the sea.

Zheng stormed out of the control room and headed for the deck. He glared at the sky where American spy satellites had witnessed everything. Instead of recording China's triumph, they had witnessed China's shame.

Chapter Two

Black Canyon City, Arizona

On the other side of the world, Erin Davis pulled a strand of curly blonde hair to the corner of her lips. In the heart of the central Arizona mountains, she lay curled up on the worn loveseat of her furnished apartment. She picked up the remote and flipped through Roku.

When she moved here two years ago, she had high hopes for her business systems consulting business. Unfortunately, this backwater town was stuck in the past. All the local businesses had been using Puget Information Systems for years and didn't want to trust a young woman they had never met before. And what was she doing in Black Canyon City, anyway?

Erin couldn't answer that question. She also couldn't bring out her Master's Degree from MIT or references from a Silicon Valley giant where she was a rising star in developing software. Those credentials belong to Cindy Lestrade. Cindy Lestrade was dead, and she had to stay that way. After the widespread media hype about her parents' treason conviction, Cindy Lestrade would never get a job in the U.S. again. The new Erin Davis could only show prospective clients how good she was—if she ever got the chance. Meanwhile, she switched out towels at the local gym and wiped down the equipment every hour. Not to mention fighting off the unwanted attention of dozens of jock-wannabes.

Her one perk was access to the equipment. She didn't have to pay to use the machines, and one of her co-workers, Diego Geraldo, was training her in self-defense. He was a former Navy SEAL. He knew a lot of cool moves, and encouraged her to enter kickboxing competitions. She was still a rank beginner compared to the others, but she liked it. Kickboxing made her feel in charge.

In exchange for Diego's help, she tutored him at the local coffee shop when he ran into trouble with his Computer Science degree at ASU. Even in Black Canyon City, Arizona loved its coffee shops.

Flipping a second time through the channel options, Erin settled on the basketball game. Shortly before halftime, her cellphone jingled.

"Davis Consulting."

"Hi. Is Gary there?" a man's voice asked.

"Sorry, wrong number." She hung up. Seconds later, the phone rang again. Irritated, she took the call. "Hello?"

A voice came through so soft and mellow that she wasn't sure if the speaker was male or female. "Ah… Hi. I'm looking for Erin Davis."

"Speaking. What can I do for you?"

"I'm the computer systems manager for Archon Energy north of Phoenix. My name's Ted Booregard. Look, I realize this is Sunday and all, but I was wondering if you can help us out. We've got a problem with the payroll program, and the checks have to be ready by tomorrow noon. I called our usual firm, but all I got was voicemail."

She couldn't let him know how hungry she was for a job. "You're right. It is Sunday. Tomorrow won't do?"

"Most of our crew is union. It's my head if they decide to walk when their checks aren't ready."

"Where are you?"

"Noterra Point. I'll text you the address."

The text came in, and she clicked the address to get a timeframe. "Mr. Booregard, I'll be there in forty-five minutes."

He sounded relieved. "Great. Someone will meet you at the front door."

She ended the call and headed for the shower, pulling off clothes as she went. She was grimy from a week's worth of depression. Seven minutes later, she pulled on her jeans and her favorite shirt. She found it at a thrift store north of Phoenix, a black T-shirt jammed into an overloaded rack. She froze when she saw small white letters on its front: M.I.T. She should have put it back, but she marched straight to the counter and bought it. She carried it to the car feeling like a law breaker. She should have made it a sleep shirt no one else ever saw, but she wore it. She couldn't stop herself. She wore it all the time.

Pulling the shirt over her wet hair, she picked up her wide-tooth comb to tame her hair but soon gave up. Black roots showed through her blonde hairline. Time for a visit to the salon. After a serious disaster, she gave up trying to color her own hair. It was too thick and curly. She had stubbornly kept the length well below her shoulders, her one attachment to the old Cindy she missed so much.

She made her way to her Jeep which was covered with such thick dust its navy color had turned to gray. It always looked like this. No sense washing it. More dust would cover it inside of an hour. This countryside made a four-wheel-drive a must. When she moved here, this vehicle, with her new name on its title, and a leased apartment had waited for her. She had no idea who funded all that, and she had no one to ask.

Since she was heading into an unknown environment, Erin opened her glove compartment and checked her Cobra pistol. She dropped it into her purse. If the company had security screening, she would pull up her best smile and say it was for protection. This was Arizona, after all. She would be fine.

The back of her Jeep had a full suite of emergency equipment. This area was prone to wildfires, so everyone had an awareness of emergency preparation. In her vehicle she kept her Bug Out Bag, first aid supplies, some camping equipment, and five gallons of clean water. She kept her gas tank full and her phone turned on, so she would hear the chime of the Emergency Broadcast System. Sometimes, she felt like packing up and going back to upstate New York where people complained about rain and snow. Here, if it rained people wrote it on the calendar.

She also had a rifle on a rack in the back. The guys at the gym were more than willing to help her learn how to shoot and care for the four weapons she now owned. After what happened to her family, she had spent a full year arming herself and learning self-defense, but not martial arts. Erin Davis knew how to fight dirty and survive. She could kick some ass if she needed to.

The Jeep floated over the miles with breathtaking landscapes in every direction. The trip down the mountain toward Phoenix was always enjoyable.

Her single contact with her old life was a woman named Nina, no last name, who was a friendly voice on the phone. They hadn't even spoken via Zoom. When Erin asked Nina who had provided the apartment and vehicle for her, Nina had simply said, "You have a guardian angel who wishes to remain anonymous." After that, Nina's lips were sealed.

Even with an anonymous benefactor covering her rent and car, Erin had spent the last two years plowing through her savings, and she was almost at the end of it. What she made at the gym barely covered gas and groceries. In the summer, the temperature stayed in triple digits for months on end. Her electric bill skyrocketed, and the apartment wasn't even cool. Besides that, the cost of water was astronomical. Arizona was an expensive place to live.

Driving slowly as she neared the address, scanning the neighborhood, Erin pulled into the parking lot of a three-story steel-and-glass office building. A heavy-featured man in a rumpled suit stood inside the front door. He had an anxious expression and thin, gray hair cut military style. He opened the door and said, "Erin Davis?"

Recognizing his voice, she nodded and stepped inside.

Bushwick, New York

Grant Collier glanced at Special Agent Levitt beside him at the window. His worst nightmare was being locked in a room with this goon. Here they were in the middle of a New York City ghetto, going on the third day. Just he and the big guy. Welcome to Paradise.

Levitt lay aside his infrared binoculars and reached for yet another slice from a flat box on the floor beside him. They were part of a multi-agency task force involving the CIA and the FBI, monitored by Homeland Security. Collier was here as an interpreter for their terrorist surveillance operation, but he had no authority as a CIA intelligence officer on American soil. Levitt was in charge of making regular phone reports to his Homeland connection. Until they nailed down exactly what these guys were up to, everyone had their ear to the ground in case they were needed.

The pizza box shuffled across the dusty floor, propelled by Levitt's foot. "Wanna piece? It's triple cheese."

Collier ignored him. The apartment was a dump. During the night, they could hear rodents scratching around. Collier grew up on a horse ranch, so rats didn't bother him much. They did bother Levitt. Last night, he squealed like a girl when he thought he had one in his sleeping bag. Pizza boxes on the floor was inviting them for dinner, and Levitt didn't seem to notice.

Levitt spoke again. "Sure you don't want some pizza?"

"No, thanks."

"Oh, yeah, I forgot. You're one of them health nuts."

Collier's mouth showed irritation. "I'm not a health nut. I just shy away from food that makes my belly look like a balloon." He glanced at Levitt's gut hanging over his belt.

"What are you saying? I'm out of shape?" He shifted in the chair, and his coat opened to reveal more evidence against him. "I can take care of myself when it counts."

Collier choked back a comment that two years ago, Levitt hadn't done so well with Cindy Lestrade. Suddenly, he had a flashback of her face close to his on the pillow, her emerald eyes full of love and desire, their breaths mingling…

Blowing out a quiet huff, Collier forced his attention back to the lighted windows of the building across the street. He had to stop torturing himself. It was over. He was never going to see Cindy Lestrade again. She wanted it that way.

Finishing his pizza, Levitt picked up his phone and started scrolling. Grinning, he held the phone toward Collier, "My grandkids," he said. "My daughter puts up the cutest pictures on social media."

Collier glanced at the phone and made an approving noise of some kind. He went back to watching, wishing again they could bug the apartment across the street. They'd tried it once, but the suspects had simply swept the place with an electronic scanner. A few minutes later, the FBI's listening device was swimming toward the city sewer. Two days ago, Collier had suggested that he might as well leave since he had nothing to interpret, but that idea got shot down by Director Mullinax, his direct report.

"Seems you're not the only one who wants pizza tonight," Collier told his FBI partner a few minutes later.

At the entrance to the apartment building, a delivery boy got out of a dark sedan with a magnetic sign on top. Slim and young, he wore a black quilted jacket. A baseball cap shielded his face from the blue-green lens of Collier's binoculars. "Some guy is going into the building with one of those big pizza-warming envelopes."

Levitt grabbed his own sights. "It's late for supper. Maybe a midnight snack?"

Collier shifted his attention to a video display from a hidden camera in the dingy third-floor hall across the way. Soon the delivery driver's long-legged, loose-limb stride brought him into view.

Levitt cranked his head around Collier's back to watch the monitor as the kid stepped into the apartment. In less than two minutes, he left with the orange warming envelope hanging at his side.

Collier said, "They must love Olympia's pizza. How many times has this been? Half a dozen?"

Without answering, Levitt returned to his scrolling. Half an hour later, Collier stiffened. "They're going out," he said. "Why would anyone go out at midnight right after eating delivery pizza?" He squinted into the eyepiece. "One of them has a briefcase."

Irritated, Levitt tossed his phone to the table next to him. "I'd hate to blow our cover for a false alarm, Collier. They might just as easily be going to get some antacid. Olympia's pizza is pretty brutal. I don't know how that place stays in business." From the pile of boxes around the trash can, if anyone knew about Olympia's pizza, it was Levitt.

Collier glanced at his wrist. 12:07. Midnight wasn't really that late. But something was nagging him. Suddenly, he swore. "Do you know what today's date is?"

Levitt glanced at his own watch. "March 20. Why?"

"Twenty years ago today, we started the invasion of Iraq after 9/11."

Levitt lifted his wrist and spoke. "They're on the street. Pick them up." He looked at Collier. "If we blow our cover for nothing, you go down with me."

Collier bit back his reply. In his book, Levitt was the king of blown operations.

In the street below, a dozen agents propelled themselves from doorways and parked cars. The terrorists scattered and ran like calves in a rodeo. Less than eight seconds later, their noses scraped the pavement.

A dozen people gathered around, gaping at the men lying prone on the sidewalk.

"Tell those guys not to touch the briefcase," Collier said.

"Hey, I'm in charge here, not you. I'll decide what happens." Levitt lifted his wrist. "Clear the area and call the bomb squad. The briefcase may contain explosives. Leave it alone."

Before Levitt finished talking, Collier bolted out of the apartment and charged down the stairs. When he burst out the door, the onlookers were rushing in opposite directions, the word "bomb" popping out like corn in a hot pan.

Collier sprinted fifty yards and drew up, sucking air, hands on hips, relieved that the leather case was still intact. It could contain enough explosive to incinerate at least one building. Still flat on the ground, the prisoners eyed him wearily. They flinched in unison when he ran his hand over the clasps on the case.

Glancing up and down the street, he saw what he needed: a twenty-four-hour check-cashing place. He grabbed the briefcase and dashed toward it. Law enforcement identification in one hand, the briefcase in the other, he stormed inside. A bald male looked up when the door slammed back.

"Everyone out!" Collier shouted.

"I'm the manager, officer. I have to remain. There's a lot of cash in here."

Collier nodded toward the briefcase. "This might be a bomb." He set off toward the thick metal door on the back of the room and almost bumped his nose on a door made of steel bars. He turned back, looking for the manager, but the place was empty.

Pulling his Glock 21 from under his left arm, he fired half a dozen rounds into the lock mechanism on the barred door. When the door swung free, he entered the vault and set the briefcase on the cement floor. He pulled the vault door closed behind him. Only the manager could lock it, but Collier was counting on its weight to absorb a significant amount of the blast, if the bomb went off. If it did, he'd never have to answer for his decision to go ahead and take a look.

Drawing a six-inch knife from a sheath at his ankle, Collier took a deep breath. He had a 50-50 chance that the side he chose would be clean. He made a long incision and started breathing again. a hole the size of an iPad revealed three sticks of dynamite connected to a timer. Any kid with internet access could do better than that.

Disconnecting the alarm clock, he pushed hard against the steel door and bounded outside. Levitt stood near a police cruiser with the perps in the backseat.

Running hard, Collier reached the FBI agent and directed him out of earshot. "We've got a problem," Collier told him.

Levitt pulled away from Collier's grasp. "What are you talking about?"

"The explosives in that case could only wreck a few cars and take out some glass. It's a decoy."

"What have they been working on all this time?" Levitt asked.

Collier glanced at the terrorists' apartment building. The answer had to be inside there. He broke into a jog.

Tapping two men from the Bureau, Levitt bounded after Collier. Slick with sweat and heaving for breath, Levitt bent over, trying to breathe, while Collier used the butt of his Glock to smash glass and reach through to unlock the door. He bounded up the narrow stairs. Three sets of heavy boots followed him. The men drew up at the door, and Levitt reached for the knob.

Collier's arm flew out, blocking him. "They may have booby-trapped the door."

The big man took a step backward. "We ought to wait for the bomb squad."

For an instant, Collier glared at the chipped door as if it could whisper its secret. He glanced at the lanky agent standing off to the left. "You're absolutely sure everyone's out?"

"Yes, sir." His Adam's apple bobbed. "As soon as you grabbed that bomb, we started clearing the building."

"Good work." Collier glanced at three tense faces, considering, then said, "You all get out of here. I'm going in."

Levitt shook his fleshy head. "No way. We wait for the bomb squad."

"We can't wait. What if it goes off?"

The men from the Bureau glanced at each other. Their leader pursed his lips. He nodded, and the agents hoofed it to the stairs. Levitt stared at Collier. "What is it with you? You got a death wish or something?"

Collier gave no reply, but the words hovered in the stale air. Since the Lestrade case, he couldn't sit at a desk anymore. He tried it and ended up going stir crazy. But more than that, he had played peekaboo with death for twenty-four months, requesting one dangerous field assignment after another. Maybe he did have a death wish.

When he heard the downstairs door click, Collier screwed up his face—expecting an explosion—and kicked in the hollow panel before him. The only bang he heard was the doorknob cracking a hole in the wall plaster. Brushing a fleck of wood from his face, he stepped inside.

Before him lay a living room with a low-backed couch, a chair covered with nubby green fabric, and a coffee table that held the cigarette burns and coffee stains of twenty years' hard labor. Food cartons and empty whiskey bottles sprawled over the faded carpet and every piece of furniture. Whiskey bottles? Those guys didn't drink. They took their Islam seriously.

In the kitchen doorway, he stopped, chilled to the core.

Segments of different-colored wires littered the table and floor. Shavings of a puttylike material dusted the entire tabletop. In a corner lay a pile of small boxes with pictures of a travel alarm clock on their covers. Instantly, he knew what had happened.

Levitt's voice came over the talkie. "All clear?"

"Yeah," Collier replied. Squatting, he counted the small boxes. "They've made eleven timer-activated C-4 bombs."

"How did they get them out? We've seen everyone coming and going. Not one of them had so much as a paper bag in his hand."

Standing, Collier nodded toward the empty pizza boxes on the floor. "Everyone but the pizza guy. He probably brought in the raw materials and took out the finished product."

Levitt appeared in the doorway. Behind him, the suited up forensic team came inside with their gear. Levitt reached for a handkerchief to wipe his face. "Okay, Collier. I admit it. I'm over my head. What happens now?"

"We don't have a clear picture of the delivery guy, and we can be sure their car has been dumped. We have to beat these guys with brains not brawn."

Levitt grunted as he got to his feet. "Now you've got me scared." For the first time since he'd met him, Collier saw a hint of humility in Levitt's eyes.

The forensic team trashed the apartment, tearing open the scant furnishings, kicking holes in walls, even to the point of ripping the toilet out. Dirty and sweaty, they finished their search empty-handed.

Collier strode to the living room window and peered down at the police car holding the prisoners. What would their weakness be? According to their religion, torture and death only added stars to their crowns in the hereafter. American tactics fell way short on that score. Psychological maneuvering was the only option, and a slim hope at that. He turned to Levitt. "I've got an idea," he said. He slipped a notebook and pen from his pocket and scrawled a list.

He handed the slip of paper to Levitt, who raised his eyebrows. "What you got cooking now?"

Collier grinned. "Trust me. It'll be good."

"I'll have to break a few laws to get this stuff."

"That a problem?"

Levitt shook his head and grinned. "Not at all." Stuffing the list into his inside coat pocket, he headed toward the stairs with Collier behind him. On the street, Levitt jerked open the door of a black SUV and roared down the street.

Collier turned to the half-dozen FBI agents standing nearby. "Take those three back to their apartment for questioning."

                    Lana McAra

Without a word, the shortest one pulled open the door and motioned for the suspects to get out. Handcuffed, they shambled down the sidewalk eyes down, seemingly submissive.

Collier sized them up as they passed. Over these days of surveillance, he had memorized their dossiers.

The oldest and by far the most dedicated was Ahmed Al-Shahin. Medium height and refined, he was a prime suspect in several bombings. He had served ten years in an Israeli prison before his release as part of a peace treaty. Robust before his prison term, he was now thin and gaunt. The Mossad had put Al-Shahin through their worst, but he couldn't be broken. He lived only for revenge.

Next in line, Mustafa Farid was an Egyptian who'd never agreed with the Israeli-Egyptian Peace Accord. He ran a terrorist-for-hire business, and Iraq was his most recent customer. He was stocky with a thick, black beard, his dark eyes penetrating and angry. Farid was in it for the money. He might talk to save his own hide, but Collier doubted it. Better to rot in a cushy American prison than spend the rest of his life running from the Iraqis.

The last terrorist was a slight fellow just over twenty years old. Saad Salih was a university student, a handsome kid with easygoing brown eyes who had joined the movement after a stray U.S. bomb took out most of his family. Saad was the weak link. He loved his only remaining family members, two sisters, with an obsessive, protective passion.

As Saad shuffled past, Collier planted his hand on the young man's chest and leaned close to whisper in his ear. "You're playing with the big boys now," he said in Arabic. "By the time today is done, you'll have a whole new understanding of the word pain."

Sweat broke out on Saad's upper lip.

Collier smiled and let him pass.

Chapter Three

Phoenix, Arizona

Middle-aged with a purple nose and blotchy skin, Ted Booregard had the look of a hard drinker. His heavy jowls sagged almost to the knot in his tie. Holding the door open for Erin, he wore a deep frown. "Thanks for coming so quick," he said, waiting for Erin to pass through, so he could secure the door.

Whatever Archon Energy did, they did it all over the world. Pictures of oil rigs—at sea, in deserts, in jungles, and on farm fields—covered the massive walls. Mr. Booregard trudged across the white tile floor to a back wall lined with silver elevators. The center one stood open. He paused for Erin to enter first.

When the doors wheezed shut, he fidgeted with his rumpled tie. "Have you ever worked with COBOL? I should have asked on the phone."

"Sure," Erin replied, as though it were nothing. "COBOL is archaic, but some people still find it useful for some applications. I take it your firm still uses it."

Booregard shook his head, regretfully. "Oh yeah, we're still using it." A bell dinged, and the doors slid open. Leading the way, he stopped before a solid metal door with an electronic lock. "I signed on here three years ago," he said as he shoved a plastic card into a slot and placed his thumb on a touch plate. "As soon as I saw what they had, I suggested they change to a network, but this outfit only spends money on things that make oil." He pulled open the door. "I call this monster T-Rex. Welcome to his lair."

Erin's jaw dropped. Before her was a mainframe at least fifteen years old. Most programmers would have just said no and let Archon pay for its sins. Most programmers weren't down to fifty dollars in their bank account.

The mainframe itself was in a glass-enclosed room that was temperature controlled with halon fire-extinguisher nozzles installed in the ceiling above it, the only suppression system that worked on these babies. Unfortunately, they would kill any human trapped in the enclosure as well.

Booregard looked at her, unsure. "Are you positive you can work with this? I've got a degree in computer science but how to understand the source code for this thing is something I've long forgotten."

She smiled. "No problem." Her father had insisted she learn every programming language used by Fortune 500 companies. COBOL was her second, after she learned BASIC. She slipped her purse strap from her shoulder. "Which terminal do you want me to use?"

He led her toward the far right of the room to a scuffed work pod—a four-man unit. "Welcome to the magic portal," Booregard said, "the place where miracles happen every day. If they didn't, we'd close down."

Erin sat at the stiff desk chair. The black screen of the monitor had one word blinking on it—END. Archon was past archaic. She glanced up. "When the system crashes, what does it do exactly?"

"It says our employee records are invalid. Two weeks ago, they were valid, but this week they're not. It makes no sense."

Her fingers played lightly across the keyboard with a metallic, rattling sound. "Does Archon know that it costs more to maintain this relic than to replace it?"

Booregard folded his arms. "I told them. I almost had them convinced until they called Puget Information to do a study. Puget's report said that the total cost of reentering records, training personnel, and buying new hardware made a change unwise. They said Archon should wait five more years."

Erin crinkled her forehead. "That's crazy."

The weary lines in Booregard's face deepened. "Between you and me, I know exactly why they did it. We ended up forking over $250,000 to service the mainframe. What's really interesting is that they gave us a two-year warranty which expired a week ago.

"When I came in to run the payroll, she crashed. I phoned Puget, and they said I'm looking at about twenty-five grand to have someone fix it on a rush basis. That kind of expense has to be approved by the board, and all the bigwigs are in Caracas at that big oil summit." He drew in a bushel of air. "So…"

Erin smiled. "So, you've spent the last three days trying to fix it yourself." Suddenly, she understood why he'd looked so dour when she arrived. Poor guy.

Booregard nodded. His mouth pulled in on one side. "I know, pretty dumb. I guess you've probably figured out that my neck is on the line here. I've got a lot riding on you."

Erin's smile widened. "We'll try and keep your neck just where it is. If you'll give me the access codes, I'll go to work."

Booregard scrawled out some letters on a green sticky note, then shuffled to a glass-enclosed office at the other end of the room, his shoulders sagging, his body heavily swaying with each step.

Erin felt relieved when the door bumped closed behind him. She hated people peering over her shoulder.

A couple of minutes later, she was inside the source code. Printing it out would take hours. Fortunately, she already had a theory. As page after page scrolled down, her eyes moved with the text, looking for one particular command. As always, time stood still when Erin sat at the controls. She loved this job.

Just over an hour later, on command number sixty-four, she nailed it. Leaning back in her squeaky chair, she chewed the last bit of lipstick from her bottom lip. The system would be up and running in less than two hours. At the normal rate of four hundred dollars an hour, she'd make a lousy eight hundred dollars. She had just saved the company at least twenty-five grand.

Booregard would never know if she overcharged him, but she could not do it. After what happened to her parents, Erin had made herself an ironclad promise. Her affairs would be squeaky clean, even if she had to shut down her fledgling business. The alternative cost far too much.

Fingers flying, she repaired eighty-two lines of code, then signaled to Booregard.

He practically leaped from his desk and rushed to her. "Something wrong?"

"It's fixed."

His eyebrows reached for his hairline. "Already? I mean, those Puget guys have never fixed anything in under two days. Are you sure?"

Erin got up from the seat. "Try it yourself."

Booregard sat at the console and keyed in his payroll program. When it loaded, he looked up at her. "What was the problem?"

"A command in your system pointed to an invalid line number after a certain date, so the program didn't know how to process the employee files. I simply found the line number and redirected the command."

"Any idea why it happened?"

Erin brushed hair away from her eyes. "The command is encrypted. I can't read it, but the problem has to be in there somewhere."

"Why is it encrypted?"

"Probably because Puget people wrote the program. Since they own it, they don't want their unprotected code on client computers. Otherwise, any programmer could copy and spread it all over the world. Puget would never get paid for their property."

His face showed irritation. "If there's something wrong in their file, then they should have to fix it."

Erin hesitated. "Without breaking their code, I can't prove it."

"Just great," he said, massaging the side of his face. "You're telling me this could happen again."

"I suggest you call them. Maybe they're aware of the problem and forgot to notify you."

Booregard's mouth twisted. "Convenient for them, don't you think?" He stood. "How much do we owe you?"

"Eight hundred dollars. I can mail you a bill." Erin had to force herself to mention a bill. She was almost out of groceries.

He stared at her. "That's all?"

She slipped her purse strap onto her shoulder and turned as though ready to go. "Of course. My rate is four hundred an hour."

He stepped away from the desk, his eyes friendly for the first time since she'd arrived. "Have you got any business cards with you? I can't remember the last time I met an honest person."

Erin pulled a stack of cards from her jacket pocket and held three of them out to him.

Fifteen minutes later, Erin left Archon Energy with nine hundred dollars in her bank account. Booregard had paid her via bank transfer from petty cash and insisted she take more for working at night. Even better, Ted Booregard had promised he'd call her again, and he'd tell his friends about her. Maybe this really was where miracles happen every day.

Bushwick, New York

Collier and Levitt returned to the trashed apartment, and half a dozen agents swarmed the place. Saad sat on a kitchen chair with his feet shackled together, his hands cuffed behind him. On the other side of the table, the Egyptian Mustafa Farid looked like a middle-aged Fidel Castro. His dark eyes were glowing embers. Grim resolve showed through his thick, black beard.

Two burly agents grabbed Ahmed on the sofa and dragged him to the back bedroom. Shouts and groans followed. Grant and Levitt stood staring at the remaining two terrorists.

Saad shifted to his left hip and tried to imitate Mustafa's stiff expression. He needed more practice to pull it off.

This wasn't a domestic law enforcement operation. This was a joint operation under Homeland Security where the prisoners got no lawyers and had no rights. The men holding weapons had a blank check. Whatever it took, Ahmed and his men would tell them where the targets were and who had the bombs.

Grant knew they'd never get anything out of Ahmed or Mustafa, so he focused his attention on the kid. He was the negotiator on the team. What was happening in the other room wasn't negotiation.

The door to the interrogation room—a.k.a. the master bedroom—thumped back, and an agent came out headed straight for Mustafa. Before he reached the chair, a pistol shot in the back room made the prisoners flinch. Saad glanced toward Mustafa then at Grant.

Grant kept his stare on Saad. With a failed attempt at bravado, the kid shrank back under his gaze.

Two agents came at Mustafa who arched his back and lunged towards the smaller of the two. Shorty stepped aside, and the tall, skinny one slapped the terrorist across the face with a crack almost as loud as the pistol. Mustafa reeled. One on each side, avoiding his thrashing legs, the agents dragged him down the hall while he shouted curses in Arabic.

More groans and shouts followed. Still staring at Saad, Grant's lips formed a smirk that could be understood in any language: Guess who's next.

The voices grew hoarse, then faded. The agents returned. Saad gulped.

Another pistol shot.

Sweat streamed from Saad's forehead and dripped down his cheek. His chest heaved. When the men grabbed him and pulled him to his feet, his knees buckled.

This time, Grant followed them. The upturned bed leaned against the wall to make room for a chair in the center of the matted carpet. On the other side of the room, Ahmed and Mustafa lay stretched out on the carpet, a small puddle of blood coming out from under Mustafa's chest.

Grant said in Arabic, "I hope you're smarter than them, Saad."

The kid's eyes widened. He looked at Grant's face, as though trying to recognize him. One benefit of Grant's Asian heritage was his ability to blend in with several brown-skinned cultures. If he glued on a heavy black beard, Middle-Eastern was one of them. Today he was clean shaven, but his appearance was still close enough for what he had in mind.

The agents shoved Saad into the chair and tied him down.

Collier leaned down until he was inches from Saad's nose and bellowed, "Where are the targets?"

Saad tried to turn his head away, but powerful hands forced his face forward.

The young Iraqi kept silent, his breathing shallow and quick.

Suddenly, Grant straightened and stepped back. He spoke in Arabic, soft and melodious. "Look, Saad, I'm not FBI. I'm CIA. That FBI agent in the corner can't speak Arabic. He would arrest me if he knew what I was saying." Grant leaned in. "I want to know where the targets are, and I'll do anything to find out." He gestured toward the bodies on the floor. "I'm not going to torture you. I'm going to send my men to find Fatima and Hala in Lebanon along with their five beautiful children." He called out the names of the children and continued, "Then, I'm going to bomb their village."

Saad trembled like he had chills after a fever.

Smooth steel pressed against Saad's temple. He gasped and looked up to see Collier's heavy hand next to his left eye, fingers wrapped around the grip of a Glock 21.

"Last chance, kid," he said. "If I pull this trigger, your sisters die."

Saad squeezed his eyes shut and mumbled, "Craigmore School."

"I can't hear you."

"Craigmore School!" he shouted. Pure hatred screwed up his face.

Collier's face turned the color of an old brick. "You targeted a school?"

"Five schools. Americans must know how it feels to have children die."

Grant took a spiral-bound notepad from his pocket. "Tell me their names. If one kid dies, so help me, I'll take out more than one Lebanese village."

Saad spieled off the names. Collier reached for his cellphone and moved to a corner of the room to make a call.

Levitt leaned down to unfasten Saad's wrists and ankles from the chair.

Ahmed moaned.

Saad's head snapped around.

The second moan came louder.

"Ahmed!" Saad shouted. He yanked at the last cuff still about his ankle, trying to get to his friend.

Levitt chuckled. "They're not dead. We smeared them with goo and put them to sleep."

Growling like an animal in pain, Saad lunged for the Beretta holstered under Levitt's arm.

"Hey!" Levitt shouted.

Like in slow motion, Collier turned in time to see Levitt lunge for his weapon and miss. The young Iraqi twisted and squeezed the trigger twice. Collier felt two tugs in the lower left of his torso. He and Saad hit the carpet at the same time. Triumphant, the kid looked Collier straight in the eyes.

Someone yelled, "Collier!" and darkness closed in.

Chapter Four

Black Canyon City, Arizona

Erin squinted at a shaft of sunlight streaming through a crack in her bedroom drapes and into her eyes. She snuggled deeper into the covers. Such a beautiful dream—she was with Brad on the sofa, snuggled up for a movie, feeling mellow…

Her eyes flew open. Why was she still dreaming about that jerk!

Dreams had not been her friend since she moved here. First, she had nightmares about her parents in prison. She couldn't even talk to them on the phone or send them an email. Her heart had a constant ache that still flared up two years later. They had betrayed their country, yes, but they had also betrayed her and left her all alone in the world. She couldn't wrap her mind around that, even now. Then, she had nightmares about Brad, romantic at first, but they quickly turned into a horror show. At least this morning she woke up before the panic started.

Rolling over, she grabbed her cellphone and opened her banking app. Yep, at least she hadn't dreamed that. Nine-hundred-fifty dollars was right there in her account. She sighed and stretched. Owww… Her last self-defense session with Diego had left her sore. She stretched again, slowly this time to work out the kinks.

After a hot shower, she pulled on jeans and her black M.I.T. shirt. Leaning close to the bathroom mirror, she carefully applied sunscreen, a must in this part of the country. Rubbing the tops of her ears, she smiled, remembering her win last night. If Ted Booregard turned out to be as good as his word, she might just be in business.

She swiped up her purse, but before she could open the door, her phone chimed. Erin stared at it. Three calls in less than twenty-four hours? No one ever called her.

"Davis Consulting."

"Erin Davis?" a woman's throaty voice asked.

"Yes."

"I'm Olivia Donner. I got your name from Ted Booregard. He says you're pretty good at programming."

"That's nice of him to say so," Erin said.

"Do you know hardware?"

"Of course."

"What a relief! My technician was in a car accident last night. He's okay, thank God, but he'll be off work for six weeks. He broke his right hand. If you haven't had breakfast yet, could we meet somewhere and talk?"

Hardware and loading software were way below her skill level, but who cared? "That will be fine," she said.

"How about Muffin Mania at Cordata Place? A quarter to ten? I'll text you my photo, so you can recognize me."

Erin glanced at her watch. She'd better wait on groceries until after the meeting. Her phone chimed. The image of a middle-aged woman with a curly brown perm showed up.

"Got it," Erin said. "See you then." She locked her apartment and headed to her Jeep. Things were finally looking up.

The moment she pulled open the door of Muffin Mania, the warm aroma of coffee and pastries closed around her. This place had a bakery in the back. No plastic-wrapped pastries here. Every table was full, and the line almost reached the door. At a corner booth, Olivia Donner sent Erin a big wave. She had a round face and puffy cheeks.

Erin navigated through the crowded restaurant, avoiding elbows and skirting chairs. When she finally reached the corner booth, Olivia Donner smiled and said, "You're right on time." She eased herself out of the booth. "What will you have?"

"Black hazelnut coffee and a blueberry muffin. Thank you." Erin slid onto the wooden bench.

"I'll be right back." Olivia trundled toward the counter.

While she waited, Erin watched the TV mounted near the ceiling, reading the closed captions because the conversation in the crowded coffee shop drowned out the commentator.

Joy Epson was at the Channel 7 News desk. "FBI agents thwarted a terrorist attack on five elementary schools in New York City earlier this morning. Unconfirmed sources say one of the officers working the case is in critical condition after he was shot in the line of duty." A video clip showed a hospital emergency entrance, then focused on the injured man's face.

Erin caught her breath. On the screen, Brad Hillcox lay on a stretcher, his eyes closed, his mouth twisted in agony.

Erin shivered. A dozen emotions washed through her as Brad's stretcher disappeared through the glass double doors.

"Are you okay, honey?" Olivia asked. She placed two tall mugs of coffee on the table, both with a muffin balanced on top. "You're as white as a ghost."

With a shaking hand, Erin reached for her cup, hoping the heat of the cup would stop her trembling. She glanced at the TV. "I think I just saw one," she murmured.

Bushwick, New York

Inside the hospital, a man's voice said, "Get him to surgery. He's bleeding."

Collier gritted his teeth and prayed he'd pass out. The left side of his abdomen was an inferno. An oxygen mask covered his mouth and nose. An IV drip ran into his arm. On both sides of the gurney, men and women whisked him down a wide hall.

One of the people holding the rail of the stretcher had a freckled forearm. Collier's pain-dazed eyes moved upward. Her face was turned away, but he saw her cheek was lightly freckled as well. Her dark, curly hair lay coiled in a wispy bun.

Cindy!

Wincing against the pain of moving, he touched her hand. She was here. She must have forgiven him.

Glancing at his hand over hers, the nurse smiled down at him. "We're going to fix you right up." She was a stranger.

Collier moaned and clenched the blood-stained sheet. Cindy, where are you?

Three wide lights glared into his eyes. Someone yanked off the plastic oxygen mask and replaced it with a black rubber thing. A masked doctor held up his gloved hands while a nurse slipped a second pair of gloves on them. The room swirled, and the pain eased back. Collier closed his eyes.

Black Canyon City, Arizona

Sitting across from Erin in the coffee shop, Olivia turned to look up at the TV screen. "Terrible thing, that. I caught the full newscast earlier. Those terrorists planned to set off a small bomb at one end of the school, then put a larger bomb at the other end where the children would run for safety. Imagine killing innocent children for some political cause! I can't imagine." She handed Erin a small stack of napkins.

"I guess not." Erin was so distracted by the TV broadcast she could hardly answer. Cindy Lestrade had loved Brad Hillcox. Erin Davis did not. She never wanted to see Brad…or Grant…or whoever he was…again.

"So, honey," Ms. Donner said, as they sipped coffee and broke into their muffins, "tell me about your computer background."

Erin shifted in her seat, trying to force her mind back to the interview. "I have a degree in Computer Science from Texas A&M." She had a framed document to prove it, provided by Nina, along with a driver's license and birth certificate.

"According to Ted, you did in two hours what those crooks over at Puget do in two days."

"I wouldn't go as far as to call them crooks."

Olivia leaned in. "Honey, you don't know half of it. Ten years ago, Puget went on a hiring binge and snatched up every decent programmer in the area. They hired one away from me. There was no way I could match the salary they offered. Once they had the market sewn up, they gouged every business around here."

She sipped coffee, then said, "Anyway, let's talk about you and the job. Our focus is giving customized service and training to local businesses and individuals. Then, we put a system together and load their software. We also do in-house and on-site training. Can you handle that?"

"Sure. I can build a system from the case up, load the software, and configure it for whatever the user wants. If they're into games, I can tweak it for that. If they're into business applications, I can do that, too."

"Sounds like you're the woman I'm looking for. What about your consulting business?"

"Will I have to put that aside while I work for you?"

Olivia's grinned. Her eyes disappeared behind her cheeks. "Not in the least, dear. I'm thrilled to have you. I was thinking, as long as you can give me a day's notice, if you get a consulting job, go for it. I can only pay eighteen dollars an hour, so it's hardly fair to hold you back. Can you live with that?"

"It'll cover my rent. And thanks."

"When would you like to start?"

Erin slowly set the cup down. "How about tomorrow? I have a few things to do today."

Bushwick, New York

Someone had built a bonfire over Grant's midsection, and the fire was spreading down his left leg. Trying to figure out if the nightmare was real, he forced his eyes open. He was in a dim hospital room with tiny flashing lights everywhere. He lifted his hand. The movement created a fresh spasm, so he let it lay where it was. Four years ago, he'd taken a bullet in the arm, but that had never hurt like this.

What happened? He tried to remember. The kid confessed. He called it in... That's right. The kid had grabbed Levitt's gun.

Collier tried to lick his lips, but his tongue was too thick to move. He managed a groan.

Immediately his mother was beside him. "Grant!"

"Water," he mumbled.

Her face was worried with deep lines of fatigue on her forehead and around her mouth. How long had he been here? Hot tears welled up. Suddenly, he felt like a scared six-year-old. He was so glad she was here.

Faye Collier wasn't his real mom. She had started out as his foster mom, but when he was eight, the Colliers had adopted him and Andre, his foster brother. Andre was African-American, and Grant had undefined Asian roots. All he knew is he looked a lot like Grant Imahara from *Mythbusters.* Imahara was his childhood idol, especially because they shared the same name.

His mom held up a pink sponge on a stick. "You can have this." She swished it in water, and placed it against his lips. When he opened, she swabbed his mouth.

When she finished, he said, "Am I still in New York? How did you get here?"

"You were on national television, son. I called your field office, and they told me where you were. Andre drove me to the airport." She lifted his free hand and cradled it in both of hers.

Andre was the same age as Grant, except he came to the family when he was five. That was thirty years ago. Grant always felt like he was lucky because he arrived at the Collier's horse ranch when he was two years old. He couldn't remember any other parents than the Colliers. Andre could remember, and he agreed that Grant was lucky.

Grant and Andre had so much fun in school telling everyone they were twins and watching the kids' faces. They did have the same last name and the same birth year. They weren't lying.

Grant's eyes closed, and he drifted into a morphine haze. The image of his dad's face came up. Warren Collier and Grant had been inseparable. Grant's first memories were of riding with Dad on the tractor. Later, he rolled out before dawn to help Dad hook up the milking machines. That wasn't a chore. It was working with Dad, far better than meat and potatoes to a growing boy.

When they were seventeen, Grant and Andre tossed hay bales from the truck bed to the ground where Dad stacked them inside the shed. Everyone else used rolled bales, but they didn't have a skid steer to move the heavy rolls, so they still bought bales.

"Getting tired, old man?" Grant called to him, laughing. It was an old joke, but one they both enjoyed.

"I can still beat a young pup like you," Warren called, his face glistening with healthy sweat. Suddenly, he bent over with a coughing fit that left him on the ground gasping for air. Andre and Grant rushed to him, supporting him, more scared than they'd ever been in their lives. Andre ran for help.

When he could talk, Dad said, "Hay fever." He held out his hand for a pull up. "That's all it is. Hay fever." Pulling a blue bandana from his back pocket, he wiped his face. By the time Mom arrived in the pickup truck, he was on his feet, but he crawled into the truck and spent the rest of the day in the house. Grant and Andre finished stacking the hay and loading the feed stands in the field.

The rest of the summer, Warren had to stop often to rest. At night, Grant lay in bed unable to sleep, listening to his father cough.

In September, Warren Collier stepped from the doctor's office with the verdict in his hand. Lung cancer. He died before spring warmed the Arizona hills he loved so much.

Grant came apart. He refused to bathe or change his clothes. He wept for days and spent long hours in the hills, tramping nowhere, filled with helpless rage. When his mother mentioned counseling, he took a shower and tried to act normal, but the rage still gnawed him to this day.

When Grant woke up, the room was brighter. Light came through the window. This time his mother stood nearby. She touched his forehead. "You've been sleeping a long time. How do you feel?"

"Rotten."

She reached for the lollipop sponge.

"How bad am I?" he asked.

She swabbed his mouth and didn't answer.

"How bad, Mom?" His voice grew louder, more insistent.

She laid down the sponge. "Let me get the doctor."

"No!" he gasped. "You tell me."

She shook her head, a frightened expression on her face. "I don't know how to explain it. I'll get the doctor." She soon returned with a blond young man in a white lab coat.

The doctor stood near Grant's shoulder, his manner professional. "I'm Dr. Alfred Henley." He lifted Grant's eyelids, shone lights in his eyes, and touched here and there.

"How bad, doctor?"

"Patience, Mr. Collier. I'll let you know in a moment. I need to do some tests."

Dr. Henley paced to the end of the bed and lifted the blanket. "Hold that for me, will you, Ms. Collier?"

Grant couldn't see what was happening. He felt a surge of panic.

"What do you feel?" the doctor asked.

"You're pressing your finger against my left foot," Grant replied, impatient.

"Thank you, Ms. Collier. You may lay the blanket down now." He returned to the head of the bed. "You lost about half of your large intestine, but that will be fine. You'll have no after-effects once you recover from the surgery." His tone changed. "You also have some nerve damage in your left hip that's affecting your left leg. With therapy, you should get around okay. More than that, we'll have to wait and see."

Grant felt a cold chill. "But I'm okay. I mean, I could feel your finger."

Dr. Henley slipped a sharp instrument from his coat pocket. "I pricked you with this, not my finger."

Collier looked at the pick like it was a cobra. "What does that mean?"

"Your leg is numb. You'll be in a wheelchair for a while, and you'll need therapy."

"But eventually, I'll be okay." It was a demand, not a question.

Dr. Henley returned the sharp piece of steel to his pocket. "With nerve damage, it's hard to say. If you work hard…" He shook his head. "We'll have to wait and see."

Grant leaned back into his pillow, his chin stretched up, his teeth tight. How could he be a field agent if he couldn't run? He squeezed his eyes tight, holding back the emotion that wanted to break him down.

His mother touched his forehead. Tears filled her eyes.

The doctor's voice grew firm. "Mr. Collier, you have a lot to be thankful for. A fragment from the bullet barely missed your kidney. You could've bled to death in three minutes. Let's keep things in perspective."

Collier glanced at his mother. Tears coursed down her weathered cheeks. "We came that close to losing you, son," she said.

He reached up for a hug. "I'm sorry, Mom," he whispered.

She leaned down to press her cheek against his, and the dam inside him broke loose.

Chapter Five

Rochester, New York

A week later, Grant was sick to death of sucking ice cubes, but at least they were better than those awful sponge lollipops. Dr. Henley said it would be a couple of days before he could take liquids, then soft foods.

He was bored out of his mind. Nothing interested him. He had a pile of books, his iPad and the TV to choose from, but staying in bed was driving him insane.

Exhausted, his mother had gone out for some fresh air. Collier couldn't blame her. She had been a real soldier through all this. A soft knock at the door drew his attention from the YouTube video he wasn't watching.

Jack Fitzgerald, Assistant Director of Operations stepped in. A powerfully built African-American, he had the look of a Denzel Washington in his older years. Jack smiled as he entered the room. "Grant, you're looking good."

Collier returned a wry grin. "Thanks. Excuse me if I don't stand." He flipped his iPad over.

Fitzgerald chuckled. "How long until you're up and about?"

"Two weeks, if I behave." He glanced down at the bandage covering his fifty-seven staples. "I'm at the mercy of a ruthless nursing staff. Every time I step out of line, they come at me with the needle or a bedpan. Believe me, I'll behave."

Fitzgerald eased into the vinyl lounge chair near the side of the bed. "Have you been following the news?"

"Yeah." Disgusted, Collier scowled at the dark TV screen high on the wall. Practically every American in the United States could recognize him on sight. Worse than that, sooner or later, he'd have to speak on the media. So far, the medical staff had kept them at bay, but once he left the hospital he was on his own. Even worse, he was trending on social media. His career as a stealth operative was over.

Fitzgerald lifted his left ankle to rest it on his right knee. He grew serious. "I guess you've already figured out what we're going to have to do."

"Kill me?" Collier asked, hopefully. "Give me a new face and a new ID, so I can stay in the field?"

"No can do. If we killed you, it would break your sweet mother's heart. Besides, it's not necessary."

"I want to get back to work. I can't do it while I'm a celebrity."

"Collier, I'm here to inform you the director has reclassified you to public relations. You make us look good."

Grant sounded ragged. "C'mon! Don't put me behind a desk. I'll be Section 8 in two days!"

Fitzgerald's voice softened. "Face it, Collier. Your undercover days are over. Take this assignment. It pays better, and you can have a life."

Collier wished he had something to throw. They couldn't do this to him. "If I refuse the transfer, then what?"

Fitzgerald raised both his hands, palm up. "You get a pension at half salary and keep your benefits." He stood up. "Get some rest. We'll talk again," he said and made his way out.

As he left, a delivery girl wearing skinny jeans and high-topped sneakers brought in a vase of daisies and placed them near Collier's shoulder on the nightstand. "Have a great day!" she chirped and hurried away.

The card was on a plastic stand. It had balloons around the edges and "Get well soon!" with no signature. Someone from the agency had probably sent them.

Collier flipped on the TV. He needed some noise to crowd out his angry thoughts. Eight days ago, he was an upwardly mobile intelligence officer. Today, he was a public relations man. All because of that idiot, Levitt.

The door opened a crack. "Anybody home?" a male voice said.

"Get out!" Grant yelled.

Levitt stepped inside. His blue suit looked like it had been slept in. "I won't stay long, Collier. I just came by to say that I'm sorry for what happened." He spieled off the words as though he'd memorized them. "If there's anything I can do for you, anything at all, you just name it."

Collier felt something snap inside his head. "How dare you show your face in here?" he bellowed. "You want to do something to make me feel better?"

Levitt took one step into the room. "You name it."

Collier wrapped his hand around the vase of daisies. "Get out!" The vase crashed above Levitt's head, showering him with water and broken glass. "You ruined my life! Get out!"

Shocked, Levitt backed away and scooted from the room.

A few minutes later, a matronly nurse came in to check Collier's IV, she saw the flowers and broken glass on the floor, and Collier holding his pillow over his face, moaning in a grating, guttural sound that told of agony far greater than physical pain.

Two weeks later, Grant couldn't help but smile when Andre burst into his hospital room without knocking. "Today is homecoming day!" Andre announced, beaming.

Andre Collier stood two inches over six feet tall and weighed in a hefty two-twenty, all muscle. He wore a grey T-shirt that stretched across his chest, his biceps pulling the sleeves taut.

After college, Grant had joined the Navy SEALs, and Andre did a hitch in the Marines. He still kept his hair in a military cut that made his ears stand out.

Andre had stayed close to home and became a deputy sheriff in Yavapai County. He married a lovely Latina named Rita, and they had two daughters.

Grant had disappeared into the secret world of federal investigations and hadn't been home in eight years. Andre's wife and kids were only photographs to Grant. He had never met them. He had been out of the country for most of that time, translating surveillance videos in six Middle Eastern countries, Scandinavia, and Germany. Whenever he was back in the states for a few weeks between assignments, he was rushing around to take care of his apartment and his life before getting on another flight to nowhere. Before he looked up, eight years had gone by. He couldn't believe it has been that long.

With a tearful good-bye, Mom had left three days ago to prepare the house for Grant's arrival.

Andre took a seat beside the bed. "You aren't talking, bro. Aren't you glad to get out of here?"

Collier stared at him. "Are you kidding? I'm jumping up and down, only my leg won't cooperate." He stretched to look out the window at the grounds below. "To be honest, the treat waiting for me on the lawn has got me down."

Andre looked out the window. "Oh, the press. You've got to meet them sooner or later. Better sooner while you're still in a wheelchair. They'll have more sympathy."

Right. Grant wasn't buying it. He'd seen too many mike-wielding reporters interviewing grieving parents, the camera coming in for a close-up of their tear blotched faces. If those guys had sympathy, they kept it under wraps.

Andre said, "Mom's tearing the house apart, looking for a red carpet to roll out when you get there." He leaned back with his hands behind his head. "I haven't seen her this excited since my wedding."

"The doctor won't release me unless I have someone to look after me and a physical therapist besides. At least, Uncle Sam's picking up the tab for the therapist." He reached for his tan polo shirt lying over the end of the bed. "Personally, I'd rather go back to my apartment at Langley."

Sitting up, Andre's tone became defensive. "What have you got against Mom? After ignoring her for so long, you should be glad she'll even talk to you."

Collier frowned. "It's not Mom, Andre. I don't have anything against Mom."

"Then what?"

Collier hesitated. "Let's forget it," he said finally, slipping the shirt over his head.

Skirting the empty wheelchair parked near the bed, Andre sat on the edge of the bed, one leg on the floor, the other hanging down. "Let's not forget it. Look, Grant, I'm not a kid anymore. I'm a man, and I'm your brother. Spit it out."

Collier concentrated on his four buttons. "It's the ranch. Everywhere I look, I see Dad."

Andre nodded, his face sad. "It's hard. I get that. He was my dad, too."

Grant gazed into his brother's gentle face. "When I'm there, all I see is him, wandering listlessly about the grounds, wasting away."

His brother touched his shoulder. "I'm just a dumb cop, but I've got enough smarts to know that you've got to deal with this before it gets you."

Grant reached for his pants. "I know."

A small nurse with a perky face bounced through the doorway. "It's time, gentleman," she called, her voice lilting.

"Be right there," Andre said, getting off the bed. As she darted out, he glanced at Grant. "What a babe."

Grant chuckled. "Hey, you're married. You shouldn't notice."

"Hey, you're not married. You should notice. Did you get her number?"

Grant shook his head. "All I know is that her name is Vicky." He stood on his good leg to tuck his shirt tail into his dark pants. "Unfortunately, I associate all the woman here with a dozen embarrassing situations, most of them painful."

Andre chuckled. "Ooookay. Let's get you into the chair."

With the difference in their sizes, Andre could have hoisted Grant on his shoulder and carried him down the stairs. Instead, he leaned down. Grant held onto Andre's shoulders for balance as he pivoted on his good foot and transferred into the wheelchair. His side still hurt too much for him to hop.

"I'm glad you can use your leg a little," Andre said. "I doubt mom could move you."

"I can walk a little," Grant said.

"You can walk?" Andre demanded. "How come no one told me that before?"

"I practice when no one's looking. They said I should wait until I start PT, but when have I ever waited for anything?" He lifted his release papers and instructions from the bed.

Grant's spirits rose a little as they wheeled out of the room that he had called home for the last three weeks. As they went down the hall, hospital staff called out their good wishes. He gave a loose salute, nodding his thanks while he tried to control his emotions. He was always getting choked up these days. That irritated him a little.

The elevator was open, and they wheeled right in. Vicky stepped inside behind them and touched the white button marked Lobby.

"You married?" Andre asked her, his voice teasing.

Grant scowled. Andre ignored him.

"Uh, no," she answered, reddening a little.

"Dating anyone?"

"Why are you so interested?" she bantered back. "Isn't that a wedding band on your finger?"

"Sure is, ma'am," Andre said, his Western accent showing. "I've got two gorgeous little girls, too." He pointed to Grant. "He's got no one."

"Shut up, Andre," Grant said. He glanced at the nurse. "Sorry, Vicky."

Her giggle grew to a laugh. "Don't be sorry. There was actually a pool at the nurse's station on which of us you'd ask out." She smiled into his eyes. "We were all disappointed when no one won."

Grant laughed, his first real laugh in a long time. "I'd like to make you the winner, but…"

"There's someone else," she finished.

"Yeah." He spoke the word softly, almost to himself.

"Who?" Andre jumped in, greedy for more information.

Collier stared at the shiny floor ahead of him and kept his lip buttoned.

"C'mon, bro! Give!"

He shot his brother a look that put a cork in his questions.

Conversation died until the trio reached the front doors of the hospital. Across from the covered portico, someone had cordoned off a square the size of Mom's kitchen. Collier nodded toward the men and women wearing press badges. "That's my firing squad?"

"Afraid so," Andre answered. He turned loose of the wheelchair to take a closer look through the plateglass window. "Must be fifty of them."

Vicky said, "I'll leave you now, Mr. Collier. Take care of yourself." With a parting smile she headed back to the elevator.

Andre gave the wheelchair a shove, and the sliding doors parted. Grant shielded his eyes from brilliant sunshine. A deep breath of the cool February breeze smelled wonderful after the recycled air inside the hospital. The moment he came into view, the crowd came to attention. People parted as Andre wheeled him to a group of microphones on a white table positioned across the sidewalk.

Collier scanned the sea of faces, then leaned toward the microphones. "The hospital says I have to stay in this wheelchair until I'm off the property. I will be happy to answer some of your questions." It wasn't really a lie. He could stand for about a minute.

Questions came at him machine-gun style. Even his training in negotiation hadn't prepared Collier for the intensity of the press. If this were friendly fire, he would hate to be the enemy.

A young woman in a red dress called out, "Mr. Collier, are you close to a full recovery?"

He grinned. "Give me a few weeks, and I'll be at the Olympic tryouts," he said.

A grizzled man in a rumpled suit shot his hand into the air. Grant gave him the nod.

"Bart Olafson, New York Times. Is it true that the FBI botched this operation?"

"Absolutely not true. We saved five schools, if you recall."

The same man dove in for a follow-up. "Sources say the weapon that shot you belongs to an FBI agent. Is that true?"

"I was on the floor bleeding. I didn't pay much attention."

Next was a thin, gray-haired man wearing wire-rimmed glasses and a badge saying CNN. "How did you get hardened terrorists to reveal their targets?" he asked.

Collier grinned. "I said, 'Pretty please,' and they told me everything."

Laughter wafted from the crowd like a gentle wind.

Tiring after fifteen minutes, he gave the last question to a middle-aged, sharply dressed woman sitting in the center of the pack. She stood up to say, "Mr. Collier, June Smith from Women's Universe magazine. Tell me, what kind of woman does America's hero like?"

Grant's brain unhitched for an instant. Everything he said here would be on the afternoon news. Here was a chance to talk to Cindy. What could he say?

Wetting his lips, stalling for a few more seconds, he finally answered, "A woman who would understand my failures and accept my apology."

"Mr. Collier, you sound like you're talking about someone specific," Ms. Smith said, her smile inviting him to say more.

Grant smiled, to let her know he was friendly but definitely closed to more questions on that topic.

"That's enough, ladies and gentlemen," Andre said. "Grant's got a flight to catch. We need to get going."

"Please, one last question," the lady from Universe magazine persisted.

Grant nodded, wondering what kind of hardball she had waiting for him this time.

"If the people of the United States could give you one thing as a reward for what you've done, what would it be?"

Grant considered. Not a bad question. "My privacy," he said. "Respect my privacy. My family needs time to heal."

On his way to their waiting car, Grant felt relieved. The press conference had gone well. Now, the question uppermost in his mind was, Would Cindy hear what he had said? Would she understand?

Chapter Six

Tempe, Arizona

Standing near the expanse of glass on the east side of her office, K.R. Quinn held an Inuit carving from Nunavut. The smooth figure fit neatly into her palm. Her manicured fingers slid across the face of the mother and rested on her sleeping child. In her younger days, owning a piece of artwork worth ten thousand dollars was only a fantasy. Not anymore. Through skillful maneuvering, Karen Quinn had turned Puget Information Systems into a goldmine. She preferred to be called K.R. and had used that since she founded the company. The name Puget paid homage to her roots in Washington State.

She now had leather upholstery, brass ornaments, and a magnificent view of the desert foothills of McDowell Mountains, the location of Frank Lloyd Wright's beloved winter retreat, Taliesin West. Her company leased the entire top floor of the Baker building.

A knock sounded on the door, and she dropped the bit of Jade into her jacket pocket. She called, "Come in," and sat at her desk.

Her security chief, Bart Dawkins, shuffled in and closed the door behind him. A former FBI agent who had left the Bureau under doubtful circumstances, Dawkins had been with Quinn since almost the beginning. They were as different as two people could be. He was built like an overweight linebacker. She was slight and small. He used his muscle to get what he wanted. She used brains and cunning. Quinn paid him well, and he was loyal. Best of all, they understood each other.

Quinn stifled a yawn.

"Too much racquetball this morning, boss?" Dawkins asked, taking a seat in front of the desk.

"The usual," Quinn said, stretching her sore legs a little to ease them. She had just passed her sixty-second birthday and wanted to stay mobile. She joined a fitness club last month and was paying for it with aches and pains. She glanced at Dawkins. "You look like a man with something on his mind."

The security chief rubbed his prominent forehead before answering. "Maybe."

Quinn leaned forward. "Speak English."

Dawkins looked uncomfortable. "We got a call from Archon Energy last week. When we quoted the standard twenty-five grand quick-service fee, they declined."

"You're kidding."

"Cross my heart, boss." He ran his meaty fingers across his thick beard at the side of his neck. "They left a message on the weekend voicemail, and the tech supervisor called them back. They said the problem was solved."

Quinn's heart rate elevated slightly. "That's impossible." She turned to her computer and opened the Archon Energy file. On the bottom right corner of the screen, she entered a password and read a string of text. "There's absolutely no way. That virus could never be broken by the likes of Booregard. He's way too dense."

Dawkins clasped his powerful hands across his lap and asked, "If not Booregard, who?"

"That's what I'm about to find out." Quinn lifted the receiver on her desk phone and punched in Archon's number. "Ted Booregard, please." Hitting a button to activate the speakerphone, she tapped her fingertips on the rosewood desk.

"Ted Booregard here," a voice crackled.

Her voice nicely modulated, she said, "Hi, Ted, it's K.R. Quinn. I heard you had a problem last week. Everything all right now?"

"Yeah, the program's working like a charm."

"I'm glad you were able to fix it."

"Not me. It was some young gal with a new consulting business. I managed to catch her at home. She's a real whiz. She did in two hours what you wanted twenty-five thousand dollars to do. Seems excessive, don't you think?"

Quinn deliberately slowed her breathing before answering. "Most definitely. You have to understand that our tech people were giving an estimate. That was the top end. If it only took our people a couple of hours, you definitely wouldn't have been charged twenty-five thousand." What she wouldn't tell Booregard is that the technician would have made sure to spend at least two days.

"Well, that would be a first," Booregard said. "Hey, she mentioned you might already be aware of a flaw in the program and have some kind of patch file. Do you?"

"I doubt it's a flaw in the program. If she only needed two hours to fix it, you probably had an input problem. If we'd worked on it, we would have been able to show you what went wrong. If it happens again, we'll sort it out for you."

Booregard's breath buzzed into the phone. "If it happens again, I'm calling her."

The front of Quinn's neck turned red. She kept her voice calm. "I'm sorry to hear that, Ted. We've always considered Archon one of our best clients. It seems harsh that one little incident like this would cause you to lose faith in us."

"Yeah, whatever. All I know is she was there when I needed her, and it didn't cost twenty-five grand neither."

Quinn's fingers tapped double-time. "Well, Ted, you certainly have the right to deal with anyone you want. I feel so terrible about this that I'm putting a note in your file that for the next year, all technical support for your company is free."

A long pause. "You're serious?"

"Absolutely. Customer satisfaction is number one."

"Well… I'll give it some thought."

"You do that. By the way, what was this young gal's name?"

Booregard chuckled. "Why? So, you can hire her and leave me with no options?"

"I am always on the lookout for sharp minds. You know that."

"You'll probably find out sooner or later. Her name's Erin Davis. She goes under the name of Davis Consulting out of Black Canyon City."

"Thank you, Ted. I hope we'll be in touch again. I can't overemphasize how much we value your business." She gently set down the receiver.

Dawkins's bushy eyebrows rose. "'A year of free technical support? Since when do you give anything away free?"

"Since now. Under no circumstances do we want someone else poking around our program. If this Erin Davis ever figures out what we've done, we'll be doing time, my friend. That would be much worse for you than for me."

Dawkins shifted uncomfortably. "What do you want me to do?"

"For now, just find out who she is, and have someone keep an eye on her. Maybe she won't cause trouble. Then again, maybe she will, and we'll have to do more."

"How much more?"

Staring at Dawkins, Quinn said, "Whatever it takes to make sure she doesn't know enough to turn us in. It's really up to her, isn't it?"

Dawkins let loose a humorless chuckle and sauntered out of Quinn's office.

Black Canyon City, Arizona

Erin tingled with excitement. She was actually sitting in Madge's Cut and Curl, the last chair on the left. Yesterday, she couldn't afford a cappuccino. She never dreamed that today she'd have enough for foils, color and cut. She'd pinched pennies for so long, this time she was going for the max.

Slender and well-worn, Madge mixed her brush through the bowl of hair coloring. She set it down and picked up her comb. On her first part of Erin's hair, she said, "Why on earth do y'all dye your hair? I can see from the roots that your natural color is gorgeous. You sure you don't want me to change you back to what you were before?"

"No." Erin answered too quickly. She smiled to soften her hasty response. "You know what they say, blonds have more fun."

Madge's tired face cracked into a smile as she ran her fingers through her own bleached mop. "So they say, but I'm still waiting. Well, here goes." She slid the first foil in place and dabbed with the brush. "Did y'all hear that fellow who saved those school kids from terrorists is from around here?"

Erin woke up. She stared at Mage in the mirror. "How did you find that out?"

"It was in the afternoon paper. There's even a picture. Seems someone from around here recognized him. He's a Collier from over in Cave Creek."

Erin gazed at her own reflection, but all she saw was Brad's agonized face on the TV screen. Her emotions were all over the place. She curled her nails into her palms. She would never let him hurt her again, even if it was just thinking about him.

Madge finished the last foil, then dabbed a deeper color between the carefully folded packets to take care of Erin's roots. "If he's anything like his picture. He's a hunk."

She set the local paper on the counter near Erin and set the timer. "Can I get you some water or maybe some tea, Honey?"

"Water, please," Erin said. She closed her eyes. The ammonia smell made her nose burn.

Madge brought her a water bottle and left to take care of someone at the register.

As soon as Erin was alone, she snatched up the newspaper. There he was, a photo of Brad Hillcox, younger and in uniform, with that disarming grin. Local Boy Swords Terrorist Plot, the headline read. Did he break someone else's heart to do it?

She scanned down to his name. Grant Collier. Her fingers touched the lettering. He grew up on a horse ranch in Cave Creek, about half an hour from here just north of Phoenix. Why was he from this area, the same area she was assigned for her new identity? Weird.

When Erin left the beauty salon, she was a honey blond with a cut that brushed her shoulders. She paused outside the plate glass window lettered Madge's Cut and Curl and dropped two quarters into a squeaking rusted machine holding the Phoenix Herald. Tucking the paper under her arm, she headed for the Jeep. She had to get home. She felt a good cry coming on.

Standing upright from the block wall, where he'd been leaning in the shade for the past hour, Rory Critch followed Erin down Meridian Street to where she had parked. He blended in well: medium height, medium build, dark hair and the slouchy walk of a cowboy. No one noticed him, but he sure noticed the gorgeous blond ahead of him. Shadowing Erin Davis would be a pleasure.

Three weeks later, Erin left the ATM machine and drove to Hillyard's Grocery on the outskirts of Black Canyon City. She found a parking place near the door and grabbed an abandoned cart on the sidewalk. Life had changed dramatically in just twenty-one days.

Olivia Donner's sales had risen significantly since Erin arrived. Last night, Olivia had invited her to stay on the payroll as long as she wanted. The locals were delighted that they didn't have to go all the way to a big box store in Phoenix to get what they needed. Word was getting out.

A friendly woman held the door open for Erin, and her shopping cart rattled over the metal threshold. For the first time since she had arrived in Arizona, Erin was glad to be at the grocery store. She was one lady with plenty of money and a raging appetite.

In the produce department, a display of California strawberries (out of season and expensive) caught her eye. She picked up a carton. One whiff and she was lost. She bought half a pound and made sure she picked up a can of aerosol whipped cream to go with them. Lettuce wasn't cheap either, but a large head still ended up in the basket. Two years ago, she was buying shoes that cost almost as much as her rent. Now, a box of strawberries was her biggest excitement in months.

She took her time, enjoying the moment. Half an hour later, she stood in the checkout line. Ahead of her, a frazzled young mother had a squirming baby on her hip, and a two-year-old girl hanging on her leg. The woman struggled to transfer groceries onto the belt.

"I can hold the baby if you'd like," Erin said, beaming at the little boy. He wore a blue jacket with the front unzipped.

His mother looked relieved. "Would you?" she held out the boy. "His name is Scotty."

Erin made funny sounds with him. When Scotty smiled, she smiled into his little face. A heavy feeling hit the pit of her stomach. She was almost thirty. Would she ever have children? In her twenties, a career had seemed vital. Now, she wasn't so sure. Had things turned out differently with Brad… no, Grant. Whatever his real name, he was still Brad to her.

Holding Scotty close, she caught that distinctive baby scent and felt a tug deep inside her.

Her grocery cart empty, Scotty's mother held out her arms, and Erin gave the child back. The mom called out, "Thanks!" and hurried away.

Emptying her cart onto the conveyor, Erin smiled at the checkout girl, who was young but weathered. The scanner beeped as each item passed. Halfway through Sharon's groceries, the beeping stopped. The cashier groaned.

"What's the matter?" Erin asked.

The clerk waved a box of macaroni over the sensor. She shook her head. "The computers are down again."

"This happen a lot?"

"This is the third time since last Thursday. Mr. Hanson is going to blow a gasket."

At that moment, a tall man with a dome-shaped forehead came rushing out of the front office. He hurried to the register, punching buttons and getting nowhere. He swore under his breath. Sweat gleamed on his face.

"Maybe I can help," Erin said.

His gray eyes locked with hers. "How?"

"It looks like a software problem. I happen to be a computer programmer."

He turned to the keypad in front of him, tapping loudly. Nothing. He said to Erin, "I appreciate the offer, but I've already called our regular company."

"When will they get here?"

He shook his head. "Three or four hours."

The people in line groaned. One of them pushed his cart to the side and headed for the exit.

Erin said, "Do you mind my asking what company you use?"

"Puget."

Erin felt like an anxious racehorse bumping the starting gate. She stepped closer, her eyes alight. "Tell you what, if I fix it before they get here, you pay me a flat fee of $500. If I don't fix it, you pay me nothing."

"Sounds to me like you're telling fairy tales." He pinned her under his stare. "How do I know you won't foul it up more and double Puget's bill?"

"Have you heard of PTL computers?"

"Sure, that's Olivia Donner's place. She used to do our stuff before we went with Puget."

"I work with her. She's at the store. Give her a call, and see what she says."

Hanson cocked his head, his mental gears working. "Wait right here." He raised his hand toward the customers in line. "Please, wait right here." He trotted into the office cubicle. A couple of minutes later, he appeared at the doorway and motioned for Erin to come in.

Erin held her hand out toward the checkout girl and asked, "Would you mind watching my groceries?"

"I'd put them back," she answered. "Last time this happened we were down a full day."

"Not today," Erin said, flipping her curls away from her face. She marched to Hanson's tiny office and took a seat at his desk. This system was more up-to-date, but his problem was similar to the one she discovered at Archon Energy.

Thirty minutes later, initializing sounds came from the register. Ronald Hanson almost kissed her. He reached for his checkbook. "Young lady," he said, beaming, "Here's your $500, and whatever is in your cart is free. Not only did you save me Puget's exorbitant fee, but I can still serve my customers. Last week we lost $8,000 in business."

Erin handed him her card. Delighted. She dropped the check into her purse. "I live here, in Black Canyon City. If this happens again, feel free to call me day or night."

Phoenix Sky Harbor Airport

The Boeing 727 softly touched down at Phoenix Sky Harbor Airport and taxied to the terminal. Collier groaned. "We've got to get through the airport, down to baggage claim and out to the car. Today, that seems equal to ten marathons."

"We'll get there, bro," Andre said, standing the moment the seatbelt sign went off. "Let's get you out of here." He placed their two carry-on bags in a rack under the wheelchair and hustled Grant out of his seat and into the chair. They took the elevator down to baggage claim and came to a dead stop.

A crowd was gathered in the corner near the automatic doors leading to the sidewalk. Two security guards had their arms outstretched to keep them from mingling with the passengers gathering around the conveyors.

"What the hell?" Grant said. "The press again?"

In his characteristic dry tone, Andre said, "That's not the press."

Collier stared up at the underside of Andre's heavy jaw. "Who is it then, the IRS?"

Andre chuckled. "You're the local hero, bro. That's your welcoming committee."

Grant's eyes narrowed. "There's a reporter in the crowd. I can smell him."

"I doubt it." Andre shot back. "The local paper might be out there, but that's all."

Gripping the arms of the wheelchair, Grant stood up.

"What are you doing?" Andre demanded, moving in front of him in a blocking move. "Sit down, Grant!"

"I'm not going out sitting in that. I'm going to walk on my own two feet."

"Why not? Everyone knows you're injured. They love you more for it."

Grant spoke every word distinctly. "I'm not riding in that chair." He clamped his jaw in a characteristic show of stubbornness. Waving Andre out of his way, he said, "I've got my cane. If you let me lean on you, I can make it."

"You'll be sorry, bro. Believe me."

Grant stared at him.

Gripping his brother's arm, Collier hobbled toward the crowd. Cheers went up.

"Wait a minute!" Andre said. "The bags!" He left Grant for fifteen seconds to grab their bags.

By the time he returned, sweat stood out on Grant's upper lip. Intense pain shot through his leg. His left hip was killing him. He managed a weak smile and a half wave at the cheering crowd.

"This is a dumb idea," Andre whispered fiercely when they were halfway across the massive lobby.

"Just keep going," Grant urged. He suddenly felt clammy and cold. The crowd was still cheering and waving. Their smiling faces started to blur and spin. Grant shook his head, trying to get his eyes to quit playing tricks. An icy chill washed over his head and back. The tile floor came up to meet him.

Suddenly, Andre's meaty arms wrapped around him. Through a gray mist, he heard shouts and voices filled with concern. One voice, a feminine soprano, stood out above the others. "Let me through! I've got to see him!" Was that voice real? How did Cindy get to Phoenix?

Chapter Seven

Black Canyon City, Arizona

Back at her apartment, Erin made three trips to haul her groceries to the second floor. She flipped on the TV to listen to the news while she unpacked everything. The lettuce remained on the counter with carrots, celery, and tomatoes. She placed a T-bone steak next to the stove. Not much of a meat eater, Erin was determined to celebrate in style. She had a check for $500 in her purse.

She sliced strawberries and added a bit of sugar. She might as well make desert and put it into the fridge, so it would be nicely chilled.

The 6:00 news came on. She stood stock-still. There he was again. Wasn't there anyone else in the United States they could put on evening television? Joy Epson reporting. Good old Joy Epson. Petite, perfect hair, upturned nose, plastic smile, and always talking about superhero Grant Collier.

"Get a life," Erin muttered at the screen. She opened her tiny fridge and pulled out the aerosol can of whipped cream.

"And our top story… Local hero Grant Collier finally speaks, and boy, what he has to say… When we return from these messages from our sponsors."

Scowling, Erin sliced the end of a pound cake and placed it on a saucer. What on earth could Brad say that a person could believe? People were so stupid.

She spooned strawberries over the cake. She should stop torturing herself and shut the TV off, but she felt a morbid fascination. What lies would Hero Hillcox tell this time?

The news began again with a close-up of Collier sitting behind a white table, answering questions with his usual smug demeanor. Holding the can of whipped cream, Erin moved over to the TV and turned up the volume. A woman in a red dress had the floor.

"Mr. Collier, June Smith from Woman's Universe magazine. Tell me, what kind of woman does America's hero like?"

I know what he likes, Erin thought shaking the can with vengeance, a woman as dumb as a fence post and a gullible as a two-year-old.

Collier hesitated, then smiled softly in a way she remembered so well. "A woman who would understand my failures and accept my apology."

"Loser!" she shouted. "If I ever see you again, here's what you'll get." She lifted her right foot and kicked the air, followed by two jabs to the throat. Oh yeah. Just let him get close enough now.

A loud thump came from the ceiling, but Erin ignored it. Let the whole world know, for all she cared. With shaking hands, she turned off the TV and paced back to the kitchen. Squeezing whipped topping over the strawberries, she reached for a fork. Half the shortcake disappeared before Erin realized that she was eating dessert and had forgotten to cook dinner.

Rory Critch didn't know much about Puget Information Systems, but he knew Mr. Dawkins would want to know that Erin Davis had magically fixed the grocery store's computers. Leaving his post where he was watching the grocery, he started his battered orange VW Beetle and headed to Dawkins's favorite bar.

Phoenix, Arizona

When Grant regained consciousness, a familiar face hovered over him: Dr. Parker, his former family doctor. The doctor had a blue stethoscope pressed against Grant's bare chest. Six gray circles stuck to his torso, with little wires trailing from each one. On his arm, a black cuff inflated automatically, then released.

Collier tried out a shaky grin. "Doc Parker," he whispered, "long time no see."

The snowy-haired physician adjusted his black-framed glasses and frowned. "You haven't changed much, Grant. You never did know when to quit."

Looking haggard, Andre spoke from a chair off to the side. "Man, you sure scared us."

Grant looked around. A pale green curtain surrounded him. The scuffling and rattling of a hospital emergency room wafted into the cubicle. "What happened?"

Dr. Parker answered the question with a question of his own. "What hairbrained impulse caused you to refuse your wheelchair?"

Grant quirked in the corner of his mouth. "What can I say, Doc? It was stubborn pride. People were waiting to see me, and I didn't want to go out in a wheelchair."

"Well, pride doesn't cut it for me. When you're in my care, you will obey my orders to the letter or have a room in a rehab facility for the next month."

"Aw, come on, Doc," Collier said, moving his hand. "I'm not that sick."

Parker opened Grant's patient folder. "This is your chart from New York." He gazed inside and closed it. "You're sicker than you think." Moving closer to the gurney, he said, "The choice is yours. Will you stay here where we can watch you, or go home and behave yourself?"

Collier tapped his fingers against the sheet. He thought of the ranch house with its familiar log walls and cracking fireplace, the soft sofa and one of Mom's thick afghan across his legs. A moment later, he nodded. "Your terms, doc. You've got me by the short hairs."

Parker smiled for the first time. "Fine. I've already ordered a visiting nurse for you and a physical therapist." He peered at Collier over his glasses. "Do I need to put this in writing?"

"Aw, doc. I'm not that bad."

"How about the time you broke your arm and busted the cast off after two weeks because it felt better?"

Collier grinned. "I was only thirteen."

"As far as how you can see, you've gotten taller but not one whit smarter since then."

A tall blond with reddish highlights in her hair poked her face through the privacy curtain. "Is this the patient, Dr. Parker?"

Parker looked pleased. "Hello! You're right on time." He looked down at Grant. "This is your nurse, Sally Kramer." Turning back to her, he said, "Sally, this is one tough cookie. "You think you can handle him?"

Her white teeth showed as she smiled and stepped through the green drapes. "Sure, doctor, I've had experience with this one. I'll keep a lid on him." She beamed at Grant. "Hi Grant. It's me. Remember?"

He gave her a lopsided grin, not sure if he was pleased or not. "Hi, Sally."

She came close to the bed and looked into his eyes. Her voice had a soft, husky quality. "It's been a long time."

Collier forgot he was in a hospital emergency room. Sally still had that magnetism he'd always found irresistible. Everyone from his class at Cave Creek High School would remember what he had almost forgotten. Grant and Sally had been an item for more than a year.

Looking for her left hand, he saw that it was bare.

Dr. Parker said to Sally, "I'll have the service notify you when he's released." To Grant, he said, "In any case, you'll stay here for the night for observation."

Sally smiled. "I'll see you when you get home."

Black Canyon City, Arizona

The next day, Olivia Donner frowned as Erin picked at her chef salad. Her newest employee looked lovely in a silky dress the mottled color of autumn leaves. She had a snappy new hairstyle and shimmering lip gloss, yet Olivia sensed that something troubled the girl.

"You don't like the salad?" Olivia asked, finally. "Would you like to order something else?"

Erin looked up. She had fatigue lines around her eyes. "Huh? Oh, no. This is fine. I'm not really hungry." She tried to smile, then gave it up.

Olivia laid down her fork. "Look. Maybe I'm putting my nose in where it doesn't belong, but I'm worried about you, Erin."

Erin pushed a tomato slice out of the way and stabbed a crest of lettuce coated with ranch dressing. "Things couldn't be better, Olivia. Honestly. I've got a great job, and I'm expecting more consulting business since I fixed the system at the grocery store. What more could I want?"

Olivia smiled gently. "How about romance? How about that?"

Instantly, Erin's eyes flashed. "Why would you ask that?"

"I'm sorry. I crossed a line. Please, forgive me."

Erin reached out to squeeze her hand. "I'm sorry I snapped. I'm not upset at you."

"I'm no great expert on romance," Olivia said, reaching for a napkin in the metal holder, "but the way you mope around, it's like you've got a broken heart."

Erin's eyelashes flickered. "This is family related, and I can't talk about it." She made an effort to eat her salad, and the conversation dwindled.

Their waitress, a woman with biceps like a bodybuilder, stopped by their table with a pitcher of tea to refill Olivia's glass.

"Thank you, dear," Olivia said, smiling. When the waitress left, she continued, "If you ever need to talk, I'm here," she said. She picked up a small menu card propped next to the napkin holder. "How about some dessert?"

Phoenix, Arizona

Grinning, Andre Collier pushed a blue wheelchair into Grant's second floor room at St. Joseph hospital. This place was more comfortable than his sick room in New York, complete with brocade curtains and a wide, soft recliner.

Dressed in a blue shirt and khaki pants, Grant lay on the bed with the top half elevated to forty-five degrees. When he glared at the chair rolling toward him, Andre chuckled. "We're not going to have trouble with the patient today, are we?"

The patient sat up suddenly. "When I get better, I'm going to wrap that wheelchair around your head."

"Watch out," Andre said, pausing to flex his powerful arm. "Things have changed since we were kids."

Grant shook his head. "No, they haven't. You've always been twice my size." He swung his sock-clad feet to the floor and slipped them into Brown loafers. "I know some moves that'll put you on your can in three seconds." He grinned. "You know what they say, the bigger they are, the harder they fall."

Andre chuckled. "I'm going to hold you to that." He parked the chair near Grant's knee. "In the meantime, we've got to go home and eat fried chicken. Mom's cooking a huge Sunday dinner and it's only Friday."

"Who's coming?"

"It's a surprise."

Grant groaned. "I can't handle a crowd. I feel weak."

"Oh, so now you feel weak. Two days ago, you were a tough guy. Changed your tune, I see… when it suits you."

Pivoting on his good leg, Grant swung into the wheelchair, and Andre pushed him to the elevator. At the hospital entrance, Andre hurried to bring the car up. In a few minutes, they tooled through town and headed north until streetlights and sidewalks faded into rolling desert and barbed wire fences. When they reached the lane winding through half a mile of pastureland, Andre said, "Grant, there's something I've got to tell you."

Grant stared at him, sensing something was wrong. "What is it?" he demanded. "Come on. Spit it out."

"I work a lot with street kids. About six months ago, I busted a sixteen-year-old girl named Roxanne. Nice girl, pretty, smart as a whip. She got involved with the wrong bunch, and I had to book them all for B&E." He cleared his throat. "That's breaking and…"

"For Pete's sake, Andre! I got out of kindergarten almost thirty years ago!"

Andre shook his head. "Sorry, Grant. I didn't mean to insult your intelligence."

The car entered a stand of pine trees and mesquite. Their branches formed dappled shadow patterns on the hood and windows of the car. When their father homesteaded this land, he had put the house at the top of a hill overlooking the beautiful landscape. Grant stopped listening for a moment. It was good to be home.

"As I was saying," Andre continued, "Roxanne had no permanent address, and her parents are both gone. She was headed for juvenile detention followed by a life in the dregs. I told Mom about her. Mom asked me a few questions, and I thought that was it."

Grant leaned forward, his hand on the dash of the car. His face had an I-can't-believe-this expression. "I already know what you're going to say."

"You got it." His brother nodded. "While I was in court waiting for Roxanne and her friends to be sentenced, the defense lawyer stood up and announced that Roxanne had a new guardian. Then, Mom marched down the aisle. She had been sitting in the back row the whole time."

Grant stared at the ceiling of the car and shook his head, waiting for the rest of the story.

"The judge took one look at her, tough as an old board, her right arm bigger than his, and he gave custody to Mom as long as Roxanne's on probation."

"Has she been giving Mom fits?" Collier demanded, staring at him.

Andre shook his head as though he were relieved to have something good to say. "Actually, Roxanne seems to be getting along fine." He gazed out the window as though the trees suddenly fascinated him. "Mom didn't want to tell you while you were so sick, but that's why she had to get back home. She didn't feel right leaving Roxanne with Billy and Ida for too long." Farm workers, Billy and Ida Ray lived in a cottage on a corner of the property.

Grant let out an irritated gasp. "What was Mom thinking? She's too old to deal with a teenager, especially a delinquent."

"She says she's giving back. You know how she is about that. Just look at the two of us. She took us in."

The car floated around a sweeping curve. Soon the house came into view. "It's what Mom wants, Grant," Andre said. "You have to respect that."

Collier passed his hand across his face. "Why did she decide to do her charity work just when I'm coming home? Honestly, Andre. I don't feel like hearing any whining and sassing right now. That girl…"

"…Roxanne."

"…if she pulls any shenanigans, I won't stand for it. Mom doesn't deserve that."

Andre didn't answer.

Grant let his back relax against the seat, his eyes on the landscape—the horse stable, the paddocks, the hay racks, just like they were when he had left. That kid better not give him any lip, or she'd get a hard lesson from old father Collier.

Cave Creek, Arizona

From his vantagepoint above the ranch house, a watcher who called himself Ben observed the dark sedan making its way up the Collier driveway, with a brown cloud of dust behind it. His powerful binoculars couldn't penetrate the dust or the tinted glass to see who was inside. It didn't matter. Collier had to be in that car. Getting close to the local hero would be tough, but he had to chance it. Too much was at stake.

Phoenix, Arizona

K.R. Quinn didn't care for the Cattleman's Bar and Grill. It was a bar frequented by men with faces like leather from hours in the desert sun and rough hands from working the ranges. On the other hand, if she had to meet Dawkins's little spy, Quinn definitely didn't want the man at her country club.

She pushed open the door, and the cloying odors of cheap beer and cigarette smoke made her wince. Music pounded from hidden speakers.

Basically, Cattleman's was one big room with about twenty oak tables, served by women who didn't know their youth was long gone. In a dark corner, Dawkins stood up and waved to get Quinn's attention. What a choice spot for a meeting. How could anyone hear?

Navigating her way past cowboys, mechanics, and truck drivers, Quinn reached Dawkins's table. Pulling out a chair, she didn't acknowledge the greeting from Dawkins's spy. The less she had to do with that pimply faced greaseball, the better. Had anyone told the kid black leather jackets and slicked back hair had gone out decades ago?

In front of Dawkins's small wide glass half filled with amber liquid, stood a brown bottle with a green label. The moment Quinn sat down, a tall waitress with platinum hair paused by their table.

"What you having?" she asked, watching Quinn.

"A root beer," Quinn said shortly. When she left, Quinn glanced at her watch.

Dawkins nodded to Rory. "Spill it."

The young man had a nasal whine. "Well, I was following the broad like you guys asked and…"

"Wait just a moment," Quinn interrupted. "I never told you to follow anyone."

"All right, all right. Dawkins told me to follow the broad. I trailed her to the grocery store where she parked in the third row…" He hesitated while the waitress set down Quinn's drink.

When she left, Dawkins growled, "Cut to the chase. Tell her about inside… the registers."

His acne-scarred face twisted. "Man, you guys don't admire good work." He gestured with the bottle in his hand. "Okay. I'm over by the magazines watching her at the checkout when all the cash registers died." He grinned. "Hanson started running around like a girl who's lost her engagement ring. My target talks to him for a bit, and he goes into his office. He comes to the door, waves to her. She goes in, and half an hour later they're back in business." He took a sip. "I figured it was important, so I came to Mr. Dawkins, here, right away."

Dawkins flipped a twenty in Roy's direction. "Lose yourself until I call you."

Snatching up the money, Rory sauntered two tables away to join a couple of hard-faced women.

As soon as he left, Dawkins asked, "You figure she fixed their system?"

"Definitely. I checked with tech support. Hanson called for help, then a little over half an hour later, he canceled the call. He was scheduled for a surprise today. It had to be her."

"How much do you think she knows about us?"

"Since she fixed it in half an hour, she knows exactly what we've done. It's only a matter of time before she's tempted to decipher the encryption. When she does that, we start doing hard time."

Dawkins shredded his napkin. "That's not going to happen. My man in New York found her hometown today. Erin Davis currently resides in a graveyard in Gravelston. She died from leukemia at the age of eight."

Quinn's expression changed. "You don't say." She sipped her root beer.

Dawkins went on, "Before we take action, I've got to know why she's here. There are four possible reasons for a new identity. First, she's hiding from the law. I doubt that. She's not the type. I checked out the social security number, and it's solid. Only someone deep in government could do that."

Quinn set down her glass. "Maybe she's in Witness Protection. That means she testified in some big case. Was she a criminal or not? If she's dirty, the feds will notice what happens to her. If she's clean, we'd best be real careful." She glanced at Dawkins. "You said four reasons."

"The fourth is the one that's got me worried. She might have a friend with connections. Years ago, some Russian mafia guys grabbed a teenage girl for human trafficking. The kid came from a single parent home, no important relatives or friends, or so they thought. It turned out her uncle was undercover with the CIA. He went on a retaliation mission and five people ended up dead. If she's a case like that, prison will be the least of our worries."

Quinn stared at him. "Find out who she is, and why she's hiding. Do it yesterday."

"What do you suggest? We just walk up and ask her?"

A sinister grin came over Quinn's gaunt face. "No, we dig a little deeper, that's all." She pulled out her cellphone and keyed in a phone number. Leaning close to the wooden paneling, she clapped her left hand over her ear, trying to hear over the pounding music. "Do you know who this is?... Good... What's your schedule like this Sunday?... Excellent. Let's meet then." She nodded. "Yeah, same as usual."

Ending the call, she smiled at Dawkins and said, "Call Rory."

Chapter
Eight

Black Canyon City, Arizona

Guiding her Jeep out of the restaurant parking lot, Erin kept thinking about her stalled conversation with Olivia at lunch. This was the reason she couldn't have any close friends. She couldn't talk to anyone about her real family, and she was a terrible liar. Her cover story was that her parents had died in a car accident. Even she didn't believe it when she said it.

Both her parents were serving life sentences for treason. After that awful FBI raid, she had expected her father's arrest. When the news arrived that he had been detained, she felt numb.

Two weeks later, she was horrified when her mother was indicted for monitoring his fake email addresses and delivering messages for him. Because Alice wasn't an employee of the Department of Defense, she wasn't under as much scrutiny, so they took advantage of that. Cindy's parents were co-conspirators, according to the prosecution. They both got life in solitary. They were too dangerous to have contact with other people, not even a phone call.

Why hadn't they considered what would happen to their only daughter if they were caught? Did she mean so little to them?

At her mother's sentencing, Cindy sat in the first row of audience seats like she had for both trials. Her mother's knees gave out when she heard the verdict. The guards helped her out of the room. Cindy adored both her parents, and she didn't have a chance to say good-bye.

How had she been so gullible? She had no idea what they were up to. Brad Hillcox had so completely taken her in. One moment she was about to be engaged. The next, she had her identity erased and landed in the desert with a blank life to fill in all on her own. She had never been completely on her own before. How was she going to pull herself together and start living again?

She sighed, easing into traffic and immediately changing lanes to make a left at the light. Was it possible that Brad really had cared for her? Why had he said that on TV?

Deep in her thoughts, she drove home on automatic pilot, somehow managing to stop for every red light and make the correct turns. Parking in her numbered space in front of the apartment building, she felt the world closing in on her. Was she going to live like this for the rest of her life?

She dug out her apartment key as she walked and pushed open the door to the red brick building. She no longer needed a key to open the outer door. The Wilson teens on the third floor had kicked it in when they forgot their key. That was a month ago, and the landlord still hadn't bothered to repair it. She clumped up the dark stairs, wishing she could afford a better place to live.

When she inserted her key into the deadbolt, her door creaked open by itself. She froze, every sense screaming. Her heart thumped like a jackhammer.

She started to push into her apartment… then stopped. How many times had she yelled at a TV character, "Don't go in there, you fool! He's waiting around the corner. Call the cops!"

Spinning on her heel, she trotted downstairs to the superintendent's apartment and pounded on the wooden door. The varnish had worn off where her hand hit.

Somewhere inside, bottles clinked. Then came language. Wouldn't that manager ever come? She pounded louder, bruising her palms on the wood.

Shuffling footsteps, and a chain lock slid off, another chain lock, a deadbolt, and the door opened. A gnarled face covered with thick, white stubble appeared in the opening. The smell of stale whiskey, and cigarette smoke hit her in the face when he spoke, forming the words carefully, each one drawing out longer than normal. "Whadda ya want? It's Sunday. Can't it wait?"

Erin cried, almost hysterical. "Mr. Iverson! Someone… My apartment!"

His watery eyes tried to focus. "Can't you see I'm busy?" He rubbed an arthritic hand across the front of his t-shirt, once white, now gray.

Eyes wild, Erin gulped, then breathed deeply, forcing herself to be coherent. "Someone broke into my apartment."

The old man's hunched frame straightened up. His jaw tightened. "I warned those kids to stay away from you. You're the nicest tenant I have ever had." He paused a second, considering, then said, "I'll be right back."

Leaving the door ajar, he headed into his apartment. Liquor bottles covered the dining room table and littered the filthy carpet. A moment later, he returned with a weathered baseball bat in his hand.

"Shouldn't we call the police?" Erin asked, wincing at the sight of the bat.

Weaving, the old man stared at her, amazed. His words ran together. "Why? So, they can give those Wilson boys some milk and cookies?" He got louder as he spoke. "Not a chance. If I survived Viet Nam, I can survive those punks. Let's go."

Erin followed Iverson up the narrow staircase, staying a few steps behind him. She scolded herself. She should have called the police first.

When he reached her apartment, he held up his hand. "Wait here. I'll make sure everything is all right."

Using the bat, he shoved her door open the rest of the way, then walked in with his club high, anxious to score a grand slam. Waiting in the dusty hall, Erin heard him muttering obscenities. A few minutes later, his blotchy face appeared at the door. "Come on in, Missy. No one's here."

Harsh in the glaring light of an afternoon sun, her couch cushions lay in tatters, her few dishes broken and scattered across the floor. The little fridge lay on its side, its contents running over the scuffed tile. The mattress hung half off the bed, its stuffing spread throughout the room like a grotesque snowstorm. Crumpled clothes lay everywhere.

A one-bedroom micro apartment, it had come furnished and Cindy hadn't bought much in the way of furnishings except for an espresso machine—something she had a hard time living without. Yes, money was tight, but more than that, she didn't want to "settle in" when the place looked so run down and the other tenants were so sketchy. She kept thinking that her days in that building would soon be over, and she could go back to something like normal life. Two years she had waited, and she was still waiting.

A lump next to the couch caught Erin's attention. Moving closer, she bent over for a better look. On her back, spread eagle, Mary Sue's torso lay wide open, her life's blood spilled out around her.

Moaning, Erin's knees buckled. She felt Iverson's stiff hands on her shoulders, guiding her to a wooden kitchen chair that had escaped destruction.

Her eyes stayed on the doll. The feds had never discovered what they wanted from her father. Had they found her and come back to finish the job? Was it coincidence that this happened the day after Grant Collier came to town?

Covering her face, she wept, her gasping sobs muffled yet strong. Mr. Iverson awkwardly patted her back. His voice had tightened up. "It'll be all right, Missy."

Raising her head, she spotted a pile of clean tissues on the floor by the window, the torn box nearby. She left her chair to pick up a handful and wipe her face.

Mr. Iverson asked, "Is there anything missing?"

Erin looked about and groaned. "My TV and electric piano are gone."

"Those little…" he looked at her, "…monsters."

Erin stifled a hysterical laugh. After the language he'd used that day, why turn into a gentleman now?

The bat hanging from his hand, he headed for the door, saying over his shoulder, "I'll be right back." A moment later, he pounded up the stairs to the next floor. From the apartment above came muffled yelling, erratic thumping, and slamming of doors.

Red face and panting, Iverson reappeared. "The little brats deny it. I looked through their place, and I didn't see your stuff."

Scooping up Mary Sue, Erin said, "Thanks anyway, Mr. Iverson, but it probably wasn't them."

He looked around. "We've got to call the cops."

Erin knelt to gather the doll's white stuffing. Maybe major surgery could save her life. She wiped fresh tears with the back of her hand.

What did they think she had? Any answers would be in her father's head, not hers.

Cave Creek, Arizona

When his parents' log home came into view, a powerful surge of excitement welled up inside Grant, surprising him. His father had built the house, using timber from the logs felled on the mountains above them. A stickler for detail, he had scribed each one, so they fit tight.

With two stories visible, the house had a solid concrete foundation and a full basement that gave it three floors with a wide front veranda and large deck that ran off to the left. His father had spent weeks blasting through caliche, the hard soil common to the desert of the Southwest, so his family could be comfortable below ground during the intense heat of the summer.

He had saved up to put on a steel roof. Red cost less than green or silver, so he chose red. What a great day when that shiny red roof was finished. For the rest of his life, he would grin as he walked in from the barn. He would look at that steel roof and say, "She'll last longer than I will." Those words turned out to be tragically true.

That sprawling roof looked beautiful to Grant today. He drew in a slow breath and felt his whole body relax. He was really home. If any good had come from his injuries, this was it. They forced him to come home.

As the car drew close to the wide front porch on the north side of the house, a massive dog with a bear-like head came at the car, barking wildly.

"Gus!" Grant cried. "Is he still around? He must be twelve years old."

Andre grinned. "He's just as lively as ever. He follows Roxanne around like he was still a puppy."

The front door burst open, and Faye Collier trotted to the top of a new ramp where the steps used to be. She dabbed at her eyes with something white. Two dark-haired little cuties joined Faye, watching with wide eyes.

Grant leaned toward the window. "Say, Andre, are those…?"

He grinned broadly. "Yep. My girls."

"They look like you did when you were a kid," he said, smiling. "How old are they now?"

"Janine is eight, and Mary is six."

Grant glanced at his brother. "Is Rita here?"

"Uh huh." He nodded. "She can't wait to meet you."

Grant seemed to grow. His shoulders squared off and his head lifted as though drawn by a string at his crown. He burst out, "This is great!"

Andre cocked his head. "You serious? At the hospital you said you didn't want to come here."

Grant paused, shocked at the change in himself. He gazed at his brother, a new light in his eyes. "I've never been more serious in my life."

Andre's big hand reached across to press against Grant's forehead.

Grant jerked away. "What are you doing?"

"Checking your temperature. You must be delirious." He chuckled deep in his chest and pulled the door latch.

When Andre stepped out of the car, his daughters rushed, squealing, into his arms. With a whoop, he scooped them up and spun them around, their laughter like musical chimes. Finally, he dropped to his knees, holding them close while they hugged him hard.

Waiting inside the open car door, Grant held up his hands in a feeble attempt to ward off a Gus attack. Wagging his stub tail twice a second, the giant hound tried to act like a lap dog, licking Grant's face and leaning into his chest.

"Howdy, old fella!" Collier said, rubbing the dog's head. "Miss me, did ya?" His heart was glad that Gus remembered him, but his left hip was protesting.

Finally, Faye came to Grant's rescue and got hold of Gus's collar. "Back, Gus!" She called, pulling firmly. "Out of the car!" Turning to lick her free hand, Gus retreated, and Grant breathed.

Holding to the tugging hands of his daughters, Andre stood up and looked at his mother. "Where's Rita?" he asked.

"Down at the horse barn with Roxanne," she answered, stepping toward the limo. "We'd best get Grant inside. He's probably worn out."

Andre turned to his brother. "Girls, this is your Uncle Grant." Mary stuck her index finger in her mouth and shied behind her dad, but Janine stepped forward, her slim arm outstretched. Grant gently shook her hand.

"I'm Janine," she said, watching him, her busy eyes curious.

"I'm Grant." He smiled softly. "How do you do?"

"I'm great." Her eyes flickered toward his leg. "How are you?"

The leg hurt like a son of a gun, but his smile stretched wider. "I'll be fine."

Andre pried himself loose from his offspring and opened the trunk. He set the wheelchair to the ground. Flipping open the seat and locking it down, Andre pushed it to the open door, saying, "Okay, Janine, step back. I'm going to help Uncle Grant get into his chair." He got it into position. "Nice and easy now, bro. Let's not have an accident and spoil your homecoming."

Waiting until he got into the chair, Mom let Gus go and bent over him for a hug. "Welcome home, son."

He swallowed the lump in his throat so he could whisper, "It's good to be home."

"Janine, go down to the barn and tell Mommy and Roxanne we're here," Andre said.

As lithe as a blade of grass, Janine sprinted the forty yards to the horse barn, her sister three strides behind her. Barking, Gus followed them, his round belly bouncing with each stride.

Grant watched them, his gaze lingering on the wide barn door. Many fond memories hid in that barn and the corrals behind it.

The mouthwatering smell of baking chicken wafted over them as Andre rolled Grant through the front door. Once inside, other odors caught his attention– fresh paint and dust, like a construction site.

"Have you been painting?" he asked his mother.

"Come and take a look," she said proudly.

"Turn loose, Andre," he said. "I'm driving from here." Taking charge of the wheels, Grant propelled the chair down the hall. Past the living room, the kitchen—where Andre left them—and on to his father's study at the end of the hall.

Rolling inside, he looked around. The room was no longer a study. His maple bedroom furniture stood there with a new queen-sized bed at center stage. A wide door stood open to the right. He wheeled toward it. "What's in there?"

Mom came near the back of his chair. "It's a wheelchair-accessible bathroom."

He looked up at her, chagrined. "You shouldn't have spent the money on this, Mom. I won't need it for long."

Wearing that decided expression he knew so well, she stepped around to look him in the eye. "You don't like to be fussed over, Grant Collier. If I hadn't done this, you'd try to use the powder room down the hall and hurt yourself." She glanced at her watch. "Besides, several handicapped people attend our church. Now I have a friendlier place for them." She headed toward the door. "Don't worry. It won't go to waste."

Grant reached the dining room in time to see Andre hugging his slender wife, her honey-colored hair swishing against her shoulders. When her husband let go of her, she turned and smiled at Grant.

"Hi, Rita," he said, liking her right away. "I'm glad to finally meet you."

She darted a glance at Andre then back to him. "I wanted to come to the hospital, but someone had to stay with the girls." She reached down and gave Grant a warm hug. "Welcome home."

That pesky lump in his throat showed up again.

Rita moved away. "I've got to see that Janine and Mary wash their hands."

As she passed, Andre pinched her.

"Oh!" Her cheeks turned brilliant red. "Andre Collier! In front of your brother?" She pushed his chest, and he took a step backward, arms flying wide. Laughing and dodging another attack, she skipped out of the room.

"Don't worry about Grant," Andre called after her. "He's been wearing long pants for at least a year or two. He knows the score." He chuckled.

Grant moved the wheelchair near the table to keep his face turned away. His loss hit him with fresh force. *Cindy, will I ever see you again?*

A sharp knock, and Sally strode in wearing a black jumpsuit with a glittering blazer in maroon, green, and gold, her wide heels loud on the oak floor. "Hello, Grant," she said, beaming at him as she flicked her green nails through her hair in a practiced move. "I hope I'm not late."

"We're just getting the gang together for lunch," Andre said, moving toward her. "I'll show you to Grant's room, so you can get set up."

She slid the strap of a massive leather bag from her shoulder and followed Andre down the hall. They both reappeared in less than two minutes.

Sally sank into a chair next to Grant. "How's my patient? Exhausted yet?"

He tried to smile. Now that she mentioned it, he was a little tired. "I'll live," he said. "Just don't fuss over me, okay? Mom will do plenty of that. I can't take it if you do it, too."

Her smile faded, "Sure, Grant. I was just being friendly."

"I didn't mean to snap at you," he said, sorry for his retort. "I guess I'm more tired than I thought."

"No problem." She put her hand on his bare arm. "This is Sally, remember?" He caught a sudden whiff of perfume.

That moment, Mom appeared, carrying a wide bowl of succotash. She drew up when she spotted Sally. She nodded at the newcomer. "Hello, Sally." Her lips smiled, but her eyes didn't. She placed the bowl in the center of the table.

"Do you want us to sit any place special, Mom?" Grant asked.

"We removed a chair from that spot for your wheelchair, Grant." she said. She nodded at a chair two places down from her son. "You can sit there, Sally."

Mom hurried back to the kitchen. The rest of the gang arrived before she returned. Janine pulled out the chair next to her Uncle Grant. Mom sat at his other side, between him and Sally.

They were all seated when Roxanne came through the back door with Gus close behind her. About five feet eight, she had soft features and black hair that fell to her hips. She was out of breath. "Mom, we'll have to keep Gus inside," she told Faye. "He keeps barking at something in the hills. I had to drag him in." She patted the dog who was sitting beside her. He grinned upward as though proud of himself.

Faye frowned at Gus. "Will you look after him, Roxanne? I've got enough on my mind without having to run after that giant furball." She tsk-tsked at the dog, her eyes smiling in spite of her frown. "You're more trouble than you're worth. You know that, Gus?" she said.

Wagging his stumpy tail, he gave a short bark.

After washing her hands, Roxanne sat across from Grant. She was around sixteen years old, but her streetwise manner said she had been around the block and then some.

When Grant tried out a friendly smile on her, she avoided looking at him. Gus lay down by the door, his wide nose between two wide paws.

"Andre, would you say the blessing for us?" Faye asked when everyone had taken a seat, and the meal began.

As usual, dinner was outstanding—baked chicken that fell off the bone and a sweet potato casserole that used to make Grant want a third helping. Maybe next time, but not today. He was already feeling queasy with pain and fatigue.

Andre's oldest daughter held a chicken bone out toward Gus. The dog stood up.

"Janine! Not while you're at the table!" Rita called. "And certainly not a chicken bone."

"Why, Mommy?"

"Because it can splinter and choke the dog."

The girl lay the bone on her plate, and Gus went back to his corner, his black eyes alert.

"Uncle Grant, is it true you're a spy?" Janine asked, watching him closely.

He picked up his water glass, buying some time. "Who told you that, sweetheart?" he asked.

"It was on TV." Her face said she was eight going on twenty-five. "They say you're a spy, and you saved a whole bunch of kids."

He shifted in his chair, wishing that Andre would help him out with an answer. "Many people helped those children," he told her, finally. "Not just me."

Her brow pulled down, and her mouth pulled up. "Have you ever shot anybody? You know, like James Bond."

"I told you she was too young for that movie," Rita told Andre, who was cluelessly chowing down.

Grant leaned toward the little girl, speaking softly. "No, Janine, I've never shot anybody." He'd broken limbs, noses, the odd jaw, true. He hadn't needed a gun to get the job done.

"How do you catch crooks if you don't use a gun?"

Whew! This kid was more persistent than a snapping turtle clamping on a stick. "By being smarter, Janine," he told her. "It's what's up here that really counts." He tapped his temple.

"Daddy shot someone," little Mary piped in, bursting with information. "A bad man was going to hurt this lady and—Um, Daddy was there, and he shot him to save the lady."

"That's enough talking about shooting, girls," Rita announced, passing the pickles to her husband. "This is supposed to be a welcome home dinner for Uncle Grant."

"So, Andre," Grant said, speaking loudly. "How's life in the Sheriff's Department? You haven't told me about your job yet."

From there the topic turned to a dozen cows mom wanted to sell and the ranch's daily milk production.

Twenty minutes later, Faye Collier stood up. "I've got an apple pie in the kitchen."

Andre groaned and rubbed his stomach. "Why didn't you tell me that before?"

Everyone laughed.

Suddenly, an FBI agent wearing the standard blue with yellow letters burst through the back door and into the dining room. "Everyone, get to the interior of the house, away from the windows!"

Gus lunged toward the man, growling like the bear he resembled. "Down, Gus!" Andre yelled. Scraping back his chair, he grabbed the dog's collar and pulled him toward the hall. "Come on, boy. here." He urged the animal inside the powder room and closed the door. Barks and scratching came from the other side.

"Andre!" Rita shouted, gathering her girls close to her. In seconds everyone was lined up in the hallway. "Did you know about this?" Rita demanded of her husband.

He grimaced. "I got a call that the feds were watching the place. They got intel that there's a terrorist revenge plot against Grant."

"What?" Grant stared at Andre. "And you didn't tell me?"

"It was need to know, bro. They said it wasn't confirmed, but they were sending a team out just in case."

Sally looked terrified, but Roxanne leaned back against the wall like she was bored and waiting for class to start. Faye came to Grant. "You're in pain. We need to get you to bed."

"Not yet!" Andre said. "They'll give us the all clear when we can go."

An officer with an assault rifle positioned himself by the nearest window, peering around the edge.

"What's going on?" Collier demanded.

"Perimeter alarm," the first one said. "We have an intruder."

Chapter Nine

Black Canyon City, Arizona

While waiting for the police to arrive, Erin sat yoga style on the floor and cradled Mary Sue. Gently, she pushed white cotton balls into her empty abdomen. With great care, she squeezed the fabric together, then sewed it closed with needle and thread from a travel kit in her purse. A quarter way into the job, the fabric tore away from the stitching. The doll was more than twenty years old. The fabric had become brittle. Biting hard on her bottom lip, Erin whispered a curse on whoever had done this to her only remaining childhood memory.

Laying the doll on the carpet, she searched the kitchen floor and found a roll of brown packing tape. Using a short strip, she wrapped the tape around the doll's abdomen the best she could, leaving a lumpy ugly scar.

A light tap on the door frame brought Erin around, her heart racing.

"Ma'am," a young voice called through the door. "I'm Deputy Wesley Anderson, Yavapai Sheriff's Department." Still holding Mary Sue, she peeked through the door opening to see a freckle-faced redhead in a brown uniform. He looked like an overgrown boy. His head barely cleared the top of the door.

She pulled open the door and he stepped inside. He glanced around the apartment. "What happened?"

"I got home from lunch and found the deadbolt broken."

He grabbed the door and flipped the lever on the lock. Nothing happened. "I see."

"Should you be touching that? What about fingerprints?"

Jotting something in his notebook, Anderson shook his head. "This isn't going to make you happy, but B&E is a minor crime. We don't do fingerprints anymore. We just take a statement and hope to find your stuff."

"You're kidding."

"I wish I was."

At first, Erin was furious, then she realized that this was a stroke of good luck. What if the CIA or the FBI were involved, and they realized who she really was. Wouldn't that blow her identity wide open? She wasn't sure who to trust, even the police.

"I'm really sorry, Ms. Davis," he said. Erin looked into his eyes and saw genuine warmth there.

He cleared his throat. "Can we sit down? I need to ask you a few questions."

Erin looked around and spotted a kitchen chair on its back in the hall. Anderson saw it at the same time and reached it in four strides. Lifting it with one hand, he placed it near its mate in the living room, knee to knee with the one she had been sitting in.

He asked the usual—name, phone number, what had been taken, any known enemies. That one was a laugh. How about the CIA and the FBI for starters? "None," was the only safe answer.

Ten minutes later, he got up to poke about while Erin stayed in her chair. Her trembling had stopped, and she watched him in a detached way, like the apartment belonged to a stranger.

"Strange kind of B&E," he said, on his knees by the sofa.

She crossed her arms tightly across her waist. "What do you mean?" she asked.

"I know they stole some things, but this destruction looks more like a search."

She chewed her bottom lip, her eyes frightened. "I know."

He looked surprised. "You do?"

Erin swallowed. What an idiotic thing to say. She laced her next words with heavy sarcasm. "Anyone who lives in a penthouse like this must have a bundle of cash stashed away."

Anderson chuckled. He stood and dusted off his hands. "There's only one thing left to do here. Start cleaning up." He strode to the kitchen. The next moment, water splashed into the sink.

She darted after him. "What are you doing?"

He smiled down at her. "I'm going to help you get this place straightened up," he said. "Unless you don't want me to."

"No, it's not that." She allowed a quick breath. "I can use the help. That's obvious enough. But don't you have to get back to work?"

"Nope." He checked his watch. "In ten minutes, I'll call in my report, and they'll punch my card." He squirted blue soap into the sink.

Erin bent down, picking up plastic food containers that had fallen out of the fridge. Her sneakers crunched over broken glass. She set the dishes on the counter and reached underneath to find the box of garbage bags. "I guess I'm the one who knows what to throw away."

He smiled and turned off the water. "Take your time. I'll tackle that fridge while you're picking up stuff." He grabbed a dustpan and the trashcan and began scraping up broken eggs and yogurt smeared over the floor. Thankfully, the milk jug was still closed.

Picking through the jumbled pile in front of her dresser, Erin had a sharp impression that she was reliving that painful day two years before, when she was the victim of the FBI's heavy hand. Was this a second try to find something on her, or was it the work of some new invisible enemy?

She shivered. Why was this happening to her? She was the kind of person who returned extra change to a careless cashier. She put money in the parking meter even when the attendant was off duty. Life was definitely unfair.

Glimpsing her M.I.T. shirt half under the bed, she snatched it up, along with her favorite jeans and sneakers, and started folding.

The bathroom sink contained a sludgy mass of broken cosmetic bottles and smashed lip gloss containers. Cough medicine and chalky white antacid smeared the linoleum.

When she returned to the kitchen, Anderson had his coat and tie off, his shirt sleeves rolled up to the elbow. The fridge sat in its former position, and he held two plastic bowls over the trash can, shaking them.

"Welcome to the palace," he said. "How about some music? Do you have a radio?"

"I'm not sure. I'll look," Erin said, her mood lifting. Having someone to share the work made the task so much easier, especially when he was fun to be around. She found her clock radio with its cassette cover torn off and carried it to the kitchen. Miracle of miracles, the radio came on. She tuned in an easy-listening station, and Spanish guitar music filled the room.

She smiled, "That's much better, Deputy Anderson. Thanks for suggesting it."

"Please call me Wesley," he said, dipping his hands into the steaming water. Dishes thumped and suds sprayed under his energetic movements.

"Call me Erin." She looked around. "Let me find a broom. I can't stand things crunching under my feet."

When the dishes lay neatly in the cabinet, Wesley said, "I'll scrub this floor next."

"You'll spoil your uniform."

"No problem," he said, grinning. "You'd be surprised what I've had on these pants. They do clean up." He glanced in corners and peered at the jumble outside the kitchen door. "Do you have a mop and a scrubbing brush?"

"Sorry, no mop, but there's a scrubbing brush around here somewhere." She paused and looked up at him, realizing again how tall he was. "I still can't understand why you're doing this."

His expression grew serious. He spoke gently. "I live alone, too. I know how I'd feel if I came home, and my place looked like this." His lips formed a soft curve. "Besides, what do I have to do tonight besides babysit my television?" His blue eyes smiled and seemed somehow close. "I want to help you. Is that okay?"

"Thank you, Wesley." She felt a slow warmth fill her as she lifted a bottle of cleanser and handed it to him. Maybe there really were some good people left in the world.

Cave Creek, Arizona

On the Collier homestead, the watcher named Ben landed face first on the red dirt. He took in a mouthful and choked. When he rolled over, dirt slid down the back of his pants. He sat up, trying to figure out what hit him. Sunlight glinted against a thin wire. A perimeter alarm.

He counted six FBI agents on the Collier property. In minutes they would zoom in on him. Could he cross the open hillside and return to the abandoned barn where he had been hiding since yesterday? Not likely.

He stood up, desperately scanning the area for a place to hide. The terrain had no bushes to crawl under. Not so much as a tumbleweed, not that he'd get near one. They were full of thorns like most everything in this area. He had only one direction left.

Ben raced a hundred yards northeast of the wire to a large pine with thick branches. Unfortunately, the first limb was ten feet up. Wrapping arms and legs around the tree trunk, he shimmied upward. His leather jacket and jeans gave him some protection, but the rough bark scraped his hands and face. The acrid smell of pinesap filled his head. Stabilizing himself with his legs, he grabbed the lowest limb and hauled himself up.

Moving like a ghost, he slipped up the tree, placing a dozen wide branches between himself and prying eyes below. Fifty feet up, he stopped, schooling himself to breathe silently when his chest cried out for gallons of air.

Running footsteps, then twenty feet to his left, two agents paused—one wide and one high. "This is the spot," the stocky once said. He had a deep voice.

Neither spoke for the space of five breaths.

"I don't see anyone," the tall one answered.

Sounding disgusted, Chubby said, "It was probably a coyote or a javelina."

"We should look around some, anyway. We'd have to pay the piper if something happened to that big-shot hero during our watch."

Chubby swore. "If you ask me, this detail is total overkill."

"You've got that right. You'd think this guy was the President."

"As far as you bozos are concerned, he is the President." It was a third man tall, big, and mad.

"Perkins!" Gary said, acting pleased. "How you doing?"

"I'm doing fine," Perkins barked. "But you won't be if I hear any more bellyaching about this detail. The President made it clear that if anything happens to Collier, whoever goofed up will be doing wiretaps until he retires."

They moved out of earshot, but Ben didn't move. His tripping the perimeter alarm was a lucky break. If he was careful, he might get close enough for a shot. He preferred to shoot during the day, but night wasn't out of the question. He had the equipment. What he didn't have was time.

Pocono Mountains, Pennsylvania

On the other side of the country, CIA director Joel Mullinax surveyed the landing area below him. His Jet Ranger hovered over a cabin nestled in the Delaware State Forest on the back side of The Poconos, totally illegal but also totally private. Three choppers already sat on the ground. Since all four of the people attending this conference were helicopter pilots, they could meet far from prying eyes.

Mullinax hadn't given out this location until they were all four in the air. This was too big to risk a leak. For the first time in history, America had a chance to destroy the military standing of China, Russia, and a dozen other nations in one fell swoop. Nothing must stop it from happening. Not even the so-called ethics of the Secretary of Defense.

Reducing power, Mullinax lowered the chopper to a vacant spot and shut down the engine. As he scuttled from the helicopter, a gust of cold wind knifed through him. Jogging to the log cabin, he had a briefcase in one hand and a hard-shell black suitcase in the other, both banging his knees as he ran.

He had borrowed the cabin from an Air Force colonel who thought Mullinax wanted some R&R. A solid growth of timber separated this place from the nearest human being by ten miles. There was only one way to get here, and Mullinax had just used it.

He pushed open the plank door on the cabin, and the smell of wood smoke caught the edge of his consciousness. Good. Someone had enough sense to light a fire. The cabin was rugged but neat, no curtains or rugs. In a dark corner, two cabinet doors and a chipped sink made up the kitchen.

Mullinax nodded to the other occupants, two men and a woman. Following orders, no one spoke. First, he had to sweep the place for bugs. He was taking no chances that someone had this hideaway under surveillance for some other reason. An unseen listener would ruin everything.

Mullinax opened the black suitcase and pulled out some electronic equipment. He slipped a couple of switches and moved about the room. Finally satisfied that it was clean, he put the case away.

This humble cabin held four of the most powerful people in the United States. Sitting on the leather sofa was Gary Jefferson, the tall, balding African-American who directed the National Security Agency. Beside him sat General Tony Ferretti with the face of a lion and a stiff shock of black hair, who chaired the Joint Chiefs of Staff. Secretary of Defense Nancy Cartwright had a chair at the thick plank table. Elegant and refined, Nancy looked like an aristocrat, but she was one of the first women in U.S. history to go under fire as a naval aviator. Her military record was impeccable.

"Nice of you to join us," Cartwright said. Her deep voice held a tinge of irony.

"Sorry for the delay, "Mullinax replied. "I hung back for a while to make sure no one followed us in."

"Good thinking," Ferretti said. "We can't afford to let this get out." His tone made one think of eighty-grit sandpaper.

"So, Director," Cartwright said, making a point of checking the time, "What is so imperative that it merits these extreme measures? I had to cancel four important appointments."

Mullinax joined her at the table, his words coming fast. "Three days ago, the Chinese fired two cruise missiles at Taiwan."

Cartwright's eyes widened. "That's old news, Joel. The report came over my desk that same day."

"Hear him out, Nancy," General Ferretti rasped. "There's more." He leaned forward, his elbows resting on his thighs, his expression intent.

Mullinax continued, "The interesting item is that the missiles held true for approximately four minutes before altering their course back toward the sending ship."

Cartwright crossed her legs. "The Chinese have never been famous for their accuracy."

Mullinax said, "Shortly after the incident, we fired a couple of our cruise missiles with the same exact results."

The men waited for her reaction. They were disappointed. She simply stared at Mullinax.

Jefferson spoke for the first time, "Harrison Lestrade's guidance system has shut down. Our smart bombs, ICBMs, tomahawks, and pretty much everything using computer guidance has just turned to garbage."

"He's right," Ferretti said. "We set off ballistic missiles from both land and submarine with the same results. They travel for four minutes then turn back upon the launching site."

Cartwright's face turned pale. "How many people know about this?"

"That's the good news, ma'am," Ferretti said, wryly. "As soon as we realized what was happening, I called off all further testing. I told my staff that the reason was budget restraints."

Jefferson said, "As you know, two years ago Harrison Lestrade and his wife went to prison for selling that technology to the Russians, the Chinese, the Iraqis, the Israelis, and who knows who else."

"It's a worldwide crisis," Mullinax said tersely.

Ferretti said, "Sooner or later someone is going to fix the glitch and gain nuclear supremacy."

"How did he do it?" Cartwright asked. She'd suddenly aged by ten years.

Mullinax nodded toward Jefferson.

The dark man spoke clearly. "During the Iraqi War, several of our high-tech missiles malfunctioned. After the war we contracted Dr. Lestrade to rework our high-tech systems. He's the most brilliant weapons specialist in the world."

Cartwright said, "Tell me you did a security check."

"Yes, ma'am." Jefferson nodded, his head gleaming. "Nothing showed up to give us the first clue that Lestrade was dirty." He paused to draw in a deep breath and continued, "His task included reprogramming software and overhauling hardware. When he finished, we could blow an eyelash off a gnat." He turned toward Mullinax. "C'mon, Joel, give us the rest."

Mullinax picked up the ball. "Last night, our people found an encrypted program within the guidance system that seems to be the source of the trouble."

"You've got the best programmers in the world," Cartwright said. "Crack the code."

"We've been working around the clock," Jefferson told her.

Mullinax added, "Harrison Lestrade is fluent in eight languages, including Navajo and an African tribal language.

The key could be a little-known language, a seemingly random set of numbers, a passage in a book, anything. Our computers are firing away with every combination of symbols, languages, and numbers they can find, but with no success. Breaking that code could take years."

Cartwright drummed her short, manicured nails on the rough oak. "Buy Lestrade off. Threaten him."

Mullinax said, "He wants ten billion dollars and full pardon for him and his wife."

"Unacceptable," Cartwright said. "You'll have to find some other way. Try negotiating with him. Ten billion and a pardon are out of the question. But something lesser may work." She glanced at the faces across the room. "Here's a thought. Why don't we just reinstall our old programs?"

Ferretti exhaled slowly. "In about six months, we could probably get them ready, but they still need to interface with our launch systems. You see, Lestrade changed both the software and the hardware. Our programs won't work with his hardware. Some of that hardware is in orbit. We'd need several shuttle missions to change it."

"You're sure the Chinese and Russians also have this problem?"

"Yes, ma'am," Mullinax said.

"The encryption could be broken at any time," Jefferson added.

Cartwright looked at Mullinax. "I thought you just told me it would take a couple of years."

"I said it could take a couple of years. We also could get lucky and hit the right combination like a slot machine."

"So could the Chinese," Cartwright murmured.

"Exactly," Jefferson said.

Watching her closely, Mullinax said, "If Lestrade came to headquarters and spent some quality time with our boys…"

Cartwright pursed her lips. "For your information, Mr. Mullinax, pounding a U.S. citizen to make him talk happens to be illegal."

"But, ma'am," Ferretti said, indignant, "He's breached national security."

"General Ferretti," She turned cold eyes toward the sofa. "You will have to find some other way."

She stood and adjusted her long, navy coat. "That's all the time I can spare, gentleman. I've got a cabinet meeting in," she checked her watch, "Two hours. I'll brief the President." She looked at Mullinax. "Joel, keep me posted. Mention the Pocono Project, and I'll know what you mean." She nodded at the others and left the room.

Ferretti rose and moved to the window. Within minutes, the helicopter's engine revved, and it moved skyward. "She's in the air," he said, turning toward the room.

Jefferson spoke to Mullinax. "What about Lestrade's daughter? That's a bit of leverage you didn't mention."

The CIA director gave his friend a cynical grin. "You have a devious mind, Mr. Jefferson." He reached for the handle of his briefcase. "We're working that angle even as we speak."

Chapter Ten

Black Canyon City, Arizona

Scrubbing the bathroom floor, Erin looked up when Wesley appeared at the door, the vacuum cleaner rolling in front of him. "It's after seven," he said. "I'm starving. How would you like to grab some dinner at Mojito's?"

She rocked back on her heels, brushing hair from her eyes with her wrist. "I'm dressed for the McDonald's drive-thru, Wesley. I can't go to a restaurant now."

He rolled the vacuum farther down the hall. The closet door creaked. A moment later, he returned and leaned his forearm on the door jamb. "I live ten minutes from here. I could go home and shower while you get ready. I'll come back and pick you up." He smiled hopefully. "How about it? I don't feel like opening a TV dinner tonight."

She sighed and got to her feet, bone weary but also famished. "I'll meet you there in about an hour. Okay?"

His face showed his delight. "Great! See you then." He stepped away and seconds later the front door bumped shut. The new lock—purchased and installed by Wesley two hours ago—closed with the loud click. Erin hurried to slip the chain into its slot.

Why was she hesitant to ride in Wesley's car? She reached for the bottom edge of her shirt. A shower would feel heavenly.

Cave Creek, Arizona

Ben would have preferred to wait, give it a couple of days, let things cool down. Unfortunately, time was something he just didn't have. He would have to get near Collier under cover of darkness. With night equipment slung over his shoulder, Ben crawled down the ladder of the barn's hayloft and slipped out the crack between the wide double doors. After the close call with the FBI earlier, he'd moved his car down the road instead of keeping it in the barn.

From the barn to the tree line of the Collier property was a long way. Crawling through cactus and manzanita was not his favorite occupation, but for his family he would do anything. He must not be caught. Too much depended on him.

Soaked from the earlier rain, mud and dirt clung to his jeans and dark jacket in seconds. This pleased him. For good measure he did a roll to further camouflage himself with local soil.

Pulling with his elbows and pushing with his knees, straining to see through the faint moonlight, he reached the ditch separating the road from the field, the most dangerous point. If the FBI agents were waiting, they might spot him.

Crawling down, then up the ditch, Ben started his slow slither across the gravel road. Rocks dug into his body, gouging his skin through his clothes. He winced but didn't complain. The payoff would be worth it.

This job wasn't personal with him. Collier happened to be in the way of what Ben desperately needed. Money.

When he was within three feet of the edge, headlights streaked down the road toward him. Left with no options, Ben scrambled into the other ditch, cursing under his breath. If his special lens had been damaged, getting a clear shot would be impossible.

He lay in the ditch, freezing in the nighttime desert chill but afraid to move. As the vehicle drew closer, the headlights went out. The car passed him at a crawl. Was it FBI? Police? Had they seen him? Ben flattened deeper in the ditch praying he wasn't surprising a rattlesnake. He ground his teeth to keep them from chattering when a roving spotlight destroyed his hopes.

Gravel crunched under slow-moving tires, torturing him. Just get it over with, he repeated in his mind, chanting it again and again.

Finally, the car rolled past Collier's driveway and sped away. Ben slowly released his breath. It was forty-five degrees outside, and he was damp.

Pulling himself out of the ditch and flopping down on his belly, he continued toward the tree line. Ten long minutes later, he reached the safety of the trees. Now to pass through without tripping another perimeter alarm. Slipping on the night-vision goggles, he inched ahead. As long as he moved slow and kept scanning for wires, he should be all right.

He stopped often to listen. So far, the night air carried only the hoot of an owl and the howling of coyotes in the distance.

Fifteen minutes later, he saw lighted windows twinkling through the trees. Only another fifty feet to reach the edge of the clearing. He'd wait there. Shooting through a window wasn't the best, but hopefully it would be good enough. He eased forward, placing each foot with care.

An upstairs light went on, but he couldn't see who was inside.

Crouched behind a tree, his leg got a cramp. He desperately wanted to move, but movement attracted attention. Didn't Collier ever look out a window?

The front door opened, spilling a yellow shaft of light across the dark verandah. Ben retreated further behind the tree, one eye peeking out. His heart started to race, elated, as light glinted off a metal wheelchair. Collier was on the verandah. Perfect.

Shifting slowly to the side of the tree, Ben lifted the sight to his eye. Beautiful. He slowly squeezed... Crack!

Bark sprayed Ben's face. Something sharp stung his shoulder. He dropped to the ground as three more bullets whistled over him.

"Stop! Don't shoot! I'm unarmed!" he screamed.

"Come out with your hands up!" a voice boomed from the dark side of the house.

Moving slowly, Ben raised arms. His left arm refused to go all the way up. His left shoulder felt wet.

"What's going on?" shouted Collier.

Ben moved into the driveway illuminated by the yard light. Boots crunched gravel behind him. The next instant, Ben's face smashed into the stones covering the driveway. His arms were yanked behind him and handcuffs clamped on.

"Intruder," a deep voice called.

Ben felt hands grab under each of his armpits. He grunted as pain shot through his side. "Hey, take it easy! I've been shot."

Black Canyon Creek, Arizona

A few minutes to eight, Erin reached the parking lot of the long, low restaurant with a giant sign out front: Mojito's. She drove around the building and slid into the last available space next to the dumpster. When she got out, she adjusted the French tuck on her cream blouse and emerald pants—both brand new. (Thank you, Olivia Donner.)

The moment she stepped inside, Wesley came to his feet at a two-person table near the door. He wore a black turtleneck with a gray blazer. His hair looked auburn under the lowlights.

Erin smiled as she slid into the seat and propped her purse against the wall beside her. Two long menus lay on the table.

"I ordered coffee," he said, beaming at her. "I happen to know that the T-bone here is out of this world." He looked up. "Here comes the waiter now."

Gentle music soothed Erin's jangled nerves. Though diners filled every table, the place had the hush of quiet distinction—mellow laughter and the soft clinking of glass and silver, quite different from the plain exterior of the building.

When they'd ordered, Wesley opened an individual creamer and dumped it into his coffee. "How long have you lived in Black Canyon City?" he asked.

"About a year," Erin said, stirring sugar into her own cup.

"Are you from California?"

"Texas." She arched her eyebrow. "Hey, am I a suspect here? Why the interrogation?"

He grinned. "Can you blame me for wanting to know more about you? We've worked our heads off for about six hours straight, and I've had the time of my life."

Erin blushed. "Sorry. I guess I'm still edgy." She sipped coffee, forming her next words. "I'm originally from Texas."

"C'mon. With your accent?"

"Why, thank you," Erin replied in a thick drawl. "It's so nice of y'all to say so."

He stared. "That's how you normally talk?"

"Not anymore," she said in her usual voice. "It took me months to learn to talk like this, but I stuck it out." In truth, she'd worked hard at developing the Texas drawl, for times such as this. Nina had insisted on it.

"Why?" Wesley asked, surprised. "I think it sounds great."

"What's the first thing that comes into your mind when you hear a Texas accent?"

His shoulders came up. "I don't know—horses?"

"Exactly. When I open my mouth, I don't want customers to think horses. I want them to think of a professional computer consultant."

"You saying Texans don't know computers?" he said. "Tell that to Dell and IBM."

"That's not what I meant," she said, irritated. "Look, I'm a single woman trying to build a business. I can't afford any hindrances, that's all."

"I never thought of it like that." He finished his coffee and pushed the cup away. "So, are your folks into computers as well?"

"Are your parents cops?" she asked sharply. This conversation was heading south fast.

Wesley held his hands up. "Hey, I was just trying to get acquainted."

Their food arrived, breaking the tension. Steak and fat baked potatoes smothered with sour cream captured their attention for a full ten minutes.

"Hey, Anderson!" A short, balding man stopped at their table. "I must have left ten messages on your machine. We've got to talk."

Wesley's head jerked around. "Hi, Boswell," he said, his voice smooth. "I've been out all day. I'll call you in the morning."

Dark, deep-set eyes stared at the young policeman. "See you do." Without a glance at Erin, he headed for the door.

Wesley smiled. "He's the coach for the force's basketball team. They want me to play, but I don't have time. Boswell has been on my case for weeks." He stabbed the last morsel of steak. "Didn't I tell you this T-bone was great?"

While they waited for strawberry pie to arrive, he said, "The piano is sitting empty tonight. I wonder where Solly is."

"I play a little," Erin murmured, eyeing the baby grand in a corner nearby.

"You don't say!" Wesley smiled, his eyes bright. He stood. "Let's hear what you can do."

She blushed. "Not here, Wesley. I couldn't."

He reached for her hand. "Sure, you can. I know the boss here, and he'd love it." He tugged. "C'mon."

She let him draw her from her seat, and she slid onto the gleaming bench as Wesley pulled the chain on the music light. Automatically, her fingers tinkled out a simple practice piece her father had written for her when she was six years old. Just twelve measures, she had played it so much that her fingers automatically went into it while she was thinking of which piece to play. Then, she launched into Bach's "Air on a G String," one of her absolute favorites.

"Say, that's good," Wesley said, smiling down at her.

Dreamy from the music, she smiled softly. Happy times—almost forgotten—came over her. As the last note faded, she slid from the seat. "Concert's over." Light applause wafted through the restaurant.

He clasped her elbow. "This has been an over-the-top night for me."

In a warm glow, Erin nodded. It was a special night for her, too.

Later, dipping her spoon into her dessert, she said, "You've heard my life story. What's yours?"

He leaned back in his chair, one arm resting on the table. "I used to work a beat in Phoenix, but when my parents were killed in a car accident five years ago, I had to get away. Someone told me the Sheriff's Department was hiring, so I came up here." He smiled. "Now I'm glad I did."

"I'm so sorry about your parents." Erin was deeply moved. "I know what it's like to be alone in the world." She looked down. "It's horrible."

"You don't have to be alone anymore, Erin." His hand reached out to cover hers.

She jerked her hand away.

"I'm sorry." There was that little-boy expression again. "I'm always such a jerk around pretty women. I knew I'd do something to spoil everything."

Now Erin felt bad. "I didn't mean it that way. I'm just not ready for any kind of a relationship right now. I've got too many things to get settled first."

He leaned toward her and looked deeply into her eyes. "I want to help you, Erin. Will you let me?"

Something inside Erin wanted to respond, but another man's face rose up just behind her eyes. She looked away. "It's late," she said, reaching down for purse. "I'm awfully tired."

"I'm sorry. I shouldn't be keeping you out after such a hard day." He picked up the check and hurried to the register. A few minutes later, he held the door open, and Erin paced through it.

"I'm parked around back, next to the dumpster," she told him, reaching into her purse for her keys. They turned the corner of the building and Erin stopped, her heart racing. The parking space was empty. Her car had vanished.

Chapter Eleven

Cave Creek, Arizona

During the commotion in the Collier driveway, a tall, bulky man stepped from the darkness at the side of the house. In the dim light, his eyes were black shadows in a stone face. He stopped inches from Ben and stared at the camera hanging around his neck. "A photographer!" he ground out. He curled up his giant fist, and Ben shrank back.

The big man said, "I ought to knock you into next week. You know how much trouble you've caused?"

All Ben knew was that he was cold and damp and hurting something fierce. Could it get any worse than this?

Rough hands hauled him to his feet, and a deep voice said, "He's bleeding, Perkins."

The deep voice said, "We'd best take him into the house before he gets hypothermia."

    Lana McAra

When they entered the dining room, a black man built like a refrigerator lunged to his feet, ready to assist. With him, approached an older woman in a housecoat.

"What's happened?" the older woman cried out.

"Who is that?" the bodybuilder asked.

Perkins said, "Some guy hiding outside. He's bleeding, so we brought him in."

Ben squirmed in pain and humiliation. He gasped, "My side."

"Bring him inside," the woman said, edging closer for a better look. "He doesn't look dangerous." She glanced at the woman on the couch with two little girls. "Call 911, Rita. He needs a hospital."

Rita picked up her phone. "I'll call, but they always take an hour or more to get out here." She dialed.

Perkins nodded to the two men holding Ben, who was now shaking like a leaf in the wind. They brought him forward.

The woman gasped, "He's been shot!" She sprang into action and headed into the house, calling behind her. "Bring him in here." She led them to a spare bedroom and grabbed a couple of clean towels from the closet. She threw back the duvet and spread the towels over the sheet. By this point, Ben's head was bobbing. His eyes fluttered closed.

Black Canyon City, Arizona

At Erin's dismayed cry, Wesley stared at the empty parking space and asked, "You sure you parked there?"

Already at the breaking point, her temper flared. "I know where I parked my Jeep!"

"Sorry." His face filled with concern. "I just wanted to make sure. You'd be surprised how many times we get a car reported stolen only to find the owner forgot where he parked it."

Erin glared. "Do I look that dumb?"

Wesley held up his hands. "Hey, not in the least. Just part of my cop training."

"Then do your cop thing and find my car!"

"Don't get mad at me. I didn't steal your car."

Immediately, Erin's expression eased. "I'm sorry. First my apartment and now this." Tears filled her eyes. "Why is this happening to me?"

His jaw tense, Wesley said, "I intend to find out." His voice softened. "First, let's get you back inside. You're shaking. You need to sit down."

Dazed, she felt his hand on her arm and followed him inside the restaurant. Wesley seated her at their table. "My cellphone is in my car," he said, leaning closer to make eye contact. "I'll make the call from there."

"Thanks." Erin wiped at her eyes with the back of her hand. The people moving around her were blurry shadows, the noises faint echoes. Maybe it was true. The sins of the fathers were visited on the children. Suddenly she remembered something. Wesley!

She popped out of her seat and ran to the door. Pushing it open, she saw him near the edge of the parking lot. "Wesley!" she called.

He spun to face her. "Yeah?"

"Don't you need to know what kind of car and the license number?"

He slapped himself on the side of the head then jogged toward her. "Boy, some cop, huh? I guess I'm kinda upset, too."

When he reached her, he pulled out his notebook. "So, give me the description." He wrote down the details as Erin gave them to him. "Great. Now go back inside, and I'll come for you as soon as I get this in."

As he started to turn away, Erin put a hand on his sleeve. "Thanks."

He smiled into her eyes. "My pleasure." With that, he stretched his long legs toward his vehicle.

Back in the restaurant, Erin returned to their table, which was now cleared of dishes. The waitress stopped with a coffeepot in one hand and wad of tissues in the other. "Here." She handed Erin the tissues. "Would you like some coffee?"

"I won't be staying long," she said, "but thanks for these." She blew her nose.

"He can be a pretty decent guy when he wants to be," the waitress said. Her name badge had Terry on it.

Erin stared at her. "What?"

"Didn't you just have a fight with Wesley?"

"No. Someone stole my car."

Terry's face blossomed scarlet. "I'm so sorry. The way you ran out, I thought... you and him…"

Erin shook her head, trying to concentrate. "We're just friends."

A man across the restaurant waved. Terry nodded toward him. She smiled at Erin. "Stay here as long as you like, honey. I'm sorry about your car." She hurried away.

The door of the restaurant swung open, and Wesley strode in, his expression intense. He sat down across from her and took hold of her hands. "They've found your Jeep."

"Great!" Looking closer at him, she asked, "What's wrong?"

"It's in a ditch."

"Wrecked?"

"Probably. They found it on a country road."

Rage came out in a rush. "Why would someone wreck my Jeep?"

"Probably some teenagers took it for a joyride. It happens."

Erin pulled her hands away and clenched her fists. "The miserable…"

Wesley reached out to cover her fists in his gentle grasp. "Try to calm down. You're going to give yourself a stroke."

"I want to see my car." She got to her feet, and Wesley followed her outside. In the night air, Erin pulled her coat tightly about her. When they reached Wesley's car, he held the door for her, then closed it with a thump. She stared straight ahead as he got in beside her.

Pausing before he started the car, he asked, "Are you mad at me?"

Erin jammed her lips together. "I'm mad, but not at you."

They drove in silence. Wesley guided the car out of Black Canyon City and headed up toward Bumblebee. Turning left, they drove a short distance past the New Beginnings Church to the scene of the accident. The orange strobe of a wrecker played across their faces and mingled with the flashing blue and red of a Yavapai County Sheriff's patrol car.

Wesley said, "I'm glad this is still in our jurisdiction."

"Why does it matter?"

Wesley parked his vehicle near the sheriff's cruiser, a white SUV with brown and gold letters on its side and a black rack covering the front bumper. He turned to face Erin, his expression serious. "It means I can give this my personal attention." He reached over and squeezed her hand.

"Thank you, Wesley," she said quietly. She felt for the door latch beside her and got out, her shoes crunching over loose gravel on the shoulder. The closer she got to her Jeep, the more furious she became. Shoulders tense, eyes blazing, she walked over to the wrecker operator while Wesley left her side to talk to the officer on the scene.

"How bad is it?" she asked.

Grease-covered and wearing blue coveralls, the operator had a flattened nose and a mop of salt-and-pepper hair. "I just pulled it out of the ditch," he told her. "Let's have a look-see." He held out his blackened hand. "My name's Jerry." He followed Erin's eyes to his hand, and his face broke into a sheepish grin. "Sorry." He wiped his hand on his dirty coveralls but didn't offer it again.

Shining a powerful flashlight, Jerry circled the Jeep. The right side had several deep scratches and a long dent. The right front fender lay against the tire.

Leaning over the fender for a closer look, he said, "That'll probably interfere with the wheel turning. It won't take long for a body shop to straighten it, though."

"I can't afford a body shop," Erin said, her voice brittle.

Jerry glanced up at her. "You have insurance?"

"Of course, but I doubt they will cover this."

"Tough break." He aimed his light at the interior, and Erin gasped. The seats had been ripped apart, and the dash torn open.

Erin covered her cheeks with her trembling hands. "Why won't they just leave me alone?"

"Hey, Honey, it might not be that bad." Jerry slid his large frame behind the driver's seat and turned the key. The Jeep jumped to life. "That's what I thought. It's just banged up."

Wesley came up behind her. "How bad is it?" he asked.

Erin took a tissue from her purse and pressed her nose. "Someone destroyed it on purpose."

Wesley peered at the front end. "You won't be able to drive it like that."

"I've got an idea," Jerry called from the inside of the car. Turning the wheel enough so that it barely scraped the fender, he managed to turn the Jeep until it sat sideways on the road. He lumbered to his wrecker and pulled out a massive hook. Attaching it to the front fender he motioned for everyone to step away, then he returned to his truck and pulled a lever. The winch turned, the chain pulled taut, and seconds later, the fender creaked and groaned. The metal backed away from the wheel.

Jerry walked over to inspect the job. He smiled at Erin. "See there," he said, smacking his hands together.

"That's great, pal," Wesley said, "but she can't sit in that seat."

Jerry rubbed his jaw. Erin watched him, feeling like an extra at her own show.

The mechanic said, "You're right, Mister. I'll be right back." He disappeared into the cab of his truck and soon returned with two rolls of silver tape.

"What's that?" Erin asked.

"Duct tape, a poor man's upholstery repair kit." Working smoothly and quickly, he wrapped it across the back of the bucket seat and across the bottom. When he finished, he stood up and said, "At least it will do until you can get a new seat." He grinned. "Or a new car."

She touched her purse. "How much do I owe you?"

"Nothing." When her mouth came open in disbelief, he went on, "Five years ago, someone loaned me enough money to set myself up with this truck and a garage. I love paying it forward." He grinned, his eyes kind. "God said not to charge you, and I ain't charging you."

Erin's anger simmered down. "Thank you, Jerry. I'll never forget you."

He saluted with two fingers, pulled himself up into the truck, and drove away. The police car followed him, leaving Erin and Wesley alone on the solitary road.

"I hate to say it," he said, "but this is the second time today that someone has torn up your belongings looking for something. Is there anything you ought to tell me?"

She looked into his eyes—so close, so concerned for her—and murmured, "I can't."

Cave Creek, Arizona

Grant Collier wheeled into the spare bedroom as Perkins was lifting Ben's camera from around his neck. "A photographer?" Grant said. "You shot a photographer?"

"I saw light reflect off a lens. It could have been a rifle scope."

Grant focused on Ben who had come around and lay against the pillow looking at them all like a rat in a cage. "What do you have to say for yourself, Mr. Cameraman?" Grant asked.

Faye came in with a first aid kit and a worn blanket. "He's not saying anything until I get to look at his wound. He's bleeding."

Two agents stood at the foot of the bed, watching the prisoner. Two more stood at the door. Perkins produced the key and removed the cuffs. When his hands were free, Faye stripped off Ben's jacket. When his shirt was off, she tucked the blanket around him, leaving his wound exposed. Ben snuggled into it and closed his eyes for a moment, then looked down.

Faye pressed a pad over the wound. "I need to get a look at it. Right now, it seems to be just a flesh wound across the edge of your side." She poured antiseptic, and Ben groaned. "Almost done," she said, smiling sympathetically. "You'll have a story to tell your wife tonight.'

Pulling a penlight from the bag, she peered at the wound while Ben held his breath, afraid she'd decide to touch it. He blew sandy brown hair off his clammy forehead and wished he were in a hot tub drinking Pinot Noir.

She smiled at him. "You're lucky, Ben. It's not deep at all. I'll butterfly it for now. The E.R. can stitch you up. You also need antibiotics. Gunshot wounds always get infected."

Collier asked him, "You know him?"

"That's Ben Jarosh," Faye said. "I didn't recognize him at first, but I do now. He's with the Phoenix Times. He came out and took some pictures when the paper was doing a feature on the local dairy industry." Faye smiled kindly at the pale young man. "How's your baby, Ben?"

He sent her a sideways glance. His voice was strained. "How do you know about Jason?"

Faye spoke gently. "My whole church knows. Our pastor was at the hospital the day he was born. We've been praying for the little guy ever since. How's he doing?"

Ben's eyes glistened. He tried to sturdy his voice. "We have to fly him to Dallas for heart surgery."

Collier's forehead creased. "What's this all about, Mom?"

His mother replied, "Ben's little boy almost died two days after he was born. He has a hole in his heart. It's been touch and go ever since." She looked at Ben. "How old is he now?"

His chin quivered. "Two months."

Collier looked the man in the eyes and said, "That's tough, pal, but why are you sneaking around our home with a camera?"

"Insurance won't cover all the medical expenses. A single photo of you could bring in enough to pay for the surgery, my wife's motel bills while he's there, everything."

Faye said, "I'm not a rich woman, but I have some resources. Why don't you let me help? I'll tell my church, and I'm sure they'll take up an offering."

Ben stared at her, shocked. "Why would you do that? You don't even know me."

Grant said, "Because she's a super lady."

One of the men said, "I can pitch in a few bucks."

Grant held up his hand and said, "That won't be necessary."

Everyone looked at him, surprised.

"Why not?" his mother asked.

"Because I'm going to let him take the picture."

"That could trigger a media frenzy," Perkins said, warning in his voice. "We'd have hell to pay, trying to keep people out."

"Not if we do it right." Collier's expression showed he was thinking hard. "He'll take the picture as if I'm unaware. When it's published, we'll make so much noise, no one will know Ben had my permission."

Ben watched them with disbelief on his face. Faye finished the bandage and pulled down his shirt.

"I don't advise this," Perkins said, shaking his head. "You're asking for trouble."

Collier ignored him. "Let's go, Mr. Jarosh."

Stunned, Ben followed Collier down the hall and out to the verandah. The younger man looked pale and walked gingerly, as though afraid he'd fall.

Collier spoke to the family members who had come to the doorway. "Just act naturally. Come out and say good night."

Still not believing what was happening, Ben stepped across the gravel. Collier brought his chair to the edge of the porch. Looking off to the left, he sat like a statue.

Ben focused the camera.

Faye came out and leaned over Grant's wheelchair. She kissed his cheek and went back inside.

Ben quickly snapped the shutter. His pain faded as excitement took over. Jason might be okay after all.

Black Canyon City, Arizona

Monday morning, Erin shuffled around her apartment with red, bleary eyes. Morning traffic moved on the street outside, calling her to join it, but the only thing she wanted to join was the borrowed foam mattress on the floor. Sunday had been the second worst day of her life.

She frowned at her reflection in the bathroom mirror as she applied makeup to hide circles under her eyes. The CIA had to be responsible for the mass destruction of her life. She remembered Brad joking about how the FBI would rather let a criminal go free than jaywalk to catch him, but the CIA had no such compunctions. Erin felt certain that included a slash-and-burn illegal search.

Picking up her shoulder bag, she yawned deeply. If there was ever a day to call in sick, this was it. Alone and afraid, she'd lain awake most of the night, hearing intruders who weren't there.

In spite of everything, she had to go to work. Saturday had been a record day at PTL, and she had five computer systems to build today. At least she could spend the day in the back room out of sight. For that reason, she wore a comfortable pair of jeans with her uniform PTL shirt and sneakers.

She skipped down two flights of stairs and stopped short beside old Mr. Iverson working on the front door of the building. "Hi," she said with cheerfulness she didn't feel.

He turned and smiled up at her. Still unshaved and wearing that same dingy T-shirt, his eyes were alert. "Hi yourself, Ms. Davis. I'm replacing the old lock. We can't have just anyone coming into the building, can we?"

"How will I get in later?"

"Don't worry," he said. "I'll leave it unlocked until I can get keys cut for everyone."

Stepping aside, he held the door for her. Erin moved down the short flight of steps and over to her Jeep, still wounded and looking forlorn in the morning light.

She found a parking space on a side street a couple of blocks from the store. She turned off the ignition, got out, and locked the door. She stared at the key in her hand and laughed at herself. Who'd steal it now?

Meridian Street was quiet. Most of the stores didn't open for another hour. Outside a hardware shop, she stopped and turned around. Was someone following her? Continuing on, Erin took a dozen steps when a heavy hand landed on her shoulder. She let out a small scream, her heart pounding.

Eyes bulging, she whirled around and looked down into the milky eyes of a gnarled old woman wearing a man's torn overcoat and enormous rubber boots, a shopping bag in her left hand.

The woman jerked away. "Sorry, Miss," she rasped. "I didn't mean to scare you."

"Where did you come from?" Erin asked, trying to catch her breath.

The old woman passed a thick hand over her filthy face. "Could you spare something, so I can get some breakfast? I didn't eat at all yesterday."

Erin started to say no. After all, the bag lady would probably just drink up anything Erin gave her. The next moment, Erin remembered Jerry, the tow truck driver who had been so kind to her the night before. Reaching into her purse, she pulled out five dollars.

The old woman looked at the bill and hesitated. "That's too much," she said. "I only need two dollars for McDonald's."

Erin pressed the money into her hand. "Then have lunch there, too."

The lady's mouth hung open, "Uh… thank you. I will."

Suddenly, Erin felt better. A few more minutes and she'd be in her warm shop doing what she loved best.

A sharp pain jabbed her shoulder. Erin spun around, hands wide, trying to catch her balance. She sprawled to the ground. A skinny man with a stringy red ponytail stood over her, yanking her handbag and her shoulder with it. "Give me the purse, Lady!" he growled.

Common sense told her to give it to him, but her rage boiled over. "No!" She jerked the bag and made him stumble. He twisted his arm into the purse strap and pulled it loose from her. Her hands curled near her face, she gave him two kicks to the stomach. He grunted but held on.

Erin froze as a brown carved handle appeared in his hand. She heard a short click and saw a gleaning blade. With quick movements, he sliced the straps and sprinted away, the bag under his arm like a running back heading for a touchdown.

Vibrating with fury, Erin jumped to her feet and set off after her attacker. In a surge of adrenaline-laced speed, she closed the gap between them.

When she was half a block from him, she heard a dull thud, and the man landed face down on the sidewalk. Still racing, Erin grabbed her handbag out of the street.

His hands covering his face, the mugger rolled over and moaned. Blood streamed from his nose.

Her breath ragged, Erin stepped nearer to him. She had a strong urge to jump on him and beat him senseless. Her foot lifted for a kick to the ribs, but she stepped back. She would not stoop to the tactics of those lowlife slimeballs who were tormenting her.

Holding her purse cradled in both arms, Erin marched away from the wounded thief, her sneakers eating up the distance down the sidewalk. A hand grabbed her elbow, and Erin spun, fist ready. She froze when the bag lady beamed at her.

"No one notices us," she said and laughed. She stuck her boot far out, demonstrating what she had done.

"Thank you," Erin said, feeling an urge to hug her.

The old woman chuckled. "Don't thank me. Thank God." She shifted the greasy shopping bag to the other hand and shuffled off toward the golden arches up the street.

Dizzy, Erin headed to PTL Computers. She had a gut feeling that the thief had been hired, and the man behind the crime lived on a homestead in Cave Creek.

She made a sudden decision. The time had come to confront Mr. Big-Time Hero Brad Hillcox.

Chapter Twelve

Cave Creek, Arizona

After four days cooped up inside the house, Grant was climbing the walls. With adequate sleep and Mom's great cooking, he was feeling much better. His wounds had closed, and he no longer needed pain medication.

With nothing to do but move from the bed to the couch, he couldn't stop thinking about Cindy. She was thirty miles from him right this minute. That was driving him mad. The better he felt, the more he wanted to drive out and find her. To at least see her, even if he didn't talk to her.

On the other hand, she would probably shoot him on sight.

He didn't blame her. Cindy didn't know that he had pulled favors to set her up with her new birth certificate, social security card and college credentials. She didn't know that he had commissioned Nina Elias to find an apartment and a four-wheel drive vehicle for her. She didn't know he was still covering her rent and car payment. She didn't know that Nina was still on his payroll to be there for Cindy in case she needed anything.

Cindy didn't have the US Marshals Service to keep her safe. She wasn't in witness protection and never had been. She wasn't a witness at all. She had the misfortune of being the child of the greatest treasonous couple since Julius and Ethel Rosenberg back in the 1950s. And now she was alone in a godforsaken desert town with no prospects for a better life. She deserved so much more than that. She wasn't only beautiful. She was brilliant.

That afternoon Sally had just finished Grant's physical therapy when Andre dropped in after work. Grant felt like he would explode if he didn't talk to someone, but Sally definitely wasn't the right person. Neither was Faye.

Grant had a compulsion to go out and find Cindy. That shouldn't be difficult with the population of Black Canyon City at 2,837.

Totally unaware of his brother's distress, Andre plopped into the chair beside Grant's bed, a slab of pepperoni pizza in each hand. "Rita and the kids are out this evening for a birthday party at Bouncers Bonanza for one of their school friends. They won't be home for hours." He took a big bite off the tip of a slice.

Sally waved good-bye and headed out the bedroom door.

When she was gone, Grant said, "Look, Andre, I'm going to tell you something. You can't repeat it, even to your wife."

Still chewing, Andre frowned. "Are you serious? Then don't tell me."

"Even the FBI and CIA don't know this," Grant went on.

Watching him carefully, Andre slowly replied, "Okay, Grant, you're the boss. Whatever you say won't leave this room." He got up and closed the bedroom door.

Grant opened his mouth, then paused. Watching his brother take a second massive bite, Grant made a spider motion with his hand, then put his fingers to his lips. "On second thought, I don't think I should tell you."

Andre's face assumed a deadpan expression. "You probably shouldn't," he said. "That's what I was trying to tell you."

"Good. It's nice to have my judgment trusted. Hey, it's stuffy in here. Let's go outside and get some air."

"Great idea."

Grant shifted to the wheelchair in two seconds. He wheeled toward the front door. "In another three or four days, I probably won't need this thing anymore," he said, heading for the hall.

Following him, Andre said, "Why do you need it now?"

"My hip hurts like hell when I stand on it for more than five minutes, even with crutches. Sally has been working with me on stretches to loosen it up. She says we're loosening up the scar tissue now that the injury has healed."

Sally stood in the ranch kitchen eating a muffin and talking with Faye and Roxanne. As they passed, she said to the guys, "That's right, Andre. Don't get him too excited. He'll do too much and hurt himself."

Grant rolled outside. He soaked in the fresh air. The late afternoon breeze felt deliciously warm. He tried to move farther into the yard, but the chair bogged down in the gravel driveway. "This is just great. I guess I'm going to have to stay on the porch."

Andre grinned. "We were going to wait until later to show you this, but now is as good a time as any." He trotted to the garage about fifty feet from the house. A minute later, the roar of an engine came through the open door, and Andre burned out of the garage on a four-wheel Polaris all-terrain vehicle.

Grant groaned. "Where is Mom getting all this money?"

Andre let out a loud laugh. "This little gem did not come from Mom. It came from Phoenix Power and Sports. It's a loaner until you get on your feet."

Grant's eyes lit up. "Really?"

"Yeah."

"Cool!"

Sally came out on the porch with her purse and her black medical bag. "Hey!" she called. "What's that?"

Grant laughed. "My new toy!"

Sally looked it over. "My brother has one like this. He's got it all dented up from racing in the rocks." She patted the front fender and bent over to check out the wheels.

Andre gave Grant a look that said, "Oh my God!"

Grinning, Grant shook his head.

With a final pat, she called out, "Later, guys! See you tomorrow!" She headed for her car and was gone in less than two minutes.

"Hop on," Andre told Grant. "I'll drive."

Grant shook his head, his face full of life. "Not in a million years. People have been pushing and pulling me for weeks. That baby is going to make me mobile. Off you get."

With a feigned pout, Andre got off the machine. "Need a hand?"

Grant turned his back to the four-wheeler and eased onto its long, padded seat then swung his right leg over. The next moment, he was in charge of the machine.

"Get on," he called to Andre.

Ignoring the warning on the bumper not to carry more than one passenger, his brother hopped on behind him.

"It's an automatic," Grant yelled over the gunning motor.

"That's right," Andre called into his ear, "No clutch."

Grant turned the throttle, and the ATV tore down the driveway, leaving a shower of stones and dust behind. The years rolled away. Grant and Andre were kids again, the wind sailing around them as they tore down the driveway ending in a narrow trail to the hills. Five minutes later, eyes full of absolute delight, Grant came to a stop in the middle of the one-hundred-acre field. "This should be far enough," he said, laughing.

"You really think your room has a bug?"

"No, but I'm not taking any chances. I wasn't kidding. What I've got to tell you only half a dozen people in the U.S. government know. You can never repeat it."

Andre got off the ATV and leaned against the front fender, facing Grant. "I hope you know what you're doing, bro. I'm not so sure I want the responsibility of knowing whatever it is. But if you think it's necessary, you've got my word. I'll never tell a living soul."

"That's good enough." He switched off the motor and leaned both arms against the handlebars. "It's like this."

Over the next ten minutes, Grant told Andre about his involvement in the Lestrade case, and his pretend relationship with Cindy Lestrade that wasn't pretend after all. "She hates me," he said, misery in every line of his face. "She hates me, and I'll never have a chance to make it right."

"Do you know where she is now?" Andre asked.

"She's right here in Yavapai County, up near Black Canyon City," Grant said. "So close every fiber of my being wants to get in a car and go up there. I want to find her."

Andre nodded and rubbed the black stubble on his jaw. "If that was Rita, no one and nothing could keep me away from her," he said. "It's tough, bro. I get that. But you have to get yourself better. You have to lay low and heal."

Suddenly tired, Grant realized his hip was aching. "I don't feel so good," he said.

"We better go in," Andre said, moving to the back of the ATV.

Grant tried to turn the throttle, but the effort was too much for him. He leaned back against his brother. The big man reached around him to handle the controls.

"You're a great brother, Andre," Grant said as the four-wheeler moved ahead.

"You're an idiot," his brother replied. "Mom is going to put me on bread and water for this."

Phoenix Sky Harbor Airport

Two days later, Alex Popov yawned as he waited for traffic to move out of the rental area of the Phoenix airport. He was driving a black Charger today. He put his hands behind his head and leaned back. Yesterday's phone call had surprised him. Now a Canadian citizen, Popov was a professional hockey scout. For the last ten years, he had traveled throughout the U.S., Canada, and Europe, searching for hot young talent. He'd assumed Mother Russia would have no more use for him. Apparently, he was wrong.

Last evening, a courier had brought him a long envelope containing photographs of Grant Collier and Cindy Lestrade. His orders were simple. Keep an eye on Collier. Where he goes, you go. If he connects with the woman, switch to following her and contact the boss. She wasn't to be harmed. They didn't say why they wanted her, but Popov knew who she was. He remembered the Lestrade trial.

The line of traffic moved slowly. Bored, he flipped the radio on, and a religious station blasted him with gospel music. He frowned and hit the seek button.

Exiting the rental area, he worked his way over to Interstate 10, then 17 until he reached the two-lane road to Cave Creek. The narrow road had horse paddocks on each side. A beat-up farm truck stacked with hay to twice as high as the truck body sat at a stop sign ahead. It pulled out in front of him and settled in at thirty-five miles an hour.

Popov slammed the brakes and laid on the horn. Why couldn't he have waited? That driver had to know he was holding up traffic.

Popov took a couple of deep breaths to calm himself. Anger was pointless. He'd just have to wait for a chance to pass. Unfortunately, the road wound around and had no shoulder. Driving close to the rear of the truck, Popov peeked out every now and then, waiting for just the right chance to pull out.

The truck hit a bump, bounced hard, and part of its load fell over the tailgate. Popov swerved, but his left front tire still cut through the hay bale. An explosion followed by a thud-thud sound told him that he just lost a tire. He drove an extra fifty feet to a wide driveway, hoping the rental car had a spare.

Slamming the car door, he stormed to the trunk, all thoughts of staying calm forgotten. The Russian stared at the truck grinding north, shook his fist, and swore a red streak.

Popping open the trunk, he hauled out the spare and wheeled it to the front of the car, returning for the jack and tire iron. Twenty minutes later, Popov tossed the tire, jack, and tire iron back into the trunk. He'd drop the flat tire off at the first garage he came to and pick it up on his way home. Still muttering about stupid Americans, he headed in the direction of the Collier homestead.

Two hours later, he almost laughed when he saw the old barn across from Collier's driveway. It made him forget his anger at the kid from the tire store.

"It'll only take fifteen minutes to fix a flat," said a short, fat kid with a missing lower tooth. "Why don't you wait?"

What would another fifteen minutes matter? So, Popov waited.

The kid disappeared into the repair bay, then waddled back, frowning. "Did you drive on this tire after it blew?"

"Yeah. There was no place to pull off the road."

"Thought so. I can't fix it. The sidewall is trashed."

"Put on a new tire then."

The kid scratched his ear with pudgy fingers. "I'm sorry, sir, but I can't do that."

"Why not?" This guy was getting on Popov's nerves.

"You're driving on Goodyear tires. We don't sell Goodyear. It's best if all your tires have the same tread."

Popov's temper blossomed. "I don't care. Put anything on."

He pursed his lips and shook his head. "Nope. If I put the wrong tread on and you have an accident, you'll probably sue us. You will have to go to a Goodyear dealer."

Seething, Popov watched the kid set the bare rim in the trunk of his car. To make matters worse they were in a dead zone and his GPS didn't work. The kid then gave Popov such lousy directions that he spent an hour finding the road to Collier's place. And Americans told jokes about Russians being inefficient. Bah!

Popov reached the road just after dark. A couple of hundred yards from Collier's driveway, he found a gate to the field. Lights off, he opened the gate, drove inside and closed the gate behind him. He eased the car to the abandoned barn and parked inside.

Climbing into the loft, he pulled out his night goggles and waited, glad he had brought along a sleeping bag. The night air already chilled him to the bone, and he couldn't risk running the car for heat. In the morning, he'd call the consulate and ask for help. This was definitely a two- or three-man job.

Cave Creek, Arizona

Someone called him, but Grant refused to hear. He burrowed deeper under the covers, so warm and relaxed. He felt no pain. If he held still, maybe the blessed relief would last a few minutes longer.

"Come on, Sleepyhead. You're not fooling anyone."

Blinking, he rolled over to face Sally. "What time is it?"

"Nine o'clock."

He tugged the quilt higher. "Too early."

Sally shook her head. "Sorry, dude. If you're going to get better, we have to keep a schedule."

He stretched, savoring a few more seconds of comfort.

Dressed in a black shirt and yoga pants, Sally pushed his wheelchair near the bed. Grant stood on his good leg and shifted into the wheelchair. He rolled toward the bathroom. "No. You can't come in," he said. Inside, he twisted and shoved the door closed behind him.

"Meet me in the living room," Sally called to him.

A few minutes later, he wheeled his chair into the great room. "Where's Mom?" he asked.

"She drove Roxanne to school. She said something about spending this morning with the cows. The vet's coming or something. She took Gus with her."

Collier grinned at her. "You mean we're alone?"

"Yep." Her eyes laughed at him.

"Now wait a minute. I don't like the way you're looking at me. What gives?"

She gestured toward a couple of blue exercise mats on the hardwood floor. "Transfer out of the chair and lie down on the mat."

He flipped the footrests up, put on the brake, and stood up, balancing carefully as he made the move with little trouble. Favoring his injured left side, he moved to the edge of the mat and eased into a squat—his left leg stretched out in front of him—and let himself fall backward onto the mat.

"That's excellent," Sally said. "I didn't realize you had that much mobility." She studied him. "There's only one problem."

"What?"

"Your right leg is so strong that you're using it too much. The injured leg will only improve if you use it." She smiled. "Today is the day that happens."

He moaned. "Now I know why you had that gleam in your eye. Have a heart, Sally."

She chuckled. "Believe me, this will hurt me more than it does you…not." She sobered. "I'll make it easy on you as I can, but you're going to have to work. Hard."

"I gotcha." He stretched back. "Bring on your thumbscrews."

Sally knelt beside him to stretch and push the injured leg until he was saturated with sweat.

"You're doing good," she said, leaning back.

"Thanks," Grant replied, his voice muffled by the towel pressed over his face. He reached back to wipe his neck. "What drives me crazy is the constant numbness. It's like walking on a stick of wood. I just want to drag it."

Sally brushed a strand of hair from her smooth cheek. "If you do that, you'll become permanently disabled. The left feels numb, but the muscles are okay, and they can work. You've got to retrain them." She stood, watching him. "Now, how are you planning to get up?"

Grant thought about it for a moment. It wasn't his leg but his stomach muscles that caused the problem. The lower left edge of his six pack had taken a bullet.

Rolling to his side, he used his hands to push himself to a sitting position. With his strong leg bent, he came to his feet in one sweeping motion and stood swaying, arms out for balance.

"Excellent!" she said, reaching for the white terry-cloth towel draped around her neck. "Now, for the rest of the day I want you to walk every hour for five minutes. It's important you walk for only five minutes. If it goes well today, then we'll do ten minutes tomorrow and so on."

Grant looked at the sweat stains on his T-shirt. "I think I'll use my first walk to get into the shower." Touching the wheelchair as he passed, he carefully navigated down the hall. Boy, did it feel good to be mobile again.

In the shower, he braced his hands against the wall for balance and closed his eyes, savoring the easing of his muscles under the pounding hot water. An image of Cindy flashed into his mind. His chest tightened. She was in trouble. He could feel it.

At that moment, Erin stood in the Colliers's gravel driveway, glaring at two men in black fatigues with FBI in yellow on their backs. A tall, slim agent had his weapon across his chest, blocking the lane, while the stout one stood next to her and stared at her driver's license.

"What's her name, Carl?" asked the one holding the long black gun.

"Erin Davis." He handed her license back. "Sorry, Ms. Davis, you'll have to turn back."

Erin's nerves were tense as a piano wire. "This is still a free country, and you can't keep me out. I'm not a spy or a crook, and I want to talk to Grant Collier."

"We've got our orders, lady," the armed man told her, moving a few steps forward. "Don't make us get rough with you."

Tugging at the bottom of her shirt, her hands itched for something to throw at them. "What are you going to do, shoot me?" she demanded.

Carl's nostrils flared. He stepped closer, towering over her. "I won't say it again. Get going."

Erin's chin came forward. She didn't give an inch. "Just call him and tell him Cindy is out here, and I want to talk to him."

His mouth quirked in on one side. "Oh, so your name is Cindy now? Tell me, are you planning to feed us names until you find one on the list?" His scornful expression showed he doubted her intelligence. "In case you forgot, I've already seen your ID."

From the driveway, the other man said, "How much longer do you want to argue, lady? We've got all day."

Seething, Erin put the Jeep in reverse. Of all the ridiculous! She backed onto the road. Across the road, an old barn stood in a field. Erin's blind rage changed to cool calculation. From the look of the ranch, it was massive. How many guards could they have over all that acreage?

At the first curve, she pulled into a field entrance with a closed gate in front of it and cut the engine. She sat still for a moment, staring at nothing, considering her next course of action. Finally, she picked up her mutilated purse and got out, closing the door gently so it wouldn't make a noise.

Instead of heading straight toward the house, she continued down the road, scanning the field. If she couldn't get to the house from the front, maybe she could come in the back way. The man said he had all day, well, so did she.

Watching from the barn, Popov was chilled to the bone, but he didn't dare leave. A woman wearing a ballcap was standing in the lane arguing with the guards. In another hour, the sun would start to warm up. He slid down the ladder and stood at the gap between the wide front doors. If she left, he could get a clearer look at her from here.

In a few minutes, she backed out the lane, but the windows of the Jeep were tinted too dark for him to get a good look. All he could see was curly blond hair. He focused his high-powered binoculars on the retreating vehicle, memorizing the plate number.

When she parked a short way down the road, he grinned. After a long, dull night, this job was finally getting interesting. In a few minutes, the woman got out of the car and walked away.

Popov studied her until she disappeared over the rise. She'd left her car, so she'd be back. When she came, he'd be waiting.

Chapter Thirteen

Cave Creek, Arizona

Swinging wide to the side of the property, Cindy Lestrade jumped the shallow ditch beside the road and jogged across the field. Stickers and burrs clung to her pants legs. She ignored them and plunged ahead. A stand of pines and brush lay a hundred yards ahead.

She slowed her pace when she reached the trees, afraid she'd trip over a root, or worse, surprise a snake. Fifty paces in, she came upon a thin silver wire and carefully stepped over it.

She stopped, pulling in both lips, thinking hard. Ahead lay the side of a log house. Its porch rail looked like grinning, taunting teeth. Getting that far would be nothing short of a miracle. She glared at the house as though it were to blame for her problems. Since Brad Hillcox had waltzed into her life, nothing had been the same. Today was payday.

Keeping low, she wound around to the backyard and hunkered down, watching for the guards. What was it with this guy that he had to have such heavy artillery around him? Was he public enemy number one or something? What was going on?

The LED reading on her watch said ten-thirty. She'd been in these woods almost half an hour already. Peering around and seeing no one, she left the woods at a full run aimed for the back steps. She vaulted up the short stairs and slammed into the broad chest of a Special Agent of the FBI.

He took a step back under the impact, grabbing her shoulders in the same motion. "Whoa! Where do you think you're going?"

"Let me in!" Cindy cried, struggling to loosen his hold on her. "I've got to see him!" She twisted and yanked, desperate to get away. "Grant!" she shouted. "Grant, I have to see you!"

The agent turned her arm behind her back and hooked his elbow high against her shoulder. "You want to fight, do you?" He growled. "Keep at it, and I'll add some pressure.

Coming around with her free hand, she punched his Adam's apple. Whooping for air, he coughed and gagged, but he didn't turn her loose.

"What's going on here?" a deep voice asked from the door. "Perkins, what are you doing to that girl?"

The big agent gasped and swallowed, unable to talk. Cindy slipped away from him and turned. Grant Collier stood framed in the door wearing a navy sweater and tan slacks. His jaw dropped, and his face paled. "Cindy."

"Yes, it's me." she said. "Don't look so surprised." She glared at Perkins.

Collier stared at her. "What are you doing here?"

"You know perfectly well why I'm here." She stormed toward him. "Haven't you done enough, you… Homewrecker!"

He held up both hands as though warding her off. "I don't know what you're talking about. Let's go inside where you can tell me about it."

"Yes, let's." She brushed past him and entered the expansive kitchen. Leaning against the oak table, she watched him limp into the room.

"You didn't do enough the first time, did you?" Her voice vibrated with anger.

"Would you take a breath and tell me what you're talking about?" His expression changed from shock to exasperation.

"Don't give me that! I've had enough of your phony playacting." Her mouth drew up as though her words tasted bad. "All I have to say to you is this: Leave me alone!"

He let out a short harsh laugh. "What do you mean? I haven't…"

"Done anything? Is that what you were going to say?"

"Yeah."

Cindy sneered. "Can you ever tell the truth? Is it so hard?"

"Not when it is the truth."

"Oh, please!" She spat out the words. "You've done nothing but lie to me since the first day we met, Hero Hillcox. I saw you on the news—so pious that people think you're some kind of saint." She glared at him. "I know different."

"If you'd just…"

"What, fall into your arms or swoon or something?" Her eyes were emerald points. "Not in this lifetime, Brad Hillcox!" She sprang toward the door, fighting furious tears. She would not break down in front of him.

He reached out and grabbed her arm, stopping her. "In the first place," he said between tight lips, "My name is Grant Collier. It always has been and always will be."

She tried to jerk away, but he tightened his grip. "Let go of me, you liar!"

"In the second place," he went on, "I've never wanted to hurt you or your family…ever."

For an instant, she met his eyes and caught her breath, stunned by their intensity. "Cindy," he said, his voice harsh, "I hope I can prove that to you someday."

Pulling away, her voice sounded low, threatening. "Let me go and stay out of my life."

He turned her loose so quickly that she stumbled, caught her balance, and headed for the door. As she reached the porch, Grant yelled, "Perkins! come here!"

The big man appeared, still looking a little green. Collier said, "See that she gets off the property without having a Glock pressed against her spine, will you?"

Giving Cindy plenty of space, Perkins followed her out.

Alone in the kitchen, Collier sank into a chair at the table and rested his face in his hands. For two long years he dreamed of meeting Cindy again. Even his worst nightmares about her had never been this bad. He could still see her furious face, her flashing eyes. She was the most desirable woman he'd ever known. And the most exasperating. He'd tried to forget her, but he couldn't. What was he going to do?

An hour after she disappeared, the girl returned by way of the driveway. She walked directly toward Popov, who watched her from the shadowy barn door. A broad grin covered the Russian's face. She was the target, all right. The hair was different, but she was definitely Cindy Lestrade. He let himself sigh and stretch a little. Finally, something in this operation had gone right. He watched her until she got into her Jeep and closed the door.

Leaving the sleeping bag behind, Popov eased his stiff muscles onto the upholstered seat of the Charger and hit the starter. Soft leather never felt so good. He was getting too old for this game.

Easing the car out of the barn's rear door, he crossed the bumpy field to the gravel road. The Jeep had already moved out of sight. If he didn't catch up before she came to the T at the end of the road, he might lose her. The Charger's powerful motor shot the car forward until he saw the Jeep at the stop sign.

Popov followed her to Interstate 17. Merging into traffic, he allowed a car or two to get between him and his target. In Black Canyon City, she slid into a parking space on the street. Popov drove past her to park a dozen spaces down. He jumped out of the car in time to see her blond head bobbing down the street headed away from him. Carrying a black case, she went into a store with tall red letters painted on the front windows. He came closer, noting the name. PTL Computers.

Crossing the street, he found an iron bench three doors down in the shade and sat down, wishing for hot coffee and a fat piece of bread with some cheese. Instead, he pulled out a cigar and lit up his breakfast.

After a while, the cigar went out and grew stale. In spite of brilliant sunlight, the air was still chilly, and Popov was still cold from his night in the barn. He decided to watch PTL Computers from a cafe down the block. Throwing his dead stogie into a metal trash can, he shuffled down the sidewalk, his hands pushed down into his deep coat pockets. A hot shower would feel so good right now.

The restaurant smelled of old grease. A tired-looking Hispanic woman poured him coffee that could patch potholes. Popov didn't care. The place was warm, and the vinyl-covered chair felt good. Best of all, the greasy spoon had a pay phone.

He could have used his cellphone to call the Russian Consulate, but he didn't want to risk it. A landline was safest. He dialed an unlisted number, waited to be told the cost of the call, and plugged in quarters.

"Hello," a guttural voice answered.

"You put an ad in the paper for a lost dog?" Popov had never quite managed to get rid of his Russian accent.

"Yeah, you seen it?"

"I saw it in Black Canyon City."

"Whereabouts?"

"Running loose in the neighborhood. I'll keep an eye on it and let you know. Maybe you should send someone over to take it back."

"Where should they meet you?"

Popov glanced at the back of a menu. "Bloody Basin Burgers on Meridian Street."

"They should be there in two or three hours."

Popov hung up the phone. He returned to his table and sipped his coffee. The girl must work at PTL Computers. She'd been in there for an hour, and she was, after all, a computer specialist. His men shouldn't have any problem getting there before her workday finished.

Two hours, two burgers, and a bowl of soup later, Cindy Lestrade emerged from the store. Too soon! His backup hadn't arrived yet. Popov threw cash on the table and grabbed a take-out menu to get the restaurant's phone number.

Moving as fast as he could without attracting attention, Popov rushed to his Charger. Fortunately, Cindy Lestrade took her time. Her head was bent down as though she were tired.

Popov's engine sprang to life. He shoved it into gear, watching his mirror to see when Lestrade's vehicle passed him. The battered Jeep rolled up and stopped. The girl inside waved for him to pull out.

Popov swore. Why'd he land a Good Samaritan for a target? Still anxious about attracting attention, he smiled, waved, and pulled out in front of her. Driving was tricky, keeping one eye on the rearview mirror and the other on the road.

At the intersection, the Russian kept a sharp eye on the Jeep's signal lights. They stayed dark. Good. He pulled through the intersection and checked his mirror. She was gone.

Swearing in Russian, he turned around in his seat and caught a glimpse of the Jeep's rear fender disappearing to the right. Flooring the accelerator, he sped to the next intersection and cut right. He was doing twenty miles over the limit, but he had to chance it.

At the next intersection, he cut right and shot down the street. The light was red with three cars waiting to make a left turn. He got in line and drummed his fingers on the steering wheel.

When the light turned green, the first car edged out to the center of the intersection and waited. Four oncoming cars stretched out ahead of them. Two cars later, a gap formed, enough for the lead car to slip through, but the driver didn't go. Popov resisted the impulse to hammer his horn. At this rate, only one car would get through.

The instant the yellow light came on, Popov cut into the right lane, surged into the intersection and cut ahead of the lead vehicle. An orchestra of horns followed him, but he didn't care. He had to catch that girl.

Weaving through traffic, he found her four blocks later. Grinning, he felt inside his coat for a fresh cigar. He had her now. The short burst of a siren made him jump. A flash of red and blue reflected in his mirror. He swore in Russian. The cop must have seen that stunt back at the intersection.

Right signal on, the Charger moved to the shoulder. The cop whizzed by and edged in behind the Lestrade girl. What was she getting a ticket for? Going too slow?

When she pulled over, a tall policeman got out of his car. He placed both hands on the Jeep's open window and leaned over to talk. In a moment, he laughed and touched her shoulder.

Popov glared at them. The girl's boyfriend was a cop. He'd have to be extra careful when he made his move. The Russian thought of the years he'd spent crafting his new life. To fail would mean disaster.

After about five minutes, the cop banged on the Jeep's roof a couple of times, waved, then returned to his cruiser. Popov eased back into traffic as soon as she started out.

They left the downtown core and ended up at a three-story apartment building with a parking lot off to one side. Popov waited across the street while she parked.

After she slipped into the building, he kept his eyes on the front windows. He was rewarded with a light shining at a window on the second floor. He pulled out his binoculars and reached for his cellphone to call for reinforcements. The next instant, his devices clattered to the floor of the car. He had no time to call. Pressing the accelerator, he shot into the small parking lot and swung the Charger around the building.

Undisclosed Location

Holding his cupped hands over his white beard so he could blow on them, Harrison Lestrade wrapped his prison-issue overcoat tightly around his thin chest. Wherever this was, the evenings were cool, much like New York.

The powers that be had moved him four times since his conviction two years ago—each time to a solitary jail block, each time with strict orders that he know nothing of his location. For that reason, they wouldn't let him into the exercise yard with the other inmates during the day. Instead, he got one hour at night. Shivering, he looked upward. He couldn't see the stars.

When the military had discovered that he tinkered with their computer systems, federal marshals showed up at his cell and whisked him onto a Lear jet with the windows covered. Off they flew to…somewhere. At first, he was terrified that his broad-shouldered Marine-type escorts were really from some foreign power. He wondered if he'd end up tortured or worse.

Fortunately, they were legitimate. His strategy was working. In federal custody no one could touch him.

High humidity told him a body of water wasn't far away. He guessed that he was somewhere on the Eastern Seaboard. Maybe the feds wanted him near Washington. Still, he couldn't figure out why his location had to be such a grand mystery. It wasn't as if he could tell anyone even if he wanted to.

An orange dot glowed by the door. Standing in the doorframe his guard, Marv ground out his cigarette and called, "Time's up, Lestrade." He had a voice like an iron griddle, flat and hard.

Harrison glanced at the sky, hoping for just one twinkling light, but only darkness showed overhead. He trudged across the yard, dampening his shoes in the dewy grass. Marv pulled open the door, and Harrison plodded down the concrete hallway that led to his home.

With Marv following five feet behind him, they made a right into a block of ten cells, five on each side of a narrow aisle. Each cell's front wall consisted of steel bars painted a muddy yellow. The stench of an unwashed toilet made it difficult to breathe. Lestrade had almost forgotten the meaning of privacy.

He paced to the middle cell on the left. He was the sole occupant on the block except for Marv, who would spend the evening sitting in a chair on the other side of the bars. No television, no books, no radio. Just Marv.

"Open cell five," Marv called into his radio.

A deep, grating buzz, and the door slid back. Harrison Lestrade moved inside, hands in his coat pockets. The door slid shut with a thump.

On a small stand in front of him sat a tin plate filled with cold meat loaf, mashed potatoes coated with congealed gravy, and a limp salad—his supper. Pulling off his coat, he sat on the cot and picked up his fork.

A wide man with a paunch, Marv sank into his metal folding chair, his eyes on the prisoner.

"Do you think the Phillies will do much this year?" Harrison asked him, lifting a cube of potatoes. His voice was husky with a cultured undertone.

Marv's pudgy cheeks swelled as he chuckled. "Nice try, Lestrade. You find out my favorite sports team, and you'll know where you are." He leaned back and crossed his arms across his belly. "No soap."

Lestrade pressed the side of his fork into a slab of meat loaf. "If we can't talk about sports, what can we talk about?"

Marv leaned forward in his chair, resting one elbow on his knee. "If you really want to talk, you could tell me what all this fuss is about. Why are you on ice?"

Harrison shook his head. "I'm sorry, my friend. That is top secret. In fact, I believe you were ordered not to ask me about it."

Marv smiled. "Yeah, but a guy can always try. Listen, there is one thing that has always bugged me."

Lestrade shoved away his plate. Two bites of that stuff was more than enough. "What is it?"

"Is it true what they said in the papers? That you betrayed your country for nothing but money?"

Harrison looked up at the yellow bulb set into the ceiling and protected by steel mesh. He turned to Marv, his voice stiff and emotionless.

"Yes," he said, "it is true."

"I thought you computer guys made tons of money. How much does one man need?"

Harrison ran his fingers over his beard, feeling it carefully. It needed a trim. "I earned two hundred thousand dollars a year for restoring integrity to our high-tech defense systems while children barely out of their teens were bringing in millions from websites and computer games." He smiled, a sad expression. "I'm afraid I wanted to even the score."

Marv peered at him as though trying to figure him out. "What about your family? Weren't you worried about what would happen to them if you were caught?"

"No one plans to get caught." Harrison clenched his teeth, highly insulted at Marv's question, and all the while knowing that he was lying. He'd always known he'd be caught. The espionage money was supposed to hide his wife and daughter until he got out of prison. He'd planned his release, too. That still lay ahead.

"But you did get caught," Marv said. "What happened to your daughter? Where is she now? I saw her picture once. She's gorgeous."

Lestrade picked up his plate and flung it at the bars. Gravy and potato flecked Marv's brown khaki uniform. He jumped out of his chair, turning it over. "Hey! Watch it!" He swelled up like he wanted to fight. Then slowly a wary, knowing expression came across his face. He righted his chair to sit down again. Leaning back, he brought his ankle up to lay across his wide knee.

Ignoring him, Harrison pulled off his shoes and damp socks. He stretched out on the cot with his back to the bars. He wasn't worried about a reprimand for his outburst. What more could they do to him, put him in a black hole?

He slept lightly and woke to the tramp of heavy footsteps coming down the hall. Turning over, he shielded his eyes from sudden brilliant light. Marv and Ellard—one of the other guards—stood beside his cell with a short, heavy man dressed in an expensive suit and a black overcoat.

Marv said, "Your lawyer showed up at the gate with the court order allowing him to visit you."

Lestrade peered at the man's face. He had a broad forehead, thick lips, and black coals for eyes. "He isn't my lawyer," Lestrade said, sitting up. "I've never seen him before."

Marv and Ellard didn't move, their faces blank. "Open cell five," Marv yelled.

At the buzz, the door opened. The three men rushed in and tackled the scientist. He lashed out and caught Ellard on the jaw. The guard's head snapped back, and he went down. Marv landed his bulk on the older man, knocking the breath from his chest.

Lestrade's fist crashed into the face of the fake lawyer who, unfazed, fastened a handcuff around his wrist, then clipped the cuff to the bed rail above his head. He grabbed Lestrade's other arm and pinned it to the bed as well.

"What are you doing?" Lestrade demanded, frothing at the mouth as he continued to flail his legs, trying to reach one of them.

Back on his feet, Ellard helped Marv grab Lestrade's ankles and shackle them to the bed.

The prisoner shouted, "If anything happens to me, they'll be so much heat you'll never live to spend the money you're getting for this!"

Marv leaned over him, his voice contorted. "We know exactly how important you are. But by the time you're discovered, we'll be out of reach." He yanked open the button on Lestrade's sleeve cuff and pulled the cloth upward about six inches. Turning to the newcomer, he said, "Mr. Chekov, he's all yours."

Marv and Ellard stepped back. Chekov sat on the edge of the bed. It squealed under the combined weight of both men. Lestrade could smell his own fear.

"You may wait down the hall," Chekov called over his shoulder to the guards. He had a slow Midwestern drawl of practiced precision. With the air of a man who has a situation under control, he turned his attention to the prisoner.

"Dr. Lestrade, I'm here to learn the encryption code."

Harrison spat out, "The price is ten billion dollars."

Chekov shook his head sadly. "You don't understand. I came to get the key, and I won't leave without it." He slipped a slim, black case from his overcoat pocket and unzipped it. Light glinted off two hypodermic needles nestled in velveteen. "Perhaps this will help you remember." He pulled one of the needles from its loop, squirted a stream of clear liquid into the air and lowered it into the inside of Lestrade's bare forearm.

Chapter Fourteen

Black Canyon City, Arizona

Cindy felt like she wore lead shoes as she climbed the steps to the front door of her apartment building. She was still shaking after her confrontation with Grant. Hearing his voice and feeling his presence had sharpened half-forgotten images to a razor edge—his dark eyes seeing right through her, his body against hers, the fire inside him that drew her in like a moth to a lighted candle. She blinked back tears, angry at herself for feeling the pain in her chest. Going out to the ranch had been the mistake of the century.

Pushing open the front door of the apartment building, Cindy opened her mailbox and pulled out a couple of envelopes. A utility bill and an offer to Occupant for a credit card with a gazillion-dollar credit limit. Occupant must have a great credit rating. She didn't have one at all. She threw the paper into the overflowing trashcan next to her.

She couldn't wait to get into her apartment and flop down on the foam mattress. She'd have to get a real bed soon, but she was so tired, the one on loan from Wesley would feel like a pink cloud. Between lack of sleep and the emotional strain, she was at the end of her tether. She blessed Olivia for giving her the rest of the day off.

She inserted her key into the deadbolt, and the lock snapped back. As she pushed the door open and flipped on the light, her heart rate picked up—a silly reaction from yesterday's break-in. Opening the door, she looked around. No surprises this time. Closing the door, she turned to slide the chain…

Instead, her face bumped into the wood. Something sharp pricked her throat. Hot breath spoke into her ear. "Don't move, or I'll cut you."

Cindy gave a tiny scream. Her knees buckled, and she collapsed on the floor.

A strong hand grabbed her under the arms and dropped her to the living room carpet.

Cindy looked up and groaned. It was the pony-tailed freak who tried to steal her purse. Flipping the crudely tied strap of her handbag off her shoulder, she held it up to him. "Here, take it. Just go away."

His face contorted. "I don't want your damn purse." Grabbing the black leather bag, he slung it behind him. It slid under the sofa. He dropped to one knee, holding the knife to her cheek. "I want some respect."

She looked for an opening to strike his throat, but his other hand grabbed her hair.

The knife pressed closer. "Tell me who you are, or I'll rearrange your pretty face."

"Why are you doing this to me?" she wailed.

His smile was cruel. "Tell me who you are!"

"Erin Davis," she whispered.

"Wrong!" He moved his hand over her mouth, pushing her head hard against the floor. "I want your real name."

Starting to recover from her initial shock, Cindy's brain slowed down. This is what she had spent more than a year preparing for. She mumbled something.

He pulled his hand away, his knife hand relaxed as he waited for her answer.

Twisting her body with the force of desperation, Cindy struck the arm holding the knife, knocking it to the side and throwing him off balance. A sharp kick to his stomach put him flat on his back. Jumping up in one lithe motion, she darted to the kitchen. She could hear him cursing, lunging for her. Reaching around the fridge for her secret weapon, she turned toward the door and set up. When Ponytail dashed in, she scored a homer with the bat her landlord had left her.

He staggered, spun... and collapsed backward into the living room.

The apartment door clicked open. Bat at the ready, Cindy peered around the corner. A man of medium height looked down at Ponytail. He had a thick neck and wore a tan hat and matching trench coat.

"Who are you?" she asked, posing for another swing.

The man smiled. He had deep creases from the corners of his mouth to his chin, a nutcracker mouth. He spoke with a guttural accent. "I saw him moving past the window. I come to help you."

He ambled over to her window, sliding it open. "Bad lock. Easy to get in from the fire escape, no?"

"Who are you?" Cindy repeated.

"Ah, a good question, Ms. Lestrade."

She suddenly felt cold. "You know who I am?"

"Da. Your father's very famous where I come from. His daughter, if you don't mind me saying, is very beautiful."

"My father." Cindy's mouth twisted. "I don't have a father."

"Perhaps. But I'm sure he still loves you. That is why you must come."

Cindy raised the bat higher. "I'm not going anywhere. I'm calling my boyfriend. He's a cop." Boyfriend? Had she really used that word?

The man's heavy face darkened. "Oh, but you will come." His hand slid into his trench coat. He brought out a pistol. He nodded toward the long barrel. "That is called a silencer. I can shoot you, and no one will hear. You come with me."

Cindy shook her head. "Not a chance. If you need me, you won't shoot me."

He stepped toward her.

"Another step," she said, "and I'll smash you with this."

He stood, arms at his sides, still smiling. "Smash away."

Cindy whipped the bat at his head. He caught it and yanked it from her.

She backed toward the bathroom, hands high, looking for a chance to strike.

He took a step forward. "You are right, Ms. Lestrade. I will not shoot you, but I will shoot anyone who comes to help you. Do you want that?"

She imagined Mr. Iverson crashing through the door only to be shot in the chest. "No."

"Come," he said, as though reasoning with a stubborn child. "No harm will come to you. Your father is a smart man."

"My father is an idiot," she said. She walked out ahead of him, biding her time, waiting for a chance to bolt.

He kept close behind her on the stairs. She started to push open the front door when a voice called from behind them. "Wait, Missy, I've got your key."

She turned to see Mr. Iverson standing in his doorway. "I'll get it later," she said.

The manager gave her companion the once-over. "Everything all right? I heard some thumping upstairs."

Cindy smiled weakly. "Everything's great."

"Who's this guy?"

Her captor spoke. "You not worry, old man. Old family friend. Right, Cindy?"

"Yeah, that's right." Her voice sounded flat.

Iverson's eyes narrowed. "Okay. Well, see you later then."

"Yeah, bye."

They stepped out of the building, and the kidnapper grabbed her elbow. "This way. To the alley."

Cindy bristled at his touch but followed his direction. They went around the building to a gleaming dark Charger, the kind policemen love.

He led her to the trunk and opened it. "Get in," he ordered.

"In the trunk?"

"I'm not taking any chances on you jumping out of moving car."

She leaned back, away from the car. "I'm not getting in there."

"Then I go back and shoot the old man." His face had a smile, but his eyes were lifeless.

Shaking and sick at her stomach, she climbed into the trunk. The lid closed out the light. God, are you there? she screamed inside. Help me!

Cave Creek, Arizona

After Cindy left, Sally came to the kitchen with her purse and medical bag in hand.

What's happened?" she asked. "I heard shouting."

At the table, Grant pulled his hands away from his face, avoiding her eyes. "Nothing that concerns you, Sally. Don't worry about it."

She watched him closely. "I heard a woman, Grant. Someone you know?"

"It doesn't concern you."

Her chin raised a fraction. "Well, I'm heading out. I'll be back at 4:00. Do you need anything before I go?"

"Not a thing, Sally. Thank you."

She left with no offer of a back rub or a board game today. What was it Grant's old SEAL commander had said? "We can't live with them, and we can't live without them!"

After today, Grant felt certain he could live without them. He stretched out on the couch and closed his eyes for a nap.

Four hours later, the front door opened. "Hi, Grant, we're back." It was Mom, home after picking up Roxanne from school. Gus trotted to Grant to say hello. Grant stroked his thick neck, feeling the coarseness of his fur.

Watching them together, Grant realized that Roxanne had a relationship with Mom that he never had. As a boy, he'd been his dad's shadow. Mom had been necessary, and he loved her, but she wasn't all that interesting. Roxanne, like Andre, seemed to bask in the glow of Mom's affection. He kinda envied them.

Her few groceries put away, his mom bustled closer. "How are you feeling, son?" She glared at Gus. "Go on, now. You shouldn't be in here."

The dog blissfully ignored her. Grant kept stroking.

"Better," he said. "I'm still walking my fifteen minutes every two hours.

"I don't mean that. I mean about earlier on. Your visitor." She watched him with that knowing look in her eye. Sally was a blabbermouth.

"I'd rather not talk about it." Cindy was a topic he couldn't deal with right now.

Roxanne breezed into the room wearing a white blouse and blue tartan skirt, her school uniform. Immediately, Gus trotted to her side. She knelt down to talk to him and run her hands over his face. The girl didn't act like a street punk, but Grant was still keeping an eye on her.

Roxanne said, "Mom, I was wondering... now that Mr. Collier is back, if I could…you know."

"Start riding lessons again?" Mom asked.

Roxanne's face lit up. "Yeah."

"Maybe tomorrow. Tonight, I've got to work on the ranch books, then get supper ready."

"I'll do supper," she volunteered. "We can have hamburgers. Please?"

Smiling, Faye Collier shook her head. "You're improving, dear, but I don't think it's fair to expose Grant to your cooking just yet."

"Can't I go riding by myself? I know what to do. I'll be all right."

"You are not an experienced horse woman, Roxanne. Duke is a gentle horse, but he could still hurt you without meaning to."

"Duke?" Grant chimed in. "You've still got Duke?"

His mother nodded. "Of course. What did you think I was going to do with him?"

"I thought you sold him. I made it pretty clear I wasn't coming back."

She chuckled. "And I made it pretty clear I would be here until you did." She smiled sweetly. "I won. You lost."

"That's where you're wrong, Mom," he said softly. "In this case, I won, too. Coming home is always a winning move." He glanced out the window at the horse stable across the yard. "Boy, I'd sure like to see Duke again. Can I go with Roxanne to the barn?"

The girl let out a little squeal. Gus barked once.

Grant gazed at her, amazed. In a single second, this teenager transformed herself into a little girl, jumping and excited. How did kids do that?

Faye laughed. "I think the problem is solved." She sobered. "As long as you don't wear yourself out, Grant. Promise me you'll make her come in when you get tired."

He held up his right hand, thumb in. "Scout's honor."

"I'll change." Roxanne dashed down the hall and up the stairs, Gus at her heels.

"Meet me at the barn," Grant called after her.

His mother stepped closer. "Are you positively sure you're up to this?"

"Sure, Mom. I'll take the ATV down there and sit on a hay bale. I can watch her ride from there."

She started to leave, then turned, "Grant, Roxanne still has a lot of hurt inside of her. Be gentle. She's a fragile little girl who needs lots of TLC."

Black Canyon City, Arizona

Though her kidnapper's car looked long and sleek from the outside, Cindy felt like a canned ham molded inside its trunk. Huddled in complete blackness, her senses came alive to every bump, every scraping sound, the smell of new carpet under her, and exhaust fumes from farther away. She felt for the emergency release. Nothing.

Her prayer became a droning repetition of, "Help me! Help me!" until after a while she sank into a strange stupor, tense and waiting, yet her mind was wandering. Scenes from her past flipped through her as though guided by a remote in the hand of a bored teenager.

Cindy didn't invite Margot Michaels to her tenth birthday party because the girl had crooked teeth, and no one liked her. High school football star Scott Kilgor convinced Cindy to help him cheat on a chemistry exam in exchange for a date to the prom. Then, there were the white lies that she'd told her mother to explain why she was late coming home from school. Starfire Arcade had drawn her like a magnet back then. Now she wondered what she'd seen in it.

Cindy groaned and moved her hand under her head to shield it from the jarring. She might as well give up. Even if she got out of this fix, everyone would know who she was sooner or later. Would Olivia still want Harrison Lestrade's daughter serving her customers? Not likely.

Cindy's knee pressed into something metal. A hard thing jammed into her back. She relived her last week's conversation with Olivia after a rude businessman brought in his crashed computer for repairs. Cindy had fixed the machine, but the man refused to pay. He claimed the computer was defective when he bought it. Olivia had smiled and said, "No charge."

After he left the small store, Cindy asked, "Why did you do that?"

Behind the glass counter, Olivia shook her head as though the incident didn't matter. "He thought the computer was defective."

Cindy grew heated. "He's been surfing the dark web. I yanked out six viruses. Didn't you tell him that?"

"He claimed he didn't get them from the Internet."

"And you believe him?" Cindy knew better.

"Of course not." Olivia chuckled and reached for a candy bar from the rack beside the register. "I was born on a Tuesday, but it wasn't last Tuesday."

Cindy moved a step closer. "Don't his lies make you boil inside?"

"If they didn't, I'd have a pair of wings and a halo."

Cindy's expression grew intense. Her eyes flashed sparks. "I'd never forget his face. And if I ever got the chance, I'd get even."

Olivia lay her hand on the sleeve of Cindy's blazer. "Let's think about this a minute, honey. If I stayed mad at the guy, would he spend the rest of his life in agony because he lied to PTL Computers?"

Cindy deflated a little, a wry look on her face. "No."

Olivia sank into her wide chair near the register and tore the end off the candy bar wrapper. "Erin, that man walked out of here thinking he got away with something." She shook her head, and her curls swayed. "God knows what he did. You know what they say about karma." She threw the wrapper in the trash can. "Why should I torture myself with angry thoughts and push my blood pressure any higher?" She made eye contact. "The only one I'd be hurting would be... me."

Lying in the dark trunk, Cindy thought about Grant Collier. What had her anger at him gotten her? Sleepless nights, buckets of tears, and endless agony. And he didn't even know about it.

When she confronted him at his house, he'd seemed fine. She thought about that some more. Or did he? She'd seen something in his eyes when he grabbed her arm. His words came to her in a rush, "I hope I can prove that to you someday." Prove what?

The car hit a bump. Cindy's head thumped the top of the trunk. The thing in her back pressed harder. Half turning to reach behind her, she ran her hands over the object, trying to push it away. A tire rim. What else was in here? Feeling around, she identified a jack, a tire iron, and some kind of metal stick.

The car slowed, then stopped. The door opened. The kidnapper's muffled voice came through the trunk lid. "Be very quiet, Ms. Lestrade. If you yell, someone gets hurt."

A couple of moments later, she heard his voice farther away. She felt the slam of the car door, and they started moving again. Before he had put her in the trunk, he mentioned her father as though he had something to do with this. Was Daddy still tearing her life apart from his prison cell? Would it ever end? She lay her head back and moaned like a hurt animal.

The car swerved, and her hand fell on the jack again. Diego's voice spoke clearly in her mind. "The worst hindrance to self-defense is blind panic." Squeezing her eyes shut, she silently screamed, "Think, Cindy!"

In a flash an idea came to her. Surely anything that had the power to lift a car could spring that lock. Groping about, she found the tire iron. At least her father had taught her how to change a tire. Feeling around the jack, she found the spot to insert the end of the tire iron and moved it up and down. Nothing happened. Was it broken?

She felt the end of the jack. It was the kind that turned! Starting to sweat from her exertion in close quarters, she wound the handle. The jack slowly expanded. Shifting her body out of the way, she slid the jack under the lock and rotated the handle.

Up it went, each turn a step closer to freedom. The top of the jack touched the lid. Metal strained, then the handle quit moving. The jack was as high as it could go. Frustrated—longing to beat the lid with her fists—Cindy kicked out. Her toe struck the tire rim. Ow!

Biting her lips, grunting from fear and pain, she wound the jack down and twisted her body into impossible contortions to slide the tire rim under the lock. Exhausted and panting, she pushed with both legs and arms until it reached the right position. Aching to rest but afraid the car would stop again, she placed the jack on the tire rim and started over. Why had she wasted so much time dreaming?

Ages later, the metal above her squawked. A glimmer of light broke through a crack.

Suddenly, she stopped. What was she thinking? She couldn't jump onto the highway at seventy miles an hour. She'd have to wait until he stopped. *Please God, when we get there keep him busy inside the car for just twenty seconds.*

Her calves ached from being cramped. She longed to stretch her throbbing back. How much longer?

The car slowed, and Cindy tensed. Would she know when to move? If she waited too long, she'd lose her chance. The car swayed into a sharp curve. An exit ramp?

She tried to peek through the crack, but there wasn't enough room to see anything but light. The vehicle stopped. Cindy rotated the jack handle a quarter turn, then paused. Traffic noises sounded fast, like a major highway. She decided to wait. On the third stop, she heard a bus starting up, and a woman shouting something. Fumbling in her frenzy, weeping and gasping, she yanked the handle around.

The lip popped up. Blinking in the sunlight, Cindy lunged onto the pavement. She turned to run as a gray SUV pulled up behind the Charger, and two men sprang out.

Chapter Fifteen

Cave Creek, Arizona

Grant rode the ATV to the barn and sat on a bale of hay while Roxanne fetched Duke from the corral. She had her dark hair tied into a yard-long ponytail. Wearing jeans, cowboy boots, and a western shirt, she had on a down-filled vest and looked the part of a cowgirl except for the helmet his mother insisted she bring.

"Please, don't make me wear that," Roxanne had said, looking at the black helmet as though it were a rattler.

Faye Collier's mouth was firm. "If you want to ride, you'll wear the helmet."

"But I've got this awesome cowboy hat." She held it up, a brown Stetson with a silver band. "Why can't I wear it?"

"That fancy thing won't do your head any good when you hit the ground."

Roxanne's entire body pleaded when she said, "Duke's so gentle. He'd never knock me off."

"Listen, little lady." Faye spoke softly with authority in every word. "It's your choice: wear the helmet or forget the ride."

Roxanne left the cowboy hat inside and took the helmet.

A gray quarter horse fifteen hands high paced toward Roxanne when she reached the corral gate, halter in hand. He stooped to touch noses with Gus, then shook his gray head and blew. The dog sniffed the horse's legs, then ambled toward the barn.

Watching Roxanne stroke Duke's nose, Grant felt the texture of the stiff bale under him and asked, "Have you worked with him much?"

Roxanne beamed. "Before you were injured, your mom gave me lessons almost every afternoon. She hasn't had time lately, but I still come out every day to talk to him, feed him, and muck out his stall. She lay her head against the horse. "We're best friends, aren't we, Duke?"

The horse blew and put his head down so she could slip the halter on. She led him to a hitching post near Grant and tied Duke with a slipknot. While she was cleaning Duke's feet, he hobbled sideways toward Grant and turned his head, snuffling Grant's shirt, his hand, his head.

"Do you think he remembers you?" Roxanne asked, prying out a rock with a hoof pick.

Grant laughed when Duke nibbled at his pocket. "Maybe. It's been a lot of years."

Duke put his head down, and Grant rubbed his face. The horse snorted then nickered. "Hmm, maybe he does," Grant said.

"You had him a long time." Roxanne tugged the back of Duke's right rear leg, and he raised it for her to hold over her knee.

"My...dad got him for me when I was ten. He was just a two-year-old then. But what a fast learner! When he was a five-year-old, we won the regional junior calf-roping championship."

He rubbed the underside of Duke's jaw, speaking more to the horse than to Roxanne. "Duke is the best horse I've ever known. He never tried to throw me. When I fell off due to my own stupidity, he'd stop and come back." He swallowed hard. "I forgot how much I missed this guy." He hugged the gelding's head, smelling that distinctive odor that said *horse*.

"Sure has been a long time, fella," Grant said. Duke nickered again.

"I love him," Roxanne said. "He's so easy to ride."

"He's twenty-seven years old. There isn't too much he hasn't seen or done."

Roxanne's blue eyes met Grant's. "That's pretty old for a horse, isn't it?"

Grant nodded. "He's getting up there, all right. But he's always been sound. He's had the best of care and feed. That helps. Unfortunately, he'd had no one to work him for a long time."

Roxanne beamed. She looked cute, even in a black helmet. "If you don't mind too much, I'd like to take that job."

Grant tapped his left leg with the cane. "I may not be able to ride for a long time."

Moving like a pro, Roxanne saddled and bridled the horse. She grabbed the reins and led him through the corral gate, then closed it behind them. Grant was just about to open his mouth when Roxanne checked the strap and tightened it some more. He smiled and relaxed. His mother had taught her right. He should have known.

Gus watched for a while from the fence, yawned, and lay down. Grant sat back and shifted his left leg up onto the bale to ease it.

After an hour, Roxanne brought Duke back to the hitching rail.

"You did good," Grant said, smiling.

"Thank you." Her face had a healthy flush.

Maybe Andre was right. Maybe she was a good kid in a bad situation.

In twenty minutes, she had Duke unsaddled and groomed and released him into the corral where he trotted to the hay rack. Enjoying this warm sun, the smell of the stable, the clear air, Grant stayed put as she strode toward him with Gus at her heels.

Roxanne dropped her slender frame onto a bale nearby, her hand absently scratching the dog's ruff. "Mr. Collier," she said, a little breathless, "do you mind if I ask you something?" She pulled off her helmet and smoothed her wispy hair.

"Call me Grant. Sure, what do you want to know?"

"This is the nicest place in the whole world. Why didn't you want to come here?"

He tensed. "Who said that?"

"When you were working in New York, Faye used to always say she hopes you get tired of running and come home." She looked into his face. "Your mother is a living angel. Why didn't you want to come home?"

Grant was getting irritated. Roxanne was treading in an area marked, NO TRESPASSING.

She sounded sad. "You have a great home. You're so lucky. I can't understand why anyone would want to stay away from here."

Grant softened. "Want to tell me about it?" he asked.

"When the application to terminate my parents' rights came to court, they didn't attend the hearing." She stared at Duke munching hay. "I hated them for it. I wished they were dead." She glanced at Grant. "You have a mother who cries over you, and you don't appreciate her."

Grant ignored the part about his mother. "Terminate parental rights? Who filed the application?"

Roxanne looked up, surprised. "Didn't anyone tell you? Your mother is adopting me."

Grant stared at her innocent face. So that was her game. He considered the situation a full minute then said, "Boy, Roxanne, you are good."

"What do you mean?" She looked scared.

"My mom is a trusting sort. My brother, too. But I'm with the CIA, and we're not that easily fooled."

Roxanne's little-girl look vanished. Her cobalt eyes had shutters behind them.

Sensing a change in her, Grant pushed ahead. "I know what happened. You found a lovely old lady and wheedled your way into her heart." His voice grew louder. "Now you've convinced her to adopt you, so you can inherit a chunk of this ranch."

Roxanne stared at him, tears slowly forming in the corners of her eyes. Ears pulled forward, Gus tilted his head, watching her. In a moment he whinnied and pushed his nose into her face. Sniffing, she jerked back and pushed him away. "Not now, Gus." The dog lay his head on her knee.

Fueled by his own anger, Grant plowed ahead. "Tears work on most people, but not me. Here's a news flash, Roxanne. My mom doesn't own this ranch. I do. This 5,000-acre property has been passed down to the oldest son in the Collier family for four generations. Dad came to this quarter to build Mom a new house, but Colliers have been on this land since before WWII. All my mother has is the right to live here until she dies. Ownership of the property remains with me or my heirs. Sorry, Kiddo, the pot at the end of the rainbow won't go to you."

Roxanne stood, shaking. She spoke in gasps. "When I first came here, I was terrible to your mom. I swore at her. I disrespected her. I destroyed things. Finally, I ran away. She always brought me back and loved me." A sob took her breath. "You don't know it, but your mother is the most wonderful person in the world. I want her to love me, that's all." She glared at him. "It's too bad you're so stupid you can't see what you've got." Roxanne's hands flew to her face, and she ran toward the house. Gus bounded after her, his tail down.

Grant stared at the hay-strewn ground by his feet. What an actress. She was almost believable.

The smell of the barn, the hay, the pine-scented breeze brought back a flood of memories. Watching the horses, he became so absorbed that he didn't hear footsteps behind him. Suddenly, his ear exploded in pain. He spun around... and cowered.

Phoenix, Arizona

Moving fast for a stout man, Cindy's kidnapper jumped out of the Charger and came for her from the left. Her only way of escape was to the right, across heavy traffic. Still half blinded by the glaring sunlight after being in the trunk, she darted into the street. A horn blared and air whooshed as a bus slammed on its brakes. It bumped her. She stumbled but kept on running.

Another horn and Cindy stopped short as a car brushed past her. Behind her, angry voices yelled, but she kept on going.

Cindy made it to the sidewalk and looked around. Spotting a uniform, she raced toward a policeman talking to half a dozen teenagers. Cindy ran to the man in tan and grabbed his arm.

The officer looked down at her, annoyed. He was writing on a clipboard. "What's the trouble?"

"Some guys... are chasing me." Cindy bent over, gasping for air.

The policeman scanned the area. "By who?"

She spun around, pointing. Both cars were gone. She gulped. They're not there anymore." She brushed her hair away, and her fingers caught in her tangles. She stared at the place the cars used to be.

"Look, lady, seems you're safe for the moment. Let me finish what I'm doing here, then we'll talk about your problem."

Cindy stepped back a few feet, watching for the dark car, not daring to leave the officer's shadow. Glancing around, she recognized the courtyard of Westlake Center. She'd come here several times to shop.

About ten minutes later, the police officer's radio crackled. "All units in the vicinity of Turgeon-Raine Jewelers—robbery in progress—respond immediately."

The policeman ran toward his cruiser, leaving Cindy on the sidewalk feeling very small and very alone. She hurried toward the entrance of the mall and stayed just inside the door. She had to stay where other people could see her. Pulling out her phone, she brought up her Uber app. Her ride would arrive in six minutes. Too long. She tapped her foot, watching out the window.

A meaty hand grabbed her shoulder from behind. The stout man with a guttural accent muttered in her ear, "Ms. Lestrade, you are becoming a nuisance." He leaned closer, looking into her eyes. "We have men at every exit. You cannot get away. Come quietly, and we won't hurt you."

Cindy backed away, watching for a chance to give him a good kick in the groin. "You'll have to excuse me if I'm a little skeptical. After all, you did just drag me here in the trunk of your car."

He shook his big head. "Unfortunate. The man in your apartment made it necessary. I could not let him hurt you."

Over the loudspeaker came, "Will the parents of Kylie Sanders please come to customer service. Your little girl is waiting for you."

The big man glanced toward the mall.

Cindy sprinted outside and into the Uber car as it rolled up. Her heart thumping, she sank into the seat and tried to breathe. The driver pulled away. For a few minutes she was safe.

No, she wasn't. What an idiot she was. They would follow her. She had to get out of this Uber pronto, before they could get their cars close enough to see. She leaned forward. "Please, I forgot something. I have to get out. NOW!"

The driver, a young guy with tattoos up the side of his neck, gave her an irritated look. "Now? We're in the middle of the parking lot."

"Please!"

He slammed on the brake. Cindy darted out the door and kept low, to stay below the level of the car roofs. She pulled out her phone and called Nina, her emergency contact. No answer, so she left a message. She had never called that number before. Nina had called her a couple of times at the beginning to check on her. Once she got settled, Cindy had never needed to call her until now.

She didn't want to call Olivia and get her involved in a dangerous situation. Sitting on the ground between an orange Fiat and a blue Chevy Cruze, Cindy scrolled until she found the number of the only man she could trust. Wesley.

Cave Creek, Arizona

Faye Collier's eyes burned with indignation. "What did you say to poor Roxanne?"

Grant held his hands up, ready to ward off another blow. Andre Collier wasn't the only one in the family with a wicked right.

Leaning away from her, Grant winced. "I just set her straight, that's all."

His mother backed off and came around to sit on the hay bale beside him. She looked like a hillbilly avenger in a jean skirt and a faded flannel coat of red plaid, her gray hair pulled into a loose ponytail.

He rubbed his sore ear where she'd boxed him. "That hurt."

Faye's blue eyes still blazed. "No kidding. If you were younger, it would have been your rear." Still menacing, she shifted toward him. "Just how did you set her straight?"

He cleared his throat and tried to drag up some dignity. "I made sure she understood how things worked around here."

She raised her eyebrows, feigning surprise. "Really? And just how do things work around here? It must be something awful. She just ran into the house crying."

He got his second wind, and his chin jutted forward. "Hey, Mom, ease off a bit. This is really your fault, you know."

"My fault?" Her mouth formed an O.

"You should have told me you're adopting her."

Some of the fight went out of her. "With you hurt, I didn't want to hit you with too much at once." The fight welled up in her again. "You need to keep in mind that you've been away for years. My relationship with Roxanne started long before you came back into our lives."

He grunted and tore at the bit of straw in his hand. "Well, it's a stupid plan. Can't you see what she's after?"

Faye cocked her head. "Why don't you tell me?"

"It's the ranch. You know… she worms her way into your heart, gets you to adopt her, then when you push off, she gets a chunk of the place."

"For someone so smart, you can be such an idiot, Grant."

His temper flared. "You're the one who's not so swift. That girl played you for a sucker."

Faye drew up, her round face tight with indignation, her words thick. "For the record, Sherlock, I decided to adopt Roxanne the day I first saw her... in the courthouse. The Lord said to me, 'Make her as if she were your own.'"

He raised his hand, palm up. "How could you do that? You didn't know anything about her."

Faye's voice grew louder. "Will you listen for a change? When I first talked to Roxanne about adopting her, I told her the ranch belonged to you, and the only thing I could promise her was my love. An inheritance has never been an issue with her."

Roxanne's stricken face and teary eyes waved through his consciousness. Grant gulped. He had a sinking feeling in the pit of his stomach. Why did he get himself into these situations?

He gazed at the hitching post and wondered if he should bang his head against it now or wait until his mother went to the house.

He darted a sheepish glance at her. "Is she okay?"

"I calmed her down."

Here he was again, feeling like pond scum. "I don't know what got into me, Mom. I keep making a mess of things."

His mother motioned toward the house, and Roxanne poked her head out the front door.

"Come on out!" Faye yelled toward the house. "He's tame now."

Shoulders bent, scuffing the grass, Roxanne made her way to them. Grant looked into her tear-streaked face and wanted to kick himself. How could he have missed it? She was a little girl hiding inside a woman's body.

He coughed, stalling to think of the right words. Looking into the girl's bleary eyes, he gently said, "I'm really sorry for what I said, Roxanne. I'm a shortsighted dufus. Please, don't ever think about leaving here. This is your home."

Fresh tears slid down her cheeks. She threw her arms around him, knocking him back so he almost lost his balance. She jostled his sore leg and planted a firm kiss on his cheek.

When she turned loose, he rubbed his leg, grinning sheepishly. Roxanne did nothing by halves. She was an all-in kind of girl.

She attacked Faye with a hug, too.

Faye patted the girl's back. "I'll be along in a second. Go ahead and pull out the flour and shortening, and we'll start on those pies in a minute."

Roxanne flew back to the house, a jump and a skip in her step.

"How does she go from the depths of despair to the heights of joy in a split second?" Grant asked, rubbing his sore abdomen.

Light came into Faye's eyes. "I don't know. I raised two boys, remember?" She chuckled, a girlish look peeking out from her lined face. "It's been nice having another female around." She stood and brushed off the back of her skirt. "You'd better get yourself to the house. Do you need me to help you?"

He shook his head. "I've got the ATV. I'm fine. I'll stay here a while. I need some time to think."

With a long stride, Faye headed toward the house without a backward glance.

Grant sat like a stone. Mighty Collier had turned into a bumbler. What was wrong with him? His intuition was good. He had come to rely on it both in the field and at home, but his Spidey sense had gone haywire. Why?

A lump pressed against his Adam's apple. His life had been so simple when he was Roxanne's age. When Dad died, all that died, too.

He got on the ATV and made his way into the barn. He had to get alone where anxious eyes at a window couldn't see him. Inside, holding onto the door of Duke's empty stall, he rested his forehead on the top rail. Sobbing out his grief for his father, he saw that dear, weathered face, heard his rough-yet-tender voice, and felt Dad's callused hand rumple his hair once more.

"Dad, I miss you so much," he murmured half aloud.

Rubbing away his tears, he raised his head and looked around. At the silo door, his mind's eye saw his father shoveling grain into a wheelbarrow, laughing, and calling Grant "Captain" because he loved the *Captain Planet* cartoon so much. At the tack room Dad was there, fixing a lead halter for their new horse named Duke. As he worked, he gave Grant gentle instructions on caring for the horse. He was in the hayloft, the feed room, and the saw marks on the board under Grant's hand.

Grant said, "You've been here all the time, haven't you, Dad?" He drew in a shaky breath and squeezed his eyes tight. Sweet warmth filled him, and he knew his dad was with him. At long last, Grant had come home.

He stayed until his leg ached to the point that he couldn't ignore it any longer.

Someone behind him cleared his throat. Reaching for a handkerchief in his back pocket, Grant wiped his eyes then glanced around. "Perkins."

The big man's granite face had a red tinge. "Sorry, sir. I didn't realize you were…" He turned away. "I'll come back later."

Grant cleared his throat and put away his handkerchief. "Now's fine. What have you got?"

Perkins moved closer. "I did some checking—like you asked—into Cindy Lestrade, a.k.a. Erin Davis. In the last three days, her apartment was robbed, and her car was stolen."

Grant said, "From the way she stormed in here, she must think we're involved."

Perkins nodded. "Your people could be doing something. They probably wouldn't tell you now that you're retired."

Collier thought about it. "I used my own resources to hide her. If the agency needed to find her, they'd have to ask me where to start looking."

"Maybe she slipped up somewhere and gave out her real name."

Collier doubted that. "Even so," he said, "she was never involved in her father's treachery. That's why I got to her so easy when I was undercover. She had no reason to be suspicious. What agency is handling her case?"

"Yavapai Sheriff's Department."

"Call them, Sam, would you? Make it sound official.

Chapter Sixteen

Phoenix, Arizona

Cindy wrapped her coat tighter as she headed for the mall entrance. The late afternoon air was cooling fast. She went into a food place and bought a soda.

Fifteen minutes later, she saw Wesley's head bobbing toward her. His face was grim, concerned. To Cindy, he was the most beautiful sight in the world. As soon as he reached her, she threw her arms around him and held on tight, feeling safe as his powerful arms pulled her close. With her face against his chest, she let tears come. "I'm so scared," she said in a moment.

He pushed her back a bit and wiped away tears with his finger. "Hey, it's okay now. I'm here. You want to get something to eat?"

Nodding, Cindy sniffed and made an effort to quiet her trembling.

Arm in arm, they headed for the Food Court. She snuggled closer to Wesley. He was a safe haven. He found a table near the back and pulled out a chair for her. "Wait here. I'll get us some burgers."

Cindy watched him make his way to the fast-food counter. How much should she tell him? She already knew the answer. Wesley had shown her nothing but kindness since they first met. He would understand.

When he returned with a tray, he sat across from her and sipped coffee, his eyes searching hers. "What kind of trouble are you in?"

Cindy picked up a fry. She said, "Today a man attacked me in my apartment."

Wesley's voice was loud and harsh. "What?"

Glancing around to see who might be listening, she leaned forward, keeping her voice low, encouraging him to do the same. "He tried to snatch my purse this morning, and when he failed, he tracked me down to my apartment."

He whispered, "Why didn't you call me?"

"I thought I knew who was responsible."

Wesley scratched his red head. "This isn't making sense, Erin."

"It won't until I give you the whole story."

Wesley set down his cup. "I'm all ears."

She hesitated. "Are you angry with me?"

His eyes softened. "I'm a little hurt you didn't come to me first, that's all."

Cindy drew in her breath and plunged in. "Do you remember that big trial a couple of years back for Harrison Lestrade?"

"Sure, the guy that was selling secrets to the Russians and Chinese."

She paused for effect. "I'm his daughter."

His eyes widened. "You're Harrison Lestrade's daughter?"

"My real name is Cindy Lestrade."

"Wow! No wonder you kept it a secret."

She ran her finger around the imprinted logo on her cup. "When that guy attacked me in the apartment, I whacked him with a baseball bat and knocked him unconscious."

"Good for you," Wesley said, impressed.

"That's when another man showed up with a gun. He forced me into the trunk of his car and drove me here."

Wesley rubbed his head. "I can't believe all that happened to you." He watched her as though seeing her for the first time. "How did you get away?"

"I pried open the trunk with a car jack and ran toward a cop." She told him about the kidnapper reappearing in her dash for the Uber. Shivering, she glanced around. "They're still looking for me. I can feel it."

She leaned forward, her voice tense. "Wesley, the guy with the gun had an accent. It sounded Russian to me."

"Whoa!" A scared look came over his boyish face. He held up both hands as though he were surrendering. "This is more than a county deputy can handle. We need big-time help here, but from who?"

"That's what I've been wondering. I mean, how do we know for sure that he's Russian? Maybe he's an FBI agent undercover still looking for something my father had." Desperation creased her soft features. "That's why I called you, Wesley. I don't know who else to trust."

He covered her hands with his. "I'm not sure how, but I'll get you out of this mess. I've got a few friends in the FBI. Maybe they can do some discreet digging and find out who's responsible. In the meantime, you have to hide."

"Where?"

His brows drew together as he considered. "I'd like to say my place, but if these guys are any good at all, they'll make a connection between us in no time. You'll have to go to a motel." He smiled. "I know just the one."

Picking up their food to take along, they left the mall. In the parking lot, Wesley held open the door of his sedan, and she slid inside. When he got in beside her, he glanced into the rearview mirror. "I hope they think they lost you, and they're out there beating the bushes looking for you." He headed north on Interstate 17. They traveled to New River, turned right and drove east for ten minutes. Pulling into the gravel parking lot of the Sabrosa Motel, he parked and shut off the engine.

The single-level building had a pink stucco exterior with a flat tar-and-gravel roof. A couple of cars sat in front of it. Cindy gasped when she read the motel's faded sign. "Wesley, they have hourly rates."

Wesley nodded ruefully. "Last year I worked on a drug case, and we hid a witness here. The owner asks no questions, and he keeps his mouth shut." He touched her hand. "Wait here while I register."

Huddled in the car, afraid someone—anyone—would see her, Cindy stared at the crumbling sidewalk and the broken–and–taped window in front of her. She'd gone from a villa in upstate New York, to a rat-infested micro-apartment in Black Canyon City, to a dive motel in the middle of nowhere. She forced back a wave of despair. Something had to change soon.

She looked around at the gray dirt and rocks they called a yard. New York had grass. She had never realized how much she loved grass until she moved here.

In short order Wesley returned, key in hand. Cindy got out of the car and joined him at the door to Room 112. The musty atmosphere inside didn't surprise her. The carpets had bare spots, the bedspread had holes, and the white ceiling was brown from years of cigarette smoke.

Cindy looked inside the tiny bathroom. No bathtub, just a rusty shower stall. The small kitchenette was probably the room's best feature, but then it probably didn't get used much.

"I know, it's pretty grim," Wesley said, watching her disgusted expression, "but at least it's safe."

Cindy sat on the edge of the bed. Creaky springs sank under her weight. "It'll have to do," she murmured.

"I've given the guy a week's rent in cash, so he won't bother you. I'll bring you whatever you'll need."

Cindy shuddered. "A sleeping bag. I couldn't force myself to crawl into those sheets." She shivered. She didn't even have her purse with her.

"Not a problem," Wesley answered, grinning. He pulled a small pad from his shirt pocket and handed it to her, along with a pencil stub. "Make a list."

Cindy started writing.

Phoenix, Arizona

Sitting in his Charger on the edge of a strip mall parking lot, Alex Popov made a call, left a message and put the phone down. Thirty seconds later, the phone chimed. He grabbed it up. "Popov here," he said in Russian. He glanced around. No cars or people were anywhere around, but he still felt as though someone watched him.

"Please hold for General Yuri Prokofiev," a woman's clipped voice answered in the same language.

"Alexander Popov!" a throaty male voice came on the line. "Do you have her?"

Swallowing and shaking, Popov forced himself to answer. "She escaped."

The other end of the line remained quiet for five full seconds. Popov resisted the urge to say something just to fill the dead-air space. The less he said, the less trouble he'd have.

The next words pelted him like bullets. "You let her escape?"

"She ran toward a policeman." He hesitated. "I can't afford trouble with American authorities."

"Where is she?"

Popov said, "I don't know."

Prokofiev exploded. "Why didn't you shoot the American policeman and take her?"

Sweat formed on Popov's face. "No one authorized such extreme measures, General. My mission was to bring her in unharmed."

The general bellowed, "She must be captured. Whatever it takes, whatever it costs, she must be found immediately!"

"General," Popov said, "why is she so important?"

A pause. Prokofiev spoke carefully. "If you repeat what you are about to hear, you will die. Is that understood?"

"Yes, my General."

Popov's breath left him as he listened. A few minutes later, perspiring freely, he set down the phone. The next time he found her, there would be no escape and no mercy for anyone who helped her.

Cave Creek, Arizona

Ending a call, Grant wore a worried frown. Over the past three days, he'd left more than a dozen messages on Cindy's voicemail, but she'd never returned his calls. Today, a computerized voice told him her voicemail was full.

He stared at the green intertwining vines on the wallpaper in his room. Where could she be?

Still using a cane, but with hardly a trace of his limp showing, he left his room and found Sally at the kitchen table. She stopped sipping Coke from a can and smiled when he strode in. "You're sure looking good," she said with a teasing smile.

"Thanks to you. Those exercises worked miracles."

Sally nodded to the wheelchair folded up in the corner. "Not much use for that anymore."

"Nope." He held up his cane. "Another week, and this becomes an ornament for sympathy purposes only."

She watched him, a slant to her eyes. "Do you still have any use for me?"

Grant studied her face—the high cheekbones, the slim nose, the full curved lips. Sally was a candidate for a glamor magazine. But she had no spark, at least not to him. "You'll always be a good friend," he said.

Hmm." Her head tilted to a provocative pose. "For some reason, that statement brings back memories from Cave Creek High, two days before the prom." She stood and made a show of straightening her narrow skirt. "It's that woman who came here Monday morning, isn't it?"

When he didn't answer, she pulled out her most seductive smile. "Boy, she must really be under your skin."

"Deeper than that, Sally," he said softly, his face serious.

She set down her soda can and moved toward him, sweet perfume wafting with her. Her lips gently brushed his cheek, and he felt her breath when she said, "I hope she blows it big-time. If she does, you know where I am."

He started to speak, but she held up her hand. "Don't say anything. I hate this kind of good-bye."

Grant let his lips curve upward a little and stepped aside for her to pass. The front door opened, then closed. Waiting for the sound of her car crunching gravel in the driveway, he paced to the front door where he pulled on his cowboy boots and slipped into a jean jacket.

He found Perkins in the front yard watching Sally's cherry-colored Camaro disappear into the trees.

"Sam," Collier called.

Perkins turned toward him, a pleasant expression on his craggy face. "Yeah, Grant?"

Holding the rail, Grant stepped down the ramp. "I've been trying to reach Cindy Lestrade since Monday. When I phoned this morning, her answering machine was full. She's not picking up her messages."

Perkins's wide shoulders moved. "Maybe she went on vacation."

"She didn't seem in a holiday mood when she was here," Collier said, running his hand through his dark hair. "In any case, I'm concerned. I want you to come with me to her apartment."

Striding fifty feet down the driveway, Perkins got into the Suburban the FBI had assigned to him and backed the car closer to Grant.

Thirty minutes later, they parked in front of Cindy's apartment building and got out. Grant looked over the parking lot. "What kind of car did the report say she drives?"

"A black Jeep."

Collier nodded toward the battered Jeep in the parking lot and walked toward it. Perkins followed him. They leaned over to peer at the slashed interior. "What a mess," Collier said. His internal trouble alarm was screeching like a wounded cat.

"Someone was searching for something," Perkins commented.

Grant gazed at the brick apartment building. He could feel Cindy's presence like a tangible thing.

Perkins said, "I know you're gone on that girl, but with her background, there's no telling what she might be involved in."

Collier's frown deepened. "If she was up to something, why'd she barge in on me? That would only attract attention."

Perkins chuckled. "She got your attention, all right."

Collier sent him a wry smile and tapped the dented fender. "The car's here, so she should be at home. Let's check out her apartment."

Crossing the lot, Perkins tried the doorknob, but it wouldn't give.

"Locked," he muttered.

"What kind of apartment building is this?" Collier asked, looking around. "There's no panel to buzz in a visitor."

Perkins pounded on the door. When no one came, he pounded again, the window rattling.

Grant said, "Hey, careful. You're going to break it."

Perkins leaned out to look up and down the street, ending with a hard stare at Collier. "You really want to get in there, don't you?"

"C'mon, Perkins, ask me something you don't already know."

The big man reached for Collier's cane. "Glass can't cost that much." He jabbed the handle of the cane at the window, and the glass shattered. Perkins grinned. "Service is our guarantee." He started to slip his hand through the opening to unlock the door when the apartment closest to them flew open.

"Just great," Collier said in a stage whisper. "Now you've done it."

A grizzled old man staggered into the hallway. He glared at them.

"What's going on here?" he rasped.

Perkins pointed down the street. "Some kids just threw a rock at us, and it hit the door. What kind of neighborhood is this?"

"A tough one. What do you want?"

Holding up his badge, Perkins asked, "Who are you?"

The old fellow glanced at the ID. "My name's Iverson. I'm the landlord. What are you guys after?"

"We're here to see…" Perkins looked over at Collier.

"Erin Davis," Collier finished. "Would you mind letting us in?"

Iverson opened the door. "It's about time you guys showed up," he said.

Perkins glanced at Collier, then said, "Why do you say that?"

"I called 911 when she left with that Ruskie. The cops forgot to send anyone over." He rubbed his hand over his stained T-shirt. "I'm glad the Bureau's on it."

Collier moved into the lobby and sat on the steps. He'd learn to conserve his energy as much as possible. "You're talking about Ms. Davis leaving with a stranger?"

"Who else?" Iverson asked, stepping toward Grant. The old man's breath was ninety proof. "Last Monday afternoon, I heard someone coming downstairs. I'd just changed the lock, so I came to the door to give her the new key, but she didn't want it.

"She had this guy with her. He was shorter than you," he nodded at Perkins, "…and older. I didn't like the looks of him, I tell you. I asked if everything was all right, and she said, yes, but she didn't sound like herself. When I asked who the guy was, he told me he was an old family friend."

His face crinkled into a wise expression. "He didn't fool me. He called her Cindy, not Erin." The old man grinned at Perkins. "I just look stupid. I see a lot more than people give me credit for."

"I don't doubt it," said Perkins.

"Sure, you do." Iverson pointed to the glass on the floor. "If some kids threw a rock, where's the rock?"

Perkins shifted his feet. "I guess I owe you for a window."

Iverson waved his hand, dismissing the idea. "Not if you find Erin, you don't. She's a great kid. If anything's happened to her, I'll be mighty tore up."

"Can we see her apartment?" Collier asked.

"Sure thing." He reached for the fist-size bundle of rattling keys hanging from his belt. "It's on the second floor."

Standing aside so Iverson could pass him on the narrow stairs, Grant followed him with Perkins at the rear. Steadying himself with the banister, Grant kept up with the old man. His leg took the stress fairly well.

The upstairs hall was dim even on a bright afternoon. Iverson led them to number 212 and unlocked the door. Stepping inside, Grant drew up short, a dull ache coming up on the left side of his chest. Is this the apartment Nina had rented for her? It was ghetto-quality. What Cindy must have endured all these months, living in a place like this.

Across the room, the mattress on the bed was a shredded lump. The sagging green sofa had its cushions sliced and gutted. A makeshift mattress lay in the center of the room on a matted brown carpet.

"I've been meaning to take that mess away for her." Iverson said, rubbing what was left of his thinning white hair. "I'll have to get a truck to come and get it."

"When did this happen?" Collier asked as he moved into the room.

"Sunday afternoon around two o'clock, she came down and got me because someone broke her lock. I came up with her and found this." He shook his head, his whiskery jowls quivering. "She didn't deserve it, Mister. That Ms. Davis is a first-rate lady."

"Grant, look at this," Perkins said from a doorway to the right.

Iverson followed Collier into the kitchenette where Perkins stood over a spot of dried blood on the floor and a baseball bat with a stain to match.

"Any ideas about this?" Collier asked Iverson.

"That bat's mine. I lent it to her for protection. I don't know about the blood. Neither of them looked hurt when they left here."

"You said you heard banging around up here?"

"Yeah."

Perkins pulled the tiny fridge away from the wall. A sharp squeal made him jump back as a mouse shot across the floor. He jerked back, stifling a shout. "I hate those things," he muttered, wiping his hands against each other.

Collier prowled around the apartment. The place was rough, but he could feel Cindy's presence here. He opened the closet door and smelled Elige perfume on the hanging clothes. Some things didn't change.

He picked up Cindy's doll from the small dresser and stared at the taped repair on its abdomen. "Whoever trashed the place did a thorough job." He set the doll down. "I hope to meet them someday." His voice was low, threatening.

The two men poked around for half an hour. "Not much to go on," Perkins said, kneeling to peer under the ruined sofa. He reached under it, then jerked his hand back and cursed as a rat raced out.

"You got something?" Collier asked.

"Nah," Perkins said, getting to his feet. "All that's under there is a dusty rat's nest." He sent Collier a meaningful look. "If you want to sift through it, go right ahead. I'm not sticking my hand under there again."

Collier turned to Iverson. "You wouldn't happen to know where she works, would you?"

"PTL Computers by Meriden and Monroe."

"Want to go there next?" Perkins asked, getting to his feet.

Collier considered. "Let's stop by the police station first. I'd like to know why they never came."

As they left the apartment, Collier silently cried out, *Cindy, where are you?*

Chapter Seventeen

Black Canyon City, Arizona

Fifteen minutes later, Perkins wheeled the Suburban into one of the visitors' slots at the local Yavapai County Sheriff's office.

When they reached the front desk, a uniformed officer with a gray flattop haircut yawned and looked up. "Can I help you gentle... Mr. Collier, what a surprise!" He turned and yelled into the back of the building. "Hey guys, Grant Collier's here!"

Grant rubbed the back of his neck, partially hiding his face as half a dozen uniformed officers came out, some smiling, some simply curious.

"Good job on those Iraqis," the desk sergeant said, beaming. "You made us proud."

"Thanks, guys," Collier said, trying to squelch the flush he felt rising up his neck. "Actually, I'm here on business."

A tall man with thick eyebrows and coal-gray eyes stepped forward, extending his hand. "I'm Sheriff Carswell. Why don't we go into my office?"

The Sheriff led them down a hallway to a room the size of a walk-in closet without a single window. He motioned for each of them to take a seat in a metal folding chair in front of a metal desk strewn with papers.

"Who's your friend?" Carswell asked Grant.

Perkins dropped his badge on the desk. Carswell held it up. "FBI, huh?" He closed the blue case and handed it back. "What can I do for you?"

Collier said, "We're here to talk about Erin Davis. You got a missing person's report on her a few days ago."

Sitting behind the desk, the Sheriff rubbed his face. "The name doesn't ring a bell." He picked up his phone. "Hang on a second."

Pressing a couple of buttons, he said, "Kowalski, come in here for a minute, will you?"

Less than a minute later, the desk sergeant appeared at the door. Carswell asked him, "Does the name Erin Davis mean anything to you?"

Kowalski nodded, showing a thin spot on top of his head. "That's the girl Anderson's been dating."

Carswell's face lightened. "Oh, yeah, Wesley's girl."

"Does Deputy Anderson know that Ms. Davis is missing?" Perkins asked.

"She's not missing," Kowalski said, stepping into the room.

"We just talked to her landlord, a Mr. Iverson," Collier said. "He reported her missing, and your department took no action."

Both officers laughed. "Iverson?" Carswell said, leaning back into his creaky chair. "That guy sees a crook under every pinecone. We've got a whole file dedicated to him. I wouldn't take him too seriously, Collier."

"No one even bothered to talk to the guy?" Perkins asked.

Kowalski nodded. "Wesley did. He phoned Iverson and told him that Erin was with him."

"Can we speak to Anderson?" Collier asked.

Carswell said, "He's taking a week's vacation."

"Personally, I think he and the girl went to Flagstaff or something," Kowalski said, "on a little romantic getaway."

Collier bristled. "That doesn't sound like Ms. Davis."

The slant to Carswell's smile made him look sly. "You don't know Wesley. He can really charm them."

Kowalski added, "He's got that innocent-puppy look that girls go for. A real heartbreaker."

"Listen," Carswell said, "she's dating Wesley, so you don't have to worry about her. If she were missing, we'd all be pounding the pavement right now."

Collier stood and picked up his cane. "When Anderson comes in, would you have him call me?" he asked, stepping away from the chair.

"No problem," Carswell said, standing to shake hands. "It's great to have you home, Grant."

Collier shook a few more hands as he and Perkins left the building.

When they reached the car, Collier sat staring at the latch on the glove box.

"I guess you don't know her as well as you thought," Perkins said, punching the ignition button.

Hearing him as from a distance, Collier didn't answer.

Putting the car into reverse, Perkins hesitated. "You want to go home now?"

Collier came out of his stupor. "We need to make two stops, first the bank, then PTL Computers. I need to pull out a lot of cash."

Easing out of the parking lot, Perkins glanced at Grant's scowl. "I take it you're not satisfied."

"Just drive, will you?" Collier growled.

Perkins drove.

When the men entered the well-lighted display room of PTL Computers half an hour later, a wide woman with a wide smile came from behind the counter and held out her hand. "Grant Collier, you're looking well. Good to see you!"

Collier peered at her. "You know me?" he asked.

"Don't you remember me? Olivia Donner. I taught your sixth-grade Sunday school class."

Grant took another look. Miss Donner. He remembered now. She was fifty pounds heavier, but that big smile was the same. She harnessed the power of home-baked chocolate chip cookies to keep the boys in line.

"I remember you now," he said, grinning. "Keep in mind I was only ten then." Suddenly, he gasped, engulfed in a big hug with no advance warning.

"It's so good to see you walking," she gushed when she let him go.

She turned toward Perkins. "Are you with him?"

The tall man held out his badge. "Special Agent Perkins, FBI."

Olivia looked shocked. She turned to Collier. "Have I done something?"

Grant said, "We're here about Erin Davis. I understand she works for you."

"That's right." Olivia stumped to a chair beside the register, "Erin's a jewel. She's the best person I've ever hired."

"Has she been to work recently?" Perkins asked.

"Not since Monday."

"Has she called?" Collier asked, stepping closer to her.

"No, but Wesley did." She glanced from one man to the other, a frown creasing her brow. "He said Erin needed some time off. I wasn't surprised. She was a real mess Monday morning, even came in late. She and Wesley must have had a huge fight."

"What makes you say that?" Collier asked.

"They were man-trouble tears, Grant." She cocked an eyebrow, coquettish despite her size. "A woman knows, dear."

Collier felt a jolt in his middle but tried to hide it. He knew that Cindy's tears were from Grant trouble at the ranch. Noticing how closely Olivia watched him, he moved on to another question. "How well does she know Wesley?"

Olivia glanced at a wall calendar beside her, moving her red fingernail on the large numbers, remembering. "The first time she mentioned him was Monday morning." She tapped the paper, then dropped her hand. "She had a kind of dreamy expression when she spoke his name."

Grant didn't want to know more, but he had to. What if she was in trouble? "Do you think she knew him well enough to go away with him for a whole week?"

Olivia looked doubtful. "Grant, to be honest, I don't think Erin's that kind of girl. Of course, I can't say for sure what she would do." She looked from him to Perkins. "Why are you interested? Aren't you with the CIA?"

Grant backed away from the counter, smiling to soften his answer. "I'm sorry, Miss Donner, but I can't tell you. Thanks for your help." He glanced at Perkins.

The agent had picked up a computer game box from a nearby rack and was reading a back cover smeared with purple, laser-wielding aliens.

"You ready, champ?" Collier asked, sarcastic.

Perkins dropped the box like it had scalded him and bustled out the door. Leaning on his cane, Grant followed with more dignity. He paused, touching the collapsible steel grate outside the doors and waved goodbye as Olivia called after them. "Thanks for coming in!"

He caught up with Perkins on the sidewalk. "What now?" the agent asked. The car beeped as he hit the unlock button on the key fob.

"I guess we go home," Collier said with a deep sigh. "It looks like Cindy did exactly what I told her to do. She's made a new life for herself."

As they headed home, Grant replayed the comments of all the parties they'd spoken to. The case seemed airtight. Cindy had a boyfriend and went off for a vacation with him. He tried to dismiss it, but he couldn't. Something was wrong.

As the Suburban turned into his lane, Grant's shoulders sagged. You haven't learned much in all your years with the agency, he scolded himself. The only thing wrong is that you don't like to think of Cindy with another man. Face it, chump, you blew it for good.

New River, Arizona

Sprawled on top of her sleeping bag with a romance novel in her hands, Cindy fought off discouraged tears. She'd been here for four days without a single breath of fresh air. The walls were closing in fast, despite the shopping bag full of secondhand books Wesley had brought her. Even his evening visits were becoming a strain. Last night before he left, he grabbed her shoulders and tried to kiss her.

When she pulled away, he let her go, but anger sparked in his eyes.

"What's the matter?" he demanded "I thought we had something going."

Uncomfortable, she turned away. "I don't mean it that way, Wesley." She paused, then faltered, "It's just that…" How do you tell someone about a ghost in your past that refuses to stay buried?

When she didn't go on, Wesley slammed out without saying goodbye. Would he come back tonight or let her stew in this sinkhole alone? Honestly, she didn't know which she preferred.

Her hand moved across the sleeping bag and a ragged nail caught on the fabric. In a sudden flash of temper, she muttered a word that would have shocked her mother and threw the romance novel at the towering stack on her bedside stand. They crashed into a heap on the rag that passed for a rug.

Using her teeth, she tried to correct the nail. If only she had thought to pick up her purse, at least she'd have her nail file. Oh, how did she get into this predicament?

Lying back, staring at a crablike stain on the ceiling, she let out a deep sob. She rolled onto her stomach and buried her wet face into the stale pillowcase. After a while, her emotions exhausted, she slept deep and sound for the first time in days.

Headlights shone through the orange curtains and woke her. Blinking, Cindy sat up and touched her tousled hair. That must be Wesley. A moment later, three knocks sounded on the door, two loud and one soft. Turning on the lamp, she fumbled with the lock, and the door swung in.

"Good news," Wesley said, setting a fast-food bag beside the broken television. The smell of burgers and fries made Cindy cringe. Not again. She had a kitchenette, but he never brought her anything she could cook.

She raked her fingers through her bangs. She must look a sight.

Wesley grinned down at her. "My FBI friends found the source of your trouble." He plopped into the only chair in the room. "It's some deep government operation."

Cindy sat on the edge of the bed. "I was afraid of that."

He leaned his elbows on his knees. "The feds want to talk to you."

"When?"

"Tomorrow. They're setting up a safe house for you." He reached for her hand. "Best of all, you'll be under their protection. No one will be able to hurt you."

She wanted to cry from sheer relief, but she felt numb. "How will I get there…to the safe house?"

"I'll take you to meet the agents at ten in the morning."

She put her shaking hand to her forehead. "I can't believe it's over."

He moved next to her, their sides touching. "This will be your last night here." He touched her cheek. "It's also the last time we'll see each other for a while. They told me I'll have to stay away for your safety."

He cradled her chin. "I care for you, Cindy, like I've never cared for a woman before."

Mesmerized, Cindy looked into his warm green eyes. She wanted to feel protected more than anything in the world. She ached for it.

Leaning down, tenderly pulling her chin, he aimed for her lips.

At the last second, Cindy turned her face, and he kissed her cheek.

Speaking against her skin, he murmured, "Cindy."

Pulling away, she got to her feet, hugging her middle. "I'm sorry, Wesley, but I think you better go." Reaching for the doorknob, she pulled it open.

"Cindy!" he said, exasperated. "Why?"

Jammed between the door and the wall, she waited. "I'll be ready when you get here in the morning."

Muttering, he paused beside her as though deciding his next action. He raised the back of his hand to her cheek.

"Please!" she whispered, intense.

Closing the door after him, she slid the chain into the lock and leaned her head against the door. She felt awful for hurting Wesley. She should have explained her feelings instead of just throwing him out. He would have understood. Grant had.

Sitting on the bed, she rubbed her forehead with both hands. Grant's face loomed up behind her eyelids. With a deep moan, she threw herself onto her pillow. Why couldn't she erase Grant Collier from her mind and get on with her life?

Chapter Eighteen

Cave Creek, Arizona

Grant limped down a California beach, his bum leg moving heavily across the sand. His surroundings were familiar yet strange. Dark waves lashed at the sand, the sky rolled with heavy clouds, and a foggy mist swirled about his knees. A wicked wind ruffled his dark hair and pierced his flesh with chilly fingers. He was alone and terribly lonely.

From behind him came laughter, two voices mingling into one.

Grant whirled around, his body twisting awkwardly to swing his left leg forward. It was Cindy, the red highlights in her dark hair glinting in the sun, her emerald eyes flashing, her smile dazzling... but not for him.

A talk, dark man without a face walked beside her. Arm in arm, they ambled toward Grant, so lost in each other they didn't notice him.

Shoulders back, head erect, Grant heard a roaring in his ears that didn't come from the raging surf.

Finally, Cindy looked up. Her expression changed. "Grant, what are you doing here?"

"Walking," he said, his heart hammering.

She looked at his leg and laughed. "Walking? With that dead stump?"

Grant turned to go.

"Wait!" Her voice sounded breathy and unreal. "You have to meet Wesley," she said.

Faceless Wesley held out his hand. Grant's fingers formed a fist. He drew it back, but before he could land a punch, Cindy and Wesley faded into the silver mist, their shrill, mocking laughter clawing at his vitals.

Thunder pounded the house as Grant pulled himself from the nightmare. The second loud bang jolted him awake—a slamming door, not thunder. Roxanne's loud, angry voice followed with his mother's as loud and firm, then feet thumping and more slamming.

Grant slid out of bed and slipped on his bathrobe. His left leg wasn't the dead stump in his dream. It was a tingly nuisance. He couldn't do the long jump anymore, but who wanted to anyway? He always felt stiff first thing in the morning, so he picked up his cane. He left his room to see what had destroyed peace in the valley on a bright Saturday morning. As he opened the bedroom door, the dream still weighed him down. He'd found Cindy only to lose her again. Maybe Perkins was right. Maybe she'd changed. He let out a heavy sigh. Somehow, he couldn't accept it.

He met his mother at the bottom of the stairs. "What's up, Mom?" he asked her.

She frowned. "Roxanne and I had a difference of opinion."

"A difference! The whole house rattled."

She sent him a calculating look. "Why don't you ask her about it?"

Catching her signal, Grant took the cue and, cane in hand, made his way up the staircase to the next floor. He knocked on the first door to the right.

"Come in!" Roxanne looked up at him from her seat on the edge of her single bed, tears smudging her face. Grant stepped into a world of stuffed animals, horse pictures, and frilly girl stuff, another reminder of Cindy.

Gus came over to meet him.

"Hey, kid, what's up?" he asked, bending to touch the dog's head.

"She says I can't ride Duke today." Roxanne sniffled into a tissue.

"That's odd. Why not?"

Her words came in a rush. "Because I got up an hour late and didn't go out and feed him right away." She sniffed. "She wanted me to go to the basketball all-nighter last night. I haven't had any sleep. I got home and crashed." She sniffed and wiped her nose. "I was going to feed him as soon as I could." She flung her tissue into the trash can. "I don't understand."

Grant held up his hand. "It's okay, Roxanne, I get it." He sat in the white wicker chair beside the bed. Gus lay down on the rug. "I hate to tell you this, but I agree with her."

"But…"

"Let me finish. Duke is an old horse. I admit that missing his hay and grain by an hour or so every now and then won't hurt him, but that's not the point." He softened his tone. "He's locked in his stall, Roxanne. He depends on you to feed him. For that hour while you were sleeping, he was anxious, wondering when you'll come. That's not fair to him."

Roxanne huffed. "I said I was sorry." She gestured toward brilliant sunlight streaming through her gauzy curtains. "It's a beautiful Saturday. What else can I do with my day if I can't ride?"

He leaned back. "You can forget about riding. Mom won't give in on that one even if I ask her. However, you can still do things with Duke that aren't technically riding."

She brightened. "What?"

"You had breakfast yet?"

"A piece of toast. I'm not really that hungry."

"Go out and get him saddled, but don't put on his bridle. I'll meet you out there in a few minutes."

"Okay!" She reached for her stained sneakers lying next to the desk.

Grant returned to his room to dress, then he hit the kitchen. Since his mobility had improved, the kitchen had become self-service. Grabbing a bowl from an oak cabinet, he poured himself some dry cereal, added milk, and sat down at the table. He caught a glimpse of his mother hurrying down the hall wearing green overalls with a red bandana over her hair.

"Not talking?" he called out.

She came to the doorway. "Sorry, son. It's Billy and Ada's day off, and I've got to do the milking."

"Hey, want some help?"

She shook her head. "Bending under cows to hook up milking machines wouldn't be good for you. I've been doing it alone for plenty of years now. Besides, Andre said he'll be over later. He can help with the evening milking."

"Why don't you get Roxanne to help?"

Faye Collier stepped into the kitchen. "No. I won't ask her to do that."

"I bet she'd be thrilled to do it."

Her mouth formed a firm line. "When I first brought Roxanne home, you know what people said?"

Grant didn't answer. What people said never bothered him.

"They said, 'Good idea, Faye. You need a helper on the ranch.'"

"So?"

"I took her in because God told me to. She's not a servant." She adjusted the bandana over her right ear. "And just so you know, the state pays me a fixed allowance to meet her needs. Every penny of it is sitting in a separate bank account for her college. I don't want anyone to ever say I took advantage of Roxanne."

Cradling his red cereal bowl in both hands, Grant grinned at her. "You bucking for sainthood or something?"

She smiled and sent a playful swat to his cheek. "I'm already a saint, son. I don't have to prove it to anyone." She turned toward the door. "See you at lunch."

By the time he finished his breakfast, fought with his cowboy boots, and headed out to the barn, Roxanne had Duke saddled and waiting. He grabbed a coiled-up line and a whip from the tack room. The feeling of walking in his old boots and the smell of leather made him want to ride.

When he reached the corral, Roxanne looked at the items in his hands and asked, "What are those for?"

He held them up. "This is a lunge line and whip to put Duke through his paces.

Leading Duke to the edge of the corral, Grant attached the line to his halter and led him to the center. He flicked the whip behind Duke, and the horse began to move at an easy walk. As he worked, Grant gave Roxanne instructions. Ten minutes later, in a sweat, he called, "Whoa!" to Duke, then summoned Roxanne into the corral, saying, "Here, you take over. I'm beat."

Retreating to a lawn chair with Gus at his side, Grant watched Roxanne put into practice what he'd taught her. The girl had a natural gift. After about fifteen minutes, she stopped Duke and turned to him. "Why did you want me to saddle him?"

He grinned like a kid. "Unhook the lunge line and get the bridle."

When Roxanne returned, he said, "Put it on him."

Her face questioning, she slipped the bridle over Duke's head. She glanced at Grant. "You're going to let me ride, aren't you?"

He got to his feet, smiling. "Not a chance. If I crossed Mom, she'd have me in the woodshed." He moved toward her. "That's for me."

She glanced at his cane. "You sure you can?"

"Nope, but I'm sick and tired of watching you have all the fun."

Approaching the animal from the right side, he said, "Most people mount from the left, but I don't have a choice." He handed her his cane. "When I get up, I may need you to push my left leg over." Sticking the toe of his cowboy boot into the right stirrup, Grant pushed himself up. As he feared, he couldn't quite bend his left knee enough to clear Duke's rump. Roxanne reached from the left side to pull his bad leg over the rest of the way and stuck his boot into the other stirrup.

"Thanks," he said. "Now hand me my cane. I might need it if I fall off."

Roxanne passed it up to him. "You look good up there," she said grudgingly.

He felt good, too. It had been years since he sat astride Duke. Clucking his tongue, Grant set the horse into an easy walk. He knew that being in the saddle at all was pushing the limit, so he kept the pace slow. Boyhood memories rushed back—rodeo ribbons, long trail rides with his father and their slow conversations in the saddle. He waited for his chest to tighten, for the old pain to wash over him. Instead, he felt soft warmth and gentle joy.

With Gus trailing behind them, he headed Duke out of the corral and onto bush trails that had doubled as much-used dirt bike tracks in his younger days. Out of sight of the house, he felt great. Over the past week, he had healed much faster than anyone had expected. Yesterday,

Dr. Parker had told Grant he was a couple of weeks ahead of schedule. Mom's good cooking wins again.

On his way back to the stable, the sound of a loud muffler reached him through the woods. The hair on Gus's back stood up. He growled deep in his throat, then barked. Grant urged the horse to a faster pace.

Emerging from the trees, Grant saw an orange Mustang parked by the front ramp. Three teenage toughs stood in a half circle around Roxanne. The one in the center wore baggy corduroy pants and an oversized combat jacket. As big as Grant, he had his shoulders far back, chest out, chin up. Roxanne had the same stance.

Setting off at a full run, Gus barked his way toward the intruders. Setting Duke up to a trot, Grant reached them as Roxanne grabbed Gus's collar and held him back.

"What's up, Roxanne?" Grant asked.

Eyes on the ground, she didn't answer. Gus was doing all the talking for her.

Calling the dog down, Collier turned his attention to the teenagers wearing leather jackets and gold earrings. They looked like reform-school rejects. "I'm Grant Collier," he said, "Who are you?"

"I used to hang around with them," Roxanne answered, keeping a tight hold on Gus's collar. "This is Kurt, my old boyfriend." She nodded toward the eyebrow-pierced soldier wannabe whose black hair looked like a thorny bush.

Grant held out his hand. "Hi, Kurt." The teenager ignored him and spoke to Roxanne. "I'm not her old boyfriend. I'm still your boyfriend, Roxanne."

Grant slipped his left foot out of the stirrup. "Roxanne, give me a hand here, will you?"

Darting quick glances at her friends, Roxanne helped him get off Duke, and he reached up for his cane.

                    Lana McAra

You a gimp or something?" Kurt asked, eying the stick.

"Yeah," Collier answered. "I've got a bum leg." He stepped closer to Roxanne and asked, "How do you all know each other?"

"These are the guys I almost went to detention with," she murmured, shying back. Gus let out a single menacing bark.

"Did you just get out?" Grant asked them, letting his eyes pause on each of them. The one on the right had his head shaved on the sides with a thick hank of hair on top. The other had a greasy, slicked-back look. They reeked of body odor and cheap cologne.

Grant spoke to Roxanne. "Are they still your friends?"

She squinted at Kurt, her eyes burning. "No!"

Kurt puffed up his shoulders a few millimeters more. "It ain't that simple, Roxy. You just don't unjoin the gang." He tried to reason with her. "Besides, we were good together. You know that."

Collier took a step toward Kurt until only three feet separated them. "You'd best go."

Kurt swore and shuffled his army boots on the grass. "Why are you butting in? She ain't nothing to you but a street punk you took in like a stray dog."

"Wrong, pal." Grant stared into the boy's dark eyes. "She's my sister."

Kurt looked at Roxanne. "Roxy ain't got no brother."

Grant glanced over at the girl beside him. "Is that right, Roxanne?"

She looked smug. "He's my brother, Kurt."

"See, punk." Grant bore down. "Playtime's over. You guys get out of here and leave my sister alone."

Kurt raised his fists. "Who's going to make me, gimp? You?"

Grant's eyes narrowed. He stepped back. "Take your best shot, kid."

Kurt faked with a left, then sent his right fist flying at Grant's face.

Collier caught it with his right hand and squeezed his steel-like fingers between Kurt's knuckles until sweat broke out on the boy's forehead. Grant bent Kurt's hand back, driving him to his knees as a car pulled up to the house. No one noticed but Grant. All were too focused on the battle of wills.

Finally, Kurt let out a grunt, fell to his knees, and pulled his fist away. Springing to his feet, he assumed a boxing stance, pumping his fists near his chin. "Okay, big man, let's see if you can take all three of us."

Grant held up his hand. "No, please. I don't think I can do that."

Kurt laughed. "Then back off."

Grant scratched the side of his face. "Be reasonable, fellas, and you'll save yourself some trouble. Don't you ever watch the news or read a paper?"

Covering her mouth, Roxanne stifled a giggle.

The boys crowded closer to Collier. "You getting out of the way, gimp?" Kurt said. "Or are we moving you?"

Holding up both hands, palms out, Collier said, "Let's be clear about what you're getting into here before you jump me. My name is Grant Collier, and I work for the CIA. That bruiser standing behind you is Roxanne's other brother, Deputy Andre Collier of the Yavapai Sheriff's Department."

All three of them looked back... then up… way up.

"Hi, guys," Andre said, smiling and full of good humor. He looked at Grant. "We got a problem here, bro?"

Kurt and company moved close together. The one on the left touched the back of his hand to his mouth. "Is this for real?" Kurt asked.

Grant said, "Roxanne is our little sister. If you toughs so much as spit in her direction, we'll make you hurt in places you never even knew you had." He jabbed his cane toward Kurt's middle. "Got it?"

Kurt looked at Roxanne as though trying to think of a parting jab.

"Get out of here!" Collier said. "I'm giving you ten seconds."

They shuffled off, trying to act as if they weren't in a hurry, but moving fast anyway. Ducking into the Mustang, Kurt waited until the third guy slammed his door before he peeled out, showering stones into the lawn.

Roxanne turned to Grant. "Did you mean what you said?"

"Every word," he answered, smiling softly.

"Goes for me, too," Andre said, stepping near them. "You're part of the family, Roxanne. We want it that way."

"I'm so sorry for this," she said, tucking loose hair behind her ear. "I tried to get rid of them before you came back, but they wouldn't go. I kept telling them that I'm not that kind of girl anymore." She picked up Duke's lead. Dropping her grip on Gus, she led both horse and dog toward the barn.

Suddenly, Grant's head jerked like he had received an electric shock. Of course! Cindy wasn't that kind of girl, either! How could he have been so blind?

He turned to his brother. "Andre, I know you came to do the milking, but I need some help. It's Perkins's day off, and I've got something that just can't wait."

"Sure, bro, "Andre said. "Where to?"

Black Canyon City, Arizona

At that moment, Wesley turned his car down a gravel road. Sitting beside him, Cindy said, "I'm surprised they're having the meeting so close to Black Canyon City." She chewed at her ragged nail. "Aren't they afraid of being found?"

Wesley shrugged. "Hey, we're talking about the FBI. If they're not worried, I'm not worried either. Besides, I think they plan to move you after I've gone. Last night was our last for a while."

She put her hand on his arm. "I'm sorry, Wesley. I didn't mean to hurt you."

He touched her hand for a brief second. "Don't worry about it. It's history."

They turned off the gravel road, then drove another mile into a hilly area. When they pulled up to the safe house, Cindy frowned at the mobile home. Its sheet-metal siding had pulled away in places. Rust stains ran down the sides, and the front window was broken. "Is this the best that they could do?" she asked.

"No one can see it," Wesley answered. "That's the whole point, isn't it?" He parked his car in the rutted driveway beside a dark limousine and a gleaming white Lexus.

"A limousine?" Cindy asked. "Who drives a limousine out here?"

"You rate top brass, my dear." He kissed her cheek. "Good-bye. I'll say it now before we have company."

She smiled into his eyes. "Thanks for your help, Wesley. I'll call you when this is over." Stepping out of the car, she drew a deep breath of clear desert air. "I sure can't complain about the scenery."

Ten strides later, Wesley held open the mobile home door, and Cindy walked in to face two people sitting in the living room. One of them was a bald, stocky man with a thick beard. The other was a tiny, gray-haired woman with her hair cut like a Marine except for long bangs that flipped forward over her eyes.

"Come in, Ms. Lestrade," the woman said. "I've looked forward to meeting you." She held out her hand. "I'm K.R. Quinn."

"K.R. Quinn," Cindy repeated, her senses on red alert. "You own Paget Information Systems."

"Precisely," she said. Her thin lips curved into an icy smile.

Cindy spun on her heels to go out, but Wesley stood against the door, his powerful arms folded across his chest. "Wesley?" she squealed. "Where's the FBI?"

"Sorry, Cindy," he said, avoiding her eyes. "I needed Aunt Karen's help. In exchange, I had to solve a problem for her. You."

She went numb. This was impossible.

"Ms. Lestrade, you've gone white," Quinn said. "Come, sit down." she waved her slender hand toward the worn sofa. "We need to discuss your future."

Black Canyon City, Arizona

As they drove to Cindy's apartment, Grant told Andre about his relationship with Cindy—how he wanted to marry her and spend the rest of his life with her, but she thought he was pond scum, which he was.

Andre scowled at a green light as they passed under it. "So, I take it you're the one who's suffering now," he said.

"That's a major understatement," Collier said.

"Serves you right." He turned the car into the parking lot. "If I'd done something like that to Rita, I wouldn't be able to sleep or eat—ever."

"I didn't know her at first," Collier said, defensive and angry. "After we got acquainted, I couldn't back out. I've been in a lose-lose situation since I first laid eyes on her." He jerked the door handle.

"Careful, bro." Andre said. "You'll tear it off." He sized Grant up. "You've got it bad, don't you?" Opening his own door, he didn't wait for an answer.

They roused Iverson from a drunken stupor long enough to let them into Cindy's apartment. "Lock up when you're through," he said, then returned to his apartment to finish sleeping it off.

"You look under stuff," Grant said, "I can bend down with this leg, but I have a hard time getting back up."

They searched in silence for ten minutes. Grant looked in places he'd already seen five times. If only he knew what he was after.

"Say, what's that?" Andre said, peering under the couch. Standing, he walked around the sofa. Its back was facing the door. Bending down, he pulled out a black leather handbag. It was dusty and the handles were broken.

"That looks like something the last tenant left," Grant said.

"Let's see what's inside." Andre unsnapped the clasp. Kneeling he turned the purse upside down on the carpet. A wallet, a folded wad of bills, makeup, a key ring. He picked up the wallet and opened it. "Well, looky here," he drawled. He held it up to Grant.

"Cindy's driver's license." Grant said, staring at the photograph. He flipped through the inner flaps. "Her debit card, everything." He glanced at Andre. "She'd never leave this and go on vacation."

"I wonder how it got in such bad shape." Andre pulled at the loose straps.

"Or how it landed under the back of the couch."

"You know," Andre said, "it is possible that she and her boyfriend got so wrapped up in each other that they took off on the spur of the moment and she forgot her purse. Rita leaves hers everywhere."

"Not Cindy." His statement had a definite ring.

"How can you be so sure?"

"When Roxanne said, 'I'm just not that kind of a girl,' it hit me." He rubbed his hand across the black leather wallet. "Cindy refused to sleep with me until we had been dating for six months. If I got too free and easy with her, she shot me down."

He handed Andre the wallet. "If she turned me down that long, she didn't say yes to someone after less than a week." He headed for the door. "Bring the purse along. We're going back to the police station and talk to that detective again. Someone is holding something back."

Chapter Nineteen

Black Canyon City, Arizona

Light-headed, Cindy eased onto a matted couch which had two springs sticking through its brown upholstery. When one of the springs made contact with her tender flesh, her shock turned to anger. She turned on Quinn. "Maybe we should talk about your future instead of mine. I know about the viruses you're installing into your customer's computers."

Quinn steepled her fingers, her mouth pulled into a tight knot. Dropping her hands she smiled, all cultured and cold. "You are your father's equal, Ms. Lestrade. The way you repaired those systems—especially the one at Archon Energy—we knew you weren't the average programmer." She smiled at her nephew. "That's why we had to turn Wesley's irresistible charm loose on you."

"So?" Cindy demanded, chin high, ready to fight. She hadn't come this far to be hijacked by some two-bit crook.

213

Quinn sobered. "How do you think the good people of Black Canyon City will react when they learn that Erin Davis is the daughter of world-famous traitors?"

Glancing from Quinn to her fat, ugly friend, Cindy said, "Is that what this is about? Blackmail?"

Still smiling, Quinn said, "You are very astute."

Cindy seemed to grow taller. "If I have to face up to my past, I'll do it. I have friends who care about me." Her stare focused on Quinn. "At least what I am won't put me in jail. How about you?"

"I told you," the stocky man said to Quinn.

Quinn sighed. "You were correct, Mr. Dawkins. She is pathetically honest."

Cindy jumped to her feet. "I've had enough. I'm leaving." She marched to the door, but Wesley blocked her way. "Step aside, Wesley!"

"I can't, Cindy." he muttered. Feet wide, he refused to move.

"Yes, you can." She grabbed his wrist and pulled, but he stood like a marble statue.

Dawkins spoke, his voice as rough as a bundle of tied weeds. "Ms. Lestrade, let me tell you the facts of life. Wesley likes to shoot dice. Last year he got into debt in Las Vegas. With the mob, no less. He'd be six feet under if Ms. Quinn hadn't picked up his IOUs. Unfortunately, he's already run up a big tab in Phoenix, and it's *dejà vu* for poor Wesley."

Cindy peered into the young policeman's red face. "Is that true?"

Turning his head away, he muttered, "Yeah."

Cindy stepped to the center of the room and demanded, "Are you going to keep me a prisoner or what?" She curled up her two fists. "If you hurt me, it'll be the biggest mistake you ever made. Someone else is looking for me. The CIA. They searched my apartment and my car." Her lips formed a straight line. "You're in over your head, Quinn."

Both Quinn and Dawkins chuckled. Quinn paused long enough to tell her, "We trashed your apartment and stole your car, so you'd run into Wesley's arms."

While they laughed, Cindy wanted to wipe the smile off Quinn's face in the worst way, but she forced herself to think instead. There had to be some way out of this.

"Gentleman," Dawkins called down the hall, "please come in." A door opened, and the fight suddenly went out of Cindy. Her knees buckled as her Russian kidnapper paced toward her, followed by two dark-haired bodybuilders.

Her stone-faced enemy clasped her arm. "Ms. Lestrade, you caused me much trouble," he said, his voice guttural.

"Meet Mr. Popov of the Russian Federation," Quinn said.

"When Wesley told us some Russians were after you, well, we just couldn't resist. We had to know exactly who. Fortunately, Mr. Dawkins has some useful contacts. It took a few days, but we learned who was looking for you, and—what a surprise—their problem solves ours."

Cindy glanced from Popov to Quinn. "What's going to happen to me?"

"We have Mr. Popov's word that within hours you will be in the air headed to Russia and out of our way. As a bonus, he's already put a million dollars into a numbered account." Quinn rubbed her manicured fingers against her cashmere lapel. "You've been a very profitable venture. We do thank you."

Cindy turned to Popov. "If you think I'm going to stay quiet while you haul me through the airport, you can forget it."

Popov shook his head. "We have a ship leaving San Diego tonight. You can help us with our problem as we sail."

"What problem?" Cindy asked. What on earth could she do to help the Russians, even if she wanted to?

Popov didn't answer.

"That concludes our business," Quinn said, standing.

Popov said, "As we agreed, we leave first, and you wait here five minutes. Yes?"

"Yes," said Quinn, nodding.

Popov gripped Cindy's shoulder. "We go now."

As she passed Wesley, Cindy squinted up at him. "How could you?"

"If it... helps," he stammered, swallowing, "I really did…"

"Don't even go there," she said, resisting a compulsion to kick him where it hurts.

Hustling her into the limo, the driver backed across the rocky yard to get around Wesley's car. They entered the gravel road and sped away.

Behind them, a roaring blast shook the car. Turning to look out the limousine's wide rear window, Popov grunted his approval as a roaring inferno rose thirty feet above the trailer.

In the rear-facing seat, Cindy watched, mesmerized. She felt an icy chill. "You killed them," she gasped.

Popov shook his closely cropped head. "Not us. Propane explosion. People need to check their gas lines more often." He chuckled at his own twisted attempt at humor.

Suddenly, he sobered and gestured to the tinted glass and thickly carpeted floor. "No trunk for you this time. You can ride in style." He put out his hand. "Your cellphone," he said.

Cindy handed over her last connection to the outside world. Her teeth chattered and she pressed both hands to her lips.

"Ivan," Popov called to the driver, "turn up the heat. Ms. Lestrade is cold."

No amount of warm air could stop Cindy's shivering. She had no idea what these insane people wanted from her. What would they do to her if she couldn't give them what they asked? And how could she give it to them when she didn't have it?

Black Canyon City, Arizona

For fifteen minutes, Grant and Andre cooled their heels in the dingy rear waiting room of the Sheriff's Department before Detective Carswell could see them.

Finally, Carswell strode into the room with an attitude of a man in a hurry. "Sorry to keep you, Collier. I've been on the radio. We've got a possible arson outside of town with a couple of burn victims. I've got to get out there." His eyebrows lifted slightly. "What can I do for you?"

Grant said, "I just learned that Erin Davis couldn't have gone away with Wesley for a week."

"How do you know that?" Carswell asked.

"We found her purse in her apartment. No woman leaves for a week without her purse."

Carswell lifted a pen from between two stacks on his desk. "That doesn't change the fact that Wesley said she was with him. Wesley wouldn't lie about something like that. Why should he?"

Grant wasn't buying it. "Anyone could have called Iverson and claimed to be Wesley."

"You may have something there," Carswell said, nodding. "Wesley Anderson was found at the fire scene I just told you about. He's burned over 80% of his body."

"Only Anderson was found?" Collier asked.

"There are two other bodies, burned beyond immediate recognition."

Grant's breath left him. His mind instantly rejected the first thought that sprang up.

Carswell continued, "We'll have to get dental records to ID them."

Collier glanced at his brother. "Let's go to the hospital." He nodded to the man behind the desk. "Thanks, Carswell."

Pushing his leg to the max, Grant rushed out of the station.

When Andre slid into the driver's seat, Collier barked at him, "Do some of your cop stuff and get me to the hospital pronto. I've got to talk to that guy before they put him out."

Without a word, Andre shoved the shift lever into drive and piloted his automobile to St. Joseph Hospital.

Phoenix, Arizona

Face down on the gurney, Wesley heard the wailing ambulance siren as though from far away. A rubber mask poured cool oxygen into his nostrils. An IV dripped the maximum dosage of morphine into his veins, but he couldn't tell it. Pain ebbed and flowed from excruciating to unbearable. He no longer feared that he'd die. Now he hungered for it.

But not yet. He only had one chance to make things right. He must live long enough to tell Collier about Erin.

The ambulance swayed, then stopped. The sirens faded, and the back doors popped open. As the gurney slid into the Emergency Room, someone shone a light into Wesley's eyes as the paramedics recited his statistics.

"Collier," he whispered through the mask.

"That's right, son," the doctor said. "We'll look after you."

Wesley shook his head, but the doctor wasn't paying attention. The gurney rattled down an endless white hall. Automatic doors whooshed open, then closed. He felt himself lifted, then set down again. A nurse wearing green touched his face and smiled. "You're going to be fine." she said.

No. He was going to die. First, he had to tell Collier. He would know what to do. Grinding his teeth, he groaned as he moved his burned arm up to pull the mask from his face. "Collier! I have to see Grant Collier!" he rasped.

"Later," the doctor said from behind him.

"Now!" he called out, pleading with all of his being.

"Sally," the doctor said, "ask the desk to call the ranch, will you?"

"Yes, Dr. Parker," she said and padded away as Wesley drifted into an agonized fog.

Sometime later, he opened his eyes to see a man's haggard face peering at him. "Wesley?" the man said, "I'm Grant Collier. Where is Cindy… Erin?"

The injured man tried to talk, then groaned under a massive spasm of pain.

Collier waited a moment, then said, "Please, try to tell me where she is."

Wesley gasped, then said, "The Russians have her."

Collier moved closer, his face inches from Wesley. "Where?"

"…ship from San Diego…to Russia."

Collier stepped back.

Another spasm, and Wesley's world went dark.

Outside the examining room, Collier bumped into Sally and asked her, "How's it look for him?"

She shook her head. "Not good. As soon as he's stable, we're airlifting him to the burn center in San Diego. He needs a miracle." She hurried back to her patient, and Grant headed toward the exit.

Andre met him in the hospital lobby. "Did he say anything important?" he asked.

"I'll tell you in a second," Collier said, pulling out his cellphone. "Mom? Hi... sorry, we didn't have time to explain. Still don't... Who called me? Okay, I'll call him later."

He shifted the phone to his other ear. "Now listen, Mom, I'm going to be out all night. I have to take care of something."

Hanging up the phone, Grant turned to his brother. "I need to find some wheels ASAP."

"Why?" Andre asked.

Grant headed for the double-glass doors. Speaking over his shoulder he said, "I'll explain on the way."

Outside the hospital, he called Nina and got voicemail. He left a short message. As he got into the car, he told Andre, "We're going to Glendale. Hurry."

Twenty minutes later, they pulled into the parking lot of Nina Elias's apartment and home office. Nina used to be the administrative assistant to the former CIA director, now retired. She had retired from the CIA at the same time and had gone into private contracting. Since she was from Phoenix, Grant had called on her to set Cindy up in her new identity.

One of their backup plans was Grant's having access to Nina's apartment codes in case she sent him an SOS. He punched in the keycode at the front door, and they were on the third floor in seconds. When the elevator dinged, and the doors slid open, Grant pulled his weapon. Andre did likewise.

"She's in 310," Grant said. "The hairs on the back of my arms just stood up. That's a sure sign something's up."

They soft-footed down the hall to 310. Grant touched the door. It swung inward. Training kicked in. Guns ready, Grant and Andre began checking rooms and calling, "Clear!"

Seconds later, Andre called out, "In here!"

Grant entered Nina's office. She sat at her desk, facing the door, her hands still on her keyboard, and a single bullet hole in the center of her forehead. On her computer screen was Cindy's address and phone number.

Langley, Virginia

Joel Mullinax stood when bulldog Ferretti and tall, lean Jefferson entered the spacious office at CIA headquarters. Mullinax motioned for them to sit on the west side of the room. Burgundy leather chairs surrounding a small conference table containing a speakerphone shaped like a UFO, along with some folders.

"Thanks for coming so quickly," the CIA director said after they were seated.

"What happened to the need for secrecy?" General Ferretti asked, his fleshy face anxious. "I thought you didn't want to be seen together."

"We're left with few options, gentleman," Mullinax said. "Secrecy has fallen from the list. National security has been jeopardized like never before in our history."

"What's up?" Jefferson asked. As usual, he remained cool and in control. His head resembled a brown bowling ball with a face carved on the front of it.

"The morning prison guards found Harrison Lestrade's body in his cell. Three of the night shift guards are missing as well as the security videotape." He lifted a folder from the table. "Our pathology people sent me this an hour ago. Lestrade's blood was loaded with truth serum." Mullinax leaned forward, a strange gleam in his dark eyes. "Some foreign power infiltrated the prison and interrogated Lestrade."

"How?" Jefferson asked.

"A man posing as Lestrade's lawyer showed up at the prison with a forged federal court order allowing him to visit his client."

"And those idiots let him in?" Jefferson demanded, his black eyes flashing.

"The papers were in order. No one questioned them until Lestrade's body was found this morning. The judge's name and signature were bogus. So was the attorney."

"Who did it?" Ferretti asked. "The Israelis?"

"Our best guess is the Russians," Mullinax said. "A background check showed that one of the guards has a brother-in-law who works for a Russian shipping company.

Jefferson spoke. "What did they milk from him? They killed him, didn't they? They wouldn't have done that if he'd held out."

Mullinax relaxed enough to tap his index finger on the polished mahogany table. "When Mrs. Lestrade found out about her husband's death, she started talking." Excitement made his voice waver. "She said that Cindy Lestrade is the encryption key."

"I thought she was clean," Jefferson said.

Mullinax ran his fingertips along the edge of the blue file folder lying on the table. "According to Mrs. Lestrade, her husband left instructions that if anything happened to him she was to say, 'Cindy is the key.' That's all."

Ferretti said, "Where's the girl?"

"Grant Collier used his own resources to hide her. He left no records. She could be anywhere in the world."

Jowls quivering, Ferretti glared at the director. "This is incredible."

Jefferson asked, "Where is Collier?"

"We're trying to locate him," Mullinax said. "We phoned his home. His mother says he's out, and she's not sure where he is." He adjusted a gold hand on his watch. "Give us ninety minutes, and we'll have him. I'm sure he'll cooperate."

Mullinax's cellphone beeped. He snatched it up. "Mullinax here... Put him on." He cupped his hand over the receiver. "It's Collier."

Central Arizona

The limousine sped south until it reached an entrance ramp for Interstate 17. From there, they glided south toward Phoenix, then took a smaller road into the desert. Too shocked even for tears, Cindy stared glassy-eyed out the tinted windows. Absently, her thumb followed the upholstery stitching beside her leg.

She drew in a shaky breath and sent out a silent call. *Grant, please come and find me. You're the only one who can help me now.*

When the limo paused for its final turn, Cindy shifted on the seat to look forward. The car parked beside a flat stretch of ground with an old airplane hangar on one end, one corner of its roof sagging almost to the ground.

The limousine bumped over a rutted gravel road and parked near the hangar. Three minutes later, a gleaming black helicopter hovered for a moment, then gently sat down, blasting dirt and small stones over their vehicle.

Popov grabbed Cindy's left hand and slapped on a handcuff. He did the same to the right one. Once again, pain brought her to full alertness. She let him lead her out of the car and, ducking low, toward the roaring cyclone caused by the helicopter.

Her senses crying for action, Cindy waited for the moment when Popov's massive hand relaxed to shift its position. Timing it to the second, she jerked back and pounded her heel into the back of his knee.

Spinning left, she raced toward a rocky outcropping like a wide receiver sprinting down the sideline.

Her head filled with a rushing sound that did not come from the helicopter. She wanted to scream, to beg someone to help her, but she didn't have breath for screaming. Every ounce of oxygen must power her pumping legs. Always a strong runner, this mad dash was a personal record for her.

Thirty feet from the end zone, one of Popov's friends came around for a shoestring tackle.

She felt clawing hands on a back loop of her jeans, felt a tug, then sailed forward. She hit the ground with an *oof* that knocked the wind from her aching lungs and tore flesh from her cheek. Rolling over, she tried to scratch him, to kick her way to freedom, but other arms grabbed her handcuffs by the center link and jerked her upward.

Mouth wide to suck in air, sobbing and shrieking by turns, she writhed and flailed as the burly Russians dragged her toward the whipping black beast that waited to swallow her up.

Seconds later, she landed on a hard flight chair, and they strapped her in. Popov and his men sat one on each side of her and one behind her. The whir of the chopper blades grew still louder as the ancient landing field grew small below them.

Her head rolled back. Moaning from pain and raw fear, Cindy knew she'd never see the United States again. Her last hope had just been ground into the dirt.

Chapter Twenty

Langley, Virginia

Mullinax spoke to the speakerphone on the table, "Go ahead, Grant."

Deep and strong, Collier's voice came into the room. "This morning a deputy sheriff who was last seen with Cindy Lestrade was badly burned from an explosion that smells like arson. He told me that the Russians have Cindy. They're taking her to San Diego and a ship to the motherland."

Mullinax's face became mottled red and white. His fist thumped the table. He swore.

"What gives, Director?" Collier asked. "Why are the Russians interested in Cindy? How did they know where she is?"

Ignoring Ferretti's disapproving expression, Mullinax told Collier of the malfunctioning missiles and Harrison Lestrade's death. "Mrs. Lestrade now says that Cindy is the key."

"That's impossible," Collier declared.

"How can you be so sure?" Jefferson asked suddenly.

"Who's that?" Collier asked.

"Gary Jefferson, NSA," Jefferson said. "How do you know the girl's clean?"

"She trusted me. She told me everything."

Mullinax grunted. "C'mon, Collier. Do you honestly believe that Harrison Lestrade would put his daughter in danger for no reason?"

After a pause, Collier said, "It looks like she made a fool of me."

Mullinax leaned toward the phone. "I'm counting on you, Collier. You pull off one last assignment for me, and I'll triple your pension."

"Just name it, Director," Collier said without hesitating.

"Go to TACTRAGRUPAC in San Diego. I'll meet you there and brief you."

"Yes, sir," Collier said.

Scowling, the CIA director hung up the phone.

"Did you have to spill your guts to him?" Ferretti demanded. He had his head pulled down between his shoulders. "What are you doing, Joel?"

Mullinax glared at him. "Extreme circumstances call for extreme action. Before his injury, Collier headed up a special unit that answered only to me. He's familiar with the Lestrade case, and I want him in this."

His tone became more congenial. "I need your help, Tony. Dispatch a couple of SEAL teams to San Diego. Once we figure out where the ship is, we've got to move. That girl must be secured at all costs."

Ferretti nodded. "You've got it."

Mullinax stood and reached for his briefcase. "Thank you for coming, gentlemen. If you'll excuse me, I've got to find a plane."

At the Nogales crossing of the Mexican border, Ruben Abrams drummed the steering wheel of his rental car. He looked at his fingers. They could make a violin sing. His parents had swelled with pride when he told them he wanted to be a concert violinist. He'd never told them that he made that decision because such an occupation allowed him to travel freely and without question.

They wouldn't be so proud of his new career if they knew how many times his index finger had pulled a trigger and silenced a life. Who would suspect that a man of the fine arts was also an assassin?

"Citizenship?" the gray-haired customs officer asked.

Ruben said, "American."

"Do you have anything to declare?"

"No."

"Please drive through."

He pressed on the accelerator and soon merged onto Interstate 19 headed north toward Phoenix. His mission was simple. Find the girl and get her out of the country. The car already had a false bottom in the trunk for that purpose.

However, the further north he drove, the more his nagging doubts surfaced. Capturing Cindy Lestrade could mean killing Grant Collier, the man who had saved his life in Lebanon last year. Could he do it? When he had received his assignment, he told himself there was no problem. Now that he was here, he wasn't so sure.

Anthem, Arizona

Andre drove Grant to a small local airport where he could catch a ride to San Diego. On the way, Collier said, "Did you tell anyone about Cindy Lestrade after I told you?"

"Are you kidding?" Andre sounded offended. "Of course not!"

"Well, the Russians have her, and the only one I told was you." Grant took a breath, thinking hard. "We were out in the field, away from everything. How could anyone else have overheard?"

"What about the ATV?" Andre said. "If we were away from buildings, that would be the only thing nearby."

"Did someone put a bug on the ATV? I don't see how that's possible. You've had it, what? A couple of days?"

Andre grew quiet. "We've got a problem on our hands, Grant," he said. "First FBI crawling all over the ranch, and now a Russian spy?"

"Maybe they are one and the same," Grant said. "Remember Occam's Razor?"

"The simplest solution is probably the right one… or something like that."

Grant said, "Work on that, will you? If we have an enemy inside the gate, we need to know about it. This is a loose end, and we need to get it tied up."

Twenty minutes later, Grant went into the airport hangar and asked for a ride. Before long, he boarded a Cessna with an executive headed to a weekend hideaway on the coast.

Grant arrived at the Tactical Training Group Pacific on Point Loma before Mullinax. Left to wait in an uncomfortable waiting room, he wanted to pace in the worst way. He had to be content with stretching his legs and leaning back to ease his side.

When Mullinax had told him that Cindy was the key, he felt like he'd been trampled by a bull. Now that he'd had time to think it over, Harrison Lestrade's plan made perfect sense. The scientist had wanted to be caught. All he had to do was wait in the safety of a prison lockup until his program brought the U.S. to its knees. A jail was the safest place in the world for him. At least, he had thought so.

Cindy is the key. Had she played Collier for a fool? Maybe she had gone into hiding because she was waiting for her father to rise from the ashes and restore what they'd lost. As reasonable as that sounded, he just couldn't accept it. Her anger at her father was very real. He had seen the way she arched her back and curled her hands into fists. No. She wasn't faking.

The office door opened. Collier came to his feet as Director Joel Mullinax entered. Striding to the metal desk by the only window in the room, the older man scarcely glanced at Collier.

Dropping his briefcase to the desktop, he turned to him and said, "Satellite logs show a helicopter leaving the roof of the Russian Consulate and landing at an old airstrip northeast of Phoenix. It was tracked from there to San Diego where they took the Lestrade woman to a freighter that's now headed out to sea."

Moving behind the desk as he unbuttoned his suit coat, he dropped into the straight-backed chair. "We've obtained permission to initiate a SEAL operation. They will attack tonight, coming at the boat at low altitude from behind."

"Why do you need me?" Collier asked. "I can't swim or run."

"I need your knowledge of the girl. We've got to decide whether to bring her back alive or just kill her there." He dug inside his coat for a cigar. "The latter would be more practical," he added.

Grant steeled himself. He must not show any emotional reaction. "What about the code?" he asked. "We can't get it if she's taken out."

"Neither could anyone else," Mullinax said. He unwrapped the cigar and reached into another pocket for his cutter.

"They have had her for six hours," Collier continued. "Who's to say they haven't drugged her and already gotten the answer?"

"In that case, she's already dead." Mullinax's voice was flat. He flicked open a brass-plated lighter and held a flame to his cigar.

Collier's stomach did somersaults. How could he think when his emotions were on the rampage? Drawing in a slow, quiet breath, he let it out and drew on his intensive training for stress management. Finally, he said, "I doubt they'd kill her. They'd want to make absolutely sure that her answer actually works. If she's given them the code, we need her alive so we can get it, too. If they've been unsuccessful, then we need her alive to get it for ourselves."

Grant paused as a thought occurred to him. "You know, there's another possibility."

"What's that?"

"There might be something rattling around in her head that only she and her father knew. She may not realize she has the answer."

Leaning forward, smoke billowing above him, Mullinax grunted. "That doesn't sound likely to me."

"What are your plans for her once she's ours?" Collier asked carefully.

"That's where you come in. You gained her confidence once; you can do it again. Get her to tell you what she knows."

"She's still got me on her list of world-class liars and villains. I don't think I've much chance of snowing her again." He shifted in his chair.

Mullinax's flinty eyes narrowed. "What do you suggest as an alternative?"

Collier grinned. "I know this may sound farfetched at first, but hear me out before you make a decision. It might just work." He relayed a harebrained scheme with the exacting finesse of a politician speaking at a ten-thousand-dollar-a-plate dinner.

When he finished, Mullinax allowed himself a small smile. He said, "I knew you were the man for this operation."

Collier added, "Once we get the encryption problem solved, it would be best if Ms. Lestrade went six feet under for good this time. We can't have anyone else getting to her, can we?"

"Take care of the details, Collier. I've got to brief the SEAL commander." He scraped back his chair and trudged out, still puffing away.

Grant's phone buzzed. Andre. "What is it, bro?" he said.

"I found the bug we were talking about. It was under the front fender of the ATV. It's one of ours, by the way."

"What? You think an FBI agent put it there?"

Andre smirked. "Remember when Sally came down the steps just before we went on our ride?"

Grant grinned. "Yeah, you about blew a gasket."

"She touched the front fender. I was too busy looking at her, uh-hum, assets to notice what she did. Who else could it be?"

"Sally, a spy? I don't think that's possible."

"Well, you've got history with her, so that's understandable. I checked around and she bugged Mom's entire house. It has to be her. She's the only outsider we've had in here. The FBI agents stayed outside."

"Put that information in your pocket," Grant said. "You can have the privilege of picking her up when the time comes."

Andre said, "With pleasure."

Grant's tone changed. "On another subject, I'm glad you called. This is gonna sound crazy, but I need a big favor."

Cave Creek, Arizona

Ruben Abrams of the Mossad stayed four cars back from the Suburban he was tailing. Last night, Israeli intelligence had heard from a wire trap that Collier wanted his brother to bring him a vehicle. Immediately, Ruben had staked out Andre Collier's home.

His hunch had paid off this morning when Special Agent Perkins had showed up, and the two men left together. Abrams followed them. Andre had promised he'd get a car to his brother. Eventually, he'd come through. The men headed straight to Cave Creek. When their vehicle turned, Abrams realized that they were going to Collier's ranch and drove on by. In ten minutes, he'd double back and pick up their trail when they came out.

Abrams turned around and parked half a mile from Collier's driveway. He slouched down in the seat and opened the glove compartment. Reaching inside, he flipped open a false bottom and pulled out his Glock 17, remembering that Grant Collier had introduced him to the Glock 17 years ago. He still loved it.

He caressed the weapon and bit down his lower lip. Why had the Mossad given him this mission? They knew about his friendship with Collier. Could he really aim this Glock at his friend who had saved his life?

He leaned his head back against the seat and closed his eyes for an instant. Damn Collier. Damn the Mossad. Why did they put him in this position?

Crunching wheels on the gravel driveway brought Abrams up. A beat-up red Bronco pulled out followed by the Suburban. Both vehicles were covered in thick dust, but the Bronco also had a caved in front fender and a wide scrape down the side.

The vehicles turned toward him. Ducking below the dash, he waited for them to pass. Two minutes later, Ruben did a U-turn and followed. They headed north on the interstate to the other side of the mountain. A road sign said they had reached 4,000 feet elevation.

Near Dewey, the lead vehicles suddenly turned west onto a narrow dirt road. He followed. A mile later, he shook his head. What were they up to? A good agent would have detected him long ago, if by nothing else but the dust he was raising.

At the end of the road, they continued straight into the Groom Creek pine forest, an area with such a steep downgrade that driving would soon be impossible for his rental car. He should have asked for a four-wheel-drive SUV.

Abrams didn't follow. Wherever they were going, they'd have to come out the same way. He'd wait for them to leave, then continue following them.

He pulled off the road behind a wide stand of brush and relaxed. His eyes had sharp needles behind them. He wanted to sleep in the worst way. Sheer force of will kept him awake.

Ten minutes later, Abrams sat up at the sound of a car's engine. The Suburban cruised past with both men in it. Where was the Bronco?

Abrams hit the ignition and followed their tire tracks, his body jarring as the vehicle lurched over rough terrain. Watching carefully ahead, he hoped they hadn't left the vehicle too far inside. If he couldn't find it easily, he'd wait out at the main highway. There was only one way out of this place, and Collier would have to use it.

There it was. The Bronco was parked next to a flat patch of ground in a clearing. Ruben did a three-point turn and headed back toward the main road. This was the break he'd been waiting for.

The Pacific Ocean

Seated in a Seahawk helicopter skimming the Pacific waters northwest of San Diego, Commander Percy Schell took stock of eight men in black fatigues seated in front of him. This team—Group A—

and Group B in the Seahawk behind them were the best the Navy had to offer—combat-seasoned men who knew their business.

Their mission was simple. Get aboard the ship and recover the woman alive.

When Schell had learned that the CIA had final command of this operation, he had bristled until he learned that the man was Grant Collier, a former colleague and a friend. Collier was top drawer, a man Schell respected, a man now seated behind the copilot of the helicopter.

Once his men landed on the ship, Schell was in charge. Collier would stay in the chopper and transport the woman out the moment they had her.

The helicopter sharply dropped altitude, causing Schell's stomach to turn a flip. The men ahead of him must have felt it, too, but not one of them flinched or even shifted in his seat.

In total darkness, Schell couldn't see the ocean, but he knew they were almost touching the waves to approach the ship below deck level. At the last moment, they'd rise over the stern and drop the men to the deck.

These pilots could fly through a mountain range in a blizzard blindfolded, or so it seemed to Schell.

His earpiece crackled. "Five minutes," the pilot said. In one movement, his men looked back at him. He nodded. Eight weapons were drawn, checked, and replaced.

A dozen sparkling white lights outlined the ship dead ahead. The helicopter slowed, then rose over the rear deck and hovered. Schell slid open the door, and his men rappelled into the darkness below.

When Schell dropped to the steel deck, he yanked the rope, signaling the chopper to back off. On the other rear corner, the second Seahawk dropped its load. The entire sequence took less than ninety seconds before the helicopters vanished into a starry night of salty winds and pervasive dampness.

Group B led by Commander Ray Wilson moved along the port side of the ship through a wide aisle between metal freight containers the size of railroad cars while Group A moved along the starboard side. Crouched behind a vent, Schell listened to deep silence. Fifty more containers blocked the bridge from view.

Except for loading and unloading, the crew had little to do on deck. This time of night they were probably below, playing cards or snoozing. He hoped they'd all tied one on and were sleeping it off.

Keeping low, Schell quickstepped toward the nearest door. Flattening himself against the steel bulkhead, he waited for his men to line up beside him.

On the other side of the ship, Wilson and his men were making their way toward the bridge.

Five minutes passed. A small eternity. Finally, his earpiece came to life. "She's on the second floor," Wilson said abruptly. "At the top of the stairs, make a right, third door down on the left."

Schell held up his hand, palm left. He unlatched the steel door beside him and slipped into the heart of the ship.

The interior felt warm and smelled dank. The dull green galley way had bare twenty-five-watt bulbs at long intervals ahead of them. Surprisingly quiet for men their size, Group A moved along the corridor to stairs that resembled a steel ladder with handles on each side.

Beretta upright at ear level, Schell eased his head around the corner then jerked back. After a second look, he motioned for his men to follow. At the top of the stairs, Schell almost bumped noses with a sailor dressed in a bathrobe. Moving instinctively, he slammed the man's jaw with his iron fist, knocking him unconscious. The last man in line would apply duct tape to the sailor's mouth, wrist, and ankles.

Two men peeled out of line to guard the stairway, two more to guard the entrance door. Heading down the next galley way, Schell hoped no one else was wandering around. He'd have to kill anyone who tried to sound an alarm.

Huddled on a creaking metal cot with a thin piece of bare foam for a mattress, Cindy stared at her guard, a blunt-featured giant wearing jeans and a black fisherman-knit sweater. She was desperate for sleep, but she couldn't relax with a thug in her room staring at her.

Sometime between midnight and dawn, a key rattled in the metal lock. The guard jumped to his feet as Popov strolled in.

Cindy's grim-faced captor didn't waste words. "Moscow sent a message," he said. "You must tell us what the key is now."

Cindy shrank back, her heart skipping in her throat. "A key to what? I don't have a key. I never had a key."

Popov's thunderous expression relaxed a fraction. He sat beside her and spoke softer. "Cindy Lestrade, I don't want to hurt you, but Moscow must be obeyed. If you refuse to tell me, I must force you. Please, make it easy on yourself."

"What are you going to do… torture me?"

He shook his big square head. "Torture takes too long." He slipped a filled hypodermic syringe from his coat pocket and repeated, "What is the key?"

"You mean where is the key, don't you?" she gasped.

"Don't play games," he said. Sharp, slim, gleaming metal came toward her. "What is the key to your father's missile encryption?"

"I don't know!" she cried, pressing her back harder against the metal wall. "He never told me."

His mouth hardened. "You leave me no choice." He glanced at the guard. "Danov."

Working with practiced skill, the guard shoved her backward on the groaning cot, held down her legs with one massive knee, and gripped her elbows. In less than three seconds, she lay helpless.

Screaming, she threw her head from side to side. Popov slapped her hard, back and forth, until she had no strength left to fight. A primal moan came from deep in her throat. Tears coursed toward her ears.

Suddenly, the door banged open, followed by spitting noises and an acrid smell. The guard collapsed across Cindy's knees. Popov fell on her chest. She felt faint. Maybe she was hallucinating.

Weight crushed the breath from her. Suddenly, it vanished, and she looked up into a blackened face with a black knit cap on top.

"Commander Schell, US Navy SEALs, ma'am," he said. "We've come to take you home."

Cindy couldn't speak. She moaned and trembled, her mouth hanging loose and open.

"We've got control of the ship," Schell said, kneeling beside her. "You're safe now."

He put his solid arm around her shoulders and helped her to stand. Moving his forearm under her armpit, he called for another SEAL to support her on the other side. Sixty seconds after they'd entered the room, the men half carried her through the ship, her feet stumbling along. She scarcely knew what was happening. She felt sick to her stomach and thought she'd vomit.

Cold ocean air blasted her face and chased the shocked numbness from her brain. When her legs began to function again, one of her escorts turned toward the other side of the ship. Commander Schell led her through a maze of containers with a massive crane in the center.

When they reached the aft of the ship, a helicopter hovered over the deck. A cable with a chair attached to it tumbled down. Schell snagged it and held it steady. "Get in, please," he said, pushing her into the seat.

The moment he belted her in, the helicopter lifted up and away while a winch hoisted her closer to the aircraft. Swirling through the darkness, Cindy knew she must be dreaming. Any moment she'd wake up in the freighter with a Russian goon staring at her.

Hands pulled the chair into the chopper. The door slid closed, and a flashlight clicked on. Grant Collier grinned at her as though she were a long-lost friend.

Numb, she stared at him while he unsnapped her safety harness. The next thing she knew she was in his arms, held tight to his chest. "You're okay now, Cindy," he told her. "Safe."

Heavy sobs caught her breath. Clinging to him with all her remaining strength, she bawled long and loud.

After a long while, he loosened his hold on her and wiped her cheeks with his fingers. "Did they hurt you?" he whispered. "Are you okay?"

She tried twice before she could gasp out, "You came just in time."

He helped her to a seat and buckled her in. "Sit here a few minutes and catch your breath. I've got something to do."

With burning eyes, she watched Grant make his way up the aisle to the front of the chopper. In one lithe motion, he pulled out his handgun and pointed it at the pilot's head.

Chapter
Twenty-One

San Diego, California

At TACTRAGRUPAC headquarters in the bustling communication center, Mullinax sat at a long table and sipped coffee from a disposable coffee cup while he listened to a radio report from Commander Schell. The commander's voice blocked out the beeps and clicks of a dozen machines jammed together with four men monitoring every blip and squeak.

The commander's message was succinct: Cindy Lestrade was in the chopper with Collier.

Suddenly exhausted, Joel Mullinax heaved a deep sigh. The fight was half over. They still had to secure the code, but at least the target was secured from America's enemies. Leaning back in his chair, Mullinax rubbed the back of his neck at the hairline.

To confide in someone would be such a relief. But he couldn't. He had an objective. Sticky points of law and high-sounding talk about ethics couldn't interfere with it. Even Ferretti and Jefferson couldn't know what he had in his mind. This was a solo flight—winner take all.

His gaze settled on the green tactical screen as he noted the various positions of the key players. One helicopter was near the ship retrieving SEAL operatives. The other moved toward Mexico. Unwilling to admit what they had done, the Russian freighter would continue on course as though nothing had happened.

Two hours before dawn, Mullinax left the communications room and found an office with a comfortable couch. He was tired. Someone would wake him when the chopper touched down. Pulling off his shoes, he stretched out and closed his eyes.

It seemed like seconds later his phone chimed. "What?" he mumbled, irritated.

A male voice said, "Sir, we've got a missing chopper."

Mullinax came upright in one motion and felt a wave of dizziness. He groped for his shoes and jammed his feet into them.

When he reached the communication center, the captain in charge pointed to the glowing green screen. "It dropped from radar coverage fifty miles offshore, and the transponder shut off."

"Is that all?" Mullinax asked, disgusted.

"Sir?" The captain's beady eyes narrowed.

"You woke me for this?" Mullinax demanded.

The small man stiffened. "Sir, it could have crashed. All attempts to contact the pilots have failed."

Mullinax yawned. "Everything is under control, Captain." He yawned again and turned away. "I'm going to catch some sleep. Don't wake me again unless something drastic happens."

At the door, Mullinax turned back. "Just to be clear. What you people saw today is classified. If it ever comes out in the media, all of you—no matter who was responsible will get a posting north. Way north."

The Pacific Ocean

Grant held his Glock steady, ignoring the shocked fear on Ken Judson's face. He and Grant were friends years ago in their first SEAL training. "Relax, guys," Grant said. "I'm not going to shoot you unless I have to. Do me a favor and don't be a hero, okay?"

"You can't shoot us," Judson said, his dark mustache twitching. "Who'd fly the chopper?"

"It's been about five years since I sat at the controls," Collier said, "but I think I could manage. Do as I say, and no one gets hurt." He handed the pilot a paper. "These are the coordinates of our destination. Get down low, shut off the transponder, and take us there."

The helicopter dropped to fifty feet above the ocean and skimmed toward the shoreline. An hour later, they increased height and set down in a clearing in the middle of a stand of pine trees.

Keeping one eye on the pilots, Collier motioned for Cindy to come forward. She unbuckled and was beside him in five seconds. He pulled a small flashlight from his pocket and handed it to her. "Go that way. You'll find a Bronco parked. Hide and wait for me there."

"What about coyotes and javelinas?" Cindy asked, her eyes round.

"You'll be fine," he told her, squeezing her lower arm. "The chopper's landing scared pretty much everything away." He smiled encouragingly. "Hurry. I'll be with you as soon as I can."

Wearing a doubtful expression, Cindy jumped from the chopper and headed into the darkness, her light bouncing along the ground as she moved.

The moment she got out of hearing range, Collier ordered the pilots out of the helicopter. Hands clasped behind their heads, each husky man stepped clear of the shopper. The wind had a biting chill. Whoever believed the desert was always hot had never been there at night.

Collier barked, "Face down on the ground." He searched them and removed their weapons. "Stay down," he said, "or you won't be eating cake on your next birthday."

Returning to the chopper, he fired two rounds into the radio and another two into the controls.

Before he left the area, he paused for one more word with the men face down on the ground. "We're about ten miles from civilization. There are bears and mountain lions in this country, so I'll leave your weapons at the edge of the clearing. When you walk out, follow our tracks and head west. East of here is nothing but broken mountains and complete wilderness."

Limping across the rutted field, he used his aluminum cane for balance. Cindy was waiting for him inside the Bronco. The moment she saw him, she got out, a stubborn tilt to her chin.

"Let's go," he said, catching his breath. "We don't have much time."

"What if I say no?" Cindy asked. She sounded like she wanted a fight.

He let out a frustrated gasp and spoke loudly. "I'm trying to help you, Cindy!"

Her words flew at him. "Since I woke up this morning, a 'friend' of mine handed me over to some Russians who almost shot me full of drugs. Then the U.S. Navy came in at the last minute and rescued me. Now someone who betrayed me pulls a gun on my rescuers and says he wants to help me." Her eyes stretched wide. "Do you see where I'm having a problem with this?"

He considered picking her up and throwing her into the Bronco, like it or not. Even as he thought it, he knew he couldn't do it. Instead, he said, "I'm telling you, we don't have much time." He stretched out his hand. "Look, if it'll make you feel better, keep this gun. On top of that, you can drive." He held the keys toward her. "What more can I do?" His tone softened. "Please, Cindy. A lot is at stake for both of us."

She shied away from the gun. "The way I see it, if I stick with the helicopter, the Navy will come, and I'll be safe for sure. If I go with you, who knows what could happen?"

Grant shook his head. "As soon as they left with you, the nightmare would start all over again. The Russians still want you, and they're not the only ones—so do the CIA, the Mossad, and the Chinese. I have a plan that gives you a chance." He sucked in a breath. "I'm trying to save your life, for crying out loud!" He pushed the Glock toward her. "Here, take the gun."

Cindy bit her lower lip. "Keep the gun. I'll drive."

Taking the keys, she handed him the flashlight, darted around the Bronco, and jerked open the door. Collier tossed the pilots' weapons to the ground, then limped to the passenger side. As he reached for the door handle, the Bronco spun gravel and peeled out.

What the…? He threw his cane to the ground. *Infuriating woman!*

Finally, he picked up the cane. He searched the ground with the flashlight until he found a fairly smooth area and hobbled toward it. He might as well sit down while he waited.

A few minutes later, when he'd had a chance to cool off, he almost laughed. Perkins had left the Bronco facing east into the wilderness. That's the direction she was headed.

Five minutes later, headlights appeared. Getting to his feet, he stood in the center of the road and held up his hands. She pulled up beside him, opening the window a crack. "How do I get out of here?" she demanded.

Collier formed his words carefully, each with its own force. "Why don't you let me show you?"

"No. You tell me."

What did he have to lose? She wouldn't let him inside the Bronco either way. All she had to do was drive straight ahead, and she'd find the highway.

He pointed west. "Drive until you get to a dirt road and keep going until you get to a paved road. Left takes you toward Prescott. Right takes you back to Black Canyon City." He reached for the door handle. "Will you let me in? My leg's killing me."

The next moment, Cindy showered him with gravel. Collier muttered a few choice words, then sat down again.

Time passed. He was getting worried. If she kept driving, she'd be captured within an hour or two. No matter who got to her, she'd die. He thumped his fist into his palm. Why hadn't he shot out the tires?

"Hey, Collier," Pilot Judson yelled across the field, "we're freezing. Are you going to shoot us if we wait inside the chopper until you get your mess straightened out?"

Grant shot a sour look in that direction. The men were in total darkness. A moment later, he second-guessed himself. Why shouldn't those guys wait in the chopper? There was no point in making them suffer unnecessarily. "Yeah, go ahead," he called.

Thirty seconds later, headlights shone through the darkness. The Bronco lurched to a halt beside him. She rolled down the window. "Get in, Collier."

He hobbled to the passenger side and pulled open the door. He was circling the door to climb in when glass exploded beside him.

Throwing himself inside, yelling, "Get down!"

Cindy lay across his lap. He grabbed the steering wheel, yanking it hard so the wheels were fully turned. A couple of dull thuds told him the door was taking punishment.

"Hit the gas!" he told Cindy.

The Bronco spun in a semicircle, and Grant straightened the wheel, keeping his head barely above the dash. The rear window exploded. A bullet whistled past his ear.

"Why are they shooting at us?" Cindy cried, hands over her ears.

"I don't know," Grant said. "Let's not hang around to find out." The Bronco bumped and swayed across the ground. Once they were out of range, Grant returned control of the Bronco to Cindy.

"I thought you took their guns," Cindy said, her breathing deep and long.

"When you took off, I let them go back into the chopper."

"Why'd you do that?"

"It's cold out there." His mouth twisted. "There must've been more weapons hidden in the helicopter."

She glanced at him. "And you're supposed to be the best?"

"I'm a little rusty, so shoot me." His joke fell flat. They rode in silence to the highway. Finally, he asked, "Why did you come back?"

Her eyes still on the road, Cindy said, "You told me the truth about how to get out of there. I figured that I'd better trust you just a little bit." She shot him a calculating look. "But just a little."

The road ahead suddenly went blurry. Grant squeezed his eyes shut and opened them again.

Cindy said, "I want to know why I'm not safe with the U.S. Navy."

The world was spinning. Grant's eyes drifted closed.

Cindy said, "You're pale to the lips." Her voice was a distant echo.

"Go to Phoenix," he mumbled, and all went comfortably dark.

Dewey, Arizona

After spending hours cramped on the front seat of a rental car with nothing for company but chirping crickets and an occasional coyote howl, Ruben saw the Bronco sail out of the wilderness and turn left with only the Lestrade woman inside. He hit his ignition. Maybe he could take the woman without having to shoot Collier. Things were looking up.

She went through the green light and turned around at the gas station. When the light turned green again, she went back the same way. About twenty minutes later, she reappeared with Collier, smashing Ruben's hope for an incident-free capture.

Not wanting a shootout with Collier in the dark, Abrams followed them. Best to bide his time. Somewhere ahead lay the opportunity he needed.

Slouched on the Bronco's seat with his head level with the back, Collier felt the Bronco lurch to a stop and pried his eyes open. "Where are we?" he asked, peering around.

Cindy said, "We're going through a fast-food drive-thru. I'm feeling faint, I'm so hungry. My last meal was breakfast yesterday. It's time for breakfast again."

She spoke into the microphone beside a wide, lighted sign, "Two orders of pancakes with eggs and sausage, a bagel with cream cheese, two blueberry muffins and two milks." She glanced at him. "Do you want anything?"

"Why would I want anything?" he asked, staring at her. "You're set to feed a Boy Scout troop."

She stared back. "I'm not going to eat all that now, dufus. I want to have some reserves in case we can't stop to eat for a while."

"Get me a sausage biscuit and some milk," he said, rubbing his stomach. "I need sleep more than food at the moment." He pulled out a wad of bills, counted some out, and handed them to her.

While they waited for their order, she said, "My last meal was a Danish and a coffee on the way to the trailer yesterday when I thought I was meeting the FBI. Last night, the Russians sent me some kind of greasy cabbage soup, but I couldn't force myself to taste it." She shivered. "As hungry as I am now, I still don't think I could have put down a spoonful of that stuff." She reached out the window for the large bag held by a smiling teenage girl with a thousand tiny braids down her back.

With the bag between them sending up a tempting aroma, she got back on the highway. "Get me something, will you?" she asked. "I can't wait until we stop."

He dug around and pulled out the bagel. She grabbed it and took a huge bite.

She swallowed and glanced at him. "You're awfully pale," she said. "Maybe we should go to the hospital."

"Can't. It's not safe."

"For who? Me or you?"

He turned his head toward her, his eyes seeking hers. "For you." For an instant, he had a glimpse of the scared girl inside the willful woman. She turned back to driving and eating.

"Don't worry about me," he went on. "I'm still not a hundred percent recovered, but I'll be okay. It's my side wound more than anything. If I get too tired, I pay. As long as I can rest, I'll be fine."

Looking ahead, Grant caught sight of a large sign. There's a hotel. Pull in."

"I don't see a hotel."

"It's family owned. Right there. I used to know these people years ago. Not anymore though. The Jamisons sold it."

Cindy turned into the covered front entrance of the hotel and put the Bronco in park. Collier started to get out, then stopped. "Will you be here when I get back?"

She paused to clear her mouth, then said, "If I wouldn't leave a wounded dog to suffer, I guess I'll stick around for you."

"Right. Thanks." She sure knew how to lay it on.

While she turned her full attention to the food, Collier pushed open the glass door and entered a dimly lit lobby decorated in deep greens and gold. The smell of old coffee lingered in the air.

Behind the high counter to the left, the wall held a rack full of pamphlets describing points of interest in Yavapai County. Collier limped to the desk and rested his elbows on it.

A sleepy-eyed college kid came from the back. "Yes, sir?" He had the slight accent of someone who was born in India.

"One room, one night. Two beds."

The clerk said, "I'm sorry. I've only one room left, but the bed is king size."

Grant looked out the glass door at Cindy sitting in the Bronco drinking milk from a carton. What would she think of this arrangement? He was tempted to look for another place. The burning in his hip ruled out that idea. He must rest.

"I'll take it," he said, reaching for his wallet.

The clerk passed him a registration card. Grant wrote *Mr. and Mrs. Tom Henna* in the top blank

"Cash or credit?" the clerk asked.

"I'm paying cash," Grant said, peeling out six twenties.

"That's fine, sir." He picked up the money. "Here's your key card. Check out time is eleven. Enjoy your stay."

Grant's limp was more pronounced as he returned to the Bronco. He got in and gently shut the door to keep the ragged glass in place.

Because the motel was full, Cindy had to park behind the main building, a good eighty feet from their entrance. As Grant limped across the parking lot, he looked the place over in the light of a new dawn. The hotel was oddly laid out in two buildings. The single-story front structure contained the lobby and the office, with a double story building behind it.

Fortunately, the elevator was close to the entrance. Down a short hallway—past a soda and snack machine where Cindy paused to buy two candy bars—they came to room 209. Grant inserted the key card, and a green light flashed.

He pushed open the heavy door to meet the pine scent of industrial cleaner and the sound of a humming heater. Dominating the room was a king-sized bed covered with a rust-and-green comforter exactly the shade of the rust carpet. On the far end of the room, double sided glass doors showed a tiny balcony.

Grant headed straight for those doors to pull the drapes closed.

"There's only one bed," Cindy said behind him.

"It's all they had," he answered over his shoulder, his hand on the drapery cord. "Believe me, the way I feel right now, I'm no threat."

Cradling the food bag in her arms, she looked him over. "Just the same, I'll sleep on the chair."

"Suit yourself. I'm too sick to argue." He sat on the edge of the bed, then gave a quick gasp as he tried to reach down and untie his hiking boots. Cindy dropped the sack on the bed and bent down to unlace them and pull them off.

"Need help with anything else?" she asked.

"No. I think I'll sleep in my clothes." He put his feet up and got comfortable. "Hand me that carton of milk, will you? That may ease my stomach a little."

She gave him the white-and-red container, then pulled an ottoman toward a soft corner chair with a high back. Lifting a carton from the bag, she tore open a silverware packet with her teeth. "You said something back there about having a plan. What is it?" she asked. She forked up some eggs and leaned down for a big bite.

"Later." He yawned and closed his eyes.

Abrams cursed when she pulled into the hotel without a blinker light, and he couldn't follow. He missed the turnaround and had to cross the bridge. By the time he found a way to get back, he'd wasted fifteen minutes. This was the most confusing and frustrating street he'd ever been on. When he reached the motel, he spotted the Bronco. But which room were they in? He decided the best thing to do was to park down the alley and settle in for a long, cold wait. Maybe an opportunity would present itself tomorrow.

Light peeked through the crack in the long drapes when Cindy stretched her cramped legs. Now she wished she'd taken half of that massive bed. She felt like a limp pretzel. With her head against the chair's back, she watched Grant's sleeping face and felt a familiar twinge.

Was he telling the truth this time? She hoped so.

Unable to stay still any longer, she stood and reached for the ceiling, urging her muscles to loosen up. She peeked out the side of the drapes, then pulled the curtain back farther.

The hotel sat on a hill with a sweeping seventy-five-mile vista. She had lived here for two years, and the silent panoramas of this area still took her breath away. Suddenly overwhelmed by an urge to breathe in some fresh air, she unlocked the sliding glass door and stepped outside. A cool breeze caressed her face. Cindy pulled in a full breath, closed her eyes, savoring. Looking across the hillsides, she understood why people came here and never left.

A deep voice behind her held a gentle tone. "Is this a private party?"

She turned and her lips curved upward.

He peered at her. "Is that a smile?"

Inwardly, she took a step backward. "Don't take it personally," she said. "Something else put me in a good mood."

He looked around. "Who?"

"You wouldn't understand."

"Maybe I would," he said quietly. He stood away from the door. "How about coming inside? We need to talk."

Cindy followed him and sat in her chair, not sure what was coming next. He sat on the ottoman facing her. Watching him, she said, "The last time you sat across from me like that, I slapped you."

He nodded. "I deserved it."

She couldn't believe he said that. "At least you admit it," she said.

Grant shifted on the ottoman. "Getting back to who were talking about... I've met Wesley."

Cindy wondered if he lost his mind. "You think Wesley put me in a good mood?"

Collier stayed serious. "I know how much you mean to him, Cindy. Didn't he get burned trying to save you?" He spread his hands. "He called me to the hospital and asked me to tell you he was sorry."

Cindy made a choking noise and sat bolt upright. "Wesley's alive?"

"He's badly burned, Cindy. The doctors didn't hold much hope for him. I've gotta give the guy credit, though. He made sure he told me where you were. That's all he cared about. He's really in love with you."

Cindy shook her head. "Not by a country mile."

"What?"

"When the Russians first grabbed me, I escaped and called Wesley for help. He hid me in a motel until his aunt could find out who was after me." She paused. "That's where I was last week." She started to shake. Her next words waivered. "Wesley and his aunt sold me to the Russians for a million dollars. That's how I got on that ship."

Collier's forehead tensed. So did his fist. "Wesley sold you to the Russians?"

She sent him an icy look. "Don't get too self-righteous. Your hands aren't clean either."

Grant looked down and consciously relaxed his fingers. "I want to make it up to you. I want to help you."

She relaxed against the chair's soft back. "What's your plan?"

Grant reached for her hands. She started to pull away, but something in his eyes made her stop. "For starters, Cindy, I have some bad news. Your father died two days ago."

At first, she thought she'd heard him wrong. Her dad was dead? It couldn't be. She gasped and started to shiver, suddenly feeling bitterly cold. She hated her father. She should be glad. Why were tears flooding her eyes?

Chapter Twenty-Two

Meyer, Arizona

Cindy stiffened and rubbed the tears from her cheeks. Her stare grew so intense that Grant forgot to breathe. "How do I know you're telling me the truth?"

He felt like she'd delivered a roundhouse punch to his midsection. He gulped. "Cindy, I wouldn't lie about something like that."

An edge came into her voice. "You could think that Dad's death would scare me into obeying you." She shook her head. "You've got to prove it."

Grant stood up and rubbed the back of his neck. The CIA negotiations manual didn't have a chapter for this one. What if the agency had killed the story of Lestrade's murder? She'd never believe him.

He grabbed the TVs remote control from the nightstand, pressed a couple of buttons, and found a news channel. He tossed the black bit of

     Lana McAra

plastic to Cindy. "Here. Sooner or later it'll show up on the news. I'm going to bring in our luggage."

"Luggage?" she cried. "You brought luggage, and I slept in my jeans last night?"

He felt more like a heel every minute. "I was hurting so bad when we arrived, " he told her, "I forgot about the suitcase. I was pretty woozy, remember?" He headed for the door, speaking over his shoulder. "I got some stuff from your apartment."

Grant crossed the parking lot at a good clip. The day was sunny and crisp. The way he liked it. His legs were cooperating nicely. He hardly limped.

He stopped short. What an idiot. He'd forgotten his cane. Another mistake like that, and they could be dead meat.

He shook his head at the sorry state of the Bronco. Windows shot out, bullet holes in the side. He'd have to replace it right away. Driving this thing around would be like wearing a placard saying, "Look at us. We're up to no good." If he hadn't been so out of it last night, he would have ditched it then.

He unlocked the rear door to haul out a single suitcase and Cindy's handbag. Back at the room, he dropped the bag on the table near the balcony windows and tossed the mangled purse to Cindy. She perched on the end of the bed, her attention on the TV screen. She hadn't looked up when he came in.

"Anything yet?" he asked.

"Just sports," she mumbled. Rubbing her fingers over the handbag, she looked up at him, grudging gratitude in her eyes. "Thank you for this."

He gave her an ironic smile. "Nice to know I have one redeeming quality." He tucked his key card back into his pocket. "I'm going down to the breakfast bar to get some coffee. Do you want anything?"

"Two of each, "she said. "Whatever they have."

He returned fifteen minutes later with four plastic-wrapped Danish pastries and two large coffees. Pausing long enough to swallow his share of the food, he unzipped the suitcase and said, "I'll take a shower while you finish watching the news."

Absently nibbling her second pastry, her eyes on the TV, she didn't answer him.

He hung his fresh clothes on the bathroom hook when a light rap sounded on the door. He froze. Another knock, louder.

Rushing into the room, he saw Cindy staring at the door like it had a grizzly behind it.

"Lie down on the floor beside the bed!" he staged-whispered.

When he removed the Glock from his jacket hanging over the back of a chair, she dropped the Danish to the bed and threw herself to the carpet, her hands covering her head.

Grant tiptoed to the door and peeped out the hole. A woman on the other side put knuckles to wood again. He couldn't see to the left or right of her. It could be a trap.

Unlatching the safety, he put tension on the trigger. Opening the door with his right hand, he hid the weapon behind his left leg.

A haggard blond, the woman spoke with a European accent. "Mr. Henna?"

Collier's eyes started left and right. She was alone. "Yes?" he asked.

She held out a ten-dollar bill. "I am the manager. Our night clerk overcharged you. Please, take this refund with my apologies."

"Uh, thanks."

She smiled. "I hope you enjoy the rest of your stay."

Grant shut the door and put the safety back on the weapon. He leaned against the door and let out a long, slow breath.

Cindy appeared beside him. "Who was it?" He could see gold flex in her green eyes.

"It was the manager. She gave me a ten-dollar refund on the room."

"Wow. Such honesty is refreshing," she said, a bite to her words. "You should take lessons."

He turned to the door on the right. "I'm hitting the shower," he said.

Bored, Cindy stretched out on the bed to watch the news. Tears sprang up again. What if Grant had told her the truth? Bitterness against her father had consumed her for so long, she was surprised at the pain his death would cause her. If he really was gone, he'd never have another chance to show her that, yes, he really had loved her after all.

The next moment, her father's face filled the TV screen. The announcer confirmed Grant's words. Harrison Lestrade had died in prison after a short illness.

Cindy jumped from the bed and ran to the bathroom door. Banging hard, she yelled, "Come quick! Now!" She sprinted back to the TV. Seconds later, Grant dashed out the bathroom, dripping water, a white towel draped around his midsection. His eyes darted about the room, shoulders tense, hands up.

"What's wrong?" he demanded.

"I'm on the news!"

Swiping his dripping hair straight back, he focused on her picture. Cindy turned up the sound.

"Further into our story on the death of Harrison Lestrade… Phoenix police are asking for help in locating this woman. She's using the name Erin Davis, but archive photos identify her as Cindy Lestrade, daughter of Harrison Lestrade. She is wanted for questioning in regard to the critical wounding of a police officer and the death of two unidentified people."

Grant groaned when his picture appeared next. "Law enforcement also advises that Ms. Lestrade may be in the company of Grant Collier, the local hero who broke a terrorist plot in New York last month. Mr. Collier is a person of interest in the case."

Grant's shoulders slumped. He tilted his face toward the tiled ceiling. "This is a disaster!"

"Should I turn myself in?" Cindy asked.

"Don't even think it!"

"Why not? They only want to ask us some questions."

"That's what they say, but it's not true. Your life is in danger, Cindy. You can't trust the police or the CIA or anyone else but me."

A firm knock at the door made them jump.

Grant ducked into the bathroom.

Another knock followed, more insistent.

Thirty seconds later, Grant came out wearing jeans and a black pullover, the back of the shirt still halfway up his back. "Lie down beside the bed again, "he said.

Cindy rolled to the carpet and heard his gun click. Squeezing herself against the wooden base on the bed, she was tempted to look out and see what was happening.

"Andre!" Grant exclaimed.

"Hi. Can I come in?"

"No."

"What?"

"I'm busy," Collier said.

Andre's voice hardened. "Can the cute answers, Grant. I know Cindy Lestrade is in there. We have orders to take her into custody."

"Show me a warrant."

"Probable cause. Get out of the way!"

After a pause, Grant said, "Okay, you can come in, Andre, but not him."

The door closed and footsteps drew closer. 'By the way, Sally Kramer is sitting in lockup, waiting for her attorney. It was her all right. We've got her fingerprints."

Grant said, "Unbelievable the reach those guys have."

"Evidently, she had a Russian boyfriend who got her to flip."

Cindy held her breath as though that could make her invisible.

"Go ahead and get up, Cindy," Grant said.

What was Grant up to now? She slowly got to her feet. Andre's blue uniform made him look massive. Despite their vast differences, she noticed some similarities between the Collier men. Both had a grim expression and body language as tense as a rock.

Andre stepped forward, "Ms. Lestrade, I need to take you in for questioning regarding the explosion near Black Canyon City yesterday."

"You can't take her, Andre," Grant insisted, reaching for his brother's arm. "She won't be safe."

Andre turned back, his eyebrows slanted. "Not safe in police custody?"

"She was in police custody with Wesley, remember? Just before that explosion. She barely escaped." He couldn't tell him the whole story. There wasn't time.

"I have orders to take her in," Andre said. He sounded as stubborn as Grant. "You're lucky it's me who got the call, or you'd both be on the floor with your hands cuffed."

Grant pursed his lips. "Any other cop would be on the floor wounded." He spoke quickly. "This is a national security issue, bro. I can't let her out of my care."

Andre shifted his weight and cocked his head. "Okay, make a call and get this straightened out. I know you CIA guys have someone to call for times like this. Do it."

Grant shook his head. "I can't."

"Then I have to take her in."

Grant dropped his hands loosely to his side. "I'm sorry, Cindy. He's my brother, and I can't hurt him. You'll have to go. I'll do the best I can to look out for you."

Cindy stared at Grant. After what he'd just told her about not trusting anyone, what was he thinking?

Andre reached forward to grip her arm.

Grant's right fist drove into Andre's kidney, causing him to drop. A solid uppercut and the big man's head snapped back. From behind, Grant wrapped his arm around Andre's neck and clamped it down with his other arm.

The big man clawed at his sleeve, trying to breathe. His cheeks swelled, and his eyes went bloodshot. Finally, he collapsed to the floor.

Grant leaned down next to him, checked his pulse, and put his cheek near his brother's mouth. He sighed, relieved. "He's breathing. I hated doing that, but I couldn't let him take you in." With Cindy helping, they dragged Andre's two-hundred-sixty pounds behind the bed.

Stepping close, he whispered, "It's time for Act Two. Keep your hands behind your back as if you're handcuffed."

When she did, he opened the door and nodded to the other police officer.

"Okay, you can take her now," Collier said.

The policeman got two feet past Grant before the Glock pressed the back of his head. "Keep going, pal," Collier said.

"You wouldn't shoot an officer," he stammered.

"I wouldn't shoot my brother, but I'll shoot you. You guys are in way over your heads. Cooperate, and you'll go home to your family tonight."

Grant knocked the man to his knees and cuffed him to the leg of a large built-in dresser. He drove his fist into the man's jaw, and the policeman laid out, unconscious.

Reaching behind the dresser, Grant ripped the phone out of the wall. Then he cuffed his brother's arm to his partner's leg. "They can keep each other company," he said wryly.

He turned to Cindy huddled by the wall. "We've got to hit the road. I'm sorry you didn't get a chance to change."

She stared at him as though he were a scary stranger. "Is this what you do for a living?"

Grant's eyes softened. He touched her hand. "After you're out of danger, I'm retiring for good."

San Diego, California

Joel Mullinax was enjoying morning coffee in the offices of the Cascade International Shipping Company—a CIA controlled corporation—when the Special Edition newscast came across a tiny TV bolted high on the wall.

His mug smashed to the floor when the photographs of Cindy Lestrade and Grant Collier appeared side by side.

He swore. If Collier had let him know about the police action, a call from Mullinax to the U.S. attorney would have resolved the situation. Instead, Maverick Collier had mauled two of Phoenix's finest. Warrants had been issued for assault.

Now the Russians, Chinese, and even some of their NATO allies would be looking for the fugitives. Collier was burnt. Mullinax would have to bring them in. Whether the woman talked or not, she must eventually be terminated.

He pressed an intercom button. "Brown, get in here."

A tall middle-aged man with permanently dour expression entered the office. "Yes, Director?"

"The mission is blown. Where is Collier?"

"He's about an hour north of Phoenix."

"Have them brought in."

"Sir, Mr. Collier can be a problem. If he should resist?"

"Take him out. Bring in the woman alive."

Meyer, Arizona

Grant threw the luggage into the back of the Bronco while Cindy hopped in the passenger side. He threw his cane in the back with everything else.

When he got in beside her, Cindy was shivering. With the broken windows, the heater was useless. Hopefully, the sun would warm them up soon. "Where are we going?" she asked.

"I have no idea," he said. He paused to wait for a red Ferrari to pass before turning right on Interstate 17. "We need to go somewhere private where we can talk."

"I know a place." She sounded a little smug.

"You do?" He smiled at the confidence on her face. He really loved this girl.

"Keep going south, and I'll tell you which exit."

"First, we have to find new wheels. This thing is worse than a beacon."

Five minutes later, he saw a gaudy sign: Pioneer Used Cars. "I've got some cash. We can buy a clunker up there." He nodded toward the car dealership and turned down the next alley.

"Is it safe to go there?" Cindy asked. "Everyone in Arizona knows our faces by now."

Collier took two pairs of black plastic sunglasses from the glove box. He handed one pair to Cindy. "Put these on. You'd be surprised how much they'll change your appearance."

Cindy looked in the mirror and made a face. "Too retro. Not my style." She giggled with a hint of hysteria. "Just kidding."

As they paced down the alley, she asked. "Should I hold your hand? You know, to make us look like a couple?"

Grant looked her over. For all she'd been through, she was holding up remarkably well. "Good idea," he said.

Her hand slipped into his. It fit just right.

"You don't need your cane anymore?" she asked.

"Just sometimes. Right now, I feel pretty good."

Suddenly, Grant stopped in his tracks.

"What's wrong?" Cindy asked, looking around for hidden gunman.

"It's Sunday. They're closed."

She groaned. "So, what do we do, drive the Bronco?"

"We switch plans, that's all." He continued down the sidewalk. "The good news is we don't have to worry about being recognized."

The car lot contained vehicles of every style and condition. "Pick one," Grant said.

Cindy walked around the lot and stopped beside an ancient Ford Tempo.

"That's what you want? A Tempo?"

"My last car was a Tempo, and it's never let me down."

"You got it." He read the sign on the car's window. "The price tag says $2,199.00. You know as well as I that they'll sell it cheaper. So, here's what I'm going to do..." He sauntered to the little trailer that served as the sales office, slammed the weathered door with his shoulder until it popped open. A minute later, he returned holding car keys and a license plate that fastened with magnets. "I left two thousand dollars in cash on the guy's desk. His alarm just went off. We've got to hurry."

He unlocked the door, started to get in, then his expression changed. "I don't believe this!" he said, getting out.

"What's wrong with it?" Cindy asked.

"It's a standard. I can't shift a standard with my bum leg. You'll have to drive."

"But I can't drive a standard," Cindy said. "My Tempo was automatic." She looked scared again.

"The cops will be here in about three minutes. You'll have to learn fast."

They slid into blue bucket seats, and she took the keys from him. On the passenger side, Grant barked instructions. "Push the clutch in and turn the key."

The motor sputtered to life. She revved the engine.

"Now, give it a little gas and slowly release the clutch." The car shot back and crunched the vehicle behind them.

"What are you doing?" he shouted.

"What you told me," she shot back. Her freckles had disappeared beneath a red glow.

"I said to let it out slowly."

"I thought I did."

He lowered his chin and tried to stay calm. "Push in the clutch and start the motor again. This time put it in first."

"Where is that?" she touched the shift stick with tentative fingers.

"Never mind," Collier said, trying to keep his voice low. How many minutes had passed? "Just start the car. I'll shift."

Jerking to the edge of the parking lot, the Tempo made a right. "What about our stuff?" Cindy asked a moment later.

"We'll go back for it."

Lurching and swaying, Cindy took the first right, went down the side street, and made another right at the next street.

"Stop here," Grant said when they reached an alley. "I don't want to be any closer to the dealership than I have to with this car. We can walk to get our stuff."

They covered the short distance to the Bronco in less than five minutes. Grant had just grabbed the suitcase when a black SUV squealed to a stop in front of them. Two men in dark suits got out. Each held a handgun with a silencer.

Chapter Twenty-Three

Desert Hills, Arizona

The small hairs on the back of Grant's neck stood up when he saw two goons with guns bearing down on Cindy and him, but he forced his face to stay calm. Idiots! What were they doing?

"Don't move, Collier," said the taller one. He stood near the open passenger door of the SUV and gripped his Beretta like he knew how to use it.

Collier's shock turned to anger. "Brown! What are you doing here?"

The big man wasn't smiling. "We're taking you both in. Mullinax's orders."

Cindy grasped Collier's arm. "Grant, what's going on?"

"I'm not sure," he told her, then moved his body between her and the CIA officers.

"Well, Collier, are you coming peacefully or the hard way?" Brown asked.

To give himself some time to think, Grant decided to stall. "Get Mullinax on the radio," he told Brown. "If he gives me a direct order, we'll come along."

Hesitating, the nose of his weapon rising, Brown glanced at his partner, then plopped onto the car's seat with one leg hanging out the door. A second later, he held a cellphone to the side of his head.

Recognition flitted behind Grant's eyes as he glimpsed the lithe form of a dark-haired man moving quietly toward the back of the SUV, using parked cars for cover.

Keeping an eye on the scene before him, Collier whispered to Cindy, "These guys are from the CIA. They plan to kill you after they get the code. I want to get you out of this alive. Will you do as I say?"

He saw something in her eyes that he hadn't seen for a long time: trust. "All right," she whispered.

He squeezed the hand gripping his arm and murmured, "Go to the back of the Tempo and stay low."

A minute later, Brown stepped out of the car, still holding the phone. "Okay, I've got the director."

Collier paced toward the Suburban, hands wide, his Glock tucked into the back of his pants and hidden by his coat. Cindy moved behind the Tempo.

"Where's she going?" Brown demanded, his eyes flickering from Collier to the girl.

"Just getting some of her stuff," Collier said, still moving.

Brown lifted his weapon. "Stop right there, Collier. Ms. Lestrade," he yelled, " Come out in the open!"

"Or you'll do what?" A gentle voice asked from behind him.

Against their training, both men whirled around to see the source of the voice. Grant pulled his weapon and aimed it at Brown's slim middle.

"Nice to see you, Ruben," Collier told the wiry Israeli holding twin Glock 17s on the CIA officer.

Ruben's narrow face held an ironic expression. "You are having a problem, I see." His voice had a definite Middle Eastern flavor.

"Are you willing to help me out?" Collier asked. He still held his gun level.

"Jury's still out," he said, raising his chin a little.

Still holding the phone, Brown's hand wavered around his ear as he asked Collier, "Who's this?"

Grant smiled. "That's Ruben Abrams of the Mossad. You know, the Israeli secret service."

"Don't get smart," Brown shot back. His pale cheeks turned red to match his nose.

"He looks like he has plans to shoot you if you shoot me," Collier said. "Is that right, Ruben?"

"Exactly." The Israel's eyebrows lifted, a silent question.

Collier nodded, then said, "So, Brown, what's it to be? Abrams is an excellent shot. He'll nail you, and I'll get your partner."

"But I'll get you," Brown said, his Beretta rock steady on Grant's head.

Grant said, "I only care about Ms. Lestrade's safety, not my own." He put tension on his trigger. "What's it going to be? Will your wife be shopping for black tonight?"

"Put your weapon down, Conroy," Brown said, disgusted. A Beretta and a Glock clattered to the asphalt.

Shoving his left gun into his shoulder holster, Abrams came behind Conroy and frisked him for more weapons. He pulled a knife from behind the agent's neck and pitched it down the alley. Digging his thumb into the man's skinny neck, Abram stepped back as the agent collapsed. Three seconds later, a karate chop put Brown out.

Stepping around the unconscious lumps sprawled in the alley, Collier picked up the black cellphone from the asphalt near Brown's hand. He spoke into it. "Listen, Mullinax, you fouled up your end of the deal, but I'm going to keep mine. If you send any more men after us, they'll pay the piper."

He tossed the phone to the car seat and slammed the door. The receiver squawked, but he ignored it.

"How long have you been following me?" Grant asked Abrams.

"Couple of days… Does it matter?"

Collier held the Glock steady at waist height. "Why are you here, Ruben?" he asked. "The truth."

The Israeli glanced toward Cindy's location. "Intelligence says that Ms. Lestrade knows the missile code. I have come for her."

"You can't have her," Grant said firmly. The Glock tilted slightly.

Abrams let his level eyes rest on Collier. "This is a great dilemma. You are my very good friend, Grant. You saved my life, and yet I love my country, too." He raised his shoulders. "What am I to do?" he asked sadly.

"If we find the key, I guarantee that your people will get it."

Abrams shook his head regretfully. "I want to believe you, Grant, but sometimes you'll promise the moon when you don't even have a rocket ship."

"I'm talking straight, Ruben," Grant said, an edge to his words. "If Ms. Lestrade finds the answer, I will make sure you get it. You have my word."

Suddenly, the second Glock lay in the Israeli's left hand. One gun aimed at Collier's middle, the other at the Tempo. "Put your gun down, Grant." Abrams said carefully. "I don't want to kill you, my friend."

Collier's chest puffed out. The ball was in his court, but he wasn't sure how to make the play. Finally, he bent at the knees and lay his Glock on the ground.

Abrams nodded and stepped forward. "A wise…" A stone clattered behind him. He flinched and turned.

Grant's hiking boot crunched into Abrams's knee, knocking him off balance. Both guns flew up and out, still tangled in his fingers. A second kick and he landed hard on his back, gasping for air.

Collier stepped from one of the Israeli's hands to the other, giant steps with his heels grinding down.

Abrams screamed.

Grant bent over to pull the weapons from the Israeli's mangled fingers and tuck them into his own waistband. "I'm sorry, Ruben. You left me no choice." A hard right to the jaw put him out of his pain, at least temporarily.

Grant dashed to Cindy, who was crouched behind the trunk of the car. She had a rock in her hand, up and ready, balanced on the balls of her feet. When he came around, she pulled back for a throw.

"Whoa!" he said. "That was great thinking!"

He jerked open the back door, threw in his phone and grabbed the suitcase. "We've got less than a minute to clear out."

"What about your cane?" Cindy asked.

"I don't need it anymore."

San Diego, California

Joel Mullinax sputtered into the cellphone for a full minute before he realized that Collier wasn't answering. Finally, he ended the call and sent for his assistant. "Get a new team and find out what happened!" he shouted.

Four hours later, Brown and Conway stood before him with hangdog expressions.

"Well?" Mullinax demanded.

"Ruben Abrams of the Mossad came at us from behind," Brown said, rubbing his bruised neck. "He must have taken off with Collier and the girl. He wasn't there when we came around."

Mullinax leaned back in his stiff chair and massaged his weary face. "Take a couple weeks of vacation, both of you. Now get out of my office."

When he was alone, Mullinax stared at the gray plastered wall in front of him. Collier had about an hour's head start on the new team. As soon as the police reported which car was missing from Pioneer Used Cars, Mullinax had every asset he had in the air for a massive search.

As an ace in the hole, his officers had located a cousin to Wesley Anderson and paid him ten thousand dollars to put up a fifty-thousand-dollar reward for information leading to the fugitives. The CIA would pick up the tab for the reward, of course.

A soft knock brought Mullinax out of his daydream. He straightened and called, "Come in."

Brown peeked his head in the door. "I forgot to tell you one thing."

"Yes?"

Brown pushed the door two inches wider. "Collier said that even though you weren't willing to keep your part of the deal, he would keep his."

"He told me the same thing on the phone."

Brown closed the door, and Mullinax's brow came down. Collier's mind games didn't matter. Cindy Lestrade must be brought in… regardless of the cost.

With Cindy at the wheel of the Tempo, the fleeing couple drove along a secondary road, passing ranch after ranch. "Isn't there a restaurant or even a grocery store around here?" Cindy wailed.

"I know what you mean," Grant said. "My belly button is almost touching my backbone."

She smiled. "That's gross."

He smiled and said, "Sorry." But he wasn't.

Rounding a curve, Cindy cried. "Aha!" Ahead on the left sat a low, flat building with a weathered sign hanging from an iron pole: Rosa's Cafe. She pulled into the lot and turned the key. "If someone comes along to shoot us, let him fire away. I've got to have something hot to eat, or I'll die anyway. Do you realize it's been over a week since I've had anything but fast food and pastries?"

He reached for the door handle. "Let's go. We'll wolf down dinner and keep moving." He grinned at her. "Just don't order half a cow. We don't have time to wait for the butcher to bring one."

Instead of half a cow, they settled for steaks that covered their plates, fat baked potatoes smothered with sour cream, and garlic bread on the side. Cindy couldn't finish her potato, so she brought it along in a small box for a bedtime snack. How did she stay so thin?

Ten minutes later, they reached Cindy's hideaway. Grant shot Cindy a disbelieving look when he saw the Sabrosa Motel.

"This is where Wesley hid me," she told him when the Tempo pulled into the ragged parking lot.

"What makes you think this is safe?" Grant asked, taking in the broken and taped windows, the missing shingles. "All kinds of shady characters come here."

She said, "We'll fit in, won't we?"

"Beggars have to take what they can get, I guess." He opened his door. "Wait here. I'll go in and pay for a room."

Hurrying down the cracked sidewalk, he pushed open the weathered wooden door and entered the office.

A cloud of smoke hung around a scraggly, thin man wearing a wife-beater undershirt and gray sweatpants. "Yeah?" the attendant asked through tobacco-stained teeth.

"I need a room."

"How long?"

"Two days at the most."

"Two hundred bucks, cash."

Grant tossed two bills on the counter. "Where do I sign?"

The man's grin looked like a broken-down picket fence. "No one ever signs. Here's your key, room 125. It's the one farthest at the end. There's parking behind the building."

"Thanks." Grant grabbed the key, turned, and opened the door, almost bumping into a well-dressed businessman coming in. Their eyes made brief contact. The man mumbled an apology, and a shot of electricity jolted through Grant. Would he turn them in?

When he reached the Tempo, Cindy asked, "What room?"

"One-twenty-five. It's at the end."

"Hmm, last time he gave me 112. I hope this one is better."

Cindy entered the room ahead of Grant who carried the suitcase. While he locked the door and set the suitcase on the leaning dresser, she stood hand on hip, looking the place over.

"Any better?" he asked, setting down the suitcase. He was suddenly very aware that they were alone together in a hotel room. The memory of another hotel room flashed through his mind... He shook off that thought and tried to focus on what Cindy was saying.

"It doesn't smell as bad, but the bed isn't even a queen size."

He made a big deal of taking off his coat and hanging it over the back of the chair to give himself time to answer in a normal tone of voice. "We can sleep in shifts. It's better that way anyway," he said. "We need to keep watch. With our faces all over the news, we can't be too careful."

She looked him straight in the eye. "Before we sleep, eat, or do anything, I want a complete and honest explanation of what is going on."

Grant motioned toward the bed. "Have a seat."

Cindy sat on the crinkled bedspread. She crossed her legs and rested her hands on her lap, watching him and waiting.

Grant eased into the nearby chair and said, "Recently your father's missile guidance system crashed and produced a worldwide crisis. His system contains an encrypted program that no one can crack. The Russians infiltrated the prison and overdosed your father on truth drugs trying to learn the code. When your father died, your mother said that you were the key. So, the Russians grabbed you.

"While the CIA was planning to snatch you from the Russians," he continued, "they considered killing you on the ship, so no one would have the answer. I talked them out of it."

Tears filled her eyes.

Grant sat in the chair and leaned forward, speaking steadily. "The CIA plans to drug you, so you'll tell them the answer. Then, they'll dispose of you."

"Why?" She sounded broken. "I haven't done a single thing."

"To keep other countries from knowing the solution. Director Mullinax is out of control. He wants total supremacy for the U.S."

She plucked at her collar. "He told you this?"

"Not in so many words, but I know how his mind works. He's gone over the edge, Cindy, and there's no one to stop him... but us."

She wiped her eyes on the sleeve of her shirt. "I'm going to spend the rest of my life on the run, aren't I?"

Grant shook his head. "Not if my plan works." He reached for her hand. "Do you know what the key is?"

Cindy shook her head until her hair swayed. "I never worked on that project. You know that."

"Did your father say anything to you that would help us figure out the code?"

Cindy's voice quavered. "My father and I did a lot of encryptions together, but nothing the government's computers couldn't crack in a couple of weeks."

Grant slowly exhaled. "Then we're sunk."

"Can't you make me disappear again?" she asked.

"No. I mean… I could, but they'd eventually find you. We're going to have to go to the Internet with the story. It's the only way to be completely free of this."

Cindy peered at him. "You'd do that?"

"Why not?"

"You're still with the CIA. Wouldn't you get into trouble?"

His lips formed an ironic smile. "We're talking jail time for breaching national security. The other option is death."

"Then let me go alone."

Grant's smile softened. "It's nice of you to offer, but it wouldn't help. I'd still go to jail for releasing classified information."

He went on, "The CIA told me to make you think you were being chased, so I could be a hero. When you trusted me, you'd tell me the code. Afterward, I'd have the code and hand you over to them."

Life came into her expression. The old Cindy stared at him. "That episode in the alley was staged?"

"No, that was real. When the police put our faces on TV, the CIA considered us burnt. That's why they sent those goons to bring you in…and dispose of me." His voice grew pleading. "If you knew the key to the encryption, you could put it on the Internet, so everyone would have access to it at once. Once the world has it, you're no longer a threat." He raised his hands, palms up. "At least, that was my plan."

"And it failed."

"Yeah. You don't know the key."

Cindy stood and peeked out the window through the crack between the mossy green drapes. A moment later, she turned to him. "How do I know you aren't lying to me again, making this all up?"

"You have no reason to believe me, Cindy. I know that."

The room stayed silent for a full minute. Cindy wandered around the room, then returned to the window and stared out the crack in the drapes.

Was he lying? She could think of only one way to know for sure. She turned to Collier who was still in the chair. "All right, I have the key."

His face had a strange expression. "You were holding out on me?"

"I think you can understand why."

He hesitated, then asked, "What is it?"

My father's grandmother was a Navajo. She lived with his parents when he was a child and taught him the language. Sometimes for fun, he would base encryption programs on it."

"It's that simple?"

Cindy nodded. She clenched her hands together. "Where do we go from here?"

"We post the code to the cloud and broadcast the link."

She watched his eyes. Did he mean it? Maybe he'd watch what she wrote, then stop her at the last second. Maybe he was just stringing her along. She ran her hand across her hopelessly tangled curls. "Any idea where we can find a computer with Internet access?"

                    Lana McAra

Grant rubbed his bristly chin. "The manager has to have one to process credit cards." He reached for the doorknob. "He's a peach. Let's go."

When they burst inside the office, the scraggly attendant strolled out of a back room, a beer in one hand, a cigarette in the other. "Yeah?" he asked.

Pulling out a friendly smile, Grant said, "We were wondering if we can use a computer. We need to use the Internet for maybe five minutes."

The attendant lowered his cigarette to get a better look at them. "I'm the manager, Matt Hardy. Why do you need a computer?"

"We need to send an important e-mail," Cindy answered.

He pulled in the side of his mouth. Looking Cindy over, his eyes lingered on her chest, then he drawled, "Your pictures don't do you justice." He turned to Grant. "Do you know there's a fifty-thousand-dollar reward for you two?"

Collier's smile faded. "Are you going to turn us in?"

Hardy drew on his cigarette and let out a cloud of smoke. "The last thing I need is to have the heat crawling over my place. Fifty thousand isn't half enough to cover what I'd lose in the process." He stepped away from the door. "The computer's back here."

He led them into a living room the size of a postage stamp. The couch's upholstery was shiny on the arms. Full ashtrays and empty beer bottles littered the landscape. On a cluttered corner desk, its blue eye gleaming, sat the computer.

Cindy dashed to the chair, her fingers on the keyboard.

"What's the first step?" Grant asked, peering over her shoulder.

"I have to search the government email addresses of all the countries involved. Russia, China, and Israel…"

Collier added, "Britain, France, Italy, Canada, and Spain."

Under her hands the keys sang a metallic tune. "Is that all of them?"

"That's enough to accomplish our purposes."

Half an hour later, she had everything she needed. She said, "I'm going to put in my real e-mail address. Then they'll be able to verify the return address as mine." She gasped. "Oh, no!"

"What?"

"They'll trace our location here. We'll have to run again."

He glanced at his watch. "It's fifteen past four. We should have at least an hour, maybe more. Once you put it out there, we're home free."

She had spasms in her stomach, and her fingers kept fumbling at the keyboard. How long would it take for those hated black sedans to reach the broken-up parking lot and take them away? But she couldn't stop now. She had to know where Grant's loyalties lay once and for all. She plowed ahead as quickly as she could. When she finished, she paused and looked up at him.

"Once I click send, there's no bringing it back," she told him, watching his face. "The world will know the key and the feds will be after us again."

"By all means, click it," he said. "Hurry!"

Instead, Cindy moved the pointer to the x in the upper right corner of the screen and closed the application. She stood and gazed into his puzzled face. Finally, she was able to admit what she had tried not to feel for a long time. She loved him.

Chapter
Twenty-Four

Sabrosa, Arizona

"What's wrong?" Grant asked. "Why are you stopping?"

"Let's go back to the room," she said quietly.

Grant threw a twenty on the desk. They waved their thanks to Matt Hardy and hurried out. When they reached the sidewalk, Cindy smiled a real, genuine smile for the first time in two years. Despite their imminent danger, she felt free. She wanted to dash out into the parking lot, arms wide, face heavenward, and twirl until she was too dizzy to stand. Instead, she laughed at him, a girlish sound.

His confusion dissolved into the wide smile that used to take her breath away. It still did. He grabbed her hand. "This is our door," he said, sliding the plastic card in the slot.

"You know what I wish?" she said, pausing on the doorjamb, close enough for their shirts to brush.

"What?" His eyes lingered on her face.

"I wish we were at the beach walking on the sand."

He touched her chin. "I second the motion. How about a raincheck?" Still smiling, he pushed the door wider, they stepped inside.

"What happened in there?" he asked her. He slid the chain lock over the door. "Why didn't you send the code?"

She gazed directly into his eyes, strong and steady. "I don't know the encryption key," she told him. "I was just pretending."

He froze, his eyes searching hers. "You were testing me?"

"Yes."

"Did I pass?"

"Yes." Her smile took over her whole body.

His jaw went slack for a second, replaced by a spark that arced between them.

Cindy felt giddy and shy with a tingle in her tummy.

He stepped closer. "This has been a living agony for me, Cindy. I've ripped myself apart every single day because of what happened to you. That day at the villa…" He looked deep into her eyes. "I never wanted that. I tried to stop it."

She opened her mouth to speak, but he covered her lips with his gentle fingers.

"The worst," he went on, moving closer to her, "was wondering if you missed me half as much as I missed you."

His hand moved to the back of her neck. "I love you, Cindy." Tears swam in his eyes. "I always will."

She plastered herself against him, allowing the hunger inside her to well up from the deepest part of her soul.

Two steps backward and she fell back across the bed, tearing at her buttons and zippers, reaching for his.

For the next hour, they devoured each other, lost in a building volcano of love and desire they had been holding down for way too long, wondering how they could have ever let go of this once-in-a-lifetime magic.

"I love you, Grant," she whispered after a while. "But there's something I have to tell you."

While Grant waited for Cindy to go on, a dozen thoughts flashed through his brain—she had secretly married Wesley... she had a dreaded disease… she was pregnant with another man's child…and worse.

"I'm not the woman you knew," she said, pulling away so she could look at his face. She had a glow he'd never seen before. "I'm a kickboxing competitor. Most people on my team think I'm a badass. Is that a problem for you?"

He lost his breath for a second. Was she kidding? He looked into her green eyes, "Cindy, I want you to be you. I want to know every square inch…his eyes drifted south… "of your wants and needs, your loves and hates…" He kissed her forehead. "…I don't care what they are, I just want to print them on the back of my eyelids, so I never forget them," He squeezed her to him. "…and never, ever let you go."

He leaned in, and they were off for a second round.

San Diego, California

The Cascade International Shipping Company had doubled its size in twenty-four hours. Electronic equipment filled its dozen offices where grim-faced men and women worked feverishly. Mullinax had called in all the troops

On the ground, his men scoured the massive Arizona landscape. In the air, a dozen military helicopters covered a grid, to make sure they didn't miss any areas.

A gray-haired woman in a navy suit stepped into Mullinax's makeshift office. "Director?" she said in a well-modulated voice.

He looked up from the papers on his desk. "Yes, Ida?"

"We've got a lead. Someone called in a lead. Someone saw them at a motel in the desert north of Phoenix," she held out her iPad, "at the Sabrosa Motel…here."

"Send the nearest units to that motel!"

When they woke up, the lights from the parking lot shone around the edges of their window curtain. Grant moved. Cindy stirred. She had her head on his chest. Her hair was tickling his chin. Nice.

"What time is it?" she mumbled.

He glanced at the glowing green numbers on his watch. "Eighteen hundred… um.. six at night."

She sat up, drew in a deep breath and dashed for the bathroom. "I'm showering first this time, you dork!" she called out.

Chuckling, to get a rise out of her, he called back, "What's a dork?"

"It's one step below a nerd!" Water sprayed and stopped any further conversation.

Grant sat on the edge of the bed. He had lost his situational awareness, to put it mildly. He had to get himself back to focus. The sex was off the charts, but neither of them had slept for days. They needed the rest. Time to shake it off and regroup.

When she came out of the shower, he was dressed and tying the laces of his boots. "We've got to get moving. We should have left here hours ago." He glanced around. "We won't be able to take any luggage this time."

Cindy pulled a shirt and jeans from the suitcase and put them on. "Where are we going?"

"We'll have to run across the back hills and figure it out as we go."

She pulled off the yellow shirt she had put on and chose a black one instead, then covered the shirt with a brown sweatshirt. She stuffed her hair under a brown knit cap. "You know how to pack," she said, appreciatively. Stuffing her pockets with whatever she could, she handed some things to Grant who did the same.

Grant said, "Take your ID but leave the cards. Those chips have trackers in them. We have to go 100 percent no electronics." He pulled a knife from his ankle scabbard and cut her plastic cards in half.

They turned out the lights, and Grant cracked the door open to eye the parking lot. Two security lights made yellow puddles along the dark building. He opened the door, and the cool evening air rushed in.

They rounded the corner of the building. The Tempo sat there, waiting for them.

Grant said, "I'll take the car and lead them away from you. You take off across the field."

She stared into the black expanse. "No way. I'm not going out there alone to meet a mountain lion or worse. We go together."

He tried to sound stern, but his heart wasn't in it. "If we split, they'll chase me instead of you."

She pushed her face to within inches from his. "Without you, I am not safe."

Just then, three black SUVs roared down the road to their right. They churned gravel and squealed brakes into the motel's parking lot.

Grant grabbed Cindy's hand. They dashed across the back lot to a cattle fence. Grant pushed down the second from the bottom strand with his foot, lifted the third strand with his hand, and Cindy slipped through.

She then did the same for him. Grant found it awkward. His leg was still a problem. The back of his coat snagged on a barb.

"I'm stuck," he said, trying to reach around to loosen the barb. "I'll have to leave the coat."

"It's too cold," she said. Gasping with frustration, Cindy jerked the coat. It seemed like hours later when he broke free, and they stumbled into the night.

Hand in hand, they hurried through the darkness. Light flickered in the distance. They automatically aimed toward it.

Uneven ground made walking a chore for Grant. His leg throbbed after only five minutes. Could he make that tingling limb carry him far enough to find safety?"

Behind them, a spotlight swept the parking lot and edged toward the field. Grant glanced back every few steps, gauging its progress.

"Get down!" He pulled Cindy's hand as he flung himself flat on the ground. She landed beside him with a thud.

"Sorry," he said. "The light's almost on us."

When she caught her breath she asked, "What are we going to do after we cross this field?"

"I'll steal a car. With wheels we can get to Phoenix."

"Will they have the roads blocked?"

"That depends on whether they call in the police and the FBI."

"Why wouldn't they?"

Grant said, "Mullinax plans to kill us. The FBI wouldn't go for that."

"Oh, great!"

A circle of brilliant yellow passed a yard from their feet. When it moved down the pasture, they scrambled up.

"Agh!" Cindy gasped. "There's something wet on my knee."

"Don't touch it!" Grant told her, pulling her along with him. "This is a cow pasture. You don't want to know what it is."

The light had come from a security pole in a ranch yard. When they drew near, a dog started barking. "Stay down." Grant whispered.

Side by side, they stretched out on the ground. On one side of the yard stood a two-story ranch house with stucco siding. A weathered barn stood a hundred and fifty feet from the house with two tall pines in the yard between.

The back door of the house opened, and a plump woman in a tent dress stepped out on the porch. She shouted, her voice nasal and harsh, "Whatcha barking at, Brutus?"

A howl sounded in the distance. "It's just coyotes, ya stupid mutt," she said. The door flapped closed.

Grant pressed Cindy's arm. "Wait here. I'm going in for a closer look."

He crept closer to the house and stood in the shadow of a tree trunk, its branches wide over his head. Both vehicles parked in the driveway—a red pickup truck and a dented Buick—were within reach of the chained dog.

Grant's leg pounded. His left side felt like someone had stepped on him. He couldn't travel on foot much farther. Then, a welcome sound came from the barn—the snort of a horse.

Grant returned to Cindy, but before he could speak the *whump-whump* of helicopter blades came from overhead. Once more, they flattened themselves into the earth, hiding their faces, as the chopper passed over them. When it reached the motel, it lit up its spotlight and hovered a few minutes, then shot down the road, the beam still searching.

"God is definitely on our side tonight," Grant told Cindy as he sat up. "If we'd left in the Tempo, they'd have us by now." He leaned toward her until he could see her glistening eyes. "We have a better way to get across country than a car."

"What's that? A tractor?" she asked, peering at the barn.

"No. A horse."

"I can't ride a horse," she said.

"Don't worry. I can. You can sit behind me. It'll be fun."

"Fun? We're being chased by the CIA, and it'll be fun?"

They scuttled to the barn and entered through a side door. The smell of horses and hay met them inside.

The yard light shown through cracks in the barn walls. Grant moved between the half-dozen horse stalls. He'd walk up to a horse, stroke its nose, then lunge forward. The animal would snort and shy away.

What are you doing?" she whispered.

"No time to explain," he said, his face striped with light.

The fourth horse was a large black. When Grant jumped, the horse looked at him and practically yawned. Grant grinned at Cindy. "This is the one. He's not skittish. He'll be safer to ride."

"Safer?" She didn't sound convinced.

"There's a door at the back. It's probably the tack room. I'll get a saddle and bridle." He picked his way across the barn through the dim light and came out carrying a saddle with a bridle hanging over the horn and a blanket resting on top. In about ten minutes, he had the horse saddled.

He tried to mount but ended up stuck. "Cindy, shove my bad leg the rest of the way up. I can't get it over." When he was settled in the saddle, he held down his hand to give Cindy a pull up. "Don't worry. I've owned horses all my life. We'll be fine."

She landed behind him with a thud. The horse never moved.

"Now comes the hard part," he whispered. "Getting the horse out of here without being noticed. That dog is going to start yapping as soon as he hears us. Hopefully, the lady will think he's barking at coyotes again."

Sure enough, the instant the horse stepped outside, the dog barked. Grant kept the horse to the dark side of the barn.

The woman bellowed, "Brutus! Shut up!"

The dog barked louder.

A man came to the porch holding a shotgun. "You trying to tell me something, Brutus?" He peered into the darkness.

"Yeah, he's telling you it's a nice night and to go back inside," Grant murmured near Cindy's ear. She shivered and squeezed his waist tighter.

He grunted. "Ease up," he said. "My wound is right were you're squeezing."

The dog kept yapping.

"Okay. Have it your way, dog," the man said. "Come on inside."

Cindy let out a sigh when the door banged shut.

They moved through the darkness to a fence and walked along it until they found a gate. Cindy scrambled down to open it, and Grant urged the horse through.

They continued for an hour. In the distance, a building with a neon light flashed the word *Tavern*. Grant headed that way and drew up within three hundred feet of it, stopped by another barbed-wire fence.

They dismounted. Grant released the horse, and it trotted back the way they had come. Crossing the fence, they approached the building from behind. A frame structure, it had the usual stucco exterior. Kitchen garbage and empty beer cases littered the back.

Stepping carefully, they reached the corner of the building and moved along the side. Cindy kept close to Grant.

When he poked his head around the corner to the parking lot, he drew back, disgusted. In a row, like soldiers prepared to do battle, stood eight motorcycles. They glittered with chrome, long forks, and banana seats.

"It's a biker bar," he told her. "You know, long greasy hair, black leather jackets. Guys who beat up people like me for fun."

"Do you know how to steal a motorcycle?"

"I think so, but do I want to? If those guys catch us, it won't be pretty."

"Do we have another option?"

Grant shook his head. "We're fresh out of options, I'm afraid." He limped around the corner and approached the chopper nearest to them. He'd never stolen a motorcycle before, but it couldn't be too much different than a car.

He unfasted two wires. A muffled scream came from behind him. He spun around to see a big, bald man dressed in leather. He had his hand clamped over Cindy's mouth, a sawed-off shotgun to her head.

"What are you doing near my bike?" the man yelled. His voice could saw logs.

Grant held up his hands. "Hey…careful with that gun. Don't hurt her."

The man shoved Cindy aside. She stumbled but didn't fall. He turned his weapon on Collier. Gritting his teeth, Grant forced himself to stay still and keep his stance harmless.

"What are you doing sneaking around the back of my place in the dark?"

The gun pressed Grant's chest.

"I was just admiring the bikes."

"Yeah, right." Suddenly, the man's body language tightened. His bushy, black eyebrows drew together. "Hey, I know you," he said. He looked down at Cindy. "You're on TV. There's fifty-thousand bucks out for you two. I could sure use fifty thousand bucks." He took a step back, and the weapon lowered a bit.

Grant had to keep him talking. "I don't suppose you'd consider letting us go if we promise to give you sixty thousand in cash later?"

The biker shook his head. "Nice try."

Cindy moved behind Grant. "Cindy, get out of the way," he whispered.

"No, I'm standing right here with you," she said loudly. He felt her hand on his lower back. God, he loved this woman.

Grant said, "Do you mind if I put my hands down?"

The biker laughed. "What, you think I'm some kind of a nut? I know what you do for a living, Mr. CIA big shot. In fact, get up against that wall. I'm going to search you."

Grant did as commanded, placing his hands against the rough stucco. The biker's hand ran across his sides and pants legs.

"See, I told you I wasn't armed," Grant said.

"Turn around," the big man said.

A click came from the left. "You turn around," said Cindy, slowly.

She had Grant's Glock aimed at the biker's chest, cocked and ready to fire. Grant grabbed the sawed-off shotgun. He kicked the man's legs out, and he fell.

Pressing the gun against his head, Grant said, "I should kill you for threatening her. Now which bike is yours? And give me the keys."

"Fourth one over," he mumbled as he dug keys out of his pocket.

"You lie here until we're gone. Then, if you want, you can run inside and get all your biker buddies to chase us. But keep this in mind. My Glock holds nineteen rounds plus whatever's in this shotgun. Is your bike worth it? I'll kill you and as many of your buddies as I can."

Keeping the shotgun on the biker, Grant took the keys and moved to the chopper. He threw his good leg over the seat and found the electric starter. Inserting the key, he revved the motor. "Get on," he called to Cindy over the engine's blast.

Cindy jumped on the back seat, the Glock still in her hand. Grant handed her the shotgun, and they roared into the darkness, anxious to put distance between them and the tavern in case the bikers decided it was a good day to die.

When they'd traveled five miles with no signs of pursuit, Grant pulled the motorbike off the road beside a field. "Give me the shotgun," he said.

Cindy handed it to him. He pumped the loading mechanism, ejecting half a dozen shells onto the ground, and flung the weapon into the field.

"The Glock."

Cindy gave him the handgun, and he tucked it under his back waistband again. In the moonlight, he could see the shadowy form of Cindy's face. She had saved their hides with her fast thinking.

"You are one fantastic woman," he said and pulled her into a hug. His lips found hers for a long moment.

Turning her loose, he fired up the Harley, and they roared off.

Chapter Twenty-Five

Sabrosa, Arizona

Speeding down the dark country road, her cap soon worked its way off and her hair was flapping in her face. Cindy felt surreal. So many sensations had hit her in the past twenty-four hours that she thought she was past feeling anything at all. All she could do was hold on and whisper a constant, silent prayer for help.

As ranch after ranch blew past, the Harley's single headlight lit up several entrance signs: Double P Ranch, Crazy Eight Cattle, Marsden Beef, Julie's piano lessons...

Piano lessons? Someone must be running a music studio out of her home.

Cindy had spent ten years studying piano. It had been a passion with her. Her father had taken great delight in finding difficult pieces of music and watching her master them.

"Stop the bike!" Cindy yelled above the rushing wind.

Grant brought the bike to a halt beside the road.

"I know what the key is," she cried, so excited she bounced off the seat and came around to face him. "About a year into the missile project, my dad brought me this obscure piece of music to learn. I was surprised at the time because it had been years since he'd done that. He was very adamant that I learn it and not forget it.

"When I asked him why it was so important, he said it might make me rich someday." She grabbed his jacket by the side seams and shook. "That has to be the key!"

Throwing her arms around him, she squeezed his middle until he gasped. "Sorry," she said, calming a little. "I forgot again."

"You mean that we can get on the Internet and tell everyone the name of the music piece?"

She shook her head. "It's not that easy. My dad changed ordinary things—such as a book or music—into an encryption key by converting it to letters and numbers. For example, if the note is a C quarter note, but is in the lowest octave, then you multiply…"

"Never mind," he said. "I get the idea."

Cindy's enthusiasm faded. "I need my laptop. It's at PTL computers in Black Canyon City. I left it there."

"No other computer will do?"

"Who else would have the right software?"

Grant sounded doubtful. "Mullinax will have your normal haunts staked out. It'll take a miracle to get you in there."

Suddenly, red and blue lights strobed toward them from the front. "Get on!" he cried. He opened the throttle, and the bike shot down the road, passing the oncoming police car. Grant glanced in the mirror and saw the cruiser making a U-turn.

"Can you outrun them?" Cindy shouted in his ear.

He yelled back. "No!"

Grant watched for something he knew every rural area had. Behind him, the police car gained ground, its siren growing louder by the second.

Grant gently squeezed the brake and edged off the road. He bounced across a ditch and onto a narrow path. Every kid in the country had a track for his dirt bike.

The motorcycle tore down the rutted path and disappeared into some trees. He could hear the sirens die out as a police car gave up the chase. They'd radio to headquarters, and all the units on patrol would keep an eye out for the stolen Harley. When the CIA found out, a helicopter would show up.

The path wound through the trees. An occasional bump gave Cindy and Grant a thrill as the bike sailed and settled back down. He'd never been so thankful for having grown up on a ranch.

At the edge of the trees, Grant stopped the bike and turned it off. They got to the ground, and he pushed down the kickstand with his boot.

"What's the matter?" Cindy asked, fear in her voice.

"Shh." he touched her arm. "I want to listen." In the distance, a helicopter buzzed across the dark sky. Soon, a bright light would be on them.

"I wish their bulb would burn out," Cindy burst out.

Grant touched her shoulder. "You're a genius."

"What did I say?"

"Wait here!" He walked into the field a hundred paces and lay on his back. Cindy crouched beside the motorcycle. Zigzagging through the sky, the helicopter worked its way toward them, its spotlight a blinding shaft that skimmed the ground

Taking careful aim, Grant fired one shot, and the light vanished in sparks. Jogging as best he could, he returned to Cindy. "We've got to go. They're going to land that baby and come in here looking for us."

The Harley roared to life once more. Grant and Cindy took off across the field. When they reached a paved road, they shot ahead until they came to an all-night convenience store, a Mom-and-Pop affair with a gas pump.

Coasting the bike to just outside the scope of the parking lot's lights, he brought the machine to a stop.

"We've got to find a phone and make some calls," Grant said.

"You never did tell me how you'll get me into PTL Computers," Cindy said, hopping off the bike. Her legs felt like soggy spaghetti.

"I'm going to bluff our way in." He took her hand. "Watch this."

San Diego, California

At Cascade Shipping, Mullinax's staff tried to stay clear of their chief—and for good reason. The director of the CIA was in the mood to find a scapegoat, and no one wanted the position. After fouling up the motel sting, the agency's best helicopter had its searchlight blown out, and Collier managed to slip away again. What was the man? A ghost?

Mullinax's office phone rang, and he grabbed it, anxious to vent his frustration.

"Director?" a familiar voice asked.

"Collier!" Mullinax's face turned the color of a ripe plum. "Where are you?"

Ignoring the question, Collier said, "I have to be quick. She's just gone to the bathroom." His words were clipped. "Director, Cindy Lestrade knows the code."

Mullinax's left hand scrabbled on his cluttered desk for a notepad. "What is it?" he demanded, picking up his pen.

"It's some piece of obscure music."

"Did she give you the name?"

"No. But it wouldn't matter. She says her father had some kind of method for changing music to code. Even if you knew the music, you'd never know what to do with it." Collier's voice grew intense. "I still want to do my job, Director Mullinax. Call off the troops and let me play this to the end. She needs to get to her computer where she can convert the music into the encryption key, and I intend to see that she does."

Mullinax let his pen fall to the desk. He leaned back in his soft leather chair, his expression tight. "I don't think I can trust you."

"Why not?" Collier sounded properly offended.

"You knocked out two of my men."

"You sent them after me, contrary to our agreement," Collier countered.

"You ditched your cane with the homing device."

"After what happened, I had no idea what your guys would do next."

"I'm sorry, Collier," Mullinax said, authority in his words. "You'll have to bring her in. We'll give her a computer here."

"She won't tell you the code willingly," Collier said.

"Then we'll drug her."

Collier kept his tone reasonable. "She tried to explain the transfer code to me and lost me after the first sentence. If you drug her, she won't be able to unravel it. Check with your own people. See if someone can explain detailed encryption technology while flying high on truth drugs." He drew in a short breath. "Sir, she's willing to do it without being forced as long as she stays with me."

Mullinax's words rang with suspicion. "What did you promise her?"

"I told her we'd broadcast the solution over the Internet. Once the world knows, she'll be safe." Collier chuckled, a harsh ring to the sound. "One good thing about all this chasing, she's convinced that I'm on her side."

Mullinax listened carefully. Collier had his full attention. "What do you propose, Grant?"

"I want to take her to PTL Computers where her software is and let her figure out the answer. As soon as she's got it, I'll shut her down, and we can take her into custody."

Mullinax's fingers showed white on the phone receiver. "How do I know you're not working an angle, Collier?"

"Sir, is there anything in my record that would make you doubt me? As we speak, the Chinese or the Russians could figure out the code and overrun our country. We're on the same side, Director."

Mullinax tilted his head back against the chairs upholstery, thinking it over. "Go to PTL," he said, finally. "I'll check with our people about the effects of the truth drug on a person's ability. If your story washes, you'll have no troubles. If it doesn't, it's over for both of you!" Mullinax hung up the phone. "Ida!" he called.

A worried look on her seamed face, his secretary appeared at his door.

Mullinax said, "I want three units to join the men watching PTL Computers. Tell them to stay out of sight until I get there." He stood up and reached for his suit coat. "Get me a chopper. I'm going to Arizona."

Grant hung up the phone and looked down at Cindy huddled against him. "I hope it worked," he said.

Cindy gave him a nervous smile. "You were so convincing I started to wonder if you were telling him the truth and lying to me."

Brushing hair from her cheek, Grant gazed into her emerald eyes. He leaned forward to kiss her forehead. "If I'm lying, you can shoot me. Wanna hold my gun again?" he asked, grinning.

She wriggled closer, with a mischievous expression. "Yes, but not the one you're thinking of." She tilted her head back, watching him. "Besides, if you're lying, I'll find a more painful way to kill you than just pulling a trigger."

He grinned. "Hold that thought. First, I need to make one more call."

Sam Perkins sat in a long line waiting to pass through a checkpoint when his cellphone rang. He touched a button on his steering wheel. "Perkins," he said, bored.

"It's me," a deep voice said.

"Well, hello," Perkins said. "Everyone is searching for you, including your mom. She's upset because you punched out your brother. Where are you?"

The caller ignored the question and said, "I can't tell you much, but I need you at PTL Computers in about two…two-and-a-half hours. Where are you anyway?"

"I'm in Tucson. Someone phoned in a terrorist threat, and the cops have a roadblock set up. They're searching every car."

"You've got to be kidding. What are you doing in Tucson?"

Perkins drawled, "Someone said it was a pretty city, so I went to see for myself."

Grant scoffed. "Get to Black Canyon City as fast as you can. It's life or death, Sam. I wouldn't kid you on that."

Perkins heard desperation in Collier's voice. He knew that Collier was on the run. That was one of the reasons he'd pulled vacation time and left the area. He didn't want to be on a search team if the locals called for FBI assistance.

"I'll get there somehow," Perkins promised. He ended the call. Leave it to Collier to ask him for the impossible.

Cindy glanced around the empty parking lot. "How do we get to Black Canyon City? Steal a car or a motorcycle? How about another horse? A hang glider?"

Grant looked over her head. "How about a taxi?"

Cindy turned to see a yellow cab at the gas pump. "That's the best idea I've heard all day." she said. "I'll go inside and pick up a couple of honey buns and a bottle of water." She stepped toward the door and turned back. "Hey, they have a cappuccino machine!"

They rode to Black Canyon City sipping hot hazelnut coffee and enjoying each other's closeness. Watching Grant's face, Cindy saw a confident exterior, but she knew he had the same doubts as she did. Everything could go terribly wrong.

Halfway there, Cindy drained her cup and suddenly felt a panic attack coming on. What if the CIA went back on their word again? What if she couldn't solve the encryption?

She forced herself to breathe slowly. Grant looked at her, squeezed her hand, and smiled, his eyes full of love. She leaned her forehead against his cheek and closed her eyes. If everything fell apart, at least she knew how much this man truly loved her.

Meridian Street was deserted when the taxi pulled up in front of PTL Computers. Grant tossed the driver some bills as Cindy got out of the car. He looked up and down the dark street. Cindy started to talk, but a flicker of his eyes stopped her.

Punching a code into the security keypad, Cindy unlocked the steel security mesh, then the glass front doors to the computer store. Inside, she locked the door behind them and turned on the main lights. Grant put his finger to his lips, then made a spider motion with his hand.

"Bugs?" Cindy mouthed.

Grant nodded. Beside the register he found a piece of paper and wrote: They may have bugged the place. Be sure to talk like you have no idea I called Mullinax.

She nodded.

"So, Cindy," he said loudly, "what do you need to break the encryption code?"

Chapter Twenty-Six

Tucson, Arizona

Putting his car into park, Perkins got out and stretched. Traffic lined up ahead for half a mile, a parking lot on Interstate 10. Dressed for vacation in loose twill pants and running shoes, he jogged along the shoulder of the road for a while then switched to alternating running and walking. A few minutes later, he reached the checkpoint, breathing heavily but still moving. Without slowing much, he kept moving past the state troopers. They were dressed in the typical khaki uniform with a Smokey Bear hat.

An officer yelled at Perkins, "Hold it right there!"

Puffing, Perkins turned and reached inside his coat for his badge.

"Don't move!" The officer drew his weapon. "Down on the ground now!"

Perkins put his hands up. "I'm FBI," he said.

The officer didn't budge. "Down! I won't say it again."

Perkins dropped to the gravel on the shoulder. Another officer ran up, weapon ready.

"I'm FBI," Perkins shouted from the ground.

"He went for something inside his coat," the first officer said.

Perkins was eating dirt. He couldn't see them.

"Where's your ID?" one of them asked.

He growled. "In my coat pocket." A rough hand reached into his windbreaker pocket and drew out a "Things to Do in Tucson" brochure. Patting him down, the officer pulled a Beretta out of Perkins's shoulder holster.

The first officer said to him, "You realize this doesn't look good."

Perkins started to sweat in earnest, and not just from the heat. "I left my badge in my car. I am FBI."

"Uh-huh," he said. "What's your hurry?"

"With you guys checking every car, it'll take at least an hour for me to clear. I can't wait. There's an emergency."

"You know," one of them said, "he does look like FBI. That Beretta could be FBI issue."

"Tell you what," Perkins said. "One of you guys drive me back to my car, and I'll show you my ID."

"Get to your feet," the first officer said.

When he stood up, Perkins took note that the guy's name was Marcus. He stepped close enough to see the individual hairs on his five o'clock shadow. "If you keep me from my duty by making me late, I'll make sure you spend the rest of your life pulling Northbound swimmers out of the Rio Grande."

Marcus got in gear. Two minutes later, they reached Perkins's car. Perkins opened the door and pulled out his blue FBI-issue blazer, flashing the back of it for Marcus to see. Reaching for the inside pocket, he found the ID folder, and opened it for Marcus to see.

"My apologies Special Agent Perkins," Marcus said. "As a courtesy, please start your vehicle and follow me back through the checkpoint, if you will, sir." He even turned on his flashing lights to make it official.

Once past the checkpoint, Perkins laid on the gas pedal and kept the speedometer at ninety miles per hour, mile after mile across the desert. The road was open. All the traffic was waiting in line back in Tucson.

In Phoenix, traffic picked up and he wove his way through it until he hit Interstate 17 and barreled north. Driving at normal speeds, the trip from Tucson to Phoenix took an hour and forty-five minutes. Perkins made it in an hour and fifteen, but even at that he wasn't going to reach Black Canyon City in time to help Grant and Cindy. Worse, he was running out of gas, and the drive north of Phoenix was all uphill.

He swore and hit the steering wheel. He had to stop or end up stranded on the side of the road in the desert, never a good option. Swerving off the exit, he aimed for the first gas station he saw. In his haste, he hit the curb. His front tire jolted hard and blew.

What now? He got out and surveyed the damage. Shaking his head, he looked at the gas station as a kid with spikey hair hurried out, slipping his wallet into the back pocket of his ragged jeans as he walked.

Perkins clicked the lock button on his key fob and met the boy at a yellow Volkswagen Beetle with a lighted sign for JimBo's Pizza stuck on top.

The delivery boy hopped in and set the engine whirring. At that moment, Perkins shoved his Beretta against the guy's cheek and said, "Get out. I need your car."

The kid wasn't impressed. "You can't do that. I'm late already." He flung his hand over the seat toward a leaning tower of pizza boxes, a dozen, at least. "I'm delivering to a birthday party. The kids are waiting."

Perkins had heard enough. He pulled open the door and grabbed the boy's jacket. "I said, I need your car!" He jerked. The kid fell out and scrambled up. He grabbed the back door handle and started to open it, but Perkins knocked him down.

"Stay where you are!" Perkins barked. "I don't want to hurt you, but I will!"

Perkins folded his big frame into the tiny car and reached for the shift lever. With a growl like a chainsaw, he floored the gas pedal. The back door rattled. Its latch had loosened when the boy grabbed it. Perkins ignored the irritating noise and kept the pedal to the floor. If the police stopped him, he'd use his badge. He only hoped he wasn't too late already.

Grant watched anxiously as Cindy tapped away at her laptop. Meaningless letters and numbers filled the screen. What she was doing was way beyond his computer training. He bent down next to her ear and whispered. "How much longer?"

In answer, she typed on the screen, "I'm going as fast as I can. Another fifteen minutes for sure."

Grant straightened and gave her some space.

The front door rattled. In one motion, Grant pulled Cindy away from the desk and pushed her down behind it. He whipped out his Glock and trained it at the door. The handle turned, and Olivia Donner walked in, leaving the steel security mesh pushed back.

"Oh, no," Grant groaned. He put down his weapon and ran his hand through his short hair.

"What now?" Cindy asked, her face white and scared.

"They're going to bust through the door any second." He looked around, his mind racing.

Her keys dangling from her hand, Olivia stepped closer. "Grant, what are you doing with that gun?"

Grant gestured, palm up. "Cindy's father did something to put her in danger. Another fifteen minutes, and we'll be home free." He turned around, scanning the barred windows and the steel doors. "They'll be on us any second. We've got to find a place to hide."

Olivia's chin came up. She moved into his personal space. "There is a place."

"Keep your voice down," Grant whispered. "The place is bugged."

She wheezed, "I've never told Cindy about it. I'm embarrassed to tell you now... but it might be what you need."

When the big woman entered PTL Computers, Mullinax didn't like it, but he decided to wait in the van and continue listening to their conversation inside. Three minutes later, he gave an order and officers descended upon PTL Computers from all sides. They blew open the steel back door and battered in the front door's glass. At the same time, they cut the power, the cable and phone lines.

In his car, listening to radio traffic, Mullinax tapped his knee, waiting to hear that his men had the Lestrade woman in custody. Finally, he barked into his wrist mike. "What's going on?"

"No one's here," Brown answered.

"What! Mullinax jumped out of the van and ran down Meridian Street. He lunged into PTL Computers—glass crunching under his feet—and turned full circle. No one was there. "What about in back?" he shouted.

"We've been all through it," Brown said. "It's empty."

Mullinax clenched his fists. "They're hiding. Tear the place apart."

He paced back and forth in front of the mangled glass doors. He had violated federal law. The cops would be here any second asking questions.

Brown and two others turned over tables, smashed computers, and ripped open walls. At Mullinax's orders, his men entered the two adjacent businesses just in case there was a common door they hadn't found. Collier and Lestrade hadn't gone out through the roof. Men had been there from the beginning.

Screaming sirens split the air. Two patrol cars pulled up on the sidewalk, and four deputies jumped out. Mullinax rushed toward them, an FBI badge in his hand.

"Special Agent Carter, FBI," he called to the approaching officers.

"Sergeant Bill Dade," the leader said, hands on hips. He was two inches shorter than Mullinax. "What's going on here?"

"We've got terrorists holed up inside there," Mullinax said, jerking his head toward the back room. "It's a national security issue. We hoped they'd come out quietly, but they're making it tough. Now, if you gentlemen would just stay back a bit, we'll finish up here."

The four officers looked at each other. "Come on, guys," Dade said, sending Mullinax a measuring glance. "The feds don't need us local yokels butting in."

The policemen retreated down the road a block. Frowning, Mullinax watched them a moment, then returned inside.

Brown emerged from the back room. "We found something."

Stepping over broken monitors, dented computer towers, and chunks of wallboard, the CIA director walked into the back room to find two of his men staring at a steel plate on the floor. He knelt and grabbed the steel ring attached to it.

"We tried it, sir," Brown said. "It must be locked from the other side."

Mullinax stamped on the plate. "Collier! I know you're in there. Open up!"

Silence.

Mullinax told Brown, "Blast it open."

"With what? We only had enough explosives for the back door. This place is like Fort Knox."

Mullinax burst out with a string of profanity. "That's it. I've had enough." He waved a hand. "Torch the place."

"Sir," Brown said, staring at his superior, "we're breaking a new law every two minutes. You may not mind a few years in prison, but I've got a family."

Mullinax's glare skewered him. "Either you obey my orders, or I'll lock you in here and have Neilsen do it."

Backing down, Brown hurried out the rear door and called outside, "Neilsen, there's a gas station at the end of this street. Buy some cans and get us some gas."

Mullinax banged his heel on the plate. "Hear that, Collier! We're going to torch this place. You're going to fry alive!"

Ten feet below Mullinax, Cindy looked up from her desk chair when he screamed those words. She raised her trembling hands to cover her ears. "I can't think, Grant. I can't!" Her voice raised a full octave and cracked.

Grant knelt beside her, peering at her through the yellow glow of a candle flame. "You're almost done, aren't you, honey?" He pulled her head onto his shoulder and held her close. She smelled good even in a musty place like this.

"Whether we get out of this or not, we'll still be together," he whispered and blinked away his own wrought-up emotion.

He kissed her damp cheek. "What's left? Is there something I can help you with? I'm handy with computers, you know."

Rubbing her cheeks and sniffing, she gestured toward her laptop. "I have to send the file attachment to the government addresses I printed from the motel's computer." She pulled a folded page from her jeans pocket.

Standing beside a shelf filled with canned goods and camping gear, Olivia spoke. "Let me do it, Cindy. I can type a hundred words a minute. My nerves haven't been torn up by a midnight chase." She stepped to the cardboard folding table where Cindy worked. "God is on your side, you know. If I didn't decide to sign up for Starlink as my backup when it first came out, we'd be sunk."

"Go, Elon!" Collier murmured. He sent Olivia a grateful glance, and wondered what it would take to get her rattled.

Cindy stood, and Olivia draped herself over the metal folding chair. She opened the paper saying, "Twenty-five years ago, when Jim from the hardware next door convinced me to convert our joint basement into a Y2K shelter, I never dreamed I'd use it to survive a CIA attack." She set the list on the desk. "Take a breather, children. I'll have this sent out in no time."

Cindy pulled Grant to a far corner of the basement bunker and spoke in low tones. "I found something else in the code."

He squinted at her in the dimness, waiting.

"My father painted a number inside Mary Sue's porcelain head. It's to a numbered Swiss account."

"Wait. Is that the doll you were fighting Levitt over?"

She nodded. "My father told me at least a thousand times to keep Mary Sue safe. He told me to keep her with me always, for the rest of my life." She shrugged. "I always have, but I had no idea why. I hope she's still in my apartment."

"She is. I saw her when I was there."

"You were in my apartment?"

He pulled her into his arms. "I've been searching all over for you." He held her close. "Do you see what that means? Your father was looking out for you. He was always taking care of you."

She nodded, sadness in every line of her face. "I just wish he understood that all I wanted was my family. No amount of money can ever replace them."

Five minutes later, his hands deep in the pockets of his tan trench coat, Mullinax trudged out the front door of PTL Computers. Three of his men scrambled out of the building behind him, taking a wide path around Mullinax. No one looked at him.

A wisp of smoke curled out the front door and Brown raced outside. Within seconds, flames engulfed the store. Black, yellow, and red shone from the windows. The fire roared and crackled.

Mullinax crossed the street to watch at a safer distance. A crowd had gathered, and sirens wailed somewhere to the south.

Brown said, "That'll be the fire department. They get pretty riled up when someone commits arson around here. They have wildfires, you know."

Mullinax glanced at the patrol cars down the street. "I think it's time for us to go."

A deep voice, mildly ironic, sounded from the shadow of the building behind him. "Nice fire, Director."

Mullinax spun, his mouth gaping. Grant Collier stepped out of the shadows with Cindy Lestrade. Olivia Donner followed them. Mullinax's face contorted, he let out an insane war cry and lunged for Collier shouting, "How did you get out?"

Aiming his Glock toward the director's left cheekbone, Grant brought Mullinax up short. Grant said, "As soon as your men cleared out for the bonfire, we left through the basement door of the hardware store."

"Brown," Mullinax said, "shoot this man and take Ms. Lestrade."

"Go ahead and shoot, Brown," Grant said. "Add that to the list of things you're going to jail for. The key to the encryption is already in the cloud. You can read it there along with the Russians, the Israelis, and half a dozen other countries."

"You're bluffing," Mullinax huffed. "We cut the cable lines."

Cindy spoke for the first time. "Ever hear of Starlink, Director?"

Mullinax nodded to four standing in a huddle on the sidewalk. "Take them into custody." To Collier, he said, "You people are going to have an unfortunate accident."

Holding weapons, Mullinax's men slowly spread out, watching Collier's gun hand, edging around him and Cindy.

Suddenly, a yellow Volkswagen Beetle with a lighted sign for JimBo's Pizza zoomed in, followed by four police cars, all with sirens and flashing lights. As the Beetle skidded to a stop, two wheels scraped the curb, leaving a long black streak and jolting the back door open. A dozen pizza boxes torpedoed across the ground, tripping up one of the CIA intelligence officers who fell on his face.

Perkins burst out of the VW's front door. Eight police officers aimed guns at him.

"Sam Perkins, FBI," the big man roared at them. "Back off! All of you!"

Grant took a firmer grip on Cindy's waist and said, "For your information, the CIA is not allowed to run operations on American soil, Mr. Mullinax. Now that Special Agent Perkins is here, I get the idea that you're the one who's going to prison."

Three fire trucks screamed onto the scene, blocking the street. They draped black hoses over police car hoods and around bumpers to reach the fire hydrants. Soon, a wide white spray arched up and into the building, a hopeless gesture. PTO Computers had already become a charred skeleton with empty, glowing eye sockets.

Relating the charges to local officers in great detail, Perkins held a gun on Mullinax until the locals cuffed him and his men, and hustled them into squad cars.

While everyone else was occupied, Grant pulled Cindy into the doorway of a closed hairdresser's shop. He wrapped his arms around her and cradled her near his heart, swaying with her from side to side.

"I've got you now, Cindy Lestrade," he murmured into her hair. "You're not running away from me again. This time I'm going to marry you." He bent to kiss her, but she turned her head away.

"I can't marry anyone with the CIA," she whispered, her voice hoarse. "Knowing you're in danger all the time would send me over the edge. I couldn't handle it." Tears filled her eyes. She tried to pull away.

"Oh, no, you don't." He held on tighter. "No more running, Cindy…for either of us. For your information, I'm not CIA anymore. From now on, I'm FBI…L."

She tilted her head. "FBI…L?"

"Yeah." He grinned and leaned down till their noses almost touched. "Family, Babies, and In Love…with you." He kissed her eyelids. "Please, say you'll marry me."

She melted against him, her forehead resting against his temple. With a deep side, she murmured, "Yes, yes, yes, yes, yes…"

Bending, he silenced her lips for a long, warm moment, staking claim to his own private niche of heaven, soft as the breath of an angel, sweet as…

"Uh-humph!"

Startled, they looked up to see Sam Perkins beside them holding a flat box in each hand. His chin had a tomato-sauce smudge. Shoving a box toward them, he asked, "You guys want pepperoni or triple cheese?"

Excerpt

Read on, for an excerpt from The Cowboy Romance Series
Tara's Dilemma **by Lana McAra**

CHAPTER 1

Mr. Mark Chambers, please," Tara Legare told the lanky hotel clerk. She had a pleasant, poised voice. It didn't give away the secret that her stomach was full of flying butterflies.

The young clerk gave her a friendly smile as his eyes approved of her large, brown eyes and creamy complexion. "One moment, please," he replied and held up his hand to summon a bellboy. "You can wait inside if you like."

Glancing around, Tara entered the hotel lobby to wait. The grandeur of the hotel snatched away her breath for an instant. She hesitated inside the door, feeling out of place and alone. She wished she could slip her hand into the warm shelter of her father's coat pocket, her habit as a child whenever she was troubled or frightened. If only he were here to help her now.

But she was no longer a child. Daddy was gone, and she would have to look after herself. And Jeremy.

"A–hem."

A woman in a stylish black hat waited for her to clear the say, an impatient grimace on her painted lips.

"Pardon me," Tara murmured and hastily stepped aside. The woman sailed past without another glance, the swish of silk skirts and the heady scent of French perfume lingering after her. Tara drew a quivering breath. She fought down the desire to turn around and escape to the anonymity of the street. Instead, she crossed the thick carpet to a chair.

She drew the newspaper ad from her handbag and read it for what must have been the hundredth time.

Industrious young woman needed to cook and clean on a ranch in the Colorado Territory. Between twenty and twenty-five years old. Orphan preferred. Top wages. Inquire for Mr. Mark Chambers at the Olympus Hotel.

The mended edge of her glove slipped from its hiding place beneath the sleeve of her jacket. Carefully, she tucked it back in.

Maybe Mr. Chambers has already found someone, she thought, mingling hope and fear. The ad had been published that morning, but she hadn't been able to get away from the shop until quite a while after lunch. Mrs. Peabody had grudgingly given her the last part of the afternoon off.

She noticed a distinguished gentleman sitting on a gold velvet sofa reading a newspaper. Discreetly observing his features, she wondered again what Mark Chambers was like. Her mind drew a picture of a short man with a middle-aged paunch who smoked smelly, black cigars and had a booming voice. His wife, no doubt, was the kind who would be constantly peering over her shoulder and making clucking noises. She cringed inwardly and again stifled the urge to run away.

How unthinkable that she, the daughter of a Virginia plantation owner, should be applying for a housekeeper's position. Her family had suffered many forms of humiliation through the last ten years, but nonetheless she was thankful her mother could not see her now.

A complete waste of time worrying about family pride, she reminded herself. Jeremy, her little brother, was desperately ill, and the sanitarium was far beyond her means. If Jeremy was to get well, she had to have more money than she could earn at the dressmaker's shop.

The years since the War Between the States had been a nightmare for Tara. The loss of her father and brother in the war, living in poverty in Baltimore, and her dear mother's death would have been enough to break the spirit of most girls.

How could they have survived without Maggie? Dear Maggie, who had been with the family for more than twenty years. Maggie, who had stayed with the family when they closed the house and left Virginia. Maggie could watch over Jeremy if Tara had to go away.

Blinking, Tara held back the worried tears that blurred her vision. She drew the scrap of newsprint between two her fingers, and the words "top wages" caught her eye. She had to get this position.

A tall, dark-haired man slowly descended the wide staircase. He scanned the lobby, pausing a moment at the foot of the stairs. He wore a tailored black broadcloth suit, white silk shirt with tiny red pinstripes, and a black string tie. He had broad shoulders and a square, purposeful chin.

Was that Mark Chambers? Her throat tightened when she realized he was striding in her direction.

"You were asking for Mark Chambers, ma'am?" he asked, bowing slightly. He spoke pleasantly enough, but his faint, polite smile didn't quite reach his eyes.

"Yes." Tara's tongue felt thick and uncooperative. "I came to apply for this position." She handed him the ad. Her hand was icy and shaking.

"I am Mr. Chambers." He sat in the chair facing her. "May I ask your qualifications?"

To her dismay she felt her cheeks growing hot. The speech she had rehearsed all morning flew beyond her reach. Frantically, she groped for it.

"I can cook and clean," she managed at last, then added with spirit, "and I can work as hard as anyone."

He looked her over, sizing her up, and his manner softened slightly. "What is your name?"

"Tara Legare. I need work. My little brother is ill, and the sanitarium is expensive."

His wife would be about my own age, she thought, not sure if that was good or bad.

"Your parents?"

"Father was killed in the war, and Mother died five months ago." She met his gaze openly, candidly, and realized for the first time that his thick black eyebrows almost came together. "I've been working in a dressmaker's shop doing fine needlework, but with Jeremy sick I'll have to earn more."

"I'd like to talk to you about some details." He glanced around. The man she had observed shifted position and turned a page of his newspaper. Two men engrossed in conversation walked past. "Would you mind stepping into the hotel restaurant where we can talk more privately? There are some things I need to explain about the position."

"Will your wife join us?" Tara asked, confused.

"That's one of the things I'll need to explain," he said, standing.

Is his wife ill? A vague doubt sprouted in her mind.

An aloof waiter showed them to a small table in a back corner of the dining room. Tara allowed Mr. Chambers to seat her. She removed her gloves, clasped them tightly in her lap, and waited. Alive to his every expression, she tried to determine what lay behind the handsome, self-assured face across from her.

"It's quite a long story," he began after ordering coffee for two. "Some years ago, my father bought a four-hundred-acre ranch near Juniper Junction—that's about fifty miles south of Denver in the Colorado Territory—from a man who left the property to come back East. It's deeded land. I guess my father was planning to go there sometime, but he never did. He died a month ago, leaving a small fortune to my sister and me. My mother died several years ago.

"My half of the inheritance comes with a condition—my father's idea of testing me." His right eyebrow lifted slightly, giving him a vaguely cynical expression. He paused while the waiter set their coffee before them. "In order to inherit, my wife and I must live on the ranch for a full year and make it profitable."

"And you want a housekeeper for her?" Tara prompted. *Won't he ever come to the point?*

He added a spoonful of sugar to his coffee and slowly stirred. Tara watched his large, well-groomed hand. She looked up to find his measuring gaze upon her.

"I don't have a wife."

"I don't understand." *Maybe I ought to leave. This doesn't sound right.*

"I mean," he spoke slowly, distinctly, closely observing her reaction, "I'm looking for a housekeeper and cook who would be willing to become my legal wife for that year." He leaned forward, speaking softly. "I'll be frank. I could find a mail order bride if I wanted to. Plenty of folks are doing it these days. But I'm not ready to be saddled down with that responsibility. I wouldn't even go this far if it wasn't for losing a fortune in the process.

"After the terms of the will have been met, I'll have the marriage discreetly dissolved. No one in the East need ever know of the arrangement. I'm willing to pay one hundred dollars per month."

"But as your wife. . .," Tara faltered. She struggled between dismay at his scheme and the knowledge that she desperately needed the amount of money he had quoted.

"A legality only, I assure you," he said. "Call it a make-believe marriage if that eases your conscience. I turned down two women this morning, but I think you and I could be partners. Why not? You need a sizable income, and I need a wife for a year. We can work together to accomplish both."

"But why would your father put your wife in his will if you aren't married?"

"He thought I was," Mr. Chambers said, ruefully. "The last time I saw him was before the war. I was engaged at the time. What a foolish boy I was." He shook his head. "She was a hostess on the *Mississippi Queen*. I thought she cared for me, but she was only after my winnings at the poker table. She dumped me when a brighter star came along." His lips tightened. "I won't be so foolish again." He shrugged, and his expression softened. "Anyway, I didn't have any contact with my father after that visit. I guess he naturally assumed I had married."

"Couldn't you go to the solicitor and tell him you're not married?" Tara persisted, still puzzled.

"It would break the will." Again that hard look. "And Georgiana, my older sister, would dearly love to chisel me out of my half of the money." He leaned back in his chair and shook his head. "No. There's no other way."

Tara's slim fingers toyed with her china coffee cup. She stared at the painted yellow rose on the inside rim, weighing the possibilities. One hundred dollars a month was twice as much as she had hoped for. And what a relief not to have to please the tastes of another woman.

"What kind of work do you do?" She looked keenly at the man across from her. He didn't look unscrupulous, but his father hadn't trusted him.

Chambers laughed mirthlessly, gesturing with his hand.

"That's a good question, ma'am," he said, sobering. "It's wise of you to ask. I left home at sixteen and found out I'm handy at cards. I rode the Mississippi riverboats for a few years, fought for the Confed'racy under Bragg, and then wandered around New Orleans after the war, trying my hand at this and that, gambling enough to keep me from starving.

"To tell you the truth, I was at a loss until this will came up. I think I'd like to have a go at ranching. Put down some roots, maybe." He shrugged. "At least I'd like to have a chance to prove I can do it even if I decide to come back East later. I don't like the idea of marriage, that's all. I've been a loner for too long."

The simple directness of his answer convinced Tara he was being honest with her.

What would a meaningless marriage matter? Wasn't marriage a commitment of the heart? All he asked was what the ad said: a housekeeper and cook. A ranch would be pleasant, too. A ranch and a plantation were practically the same, weren't they? She remembered the corrals, the riding stable, the spreading lawn, and columned plantation house she had known as a child. The ranch would be different, of course, but there were similarities.

What a relief to go back to that life, even if she were only a servant.

But I won't be a servant, she suddenly recalled. I would be the mistress. Some of the cloud lifted from her mind. Yes, she rolled the idea around on her tongue, I would be the mistress.

"When would we have to leave?" she asked.

"Three weeks." He peered at her with half-closed eyes. "Does that mean you accept?"

"I can't see that I have any choice," she said, steadily. "Yes, I accept."

"Good." His expression relaxed. He reached inside his coat. "Here's my card. I'd like you to go to the Hurlick's General Store on Market Street and purchase any household goods you feel will be necessary. I'm afraid I wouldn't know where to begin when it comes to housekeeping, and I think it would be better for you to make your own choices. Give Hurlick this card, and he'll put it on my account. Have everything packed and sent to my address."

"What should I get?" Tara asked, taking the card and glancing at it.

"Whatever you'll need to take care of the house and fix things up a mite. The house isn't large, I understand, but it has been empty for quite some time. Cooking utensils, curtains, and such like would be in order, I suppose."

Tara slid the card into her purse. Her hands were clammy, and she had the strange feeling she was somehow watching herself from far away.

"We can have the ceremony performed in a quiet corner of the city in about a week," he continued, "but I see no need to change our living quarters until we leave. If you need to contact me in the meantime, you can reach me here. How can I contact you?"

"I live at 148 High Street, Apartment 3B," she said. She pulled on her gloves and stood up. She wanted to have some time alone to adjust herself to the new circumstances.

"Thank you, Miss Legare," he said, rising with her, the shadow of a smile on his lips.

"Tara," she said seriously. "It's foolish to continue formalities."

He smiled. "Tara." He gazed into her eyes, and his lips grew firm. "I'm sure I don't need to tell you our arrangement shouldn't be known to anyone else. Will you meet me at the park near the big fountain with water spraying out a carp's mouth, say a week from today? At two o'clock?"

"I'll be there." She offered him her hand, and he clasped it briefly. His hand, though uncalloused, was surprisingly firm and strong. "Good day." With a nod, she left the hotel.

Conflicting emotions swept over her as she stepped, blinking, into the bright afternoon sunlight. A flash of exhilaration tingled through her as she mouthed the wage he had offered her. A hundred dollars a month! Her brightest hopes had never been audacious enough to rise up that high. The marriage contract was a little disturbing, but livable for a few months. However, now that she knew the problem of the sanitarium fee was solved, she had to face the dark side: leaving behind all she loved to brave the unknown. Many who ventured into the wild new territories were never heard from again.

A whole year. She was heartsick at the thought. *Can I do it? Can I say good-bye to Jeremy and Maggie?* She pushed back the walls that crowded in on her. She would not succumb to her fears and heartaches. If she caved in, Jeremy would sense it and be afraid, too. She must be strong for him.

She walked blindly along the cobblestone streets. The chilly May breeze tickled her burning cheeks as her shoes beat a steady cadence on the sidewalk.

Acknowledgments

Many thanks to my ARC readers who are always there to give of their time and encouraging feedback. I appreciate you.

Thanks also to the Vendela Publishing family for the hours of service and attention to detail that goes into every single book. I'm truly grateful.

Indie Authors

You've done the hard part—writing the book.
Now let us help you go beyond the algorithms and into the global marketplace—without losing creative control or breaking the bank.

- ✓ Recognition in all markets—without the high cost of hybrid publishing

- ✓ Access to bookstores, libraries, and global distribution

- ✓ Eligibility for traditional-only contests and industry events

- ✓ Personalized marketing support that fits *your* voice

- ✓ A true publishing partner who's invested in your success

We'll take your book from online to on shelves.
www.VendelaPublishing.com

About the Author

Lana McAra is an award-winning author and ghostwriter of 48 titles with a million books sold. She has been teaching how to write fiction for 20 years. Lana currently serves as the president of the Northeast Florida Chapter of Sisters in Crime and host of The Fiction Writer's Podcast.

She is the winner of The Christy Award for *Reaping the Whirlwind* by Rosey Dow, The Book Excellence Award, and The Literary Titan Silver Book Award with a 5-star rating from Reader's Favorite. Her mystery series, *Colorado* by Rosey Dow, sold more than 250,000 copies. Her book *How to Write a Novel That Sells: From Concept to Publication* is a training manual for aspiring novelists.

Visit www.LanaMcAra.com for news of her new fiction releases and her classes.

Complete the Puzzle

Win a Prize

Screenshot and print the puzzle.
Mail it to the author in care of Vendela Publishing
to receive a personal postcard handwritten by the author.
Mail to:

Vendela Publishing
17511 County Road 136
Live Oak, FL 32060

Across
3. The tech shop owner
6. Grant's nemesis
7. Local software company
10. The female main character's fake first name

11. The female main character's real first name
14. Grant's new sister
15. Where Erin met Olivia

Down
1. The agency
2. Erin's landlord
4. Cindy's favorite self-defense

5. Grant's Director
8. Grant's bike
9. The male main character's fake first name
12. The male main character's real first name
13. 'family, babies, and in love'
16. Cindy's alma mater

Name:_______________________________________

Address: ___________________________________